Watching the swirling blue portal shimmering like a pool of water within the metallic arch, Red stood as ready and confident as she would ever be. She extended her gloved hand close to the portal and felt a familiar tingling sensation that scared her.

"Red Rover, Red Rover, send yourself over." The portal whispered.

As the voice grew louder and echoed out into the settlement, the crowd fell silent. Many of Red's fellow Rovers removed their headphones in bewilderment.

Red took a step back and steeled her nerves for her charge. Unraveling the mysteries of the arches was a Rover's duty. Now she had the chance to do the preeminent task and learn more than any of them had ever imagined. She had never fancied herself a brazen explorer like her mother, but the universe was calling her by name to investigate its supreme secrets.

Red hoped in her heart that she would discover and return with the greatest answers the colony had ever known.

∧

Red and her colleagues must devise a plan to stop an uncaring intergalactic empire. Beasts of science, the politics of man, and their own young hearts stand in their way. But each of their unique societies can serve as part of the larger solution. Their only chance against overwhelming power is to call out to humanity while it burns, compile the best of them, and pray with all their might regardless of how misguided Red believes such faith in the Divine deity may be.

Vibrant Steel

By

Daniel G. Chou

Substantive editing by Greta Henderson.

Copy editing by Marci Chou.

Cover illustration by Daniel G. Chou with help from DALL·E 2.

Other books by Daniel G. Chou

Candii's Quest, a musical fantasy novella

The Martian Connection, a sci-fi romance novella

www.choustore.com

Summary: No one knows what happened to the civilization the people of Abeona-2 left behind. This is why the Rover Order searches for clues. Seventeen-year-old Red answers an unexpected call to travel the galaxy in opposition of the Order's scope and to hopefully clear her family's generational shame. Humanity's truth will challenge her. An intergalactic war machine may break her.

ISBN: 979-8-9884664-0-6

To my writing community and all my supporters.
It's never too late to learn a new skill.
The hardest part is the first step
and it's easier with allies.

To my wife, Marci.
You were the inspiration launching my
literary career. My muse that started a quest
which led me to the other side of the blue, wispy portal.

Contents

The Red Rover

File Under: exploration, boundaries, knowledge

Location(s): Abeona-2

Executive Summary: I, Red of Omega settlement, humbly submit this report to the Planetary Archives of the Rover Order formatted in formal Rover Code third person qualitative-compliant narrative style. This is a complete written history of my summarized oral presentation titled *Documentation Regarding the Red Rover's Journey Across the Stars* at the 701st Annual Rover Conference. I also include an appendix of subsequent events thereafter. This report explores the complex circumstances that led to the Great Answer Crisis. It encompasses my discovery of answers to arch technology, its origins, those connected through it, and how we came to be in this new post-arch era. The following first entry is of my own account. Further entries will document ethnological interviews I conducted with my known associates before returning to my own experience. Herein, the Red Rover verifies her documentation is true and free of intentional error.

ROVER ENTRY #1011

Little miss Red's cactus-fiber wrapped feet trembled half-buried in golden-red sand at the top of a blustering hill. The metallic arch before her cast a wavering blue glow. Inside its metal frame swirled a thin, undulating surface that could have been mistaken for gelatin if her family had not taught her better. No more than a few centimeters thick, the portal still had a cavern inside it and no one understood how. Gusts of indifferent wind, so much worse up here than around her home at the hill's base, ignored her craving for stability like the wilds of her galactic frontier world. Nature would not offer her peace today. Assurance would have to come from within herself.

"You always knew one day you'd have to cross this boundary," the staunch Governor said, standing beside her. He gripped a metal pipe anchored deep within the sand. It held the two of them steady despite the fierce wind. Dressed in his finest ceremonial attire, bright red leather pants tucked into his boots and a thick woven jacket adorned with jangling medals and chains, he looked uncomfortable. However, this ceremony was his to oversee. He was a man who believed duty always came first and he was expecting the same from her.

"Come now," he said, patting her back. "People aren't used to seeing a child up here. Put on a cheery smile and wave."

Omega settlement expected Red to shoulder the full responsibility of a Rover. Many believed the Great Answer of the arches was almost upon them and her profession was a necessity. Her school texts corroborated this in the history section along with recently introducing her young self to multiplication tables. No more than a week prior she would never have thought it possible that she would be standing on this hill at so young an age. She was supposed to have at least ten more years to go. Yet, the settlement believed sacrificing her childhood was worth it if it could help solve their planet's greatest mystery. The revelation, it was widely believed, would change everything.

Like the desert sand, the colonists' excitement coalesced around their new Rover during the ceremony taking place in the settlement's center. Their densely packed buildings made of rusting expedition-age metal had been Red's entire world. She knew through tales that tan sand and gray stone indeed extended indefinitely across an environment devoid of mercy for its occupiers, but she had never seen any of it with her own eyes. Instead, the novel sight, the first of many in her future, was unfolding just below her. At the base of this hill, hundreds of people held the hands of their neighbors. Their bodies swayed in unison. Lungs rang out a melody from composers whose names had long been forgotten. Linked like a fence, the people believed their ritual channeled their strength and wishes into their Rover as she took her oath to serve the colony.

"Red Rover, oh Red Rover. Send our questions on over. Red Rover, oh Red Rover. Bring answers back over," they crooned.

Despite the unpleasant dust storm whipping up, the weather was comparably kind for her first clash with the pristine metallic curve at the center of her people's society. Any other day of the year and she was likely to be facing down her destiny in the middle of a terrornado surge. This arch, about four-meters tall, had always been here on top of the hill in all its silvery glory. It resided at the base of a conductive colonist-constructed mountain of metal and wire. The electrified heap's summit held steady, defiant among the clouds of the orange sky. Together, the crag of shining debris polished over centuries by sandy gales and the arch both sparked excitedly with the electricity that powered their homes.

As the chanting grew louder, Red shook her head within her wrapped up hood. Her weather-repellent goggles jiggled upon her face, too big still for her small noggin but necessary for such an occasion. Being part of such a silly ritual felt childlike. And, despite her age, had the Governor not told her the time for childhood things was over? But when her mouth cracked open to protest with confident words directing the Governor on how *she* wished to conduct the ceremony, her pronouncement failed to materialize.

A helpful distraction or not, other worries occupied her mind and competed for her attention. What expectations would the youngest Rover in history have to bear? How could she be expected to leave her home, conduct serious research, and *learn to drive* as a seven-year-old?

She wanted to cry. She wished her grandpa could accompany her for the moment she had to finally reach beyond.

Her mother's brownish-red leather glove encapsulated her hand in the only comforting embrace she had been afforded yet today. It was well worn for it had seen decades of adventure before Red herself was even a conceived concept. Red wished it were her mother's hand that held onto hers, providing her warmth, but that was impossible. Instead, her own small fingers swam in the glove's spacious cavity, and she was beginning to resent that fact.

She glared at the glove and recalled her grandpa's earlier pleas.

"My little desert flower, please put it on. It'll bring you luck. I'm sure of it," he said while holding her arm still. His voice was quiet, almost lost in the wind. He grew more frail with every season. She would have no one left who understood her once his last grain of sand drifted away.

"No. I don't want that anywhere near me!" she cried. Try as she might to wiggle out of his grasp, the shifting ground made her unsteady. He slipped the large glove over her hand and tied it closed at her wrist. His shaking fingers could still summon a few Rover knots she had yet to learn. He loved this without-a-pair trinket because it harbored many recollections he never wished to forget. Red hated the glove because its owner chose adventure over making new memories with her.

"Trust me. You will want it in the end. You will."

"It's time," the Governor said, recalling Red to the present moment with a lull in the wind. "Quickly now before it picks up again and blows either of us off this peak." He released his grip on the stabilizing pipe and they approached the arch hand in hand.

With the arch's portal swirling near her face, the Governor guided her gloved arm and pushed it slowly through the sea of blue. There was no clue to discern what to expect out of its swirling patterns, just static. She squirmed at first, wanting to run back to her grandpa waiting at the bottom of the hill. She had heard from other young Rovers-to-be that the inside of an arch was excruciating. But just prior to her fingers piercing the veil, she remembered her grandpa said everyone expected her to be brave. She did not agree with all his beliefs, but she wanted him to be proud of her. Like how he inexplicably was of his daughter.

She settled for the comfort of closing her eyes.

Unsettling heat swathed her hand like cleaning out the organs of a freshly gutted canidauroch for holiday dinner. There were no daggers, stretching of flesh, or mind-boggling agony. She released her trapped breath. The evidence was clear; just as the adults had said, she was in no actual danger. It was almost pleasant at first. She almost smiled before the pressure grew stronger. First firm, then concerning, and finally escalating to a frightening level of crushing strength that swung open her mouth before her eyelids.

Her screech hushed the crowd of neighbors. It drew out by itself until the dry air tugged the last string of breath from her lungs. Red believed she could have suffocated if the Governor had not gently withdrawn her wrist.

Tingling aqua sparks, like little hands gripping her fingertips, came back with her painfully pulsating hand. She had never seen anything like it, but she was told that something like this may happen. Yet seeing it in person was surprising. As the end of her glove pulled away, a weak invisible force tried to pull her back inside. She struggled until it let go and snapped back to its mysterious world. All the pain was gone in an instant.

"It is done! The boundary has been crossed!" the Governor announced to the audience. He lifted Red's hand toward the crowd. "Introducing the twelfth Rover of Omega Settlement who will be known henceforth by her legacy name, Red!"

The quicker she forgot her old name, the better it would be for everyone. A life-long professional Rover had no need to be identified by anything other than their formal designation. But she never forgot the first time she touched the inside of an arch. Those sticky little metaphysical hands had imprinted on the deepest recesses of her memory.

She descended the steep hill amid the backdrop of euphoric applause and the calls of respectful remembrance for her mother. Red kicked up sand, avoiding tripping, and managed to rip the glove off. She ran into her grandpa's chest and buried her face. Moist tears trickled down her cheeks. They evaporated in the arid wind as fast as she could expel them.

"Honey. Why are you crying?" he asked with a curious smile, cradling her head between his arms like he did for her mother at the same ceremony a lifetime ago. "This is a moment of great joy. You begin a critical journey today."

She shoved the glove into his hand. How could she wish it away, make it disappear where she would never see it again?

"I heard them shouting just now! Everyone says I look just like her. But I *don't* want to *be* her!"

Embarrassment for thinking such things about the recently departed stacked upon her still mourning heart. This life was unfair and it made her weep. However, starting that day she did become the Red Rover as per ritual. Her new responsibility would leave little time for dwelling on personal concerns, so she wailed out her troubles for the entire planetary colony to hear.

Her grandpa must have understood the cathartic need to do so for he did not scold or discourage her from expressing herself despite being unbecoming of a stoic and adaptable Rover. Her adherence to the Rover Code could start the next day after she had a proper goodbye to her past self.

Nothing would have consoled her in that moment, but she could have tempered her remorse if she knew she had taken the first step on an expedition which would lead her to unlocking the mysteries of the arches, embarking to lands unknown, and ending it just as it began: recording knowledge in her Rover Journal.

ROVER ENTRY #1012

The dunes were wider. The cactuses were taller by ten years. Red's buggy maneuvered through the Lonely Basin's sun-scorched badlands. Sand stretched toward the early evening horizon. Only the occasional craggy rock formation or blooming cactus patch broke up an otherwise unremarkable Abeona-2.

She tapped the glass on the buggy's temperature gauge. The heat was cozily within the orange zone, but her sand-resistant clothing made it seem much hotter than that. She unbuttoned her hood and let her fluttering hair take to the wind. After years of her profession, she was used to the grueling conditions on the road. But on trips like this, she still longed for the days of childhood when her higher station afforded her luxury with no responsibility.

The beginning of this expedition season began on the eve of the week after her birth date. The twin-suns, burning fervently, reminded her of the candles stabbed into her aging-ceremony steak. The fresh memories of laughs, pats on her back, and kind words inscribed inside a card which she had left at home came to mind. The polite smiles of her neighbors hid their true opinions: she was either stupid or brave to do the work that she did and they were not enough of either to be like her. Several elders in attendance congratulated her on surviving long enough to finally unlock all the rights and responsibilities of her fellow colonists. She nodded amicably for she had already believed herself an adult for years. Despite the dangers of her job and the expectations placed upon her by the Rover Order, she had risen to the occasion on all accounts. Did that not separate her from her youthful peers already?

As a mature Rover, she had traveled the colony and employed her craft to observe, analyze, and draw conclusions from the planet's mysteries. Yet what her society considered a mystery was limited to the arches. The Order only provided aging tools, sonographs, radars, and software to complete the task. This might have been intentional serving the messaging from her Rover academy days: further curiosity could cross a dangerous line.

Red's deviant conjectures would be frowned upon by the colony and thus had remained unsaid. But it was becoming uncomfortable being aware of a voice inside herself, soft and low but growing with insistence each year, asking for more from this world.

Enough worrying about what she could not have, she thought. Red tapped her palms upon her fraying, leather-wrapped steering wheel. She bounced in her seat thinking about the variety of reasons for this trip, yet it was an old friend who loomed largest in her mind. The sliver of a moon was in a very different place in the sky than the last time she had seen her colleague, Green Rover of Iota settlement. After how they had left things, the secret flirting and forbidden desires spoken aloud, she hoped he was as eager to see her as she was for him.

She did not know many Rovers her own age, the profession being mostly populated by twenty-to-fifty somethings, so the few fellow youths tended to light a spark inside her. Was he equally anxious, sitting at home and playing out the scenario of her arrival over and over again in such a way that no other thoughts could penetrate his speculative mind? Perhaps. Yet, she recalled Green was not the most considerate or organized Rover. She tempered her expectations and hoped he just remembered she was coming. A clean bed to sleep on may be the best she could expect for such a scatterbrain.

Her heart was also thumping at the thought of initiating the first field test of an experimental device of her own design. The makeshift machine rattled in her cargo space. She worried the rough road would shake all the screws loose, but there was nothing she could do about that. She never told anyone about this monstrosity, not even her grandpa, but she thought Green *could* be open-minded enough to help her test it. And besides, he liked her.

The Red Rover's reputation, tarnished by her mother, was hers to correct. While her current course of action was unsanctioned, she believed history required a certain degree of measured, hushed boldness to achieve great shifts. She was sure people would understand once they beheld its results and it would be worth it in the end.

A welcome, cool breeze foreshadowed the return of a relentless winter with the evening temperatures dropping into the blue zone. With that relief, persistent sand hitched a ride and found its way in and through her still exposed, tangled hair. At least her Order-issued red jacket, complete with thermal padding and more pockets than necessary, kept this nuisance away from her core. Her trusty goggles also kept the road ahead clear.

Red dragged her finger along the map lying on the passenger's seat. Rough cactus paper against her skin helped fight the barren, unpaved road's mind-numbing effects. While lonely, she slightly preferred solitude on the road to the bustle of the settlement centers. She did not understand people that well. Was that just her or part of being a teenager?

To her delight, the map foretold the approach of a point of interest brimming with potential to break up the monotony. She scanned the flat horizon. Her goggles zoomed in on the distant hilltop peaks. Details of the atmosphere were revealed to her by colors flashing across the glass circles. Such rare and aging technology effectively helped Rovers avoid life-threatening hazards like potential conditions for a storm. A small blue pip pointed her toward an ancient colony ark.

The mountainous wreckage was from her people's first days. It certainly was an interesting sight and one she had missed the first time she traveled to Iota. This specific ship must have been a vessel that experienced a radioactive meltdown upon landing. She noted no visible tire tracks or campsite smoke pillars. Scant evidence of salvage activity lent support to this hypothesis, although she wondered how long resource-strapped settlements could avoid this dangerous yet invaluable heap of material. She recognized this same insecurity in the spurting sounds coughing out of her buggy's exhaust port.

After over a millennium since their departure from the home world, a period known as the Great Expedition, their colony had reached its near limits of self-sufficiency. They may have called themselves *The* Lost Colony, but her ancestors were just one of many ships that first explored the galaxy with no expectation of ever receiving assistance from home. No doubt other forsaken expeditions existed, but she had never read anything about them in her school texts. And without the functioning technology to initiate space-flight or communication over galactic distances, no average colonist could gather such information from what remnants of humanity remained among the stars, if any at all.

She checked her map again to see if the Order had marked this route as dangerous. She did not want to accidentally drive through the surely poisonous wind the decrepit ship emitted. Curiously, there was no such note. Perhaps this was an oversight? She assessed her battery gauge. A slight detour would not cause any trouble.

Red believed nuclear radiation was worthy of research. However, she knew it was best for her to forget about it. The wild frontiers outside the established settlements were largely a mystery even after generations of colonists. The Order wanted it this way.

She charted a path a little off-road. With a jerk of her wheel, she gave the colossal wreckage a wide berth. Yes, the undocumented trail was unpredictable, but a good Rover could handle themselves on the road. She reasoned she was taking a well-calculated risk considering the alternative.

Her eyes darted as she analyzed the rocky route ahead. She dug her fingers into the steering wheel's cold leather. The tires spun and popped over unseen rocks. She gasped as a steep cliff materialized before her. She swerved the buggy in circles until it stopped at the edge.

Still anchored in her seat, Red's hands trembled at the sight. Climbing higher than a few meters off the ground was not in her job description. Eyeing the craggy crevasse as if it would reach out and grab her, its absence from her map puzzled her. Yet the longer she spent near the brink, the more curious she became much to her dismay. Shifting mountain ranges and deep valleys, like this one which nearly took her life, were still not fully understood.

There were theories proposing an overactive molten core inside the planet or massive regular meteorite impacts. Kids often gossiped about her favorite conjecture; the land was carved by giant sand serpents. Little to no evidence existed for any of these ideas so she did not think about it much. And yet an opportunity to gather more data on that mystery spanned before her.

She climbed out of her vehicle and tiptoed toward the edge.

"As long as I take it slow and am careful, I should be safe," she muttered to her nerves.

Some things could only be learned by living, her mother used to say. This cautionary argument seemed less convincing as she crept closer. Competing in her head, the raw statistics comforted her. She had exponentially more Rover hours than anyone her age and could not recall the last intentionally stupid thing she had done. She was capable of being safe.

The open chasm stretched before her. From gold to amber to red all the way down, layers of colored rock provided a glimpse into the past. One feature which caught her eye was the large holes speckling the opposite cliff far below. Muscle moles, another of the desert's rare creatures, lived deep underground among the rock too hard for human tools.

It took her three tries to get herself to take a steady seat on the ledge. She unfurled her map to sketch the gorge. A gentle breeze still required a firm grip. She should report the aerial dimensions with her upcoming log so updated maps could be sent to the other Rovers. While attempting to estimate the distance between the vast gap, she recalled a school text which claimed the existence of fissure-filling technologies equipped on the ancient colony arks. The planet proved resistant to such terraforming efforts. Other inadequacies, like the inability to calm the green lightning storm beginning to peek over the horizon or being unable to find ways to vary their nutritional diets, were more challenges that hindered her people.

Confident with her estimates, a second sketch inside her Journal was for her alone. Her black pencil constructed the scene. Colored ones brought it to life. Chromatic pencils were not standard-issued Rover gear. She spent a month's salary at Epsilon's market for those beauties. They were worth their weight in water.

She sketched the horizon as well. The view was breathtaking. Why could this not be studied, distributed, and enjoyed by the people? She believed the image had value. Yet it took away Journal pages from the Great Answer. It was possible her desires were wrong. The Order would certainly think so.

After shading her last cloud, she retrieved jerky and a pouch of water from her belt. She enjoyed a bite of sinewy meat and double the gulps of satiating liquid. Her grandpa would have scolded her for deviating from her ration schedule, but she wanted to celebrate her bravery in some way.

A hair-raising howl echoed up from the ravine's deepest depths. Few had seen vicious canidaurochs near settlement walls in recent years. She had never seen one in the flesh before. The boundary of her curiosity approached and she was not willing to cross it. Red hopped up, cursed as dizziness fell upon her from peering down the cliff too far, and carefully climbed back into her buggy.

She had been off course long enough. She had a date to make.

ROVER ENTRY #1013

Red returned to the road energized and longing to chat about her thoughts regarding the value of new knowledge. Yet she had no co-pilot. While normally a solitary job, Rover tradition prescribed a partner on this specific trip. A Rover's predecessor would accompany them on their tricentennial excursion and point out all the sights and sounds regarding the first time they themselves visited and recorded at the destination settlement. But like her initiation years prior, she had to observe this tradition in her own modified way.

Absent her mother, her grandpa was the natural next choice. But his frailness forced her to make do with her mother's aging Journal saddled into her passenger's seat. This passive tour seemed like a poor substitute, but she did not know any better way. She occasionally flipped through her mother's Journal to reference pages upon pages of environmental sketches. It helped her navigate and shave time off her anticipated arrival. No other Rover would have expected these deviant drawings to ever have an official purpose, and yet on this trip they made their small contribution.

Later that afternoon, a pair of dueling plateaus bathing under twin ginger suns pinpointed her location upon the map. She could make up another half an hour if she drove straight through them. Her mother had always taken an interest in the planet's many characteristics. She had devoted a concerningly high number of Journal pages to visually documenting them. Red wondered if this obsession was her mother's way of rebelling against the narrow Rover objective. Curiously shaped hills, rarely seen carnivorous creatures, and terrornadoes that would vary in element and color between regions. Those were the kinds of things you could admire during your drive. But the natural world should be of no concern to a Rover.

Red stared at the peaks mirroring each other. Was she a mirror of her reckless mother? No. Her last pit stop was on the way and she was making excellent time to her destination. None of her Rover duties would suffer in the slightest. In fact, her sketches of the canyon were done with Rover maps in mind. She had committed no dereliction of duty. She was nothing like her mother. She hated that she had to occasionally fight the notion.

Red pulled her buggy into the Iota settlement carport and could not keep her fingers from rapping across her buggy dashboard.

Noticing her jitters, she whispered, "Get a hold of yourself. You're here for work." An intrusive memory of Green playfully tapping his fingers upon the back of her hand begged to differ.

She parked inside the covered garage reserved for Rovers and unloaded her survey equipment as a woman approached her, waving a clipboard.

"Red Rover, Red Rover. Running ahead of schedule, are you?" the official asked with a smirk. Her badge and illuminated safety markings upon her jacket identified her as a settlement customs agent. "You didn't cut a bunch of corners at your last stop just to rush over here, right?"

Red rolled her eyes. Some administrative factions got along better or worse with the Rover Order. Customs agents were generally allies, but they sometimes took exception to the Red Rover. Their consistent disrespect in her presence and the sloppy way they handled her paperwork indicated the reputation of her designated color preceded her personal accomplishments.

Red had endured a long drive. She did not care to reply. She simply reached out her hand and wiggled her fingers.

The agent responded, "I'm sorry. Here I am wasting your time when you probably have hugely important research to do. Oh, and could you try your best to focus on your job? Try not to get distracted by any shiny clouds like your predecessor."

The jab was anticipated, but it still stung. Somehow it always circled back to comparing the two of them. While her mother argued vocally against the Rover Code restricting their investigative parameters, Red followed the rules. Publicly, at least.

Looking this paper-pusher up and down, Red often wished she herself were not so easily recognizable. Yet the Order's color conventions made that all but impossible. On a planet of tan sand, brightly color-coded explorers were easy to spot during rescue missions when one went missing. However, that meant no way of ever claiming to be anyone but the Red Rover. Who could she be otherwise? The made-up Cherry or Scarlet Rover? Or not a member of the Rover Order at all? Whether she liked it or not, she remained an instant person of interest wherever she went.

"I'm not like her," Red said under her breath.

"Huh? Did you say something? You know, a good Rover is clear and concise."

"Never mind." Red snatched the clipboard and declared her buggy's cargo. She thankfully caught her tongue before she uttered an unprofessional quip. Besides, it would be stupid to get into an argument with one lone settlement civil servant about her mother's legacy.

"Say," the agent said, "aren't you the one who's mom left her Journal with more drawings than prose? Seems like a kick in the gut to the Order."

Red kept writing silently despite her twitching brow.

The woman paced, circling around Red. "Eh. At least they all amounted to something. I gotta say, I do appreciate the random illustration popping up every now and then in my kid's school texts. Divine forbid he ever gets lost out in the wilds, I think he could find his way home based on a few of those."

Red let her tense shoulders relax. "I've used them myself to identify storm cells hovering over the horizon long before wandering into danger."

"But what about the Great Answer? Even *you* should recognize the value of the mystery."

Lost in wrestling with the argument, Red did not notice a second clipboard waving in front of her face.

"Hey Rover!" the agent shouted. "You got to sign these pieces too. Gosh, you Reds are flighty."

Red took the bundle and signed it. She feigned a trip and sent the two sets of forms flying. The pages tumbled into a tiny tornado heading out of town. The agent ran after them.

"Sorry about that!" Red yelled. "I guess I'm wholly incompetent!" She could not contain her smile despite feeling a pang of guilt. The agent recorded knowledge just like her. As a professional, she should have respected that.

Red wheeled her bubble-shaped cart into town. Nothing much had changed for the better since her last visit. It was no surprise that the metal structures constructed from salvaged colony ark materials were covered in holes. Dirt and sand blew down the roads and seeped their way into every building. Shoddy construction meant any shack higher than two stories would likely collapse upon itself should a quake strike. At least the settlement's lights, strung along fraying wires crisscrossing the streets and rooftops, were shining bright during midday. While metal was becoming increasingly rare, they would never worry about electricity. Or so the colony hoped based on what little they understood about their source.

These people deserved better, she thought. Her settlement was certainly not gleaming, but they were well insulated from the winter. What of the research she pondered earlier about radiation? If they only knew how to protect themselves then maybe salvaging the affected ships would be possible. The Order should deem such research worthy especially in light of these conditions.

Red received plenty of polite waves from the Iota folks as she walked through the bustling public market. Settlement tourists were not always welcome, but a Rover was believed to usually bring good luck. Several dusty children approached her bubble cart and asked to see what was inside. Red politely declined. Incredibly sensitive Rover equipment could not risk tampering.

She consulted her handheld radar and navigated the streets until Iota's own glowing arch led the way to the power mountain's base. Just like her home, their Rover cabin was near its summit. She noticed Iota had fewer conductive wires running from the mound than many other settlements she had seen in the last year. Like the houses in obvious disrepair, all sorts of raw materials must have recently become more rare. Darker nights and a colder winter could be in their future.

As she climbed the hill toward the mysterious arch, it illuminated the sandy path ahead with a light-blue glow. Not every arch on the planet glowed, but those that did provided limitless electricity to anything that touched it. With only so much surface area, the mountains of conductive metal on top of them allowed more connections to power the settlements.

She approached Green's cabin. The green-painted siding was devoid of cavities. The importance of their profession's work meant his little hut stayed in good shape. As her knuckles rapped upon his door, she hoped she knocked in such a way that did not come across as too desperate but just the right amount of excitement.

Immediately the door swung open. Either he waited just beyond the other side for hours preparing for this exciting moment or had set a proximity alarm. She preferred believing the former.

ROVER ENTRY #1014

Red!" Green's goofy grin welcomed her. He was noticeably taller. His short hair had a little sand lodged in it.

She hesitantly raised her hand to clear his peak but diverted to lifting her goggles instead.

"You look great!" he continued.

She smiled. He was incredibly kind for she was mostly wrapped up head to toe.

He held the door open and waved quickly. "Please, come in!"

She kicked her boots against the doorframe and shivered her whole body to dispel as much sand as possible before shuffling inside. Taking a gander at the interior, she remembered his hut being in exactly this much disarray. Tables and chairs were piled with green clothing. Datapads were strewn across the floor. However, the corner where guest Rovers stayed was tidy and organized, devoid of equipment odds and ends dangling from hooks in the ceiling. Did he keep the corner clean during the entire year or only when he was expecting company? Or perhaps he put it together just for her. What allowed someone to be both considerate and sometimes single-minded? People were an enigma.

Everything else more or less was standard-issued Order furniture made of stone, metal, and cactus fibers. A small workbench lined one wall, the bed, couch, and dining table along another, and the austere kitchen and bathing equipment hid tucked around a third.

"I didn't think you'd make it so early. Sorry, everything's a little bit of a mess here." He chuckled and stared at the ground. "Uh, how was your trip? Safe, I hope." Stains covered his green uniform. Frayed edges hinted at all work and no play.

"Oh, you know, just a wayward rock cracking my left lens," she replied, taking one step and then two in his direction. "I almost met the road's edge on two separate occasions and barely saved myself from careening to my death."

"Ah." Green's eyes ran up her legs and stopped just above her eyes. "I bet one of those ravines was Flying Pass."

She nodded. Despite trying to attract his gaze, he seemed fixated upon something.

"Of course you'd know about it. It's…it's…in your own backyard…" She paused. "What are you looking at?"

He leaned into her face, expecting what she could not determine. Did he want a kiss? Could he be that forward? The lonely Rover life surely affected him as well. The possibility he wanted to stoke the flame of whatever relationship they had forged during her last cooperative visit was not zero.

She convinced herself it was so, pursing her lips ever so slightly, when he reached his hands to her forehead.

"Oh, that's a mean crack for sure." He gently pulled her goggles from her head. "Here, let me fix that."

"Uh, oh, yeah." She watched him walk the pair to his workbench and get right to it. She smirked. Was her mind playing tricks on her or was he just being shy?

"Can I get you anything?" he asked.

"You got any water?" Her sandpaper tongue nagged her. She hated insinuating her buggy canteen had run dry. A reliable Rover would never forget to top off before a big trip like this, yet here she was. Perhaps she embodied more of the lies they claimed about her mother than she ever wanted to admit.

"Sure. Let me siphon one for you." He handed back her renewed goggles and drifted past her into the kitchen. He seemed more confident than she remembered. His allure gripped her more strongly than she anticipated. Tan hair combed to the side and long arms capable of wrapping around her for a hug once again. She only ogled the back of him, but that was already pretty exciting.

Purely out of habit, she turned her head to see if any Order enforcers were in the hut. She felt her emotions brewing. They would very much disapprove. The Order expected their members to be as stoic as research upon the page. She had never personally subscribed to that policy for a day in her life. She was careful not to hoot and holler while visiting the Order Headquarters in Alpha settlement but allowing her heart to speak in the presence of close friends, family, or when she was alone was never a problem. Sometimes this was through tears and other times with raucous laughter. Her grandpa once said it was this doctrine that stunted the sociable growth most Rovers were known for lacking. Not very good with people is what they say about the Order. Red was no exception, yet she never wanted that to hold her back.

"You seem happy about something," she said. "So, tell me what's up?"

"Do I?" he turned the handle of his reservoir. "Lately my mind's been a big ole mess. I've hardly taken a moment away from official duties." He tapped his foot, searching his thoughts. "Well, I suppose the start of this research season has started off strong. I *did* have a breakthrough yesterday with one of the rookies present."

"It's exciting, isn't it? I always do love a good training opportunity." She understood the feeling, however, she alone had the unique experience of training colleagues who were almost always older than her. Many underesti-mated her, which only added a certain level of relish when she taught them a new trick. Too bad that after a few years of deciphering the garbled voices broadcasting from the arches, the heart of their trade, anyone would start to get the hang of it. Opportunities to be the smartest kid in the settlement eventually faded.

He strode across the room and handed her a cup. "Sorry for making you wait."

"No, not at all."

She peered into her water. A little cloudy throughout, but that happened everywhere. She sipped. A little gritty too. That was not quite right. It reinforced that Iota was going through hard times. This clue suggested that despite Green's enthusiasm for his results, he had not discovered anything new. Otherwise, the Order would have already descended upon this settlement like a terrornado and showered it with recognition and resources.

"So about my research, Purple and I completed our observations yesterday and she helped me refine two words! Can you believe it, two within the first week of the season?"

Red blinked twice. "Purple did that?" This piqued her curiosity. She knew of Purple, an up-and-coming Rover from the southern settlements about their age. Rumor had it she was also still quite expressive with her emotions having joined the Order recently and by some unplanned circumstances. She had not yet fully been indoctrinated into their customs but the Order would see to that in time.

Young, pretty, and a big flirt, from what Red had heard, were also Purple's defining qualities. But apparently she had talent too. Had Red known Purple would have been here the day before her, she would have rescheduled herself to the week prior. Her shoulders slumped knowing this other woman incited such excitement from him. But then again, where was Purple now? Out of sight hopefully meant out of mind.

"Well, maybe now that she's off to her next settlement," Red said as she placed her glass down and rose to her nervous feet, "you and I can crack the code of…"

"Oh, she's still here!"

His big smile made Red wonder if he was recalling Purple fondly. Red did not let that get to her. She lacked enough evidence to surrender. Instead, she listened for more information.

"Yeah. As she was packing up, I mentioned that you were coming in today. I suggested if she had the time, then she could watch the master herself perform a replication. She expected to take two days to get to Alpha next, but with the weather being tip-top lately she figured she could make it in one. So she decided to ask your permission to observe your work."

An unexpected smile edged across Red's face. Green wanted to show Purple the wonders of his good old friend Red. Yes, Red was the youngest person ever to be made a Rover. But her young age did not usually serve to her benefit. She lacked the deep experience many of their established colleagues had. And still, the Rover Hall of Records contained many of her contributions rivaling some twice her age. Green was right to be proud of being her acquaintance. If they expected a pseudo educational seminar, she would need to present a replication by the book. Sadly, that meant no illicit tinkering with her little invention.

Red glanced around the hut. She did not see Purple hiding anywhere in plain view. The next twenty-four hours were for science, but first, if Purple was running errands, there was a little time for Red to explore more with one of the few men she had ever known so personally.

With her confidence swelling, Red said, "I see she's out and about. I…I read an article on the research network last week about courting habits of Earth's youth during the first half of the space-age millennia. Th-the engineered differences between the test groups A, B, and the control had me wondering…"

The door burst open. "I'm back!"

A young woman stumbled inside with several sacks slipping out of her arms and spilling onto the floor. She was panting. Her purple uniform was tailored and bright. She pulled her fogged-up goggles and jacket hood over her head and ruffled her curly hair as cups of sand fell out of it. She had failed to secure her head gear appropriately and was creating a small dune in Green's living room.

This seemed rather rude to Red and she had half a mind to scold Purple, but she checked Green's expression first to see whether he felt the same. To her surprise, he wore a quirky smile. He appeared amused.

"Oh goodness." Purple continued to shake her long hair, obscuring her face while she went on. "My trip to the market was an absolute nightmare! First, I couldn't find my way to the water refueling station *and* I forgot my wallet in my buggy. So I had to head back to the carport when...get this. You're not going to believe who's already in town. I saw the buggy of..."

Purple raised her head. She and Red locked eyes. Red smiled and curtly waved but Purple's wide eyes made her believe they were sending each other signals of a vastly different nature.

"Red!" Purple squealed. "Oh my gosh!" She bounced in place. "Oh my gosh. It is *such* an incredible pleasure to meet you." She stepped forward, presumably to shake Red's hand, but paused and threw her purple backpack on the ground. "Wait! Let me just..." She rummaged until her face lit up. She yanked out a bundle of white cloth and handed it to Red.

Tiny claps of joy from Purple's gloved palms puzzled Red as she unfolded the package. Inside, Red found a spool of refined copper wire.

"This is...nice. Thank you." What exactly was happening, Red wondered? No one had ever given her a gift just for existing. Could this be some type of peace offering? But for what? They were not formally at war over Green. Right?

Purple laughed and slapped Green heartily on the shoulder. "When I saw Red's buggy in the carport, I picked that up on my way back to say, 'Hello from the southern settlements!'"

"Yeah," he nodded, rubbing his arm absentmindedly. "That's...that's a real nice and thoughtful gesture. Definitely something a good host should do..."

Red weighed the wire in her hand. There was no doubt of its decent quality. It must have been expensive in a town with a wiring shortage. Genuinely grateful and equally annoyed, it seemed Purple had money too.

Green scratched his head. "Sorry, Red. I wish I'd thought of picking you up a little care package as well, but I guess I didn't prioritize the right things."

"Please don't worry about it," Red said. "We've known each other for a bit. You've done enough just welcoming me into your home."

Green smiled. He turned back to Purple and laughed. "Since you're handing out trinkets from the market, what did you pick up for me?"

"You already got your present…" she smirked fleetingly and dived back into her pack.

What was that about a gift? And that coy little smile? Red did not understand their relationship's exact nature and it frustrated her like trying to grope for a pencil you dropped under the seat while keeping your other hand on the wheel. She wanted to figure these people out, but she lacked some form of critical knowledge. There was only so much to be gained from observing. Sometimes you needed to ask the right questions.

"Hey, thanks for this, really," Red said. "This is amazing and I can already think of a hundred ways to use it. So, uh…what exactly are you two…"

The unmistakable whine of a Rover siren wailed outside.

ROVER ENTRY #1015

Green cracked open his hut door and peeked outside.

"Red, did you already set up your site?"

"No. I just knocked when I..."

Purple secured her hood and pushed gently past Green. She stepped into the early evening. The wind was blowing softly and the suns cast a ruby glow across the face of the power mountain before them.

"No," Purple grumbled. "That sounds like my equipment. I thought I packed everything last night."

Red and Green fastened their uniforms and followed her to the arch. They found Purple's signal-detecting spectrogram. Sand almost completely submerged the little crying machine. It had found something worthy of investigation and wanted anyone from the Order to know.

Like a flip of a switch, their training kicked in.

Red shelved her personal feelings that, for a moment, she almost convinced herself were the most important matter. She pulled her cart from Green's yard to the base of the arc. Prompt, critical work needed doing and the thrill of new knowledge energized her.

As she unpacked a bundle of worn stakes from a small sack, she failed to recall any documented instance in which three Rovers set up an observation site in tandem. However, together they constructed her travel tent around the arch, unloaded the signal detectors, wavelength analyzers, audio amplifiers, computers, monitors, and all the supporting gear inside. Every machine connected to the energizing arch using small wires and adhesive strips. There were no questions regarding setup because the Order kept all Rover equipment and worksites standard. It happened so fast and efficiently, she wondered why teams of Rovers did not gather more frequently.

Red's cart was empty save for a single tarped oval-shaped lump. She kept it concealed and their hands away from it. There were one too many persons present for that now.

Once inside her tent and with their weather gear comfortably off, no one could deny it was cramped.

Purple bent to pick up her spectrogram, but Red had to squeeze herself to the side to make enough room for the maneuver. The tent's fabric strained as her back pushed against it. She had to be careful. There were no replacement tents back home.

Purple silenced the alarm and blew sand out of its vents.

Red turned away to avoid coughing. "Hey, easy now! Don't do that inside with the equipment!"

"Oh my gosh! I'm so sorry!" Purple opened the entrance flap and fanned the dirt outside. She mumbled, "How did I miss this?"

Red felt a little sorry for her. When she herself started in the profession, she took every one of her mistakes pretty hard too. Her first years were during her childhood, but she had not outgrown the desire to avoid embarrassment in front of strangers who she was to collaborate with. Feeling nervous and intimidated was normal when you were alone in a tent with someone who had been doing your job longer than you had been alive.

However, as Red thought about it more, Purple, Green, and the other Rovers learning their craft during their teenage years probably had it worse. The only thing that worried Red anymore was not doing a respectable job. Normal teenagers had a lot more going on in their head competing for their attention against their training. She, an outlier skilled and self-assured about her work, maybe represented someone of high regard to Green. Part of this career-focused logic was a self-constructed lie. Of course she fettered about other matters like feelings of the heart, but she willfully excluded the thought for a moment.

Green gently placed his hand on Purple's back. "It's okay. You'll get the hang of it. We all do eventually." He looked toward Red and made a gentle nod.

Purple followed his gaze and faced her too; her eyes were watery.

Red reasoned she could not stay silent and let a preventable loss of moisture occur. She quickly nodded. "Th-that's right." She diverted her attention back to her computer and sat on a stool while typing. "Don't expect yourself to remember everything right at the get go. You'll get it soon enough."

Purple wiped her eyes and resealed the tent. "Thanks." She tripped over a power cord and the spectrogram went dark.

Red picked up the end and taped it back onto the arch for her.

Purple nodded gratefully and held the device in her hands as she waited for it to reboot. "When it's ready to output, is it okay if I send it to your console?"

"Of course."

Red matched her computer's frequency to Purple's signal and wirelessly connected the two devices. A few minutes later, Purple's data crawled across a small monitor. The lengthy compiling time made Red a little conscious about her equipment. What were some Rovers to do if their settlement could not afford the annual maintenance pilgrimage back to Alpha? Her home could barely afford to send her on the regular excursion season. Such limitations led to her becoming a tinkerer and having to learn the ins and outs of her precious equipment.

She felt the other two staring holes into her screen until, with a chime, the output waited for their action.

Red respectfully offered Purple her headphones. "You should be first to hear. They're your findings."

"Oh no. I couldn't." Purple gently pushed Red's hand back. "This is your day and your site. Just because I forgot my equipment doesn't mean you wouldn't have found it yourself. You should have the glory."

Red placed the headphones onto the table and pushed them Purple's way again. "I've deciphered hundreds of broadcasts. Exciting as this is, it's really no issue. Just take it."

"Please," Purple protested again. "I'd rather not. Besides, I'm only here to observe your work and..." She paused. Her mouth fell agape. "Oh my gosh! I haven't asked for your permission yet, have I?" She turned to Green.

He sighed and shook his head with a quiet smile. "I should have reminded you. I'm sorry."

Purple buried her face in her hands and wept. "I'm so sorry! It's so rude of me to assume! I...I-I meant to ask your permission as soon as we met, but I got caught up in my backpack and the siren and, and..."

Red rolled her eyes and hoped she had never come across so sensitive. She picked up her headphones and placed them around her neck. "I've been offering so obviously it's fine. How about we listen together instead?"

She pulled her monitor near and grabbed the keyboard. A few commands and several desperate smacks against the side of her loudspeaker later, a message leaked out.

"ch----ren-e-e-s-reno--e-app-o--ia-e-or-h-s----f-he-ar--n".

Red strained her ears. The broadcast continued a loop as she attempted to isolate any single word.

"Did you get anything like this at your site yesterday? Are we performing a replication?" she asked the others.

"No." Purple patted her face dry and leaned closer to the speakers. "This is new. I simply performed a standard independent replication and refinement of Green's latest finding."

Green groaned. "If this is a brand-new message, then my chance to unravel the rest of mine is over. But regardless, Purple's right. This is nothing like mine. 'Critical maximum distance' and 'frontier worlds' were all we were able to decipher. Just more of the same, unfortunately."

A new message made its debut upon their world. What knowledge would it reveal about the origin and power of the arches, she wondered? Could this finally be the one that shed light on how the arches worked and ensure their continued operation indefinitely?

Green's sullen shoulders tugged at Red's heart. "No, that sounds good!" she said. He had surely achieved worthy pieces of another communique from the home world. There was still a healthy inquisitive community around that topic at Alpha.

"The signal was just so…garbled."

"Red's right," Purple assured him. "The Order believes these messages regard the fate of our ancestors, right? Despite it only being a replication of a small bit of known knowledge, I think confirming past research is still a noble contribution."

This was all true, yet the quality of the signal would ultimately define its worth. Poor-quality recordings already saturated their records. "Is it just me or are the messages getting worse?" Red asked.

"That did come up in my training," Purple said. She tapped her head. "I think statistically speaking the strength required for our instruments has had to increase over time to gather the same amount of material. Order researchers are unsure if it is the originating sources that are deteriorating, our position in the galaxy changing, or a million other possibilities."

"Huh. Was that from a new course? I didn't learn anything like that when I was at Academy," Green said.

Purple shrugged. "I don't remember what it was called but I do remember there being what some of my instructors described as a shift in perspective within the Order. My class was being encouraged to start thinking about what a post-Great Answer colony would be like. The Answer could be almost upon us."

"Ha," Red laughed flatly. "They're always saying that. Have been for decades according to what I've read."

"Yeah, sure." Purple's smile came and went quickly. "I'm just saying that's what I was told."

"Well, let's leave all that philosophical high-mindedness to the leadership," Green said. "We have a mystery right in front of us so let's get to listening better."

He scooted forward and leaned closer to Red's speaker.

His hand gently rested upon her shoulder. An involuntary smile drew across her lips. In such cramped quarters perhaps no alternative surface existed. But she liked to think he took advantage of an opportune arrangement, and she had no objection.

Stick that in your bag and gift it, Purple.

ROVER ENTRY #1016

Red's staticky broadcast looped continuously. With most of her attention swirling in excitement over Green's touch and the few remaining brain cells left focusing on the audio, she was in a happy place.

"Is it just me," Green asked, "or is anyone else picking up an Indo-European language? French? Possibly Italian?"

How bothersome, Red thought. Now that they were getting somewhere, for clues of this magnitude she needed to concentrate better and say goodbye to the fanciful pleasures. "Excuse me." She put on her headphones and fiddled with the amplifiers upon her console. Considering Green's perspective, she started to hear it too. She needed to account for distortion so she switched on her own spectrogram and attempted an immediate replication. The machine detected the signal and compiled it independently. It sounded the same.

"You're going in the right direction, but I don't think it's a Romance language." Red wondered what more she could pick up if she had more power, but she had never done *that* in the presence of another Rover. She was taught that there were rules for a reason. She did not understand them all and often deviated when alone. That was the origin of many of her contributions to the Order. Plenty of Rovers probably did the same in minor ways and got away with it, but she could recall at least a few examples of actual public reprimands. How long would her luck run? She preferred to keep her public reputation clean. Was this an appropriate risk?

She turned to the two. They smiled like goofs at her interest. "Green, you know me. I like to try stuff."

He nodded. "One of the many things that makes you interesting."

She blushed, feeling more at ease. "Okay. Bear with me for a bit. I'm going to try something."

She unscrewed the back panel of her clarity dish antenna sitting on the table. A few crossed wires and double the number of power lines connected to the arch later, she screwed it all back together.

"Uh, I don't think you're supposed to do that," Purple said with a hesitant hand reaching toward the lines. She glanced nervously at Green. "The standard equipment is standard for a reason, right?"

"It's okay," he said with a steady gaze. "Red knows what she's doing."

Red placed her supercharged clarity dish in front of the arch's portal. Its antenna emitted an errant spark. A high-pitched tone made her quickly turn down the screeching volume from her headphones before placing them back on.

Green raised an eyebrow. "It's been a while since we've last worked together. At least I think she knows."

"I know, I know," Red said. "We're supposed to do things as similar as possible to guarantee a quality replication. But…" she continued as she twiddled knobs, nudged her dish slightly about, and listened for the sweet spot. "Sometimes you can tweak the formula just a *little* bit for a morsel of progress."

Her headphones hummed pleasantly. "Ah! There it is." She switched the output back to the speaker and played the new result.

"c---l-ren-eve-s-ren-t-e-a-p-op-ia-ef-r-h-s-ze-f-heg-r-en."

The perplexed looks on her colleague's faces raised doubt in her mind. Had she done the right thing? She was aware she sometimes strayed from the Order code of conduct, but she believed it was always in service of the Great Answer. Never mind that no one knew what the Great Answer was about so it was hardly possible to claim anything was more or less on target with the topic.

"That's...unique." Purple tilted her head. "I've never heard a replication of the same source sound so *different*. They're the same length, tone, and accent. Like, I can tell it's the same message, but with new parts." She drew her face close to Red's clarity dish. "What *exactly* did you do to this?"

Green remained focused on the repeating message. "Did you just hear 'ren'? Spanish maybe?"

Red followed Green's questioning happily. She opened her Journal and flipped to all her known vocabulary words of the old world. "No. I believe this is Germanic."

"How can you tell? I don't think I have any skill for this translation business," Purple said. She opened her own Journal. "Am I right that none of these messages are ever in our native language?"

"That's right," Green said. "But don't worry. Everyone becomes familiar with the roots with enough exposure. I've only been at it for a few years and I'm already fluent in several old tongues."

Purple pointed at Red with a sparkle in her eye. "What about her?"

Red flipped through her Journal. Pages were aflutter like a breeze had wafted inside. "English, Mandarin, Pre-Awakening Arabic, German, Neo-Spanish, Kaswahili, and Plutonian. Knew them all by thirteen."

"Wow!" Purple gasped.

Green grinned and shrugged. "A real whiz kid, this one."

Red granted her mother only one redeeming quality, one which even those who made her a pariah could not deny. The decent vocabulary collection she compiled and contributed to the Order during her earliest days as a Rover were lauded. They came from a time before her other curiosities took precedence. Red too had a knack for deciphering words and adding them to the Order lexicon. Still, she was lucky to have inherited the original, much more detailed notes of her mother's etymological discoveries by right as her successor.

As Red scoured her extensive dictionary, Purple scooted next to her and said, "Incredible. You sure have a ton of words and notes. It's amazing."

Red wanted to pull away and guard her horde, her last possible remaining leverage for Green over this siren. But such an uncooperative act would have been the Rover Code antithesis and she had already deviated enough for one day. She reasoned for a moment before settling into what was right. She tilted her Journal so Purple could see better. More slowly than before, she flipped each page. Like it or not, a Rover should champion the transparent pursuit of knowledge and she felt more comfortable doing that than being selfish.

Purple raised an excited hand several times but placed it respectfully back on her lap. "Wow, you have thousands of words, possibly hundreds of thousands!"

"Well, I had a real head start because of my mother's and grandpa's Journals so I can't take all the credit."

Purple leaned back and furrowed her brow. "Your mom *and* your grandpa...were Rovers? Were they *your* Rovers?"

There was a noticeable pause. "Oh, that's right." Red smiled and turned toward her. "I'm sort of an anomaly, aren't I?"

She tried not to let the staring bother her. Purple was referencing Omega's practice of allowing their Rover to select their successor. Every other settlement on the planet had migrated to choosing their Rovers utilizing aptitude tests and a panel of Order-appointed judges. Red had zero problem with that method. Thankfully, this was one area the Order never bothered to micromanage. Of course settlements want their most talented individuals unraveling the mysteries of the universe for glory. However, with bureaucracy came politics, and with politics came disagreement.

Her settlement was fairly criticized for other quirks, but she would defend their process to her last written word. Besides, the Rovers of Omega had not always been related, just their last three. And who was to say she would have a child of her own or, if she did, they would be any good at this life? She was fine selecting outside the family lineage if her descendant did not show a talent like her at such a young age.

It was as if Red had grown a second head. Purple's prolonged staring started to get to her. She formed the words of a snippety response when Green interjected.

"I was told during training that the Red Rovers of Omega were so talented in part because of their bond with their predecessors. It seems there are perks to their peculiar arrangement."

Purple sat up straight. Her narrow eyes looked unconvinced. "I suppose, but…"

"Here!" Red shouted much too eagerly. She pointed to a page of Orderlish, a mysterious language not found in any of their archives from the home world, but one they pieced together from communiques over the ages. Red was no expert in Orderlish, but she knew enough to be dangerous. "Following the trail of 'ren', here are words that start with the letter R. There are quite a few for us to consider."

"Ren," Green repeated. He rolled the word around his mouth a few times. "What if…" He pulled a book out of his pocket. "Oh, darn it. This is my old Journal. I'll be right back."

He exited the tent.

He had doomed Red to sit inside with Purple alone.

Purple sat quietly perched next to her, eagerly watching with what she supposed was a mixture of child-like wonder and morbid curiosity as Red racked her brain over each word. Red was not doing anything spectacular. There was no magic wand waving. She had no idea what Purple expected to see but she tried to stay focused as she continued to mentally sound out each word in hopes of making any sense.

The silence was almost uncomfortable when Purple broke it. She started quiet at first but became louder as she went on. "I'm sorry. I didn't mean to sound as if I was judging you or your settlement earlier. It's just that…" Her eyes grew wide.

Red curiously turned and they locked gazes.

"Well, I've heard stories of the Red Rover."

Red sighed. She smirked against her will. "Is that so? I mean I *have* had my share of deciphered messages archived at Alpha, but I would hardly call them…"

Purple quickly waved her outstretched arms through the air. "Fantastic tales of meandering adventures on the frontier!" The tent shook when she jumped to her feet and slapped one fist heroically to her chest. Her voice changed to what sounded like a radio drama broadcast. "This explorer, an inspiration for new Rovers the world over, documents discoveries about our planet that are just as valuable as what she contributes to the Great Answer! Look at her now, charging valiantly into a terrornado with her trusty Journal in hand. What mystery of this violent planet will she shed new light on next?"

A compendium of human language in her hands and Red was at a loss for words. Purple was not referring to her, but rather her mother. From Purple's tone, Red confidently dismissed a mocking motive. Rather, Purple placed her mother on a pedestal of esteem Red herself found unfamiliar. A high amount of cognitive dissonance muddled her thoughts.

As if she had forgotten where she was and then suddenly remembered, Purple faced Red with a slight blush. She swiftly took a seat. "I never could tell which rumors were true. I thought the whole lineage thing was just another one of those tall tales. I mean, maybe lifelong Rover candidates would know the difference, but I never thought I'd be doing this work. I never really cared to know if it was all true or not."

At first, Red did not want to engage in that emotional topic. But she considered it once more and decided to believe the sincerity in Purple's voice. It was harder to argue and she was not confident enough in the skill of rhetoric to start a fight she may not be able to win.

"Those stories," she replied, "are about my mother. Although," she placed her Journal softly on the table, "I'm curious as to who told you she was any kind of inspiration to *any* Rover at all. She was one to explore and record more than just our calling for an inordinate amount of time. In her opinion, everything she crossed paths with was a subject worthy of study."

"But *I* admire her. I did before my training and I still do now."

Red revealed her mother's own Journal from a pocket. She peeled the aging pages back and showed Purple several insights. Detailed illustrations of scarce creatures, crackling clouds, and exotic rocks and minerals seemed to awe Purple much like when Red herself first beheld them long before she understood what official work suffered because of their inclusion.

"These are amazing!" Purple said. She leaned in uncomfortably close.

Red stiffened up not wanting to be cheek-to-cheek with her. She turned her face away to at least not breathe the same air. "Yeah. I guess they're pretty interesting."

"The composition. The artistry. I *know* I've seen some of these replicated in the school texts, but there are so many more." Purple pointed to one after the other. "Why aren't we shown all of these in school…or during our training? Some of these…I don't even know what they are but I want to learn."

"To learn?" Red scoffed. "What is there to learn from an illustration that doesn't relate to the Great Answer?"

Her immediate quip was a defensive response that had kept the ridicule aimed at herself to a minimum for years. However, in her heart, she agreed that these sketches were helpful. In the least, they helped her navigate terrain. Yet, saying such things to others was always a risky line for her to cross.

Purple tapped her chin. "But that isn't the question, is it? What I mean is that I want to learn about these places, creatures, and environments regardless of their relation to the Great Answer."

She pointed to an illustration of an epic mountain. "We Rovers are explorers. You and I are pioneers of the unknown. The Great Answer, how the arches work, and what information about the home world that leaks out are just a few of many mysteries waiting to be investigated. I'm not advocating for neglecting the arches. I'm just saying there are more questions, real worthwhile pursuits beyond our current scope. Both things you can touch and some that you can't." She glanced away and sighed. "Maybe some of this is coming from my perspective as *just* a *new* Rover. They loaded me up with investigative techniques and tech before pushing me out the door. What did they expect me to think? I don't know."

A perplexing thought, Red considered. There was nothing so specific about their training that *should* confine them to investigating the arches solely. Yet, that was the Order's way. She had long believed only she and her mother alone entertained thoughts such as these. Even her grandpa nodded politely when her mother went on a tirade, but he did not repeat any of her views. Now a young woman Red hardly knew also advocated pushing the boundaries of what a Rover should investigate.

Red stared at the two Journals sitting before her. To illustrate the clear line between her and the former Red's legacy, she had publicly fought against such ideals. Yet she too had a microscopic collection of non-arch findings which seemed to call to her. Could there be any bigger plan to their shared curse? Of course not, she thought. That was silly magical thinking.

"My mother," Red said, "saw this gap in our knowledge and for some reason was drawn to filling it. My grandpa said he saw a light glowing from within her and, even though he didn't walk that path himself, he supported her the best he could from afar. He said living her unapologetic truth was brave. I'm not so sure."

It was not that Red was not brave herself, just daring in different ways. She hesitantly reopened her Journal and flipped to the page with her canyon illustration. The lightning storm raged on the horizon as if it were real. The valves of her heart pumped furiously. Some would contend she was revealing the evidence of a taboo committed, precious wasted paper that could have contained clues for the Great Answer.

She slowly watched Purple's eyes for a sign of disapproval, which is what she would have expected from almost any other Rover she had ever met, but she already knew this was a well-calculated risk based on Purple's ecstatic disposition. She did not flinch when Purple reached across her and ran her fingers down the page. The mark's coarseness upon the paper always personally delighted her so she understood the allure.

Purple's face scrunched. "We should go to other places. The Order could divert some of our resources. We don't *all* have to do arches. Conceivably some of us travel, explore, and record amazing sights like this." She lifted away from the sketch. "More of us could see this for ourselves."

"Careful," Red shook her head. "That kind of thinking made my mother an outcast. Some people even said she was an ineffective Rover. It's possible soon she'll only be remembered for ignoring her call." She gazed down at her feet and sighed. She disliked uttering such a terrible future.

Purple shook her head. "But your mom did both!" She slammed her fist into her palm.

Red faced Purple with a blank face. "What are you talking about?"

Purple pointed to both Journals in Red's hands. "She left you with an amazing collection of arch messages *and* information about our world. How could anyone say she didn't answer the call? If you only consider her later years, then from what you said *maybe*." She shrugged. "But the Red Rover of the radio dramas had a lengthy career under her belt. I'd argue she did exactly as they claim. She went above and beyond!"

An unauthorized radio drama, Red realized. They seemed responsible for circulating these strange stories about her mother. A lot of fringe ideas were spread across the airwaves of the pirate stations.

"Well, it isn't the *right* knowledge, is it?" Red pointed out. "The Order's bureaucracy places value on what is worth and not worth knowing." Despite this reality, an inkling of passion sparked to life in her mind. Purple was pushing. She was pushing harder than anyone Red had ever met besides her mother. While she discounted her mother by expectation, Purple did the opposite. Was Red and the Order the ones who had been wrong all this time?

"Besides," Red waved her hand away to banish the thought, "I'm in no position to do anything about that. Even if you or I wanted to formally research more, we'd never be allowed to. Everything we do must be for the Great Answer. You're young. You'll get it soon enough."

Red believed a gulf of maturity still separated the two of them.

Purple frowned. "That seems a little depressing. And we're practically the same age, aren't we?" She looked back at the Journals. "Um, do you have other sketches that you've done? Can I see them?"

Red shut both books. "We shouldn't be talking about this. I've already strayed enough on my own and you're not exactly sounding like a model Rover either. Let's just get back to work." She tucked the books away and shifted back to her computer. She repeated the message and returned to sounding out the words. "Ren…ren…ch…rench. Wrench?"

"Wrench?" Purple flipped through her own Journal and pointed to an entry. "That's an Orderlish word. But it doesn't start with an R. Wrench, with a W. A tool. Used to twist bolts." Floating her finger in the air to help her complete some mental calculations, she screamed, "Oh my gosh! You did it, Red! You divined the first word!"

Red immediately recoiled. "Did you just say *divined?*"

"Um, yes?" Purple replied, curiously taken back. "You know, to gain knowledge directly from the Great Divine?"

For the first time, Red noticed a Divine charm hanging from Purple's neck. The golden metal circle and three thin rays emitting down from the bottom was a common symbol among believers.

She laughed. "Oh, no, sweetie. I don't *divine* anything."

She knew this was rude, but she responded in reflex. She did not know a lot about Purple's home, Gamma settlement, or the cluster of southern settlements known as the Divine Domain, but during her brief visits she had heard gossip about their culture. Rover research programs in the south were incredibly rare. They mostly left the questioning to the rest of the colony. Everyone knew they were pretty superstitious too. People from Gamma would point out they were actually *religious*, but Red saw it as the same thing. For goodness' sake, Abeona-2 was a colony of science! Science flew them here and science kept them alive. Cause and effect, a healthy interest in the unknown, and making decisions with proven knowledge was their collective culture's strength. How could the barbaric practice of tossing a kid into an arch every ten years to appease the *arch gods* not be the definition of superstitious?

She did not dare debate this with Purple out loud. She already knew the familiar Divine talking points. The arches had not destroyed the planet *precisely* because of child sacrifices. The Rovers, in their high-minded quest to unravel the Great Answer, would understand that too if they actually bothered to truly *listen* to the sacred messages. It was a simple case of cause and effect, except those fanatics had gotten it completely backward.

Red was still mentally putting words in Purple's mouth when Green jumped back inside the tent.

"Children!" he exclaimed, finger in the air and chest puffed out. "That's it!"

ROVER ENTRY #1017

What about children?" Red asked Green as he scooched next to her inside the tent meant for one. "Please don't tell me this settlement is feeling the fever too."

Purple flashed her a disapproving look which Red ignored.

Green squeezed in next to the speakers for another listen. An energy built up within him. "That's our first word. Children."

"Actually," Purple said, "our first word is wrench. Red just *divined* it a moment ago."

Red refused to engage in Purple's ploy in front of Green. Instead, she faced him and asked, "What do you need?"

"Can you replay it for me?"

Red turned up the loudspeakers.

"c---l-ren-eve-s-ren-t-e-a-p-op-ia-ef-r-h-s-ze-f-heg-r-en."

He handed her his Journal and pointed to the Orderlish word for children. "It's Ch-ren, not ren-cha. You got it backward."

Red immediately realized her error. "Okay, I hear it. Children it is."

"And I hear *appropriate* and *size*," Green said.

"Children. *Oh no*..." Purple trailed off. Her gaze receded. She looked as if her consciousness had fallen into a well. "I hope...I hope this doesn't have anything to do with the wretched rituals and..."

This surprised Red. Purple spoke ill about her home settlement. Or at the least she did not agree to a fault with all their practices. Her rebellious streak might have extended farther than just a curiosity for illustrations.

"Purple," Green said, pulling her into a hug. "I'm so sorry. I'm sure this has nothing to do with that."

Red left Green to the task of comforting Purple. She typed on her console again. "So, if we put our two slightly different messages together, I think we get something like this." She overlayed one sound on top of the other and performed micro adjustments with spinning dials. The other two watched closely as she orchestrated a process no other Rover would ever do. She played the finished result through the speakers.

"ch-ldre-evels-ren-tye-a-p-opria-ef-rth-s-zeof-heg-rden".

"Ah, yes. There it is," Red said. "I hear it now where I made my mistake…"

"Children levels are not yet appropriate for the size of the garden." Green said in Orderlish. He flipped through his Journal and checked it over again. "That's it! Children levels are not yet appropriate for the size of the garden! Oh my goodness, we just deciphered an entire message in an afternoon!"

While Purple was still translating in her head, Red and Green jumped, screamed, and hugged each other. It took a moment for Red to fully realize what those old-world words meant. She was instantly concerned. Who exactly were these message crafters with their cryptic themes? And were they indeed lost in the past never to be discussed with directly?

"Children?" Green said as he completed translating the message back into their native tongue. "You don't think this really is about…"

"…the ritual," Purple whispered. "That doesn't make any sense. What's the garden? What are the children doing there? Are they okay?" She turned to Green with a hopeful smile. "Could it be? They're actually all okay on the other side? Could my…"

Noticing her shaking lips, his voice boomed as if issuing an order. "We need to know more. Red, is there any way we can scan with your doctored dish and hear more messages?"

"That's not really how that works, but there may be something else we can try." Red felt a chill down her spine. Was there substance to the ritual after all? She too wanted to learn more. If anything, she would love to prove the Divine way was all a bunch of crock. "If this is about the children sent through the arches, people everywhere should learn the truth."

This was the perfect opportunity to test her secret invention. But could the other two be trusted not to tell anyone what she did to make it? Specifically, could *Purple* be trusted?

"You want more data? I can try to get you more data, but I need you two to look the other way on some things." Red lifted the tarp off her cart revealing her obscured experimental device.

Purple scooted in for a closer look. "What's that? I haven't seen anything like that on the equipment list."

"This is the first thing I need you two to pretend you never saw." She hoisted the delicate device onto the table.

Green inspected the rectangular metal box with a flashlight. "It looks like a custom-built machine made of mismatched Rover parts."

"Well, aren't we perceptive? What did I just say?"

"Sorry. I was just…"

Red waved it off. "I know. You're both curious. That's natural. But I think we all know how important it is that we keep this a secret. The fact that I've cannibalized older equipment is criminal. But it's for all the right reasons. It's for the Great Answer."

"How?" Green asked. "Why would you build this?"

She attached a wire to the arch and the device's lights blinked awake. "Our standard equipment is great for one thing: replicating results. When you already know what you want to know, it's easy to interpret something as being the same. But I've always thought there was more we could learn from the arches. Like, first I wondered if we could listen from another angle, gather slightly different information to cross reference and learn more."

"Like your clarity dish modifications," he offered.

"Exactly. I wondered about what else we were missing because we never dived in a little further. That's why I built this." She flipped a switch and the device hummed loudly. "Before I tell you anything else, I need your promises to keep this a secret. I'm confident this has the potential to revolutionize the work we do, but it's going to take time before I get it down to a science and produce results. I…I know you two think of me differently than most people, but I can't let this further harm the Red Rover's reputation in everyone else's eyes. Please. Do you both promise?"

Green did not hesitate. "Of course. Everyone thinks we're on the verge of the Great Answer anyway. Although I'm not entirely convinced you have something *functioning* here, I can at least keep it to myself. I trust you. Whatever it is, I'm sure it'll be interesting."

Red smiled. She turned to Purple.

"I can't…I shouldn't. You've destroyed sacred property. Whatever you're hearing, you might be distorting the Divine messages with your monster device. I think this is all against the Rover Code."

Red let out a slight chuckle. "What is your hang up on following the Rover Code to such a standard? Just a few minutes ago you were practically suggesting we mutiny over the restriction of our research. Even I have my qualms, but I'd never abandon the work."

Green's eyes shifted toward Purple.

She twirled her hair. "Well…I, um, that was really a conversation between the *two of us*, I thought. I don't think we need to hash that out again. I'm just saying there are certain lines maybe we shouldn't cross despite what you think I said."

Purple looked toward the tent's exit.

Red scrutinized her every movement. Her mechanical deviation could not become public before it was the right time. What she would do after grabbing Purple, if necessary, was a frightening mystery.

Yet, Purple turned back to the device. She said quietly, "But…I want to know. I need to know for sure the children are safe. That my brother is safe."

Red did not gasp, but she was surprised.

Purple continued. "I've always believed what we did was for the colony's safety and that every child was cared for by the Divine on the other side. But when they sent my brother into the arch, I petitioned for Iota to create a Rover program. My family's influence made it possible and I joined the Order to unravel the Great Answer and find out if that was true. This could be that proof, what with the mentioning of some type of garden. Yet, if we can learn more and I find out it's actually something terrible…then…I…" She closed her eyes. "I just need to know."

"Purple…" Red said, her arm extending out.

"And," Purple said louder. She reopened her eyes and pointed at Red. "I believe the Red Rover, *your* mother, wouldn't have feared exploring any frontier. It's still for the pursuit of knowledge."

Red froze her hand. She let it fall into her lap and asked, "So, you promise?"

"Yes." Purple nodded. "We've been given a glimpse behind the Divine curtain. The weight of possible responsibility compels me to learn more." She smiled, but not with happiness. Red recognized the look of someone struggling through pain. Perhaps she had Purple figured all wrong.

Red flashed her hands above her creation. "Okay! I present to you the Impulse Encoding Transmitter capable of sending messages back through the arches…in theory."

"No. Wait, stop." Green said with a vigorous shake of his head. "Transmitting uncompromised data through the arches? That's not possible. Every text I've ever read on the subject states anything sent through is scrambled into indistinguishable components."

"My math adds up."

He wagged his finger. "No way. You're telling me you've invalidated centuries of fact. How can you even *claim* to retain the message's integrity? No one's ever achieved that!"

Red sat at her console and typed. "I've figured out there are different classes of messages. Ironically, it was my mother's intense disagreement with our order's insistence that not all knowledge is equal that led me to investigate whether all messages from the arches were equal, in a technical sense anyway.

"First off, I've discovered there are two classes of transmissions. Bottom-class transmissions, like what you were investigating yesterday, and top-class. Bottom-class are ancient communiques from Earth, and presumably from other defunct settlements across the galaxy, that are finally making their way past our little corner of the stars. This is sort of like space noise, litter that humanity cluttered the galaxy's frequencies with. Alternatively, the tops pertain to the Great Answer. Divine clues, if that's what you want to call them, are fantastic examples of top-class transmissions. We've studied the content endlessly, but I don't think anyone's ever studied the frequency's mechanical aspect."

"They're different?" Purple asked. "Like, do they sound peculiar or have a unique accent?"

"Yes, but it's more than that. They do sound somewhat phonetically distinct, sometimes in Orderlish, English, and other languages. But that's just the start. I've analyzed the audio recordings of confirmed top-class messages many times over the last few years. I've been able to visit the originating settlements and re-record some of them from their arches using my clarity dish. Did you know top-class messages can still be detected years, even *decades* after standard Order tech stops being able to pick them up?"

Green smirked. "You're saying you can detect messages that nobody else can hear anymore? Red. I know you're different, a little out there. But this? That's…a bold claim."

"Right?" Red continued undeterred. Any other time she may have been wounded by his characterization of her, but in this moment her heart was burning with adventure. "That's when I realized their wavelengths were distinct and their strength uniquely oscillates over time. You can actually determine if a transmission is a genuine clue just by analyzing the message's technical signature."

"That's incredible! I don't know what that means, but it sounds amazing." Purple put her hands on the IET and peered inside a small observation window. She looked perplexed as she spied spinning wheels and blinking green lights inside. "What is with this glass hole? Why would anyone need to look inside a piece of equipment?"

Red squinted through the glass on the other side and their eyes met. "It's so I can see that it's working properly. Like you two, I'm not an engineer. This took me years to figure out and I'm still not sure it'll work how I hope. There are bound to be quirks." The wheels began spinning wildly and a red light flashed. She smacked the device several times, giving Purple quite a start, until it stopped squealing.

Purple stepped back and beheld the arch engulfed in their private hide-away. "Perhaps there are clues we've missed because we didn't recognize their content as part of the Great Answer. With this new perspective, we can analyze *all* of our past messages and…"

"We *could*," Red said, "but that's not what I'm after. I'm tired of listening." She took her headphones off and wrapped up their cord. She faced the two. "I want to talk back."

"What?" Purple responded, twirling her hair twice as fast this time.

Red returned to her computer. Her leg was bouncing energetically. "I've figured out how to make our equipment match the frequency. I've studied them enough. I think we can send identical messages. If there is anyone out there actively sending these so-called Divine messages, if they are intentionally trying to tell us something, then I'm betting they'll recognize what appears to be one of their own kind. It's possible we'll be able to just ask our questions directly."

"I don't know about this," Green said. "I still have a lot of questions…"

"But why send a message back?" Purple popped out of her chair closer to Red. "Clues are divine messages from the heavens. Their communication only serves to inform us."

"Or, and I add this respectfully," Green said, tilting his head toward Purple, "a more general perspective is that genuine clues are ghostly memories from the ancient past. While we don't know exactly their origin or why the arches choose to capture them, whomever sent them is no longer with us. Sending a message back out would only reach silence. And that's only if we're lucky and…"

Red nodded quickly, repeatedly. Her fingers rattled away on her keyboard. "Perhaps, perhaps! And I've mulled that over considerably. But no one's ever had the capability to try like this. This is just my wish for the machine. I understand the odds are infinitesimal. The device's ability to analyze signatures is obviously of greater value to the Order. I just want to know that I tried and to finally write off this theory before I hand it over. Once it's fully operational, the Order will most likely use it as Purple suggested."

Red reached for the broadcast button on the IET's side. Just about to activate its function for the first time near an arch, her body shivered with excitement. Her finger homed in when Green grabbed her wrist.

Her body froze. Her thoughts were ablaze.

"Wait!" he said. "This is all going too fast. Forget about all the technical problems for a minute and listen to me, please? I haven't even mentioned my biggest concern."

His palm was sweaty. Red was willing to pause for him.

"You are assuming there's someone out there to hear this. There's never been evidence the broadcasters, the gods, the creators of the arches, *whatever* you call them, still exist. For all we know, we're listening to the ramblings of the long extinct home world."

"That's not what they are," Purple said with a stomp of her foot. "Divine messages are not from humans. They only speak with our ancient languages because they must vocalize in our mortal plane while conducting business here."

"That's not real," Red said flatly.

Purple scowled.

"*Or*, and this is the scenario I most hope is too crazy to be the Great Answer, even if the senders do exist, do we want them to know we're here?" He paused. Their hands drifted apart. "Do you remember from the Academy the theory of advanced civilization hostility? That is a hard and fast boundary we should *never* cross!"

Red's heart fell into her stomach. So intent on exploring, so seemingly in complete control of her craft, she had never considered his second point and she should have. That theory was part of a standard Rover education. What would happen if she uncovered a danger to her people? Could she single-handedly be lighting a beacon for humanity's enemies? Was there a deliberate reason Abeona-2 seemed to be the last of the human species? Cut off, unable to announce their presence or even peek out among the stars, their limitations could have been their advantage.

Her hands suddenly trembled. Like the blinding beams of dawn's double suns, the realization that her story sounded dangerously similar to her mother's struck her. But this was different, right? She explored the frontiers of arch knowledge safely inside a tent, not the minutiae of wildlife surrounded by the inhospitable wilds of their planet. But how confident was she that she was not about to charge headfirst past even her own mother's limits of safety?

Purple slammed her hand on top of Greens. Both collided with Red's. "Whatever it is, we can figure it out together!" She caught Red's darting eyes and focused Red upon her.

Red's chest was tight. She was sure she had stopped breathing for a moment.

"I know what you're thinking," Purple continued. "Your mother was a fearless pioneer with no regard for the Code. You believe it was that philosophy which solely led to her troubles. *But* she did it alone. You are not alone."

Red recalled all the times in her career that she had almost died driving off ravines, being electrocuted by faulty wiring, dehydration, starvation, and numerous other pitfalls. Never had she ever faced one of them with someone standing beside her. If she was capable of surmounting all those challenges, then the odds were mathematically in their favor. The three of them were more than capable of venturing into this unknown.

A long, cleansing exhale accompanied a feeling of wonder for her colleague Purple. This was bravery. Purple's courage was in service of the Great Answer. Despite her earlier judgment, Purple was a true Rover.

"I...I need to know." Red took their hands with hers and slammed the button down. She leaned her face into the IET microphone. "This is Red Rover. I repeat, this is Red Rover. If you're receiving this, acknowledge us and send more messages. Over." She repeated her call for half an hour in twelve languages with no breaks.

They spent the entire day in that tent listening for any responding messages. No new signals emerged other than static and ghastly scream-like distortions the Order had long chalked up to space radiation. Regardless, not a moment was wasted. Three Rovers working together in-person, getting to know each other in such close quarters, comparing notes, and feeling the human connection was its own exciting excursion. The inner workings of people, Red would discover slowly, were another hardly understood area of study.

Green slept on the floor that night after refusing to accept Purple's protest about seniority and respect. She left the following morning, having arrived Red's rival but leaving as a friend. After another day of the kind of standard observation Rovers were expected to do, Red never felt more frustrated to be alone like when she embarked on her return home across the desert. Despite her frustrations with Green and her misgivings about Purple, Red did not want to go back to her status quo. Yes, Rovers were a part of a grand scientific order filled with hundreds of researchers, but they rarely ever communed with another human being like the three of them did that day.

They did not know it yet, but together they had discovered the border of a vast new frontier. The three of them would not be the first Rovers to venture outside the Order's boundaries. Red's mother had claimed that distinction and she was not celebrated for it. But they were about to become the first whom the settlements started listening to

ROVER ENTRY #1018

Many months passed and Red's friendship with Purple and Green grew. They exchanged social messages through the Rover Research Network even though that was technically a misuse of the platform. Purple had to be prodded into joining in, but eventually she caved.

"Purple! I looked at your travel schedule and noticed we could connect for drinks in Delta if I rearranged a few things. How about it?"

"Are you safe? I heard terrornadoes swept through Zeta while you were supposed to be out there."

"Did you hear that Cyan's divination was classified as another sign? I wonder if it mentioned the children or the garden."

When meeting with her new friend Purple, Red occasionally spoke of the IET in person, not daring to leave a trace of such talk on the network. They told no one else about what they attempted that day and, honestly, they did not think anything *had* been done.

However, just as winter began to recede, Red found herself standing in front of her settlement's arch because of their actions.

Just like on her Rover initiation day, colonists held hands on the blustering sand hill's base leading to the metallic mountain. The audience watched at a distance as Red stood near the arch. But this time the massive crowd, composed of citizens from settlements all over the planet, differed greatly in origin and belief. Both the scientific and religious observers sat intermingled within the viewing gallery.

Her otherwise familiar arch spewed frighteningly erratic, billowy clouds of stardust. This anomalous behavior, going on for weeks now, was the first sign of a forthcoming groundbreaking event which prompted the Order to plan and host this ceremony. Pennant and flag decorations of purple, orange, and every Rover designation flapped in the wind. Makeshift booths constructed of repurposed metal from the homes of supportive Omega believers protected the encircling aristocrats and officials from the well-to-do governing bodies sitting beside the Divine clergy hungry for validation. They together believed the speculation that the Great Answer was finally upon them. And due to the newest message broadcast by arches all over the globe, they too agreed the Red Rover was personally invited to discover it.

Rovers from across the colony were in a special observation area to Red's left. Young and old, many of which she personally knew, were recording every detail furiously in their Journals.

Her grandpa was permitted to stand by her side unlike a decade prior. He waved her close to him and asked a question with a hoarse voice barely above a whisper.

Red knew his time for eternal retirement was quickly approaching. She knelt to be closer to his words and listened intently again.

"My sweet desert flower, are you sure about this? No one knows where the arch leads or if you'll survive. Children have never returned in the past."

She placed a hand upon the back of his head and drew him to her shoulder. Red noticed how strange it was to be the source of support. Memories of her mother were limited but vivid, yet she could not recall being comforted in this way. Red took solace recognizing that putting people first was important to her, a stark contrast from how her mother felt.

But she could not turn back now. Yes, she had the same concerns. Frighteningly little information about the arch's intentions and capabilities all added up to a mistake in the making. Yet, the reputation of the Red Rover could recover greatly if she were to succeed. Unlike her mother's lonely, daring adventures on the frontier, she was surrounded and supported by her people. The Order believed she was completing a great task for the colony. What good Rover would say no to such a request?

"Yes, grandpa. I have to. The Great Answer might be on the other side. That's our calling. And mother couldn't solve it, so…"

He nodded and stepped back. From a small cloth sack, he handed her a box she had not seen in many years. It was her family's keepsake case.

"What is that? What is he giving you?" The Rovers called out clamoring to know.

Their questions passed right over her. She focused fully on the box. She hesitantly accepted it and immediately recognized its familiar weight. She ran her fingers across the scuffed metal exterior and the Rover symbol etched onto the lid. The hinges creaked as it opened. She found her mother's excursion glove waiting inside.

She cast her eyes away. "No, grandpa. Take it back. I don't need her."

His hand on her cheek, he directed her gaze to his smile. He nodded slowly. "Don't think of it as *her* glove. It can be *your* glove instead." He took the piece out and cradled it delicately in one hand. "This glove may be one of the last things that connects us to her, but it wasn't all that she was. She was so much more. And there's no denying you're like her in some ways." He pulled her into a hug. His voice cracked as he said, "But, you're different too in so many more. This is a good piece. Take it and make it your own."

She tentatively took the glove and examined it closer. Made from the blood-red hide of the canidauroch, equipment made from them was known to be impervious to almost anything. Many years after her initiation, she learned that this glove had prevented an unfathomably greater pain at the hand of the arch. Other Rovers had described the feeling of fire, electricity, daggers, and the peeling of skin which she was thankfully unfamiliar with. Because of her immature age and lack of prior training, her grandpa convinced the Governor to allow her to wear the glove despite the Order code. If it could insulate her like that, then objectively the glove was an exceptional survival tool.

Red decided to try it on just to see how it felt. Once slipped up to her wrist, the surprising warm embrace of her mother enveloped her. Her compassion, her soft skin, all the things that Red loved about her and none of the frustrating baggage. Emotion flooded her mind, spilled out of her head, rolled past her shoulders, and down her back.

She had robbed herself of this comfort all these years. And for what? Running away from her mother's legacy? Her mother may not have been wrong in all she did, just not yet appreciated. Members of the Order viewed Red's IET mostly in the same way. She was forced to reveal it to help explain the cause of the Great Answer events. After all the pomp of this event concluded, she knew she would face grave reprimands for what she did, but she did not let that bother her. Her machine was right and good and it served a purpose for the Order.

"Now, go," he said. "Find her on the other side."

She did not understand what he meant at the time. Her mother was never fascinated with the arches.

Watching the swirling blue portal shimmering like a pool of water within the metallic arch, Red stood as ready and confident as she would ever be. She turned to her audience and spotted Green and Purple pausing their Journal documentation just long enough to wave and smile at her.

She extended her gloved hand close to the portal and felt a familiar tingling sensation that scared her. She recoiled and, for a moment, the portal organized itself into a startling, clear image that was familiar yet alien.

"Red Rover, Red Rover, send yourself over." The portal whispered aloud the message that previously only their equipment could hear. The unexpected audible vocalization from the chaotic structure set her curiosity ablaze. She believed she was perceiving the first message to ever be interpreted with the human ear alone. How the arch emitted unassisted perceptible sound waves was a mystery for another day.

As the voice grew louder and echoed out into the settlement, the crowd fell silent. Many Rovers removed their headphones in bewilderment.

Red took a step back and steeled her nerves for her charge. Unraveling the mysteries of the arches was a Rover's duty. Now she had the chance to do the preeminent task and learn more than any of them had ever imagined. She had never fancied herself a brazen explorer like her mother, but the universe was calling her by name to investigate its supreme secrets.

She hoped in her heart that the Red Rover would discover and return with the greatest answers the colony had ever known.

The King of the Hill

File Under: sport, resilience, pursuit

Location(s): Balamanda

Executive Summary: Those who are seeking my field-leading ethnological research will find the anecdotal accounts of all my known associates within the following five sections transcribed from interviews regarding their perspective and experience with vibrant steel prior to meeting me. The following entry is based on one such set of interviews conducted with a resident of the planet Balamanda, my known associate King Cunningham. His knowledge brought us much of our current understanding regarding the culture and recreational life of our fellow humans across the stars. While their interests are far from representative of the larger galactic society, they are none the less equally foreign to us.

ROVER ENTRY #1021

He loved the thrill of the climb and the smashing of metal, but young King always wished for more than having to fight his brothers and sisters for the remote just to watch it all from the couch. Mauler Hill was growing into the galaxy's biggest sport. Back when he was a kid, he lived for everything Maul. One day he hoped to be a glorious part of it all.

Men of a certain age would eventually grow out of childhood obsessions. King lost interest in mud and worms but his enthusiasm for the sport never waned. Being a working adult in the big city was a struggle and he had no idea freedom came with bills. Regardless, the trade-off was worth it because he could indulge in the Maul away from his small town's judgmental eyes.

It was standing room only on his morning commute but King did not mind. The passenger train hovered over the steel tracks. Smooth electromagnetism hurtled the monorail car above the bustling port city of millions. He skimmed through the galactic news on a colorful rag he bought for a reasonable five credits. He knew one could never totally trust these types of publications, but at least he would have enough truth to hold his own during a conversation with some smarty-pants at the gym.

The front page shouted a sensational headline:

Earth Directorate Declares Boycott on Autocracy Imports

He chuckled and shook his head. That would not last. The home world gluttons could never cut themselves off from all the cheap, plentiful vibrant steel the Autocrats discovered on the galaxy's other side. This not well understood element, which emitted its own limitless energy, is what put his home, Balamanda, initially on the galactic map.

Peering out the window, the skyscrapers approaching from the horizon seemed like elevators to heaven. However, King knew they were built a long time ago using locally sourced vibrant steel. The entire construction industry had its own devilish secrets and a lot of it was connected to unscrupulous business practices. That did not sound like any divine road he had ever heard of.

Those buildings were built by his ancestors during a period known as the Metal Rush. The first settlers dismantled the enigmatic, massive steel rings discovered within the western hemisphere's mountains. The ring's rare metal ushered humanity into a new age of energy independence. As the only supplier at the time, Balamanda became a melting pot of people from dozens of colonies across the stars looking for work. In the centuries since its discovery, other small deposits had been found, but Balamanda still held the crown for largest harvested vibrant steel stockpile.

King's grandma told him that back when she was a kid, Balamanda announced on the galactic news network its intention to seriously reduce its exports due to concern of running out of it themselves. Their home-grown sport, Mauler Hill, was practically a formalized religion to Balamandans. With planetary franchise opportunities emerging and having created an entire economy around the metal, demand for the steel was high and would only intensify. Slimy home world politicians had been clamoring ever since for a competing source. This is what led them into precarious relationships with the likes of the Autocracy.

King never cared much for politics. But he kept abreast just enough to know whether elections ever concerned the regulation of anything Maul.

Sometimes that meant supporting the Autocracy, like backing those who wished to expand the sport into their realm, and other times not.

The train car entered a tunnel and experienced a moment of muted obscurity. Complete and utter darkness, his grandma warned him, would be their planet's future if Balamanda kept exporting the steel across the galaxy at rock-bottom prices. In the centuries since the Rush, the metal influenced every part of Balamandan life. The rails he traveled on were electrified by substations humming with steel. The factory gears that produced the paper he read rotated because of batteries crafted around the metal.

The light at the end of the tunnel grew brighter until the city's skyline burst into grand view. This is why King preferred standing. Settled close to the window, he had a front row seat to a majestic landscape. Almost monopolizing the scene, a titanic colony ark hovered above the city's central starport waiting to take on migrants. He pitied the ignorant saps who thought any other planet could beat out Balamanda. Best of luck finding a star system with half as much entertainment.

Nestled within the city's streets, two Mauler stadiums rose from the gray urban jungle like a pair of dueling mountain peaks. The rivaling team's colors adorned the domes. Today his shirt was Caldarado Killers red but tomorrow he would show off Glo-town Mowdown green. As a true fan of the game, he viewed the sport as big enough for everyone.

Another train whizzed by. He caught a glimpse of the destination scrolling in light across the side: his rinky-dink hometown. When he left that place behind, he knew there was only one place he wanted to be. The Mauler mecca of the world and the sole city with two teams, Caldarado had an electric atmosphere that washed over the metropolis all day and night. In-person games were plentiful, fans were everywhere, and Mauler fever infected the city's every facet. The fact that one team was a twelve-time champion and the other was practically bush league concerned him not in the slightest. They both were entertaining to watch in their own way.

His stop quickly approached so he reckoned it was time to scoot toward the door. He picked up his duffle bag. One of his steel practice boots fell out and clanked across the floor near another passenger.

"Hey, son," an old man said as he picked up the boot and returned it to him. "Are you a Mauler?" he asked with an imperfect grin.

"What? No!" King responded by reflex. He waved his hands dismissively. "That's…that's not what you think it is!"

He stopped himself and remembered where he was. "Ah, wait. Well, what I mean to say is *not yet*," he said with a wink.

No need to hide his interest anymore, but old habits die hard especially when they were tied to your well-being. The city and its wonderful people would not judge him, but this interaction did stir up the memory of more oppressive times when he was shunned for dreaming of being a glorious Mauler.

ROVER ENTRY #1022

King grew up in a quaint little town in an otherwise barbaric world. If the official planetary sport, Mauler Hill, revealed anything about Balamanda, a majority of society loved ruthless combat. But King's hometown cherished the opposite. This peaceful place had one road in and one road out. Nobody left and others only passed through. Couple that with the influence of the Harmonious Sect of the Divine Church and you had a recipe for a bunch of good ol' boys and girls.

He never bought into that narrative. While almost everyone in town was content taking their place in the mold and nestling in, you could find kids like him hidden in small, rarely seen parts who liked to push their boundaries and almost always get back up when the world knocked them down. The local leadership discouraged, persecuted, and drilled out this attitude from those stupid enough to flaunt it. Luckily for King, he was a special kind of stupid who could not be taught to quit.

One of King's most vivid memories was the glimpse of his first Mauler game. At about age seven, the sport was coming back from a slump. It received a lot of press when a large foreign star system established a new franchise.

He, his Ma, and five of his dark-haired, grubby siblings were browsing the TVs at Ted's Electronics. They could never afford a screen from there, but Ma liked to window shop. She let go of King's hand for just a second and he ran towards a monitor exploding with Mauler glory.

Static sparks, drawn inductively from the jagged beams of the vibrant steel hill, skittered up the standard alloy armor's sides. Blinking indicators upon their chest plates flashed red when another Mauler lifted their feet off the ground and threw them tumbling down the cliffside. Crimson splashed across the camera as the Ardiac City Rippers' Lieutenant Deek clobbered The Blue Bomber from Trost knocking her off the summit and clenching an epic Ardiac overtime victory. King had never in his short life seen such raw violence and by such large titans that were somehow human. To a small boy, Maulers were towering masses of strength and he wanted to be just like them.

He witnessed a true spectacle that day. But Ma and Pa would have expected better from him.

"How grotesque! Someone's gotta turn this filth off!" That's what Ma later told him was the correct response when seeing anything so unharmonious.

Instead, he screamed, "Look, Ma!" The whole store took notice with all their delicate sensibilities. That moment brought shame upon his entire family for generations, or at least Ma described it that way.

Because of *The Incident*, Pa railed on him for years about the staggering number of missed formal school hours he racked up. The town's harmony board sanctioned him to ongoing church-supervised Harmony rehabilitation. Every morning, instead of class, he went to a little marigold building behind the church for an hour and listened to what he felt were dumb lectures about being a good neighbor. He knew they were dumb because no one would schedule something important at the crack of dawn with everyone half asleep. And the teacher? She was the dumbest part.

Ms. Kennedy often paced the little Sunday school room while attempting to teach him and another boy, from the Tsu family, about the importance of being tender to others. Children's drawings of people floating into clouds and enormous brains barreling through space adorned the walls. The stained windows' colorful glass was pleasant enough but they reminded him too much of the church chamber proper and all the sugary sermons the pastor dribbled onto the townsfolk. Most of those folks seemed nice enough at first, but they ate up the silly philosophies and eventually ended up judging him just on rumors alone. He kept his distance from that type of groupthink most of all.

"And that's why you can't be watchin' this Mauler Hill scrap," Ms. Kennedy said as she circled around little King with a ruler in her hand. Smack, smack, smack, the wooden stick slapped upon her palm to keep them in line. She had never hit either of them before, but perhaps she believed threats were sufficient encouragement enough. "What part of hittin' your friends has any part of maintainin' harmony with them?"

"Well, ma'am, I didn't think 'bout that when I was watchin' it on the TV," King said through their thick rural accent. "I just reckon it's excitin'. I don't want to hurt none of my friends. I wouldn't do what I see on TV to any of 'em. And besides, ain't there a difference between bein' tender with your hands and tender with your heart?" He thrust his thumb to his chest. "I'm a good boy with a good heart! My biggest bro says so!"

Ms. Kennedy rolled her eyes. "Do you really expect me to believe that? What about last week when you were runnin' around behind the Jeppson's place with that weighted metal getup held together with tape? You nearly knocked the teeth out of little Tillie Sue!" She leaned down and hovered her stern face in front of King. "Now that there's a nice little girl. She doesn't need any influence from the likes of you."

King slowly pushed his chair back and away from her ugly mug. Standing at his desk, he cleared his throat. If he was on trial, then he would present a professional defense. Well, competent at least for an eight-year-old. "Well now, ma'am, I didn't mean for none of that to happen. I was just playin' by my lonesome, away from home on account of, well you know, how Ma and Pa don't approve of me playin' dress up, when Tillie Sue came 'splodin around the bend and bumped into *me*. It was an honest accident."

"'Splodin? What the scrap does 'splodin mean? Please explain yourself to me or maybe don't. I suggest the latter if you know what's good for you." The Harmonious Church had easy ways and hard ways of convincing people to harmonize to the beat of their drum. Anyone who truly knew King Cunningham knew he seemed to always dance to the wrong rhythm.

"You know, 'splodin. Dartin' like a skunk outta a log so fast that you can't dodge its spray. I know I wasn't too good at gettin' outta her way that time, but mark my words I'm gonna keep practicin' my dodgin' game and become the greatest Mauler you ever did see! Yes ma'am, next time..."

"King Lee Cunningham! You will *not* play Mauler Hill ever again and I'm going to personally see to that, ya little snot-nosed kid!"

That's when the hitting began. He did not have much kindness towards Ms. Kennedy, but he gave her some credit. Thanks to her, he learned how to dodge a ruler and how to grin and take it when he could not.

He also was not so dense as to ignore the Harmonious Divine Church's role. Everyone getting along was the only way their little congregation would stay together after the spiritual event known as the Singularity Rapture occurred, so claimed their scriptures. They hoped to maintain their essence as one mind amid a sea of human consciousness and float forever together in space or some other nonsense. Pamphlets on that hogwash were pervasive in their region and King made a habit of tearing them down wherever he saw one posted. It was like sticking it to Ms. Kennedy every time.

"Look, Ms. Kennedy," he would say to himself. "I'm doing it. Despite you and all the others, I'm walking toward glory."

ROVER ENTRY #1023

As primary school trudged on, everybody learned to avoid associating with King. He interacted with people around town mostly through curt interactions peppered with dirty glances. It did not get easier in secondary school. The steel nerds would not have him, the church posers thought he was evil incarnate, and the jocks were interested in boring sports like toss-ball because no one could establish a Maul league on a rural school budget.

His pariah status made for a lot of alone time lifting weights, hiding away to read Maul magazines, and catching the occasional broadcast when no one was home. However, it turned out the unlikeliest person did not see him as a complete waste. She curiously popped up every now and then whenever he experienced a newest low, offering a kind word or just her time to listen.

He decided to take his shot and ask her to the Spring Fling his Sophomore year.

Truly an angel, sweet Tillie Sue let him invite her right on her front porch, in view of the public, with a face fit for a Mauler. He had at least two scars, a black eye, and a patch of his hair missing on account of catching her straight after one of his secret training sessions down by the inductive rail tracks. His initial thought was *'gee, won't she be impressed by how hard I worked out?'* But by the time he stood at her door, he was sweating dumbbells and almost forgot his own dang name.

"Hi, i-it's me, Tillie…I mean King! You're Tillie Sue!"

She pushed her bangs out of her eyes and smiled. "I know who I am, King. What can I do for you?"

Her parents must not have been home or they would have shooed him away at the door.

"I-I was thinkin', wonderin' really if maybe you'd ever think about goin' with me to the…"

"Spring Fling?" she finished. "I'd love to!"

On the night of the dance, the silvery streamers and colored lights the school decorated with were really nice. They were slow footing under the school gymnasium glow to one of those sultry June Roberts' numbers. Tillie Sue's silver hair rested on her shoulders and shimmered in the twilight. Her poofy, periwinkle dress was just so her style.

King built up the courage to ask her about that time when they were kids. His curious mind had wanted to know what she thought for ages, but he never found an appropriate time. He convinced himself within her arms that answers never came to the meek.

"Tillie Sue, I really gotta know somethin'. Do you remember that time I was muckin' around in that alley behind your house and you ran into me?"

"What was that? What time?" she said looking up at the ceiling. "Oh, you don't possibly mean sometime between the third and the fifth grade, do you? For some reason I can't remember anythin' from that time of my life."

"Oh scrap!" The glaze in her eyes was proof that his young carelessness had literally knocked the memories out of her. The color drained from his skin. Anyone looking on might have thought the professional Blue Bomber herself tore through his body and ripped out his stomach.

"King? Are you okay?" she asked with concerned eyes.

"I, uh…just it's…"

She cracked a smile. "I was just jokin'! You didn't believe me, did you?" She threw her head back and guffawed. She punched him in the arm for good measure.

He sighed and chuckled too. She twirled in his arms as he swung her around to show her how strong he was. They gave no care to the other dancers dodging out of their way under the sparkling lights as they laughed.

"Oh please!" she said. "I can take a little bump on the head. I ain't one you gotta keep in an iron vase like those prissy miss summer flowers."

The prancing girls nearby scowled.

They ignored them.

During their remaining school years together, she accompanied him a few times down to the tracks for his self-guided Mauler workouts. He had the world's trashiest set of insulated powerboots on his feet, but once they touched those tracks and energized up, they were enough to get him used to the sensation of electricity flowing between his toes.

In pursuit of impressing her, he lost his footing trying to execute a particularly hard maneuver. He tripped over himself on an otherwise flawless stunt. As he fell, he threw his unshielded arm out and accidentally smacked against the track. A hair-tingling shock surged through his body which he would not soon forget. Mysteriously, vibrant steel itself was safe to touch, but any other metal that carried its charge punished you for it.

"R-r-rust bucketssss!" He rolled away and grabbed his convulsing arm.

"Ha!" Tillie Sue pointed with one hand over her mouth. "You're gonna have to be better than that if you're ever gonna make it pro."

She sat comfortably on the lush grass nearby. The tall trees and light breeze provided shade while King struggled to catch his breath in the midday sun's heat. "You should really pick up a couple more pieces of a suit. It'd keep you from turnin' yourself into an electric eel every other day."

He rubbed a medical gel on his arm and watched the electrical burn fade away. "I don't have the money for nice upgrades like that right now."

He decided on a break and joined her in the shade. The soft grass and gently sloped ravine they found themselves in was serene.

"And hey, this is a lot harder than it looks. I've put in years tryin' to get this back flip just right, but it's really hard to keep haulin' all this metal armor on you when it's not powered anymore. You gotta have some real strength for that brief moment of separation."

She shrugged. A cloud passed above and it looked like a mountain. "I don't see why that should even be a problem. Can't they just make them suits out of vibrant steel themselves? You wouldn't need any energy hill or whatever under your feet." She whispered, "Seems pretty stupid to miss that."

"Amateur talk. Listen. Where would the sport be without the electric hill? You gotta have some boundaries, strategy, and challenge." His face lit up just thinking of it. "Keepin' yourself on the field, being strong enough to lift the weight of all that metal! All of that *makes* Mauler Hill what it is!"

She gave it no thought. "Is that it? Just a bunch of meatheads tryin' to out brawn each other? They don't want any help?"

King rolled to face her. Would nothing impress this woman? He captured her passing gaze and held her attention. Her eyes were aflutter, chest still as if she had stopped breathing. But dropping dead was not going to stop him from setting her straight. Darn it. She needed to understand the sport.

"Well, no. Mauler Hill is about strength, sure, but the Hills are basically giant chunks of solid vibrant steel pieces because it's explosive if you try to bend it too much. Would it be nice if they shaped an actual mountain out of them? I guess so, but tryin' to do that would blow a factory sky high. Same goes for makin' whole suits out of them."

A faint crack spread across her lips and she burst out laughing. She rolled onto her back and stared at the clouds again. He followed her wandering eyes and spotted the cloud she seemed drawn to. It was the mountain.

"Actually," he continued, "I reckon I prefer it this way. If they could shape the metal, they'd just make all the Hills exactly the same. I like it more that every stadium's Hill is completely unique."

He traced the cloud with his finger. Tillie Sue leaned closer to him and watched as he said, "You gotta learn the curves, the ins and outs of your opponent's Hill to do your best. There's a lot of strategy just in that."

Hours later under the cover of night, they rendezvoused in secret in a shed of one of Tillie Sue's girlfriends. They watched a high-profile match on a tiny travel television. This was Tillie Sue's first game and King brimmed with enthusiasm at the idea of her taking an interest in the spectacle of the sport. She was athletic, competed in three school sports and would no doubt be able to follow the game. He did not know it at the time, but she was not there for that. Perhaps the urge for teenage rebellion had started growing inside of her. It did not matter what he proposed they do that night. She was simply happy sitting next to him as he whooped and hollered at the television and scarfed down a whole bowl of chips before she even had three.

They were close after that first summer, but they never quite ignited the flame many of their peers did. Possibly they were looking for different things or they saw diverging futures for themselves. King's insistence they rarely hang out together in public to lessen the occasional ridicule she suffered from their peers probably contributed. Regardless, the day came when he was leaving for the city. Whether they would ever see each other again was unknowable.

Saying to heck with his senior year, he lingered in his parent's driveway at the wheel of his idling rusted truck. He finished his goodbyes to his many brothers and sisters as they paraded past his window. Hand slaps, pats on the arm, and stuck out tongues were par for the course. He loved them all dearly.

His parents refused to show any sign of support for this grave mistake so they stayed in the house. He thought he caught a glimpse of Ma pulling back the front curtain but it could have been the wind.

His heart deflated at the thought that Tillie Sue would miss him by the time he was ready to go. She knew he was planning to be gone by noon as they had just talked about it the night prior. That fiery conversation was the closest thing resembling an argument they ever had. She considered him a fool to venture out into the barbaric world of Balamanda. Watching from their couch was one thing, but residing in the cities surrounded by all those unknown, unharmonious people? That may very well spell trouble for a country boy.

A lump in his throat almost brought him to tears as he pulled out into the street. To his surprise, Tillie Sue came sprinting through the neighborhood. His heart was aquiver.

"King! Wait up, you rusthead!"

"You're the rusthead. I reckon you forgot to see me off. Whatcha' got there?" He pointed to a small box in her hand.

She gave it to him.

Inside, he found a set of five metal rings and a thin, chainmail glove. Brushed surfaces and tiny jagged tiger-orange flecks sprinkled about, the jewelry rested upon a soft cushion of white fiber. They looked extremely luxurious.

"What's this?"

"Did you forget all your school lessons or is your head all messed up from all your falls? They're vibrant steel rings. The glove's so you don't 'splode your fingers off."

"I know *what* these are. I mean why are you givin' them to me?" Curiosity compelled him to slip one on. It fit just fine.

She gently took hold of his hand and squeezed the ring between her fingers. "They're cut out of solid vibrant steel. Drilled the hole right through the center. No bendin' necessary. Lot of waste metal that way though."

"These must've cost a fortune then!"

She pulled another ring out of the box and slipped it on his next finger. The two attracted each other like magnets. A surge ran through King's bones that might have brought a weaker individual to their knees, but his tolerance was high by now. He admired the others inside and knew this set could make a fist into an unstoppable force.

"How...why are you givin' these to me? You're crazy," he smiled, holding the box with an iron grip. He was nervous he might drop them and cast disrespect.

"Well, I figured you would need somethin' to protect yourself out there in the big city. I actually didn't spend no money on them on account of I have this and another set already at home. They're mine, left to me from my grandpa. He used them when he was working down in the old mine. Just the rocks and his fist. And seein' as how I ain't predictin' to start any fights in my future…"

He mustered all his will and quickly boxed them again. "Oh, Tillie Sue. I can't take these from you."

She pushed them into his chest and held her hands against his. He did not resist further. Instead, he tried to capture that moment in his mind so once he left this town forever, he could always remember what the only good thing about that place felt like.

"Do it, King Cunningham. You're the scrappiest, aim-for-the-mooniest person I've ever did met, and if you're gonna make it you'll need a uniform of your own one day. Consider this your first sponsorship, one that'll keep you connected to your biggest fan back home. I'll be watchin' every game back here until I see you on top of the Hill reachin' for the sky."

ROVER ENTRY #1024

From the stands of the two city stadiums, King spent a couple spectacular years watching a lot of his heroes take to the Hill and just as often get chucked by an opponent, breaking every bone in their body on the way down, and having their careers violently ended. He loved the freedom to watch his passion from a vantage point he ever only dreamed of.

Money was tight but otherwise he was doing well on his own. He counted burying his accent as his first success relieving him of being incessantly discriminated against as a crazy Harmonious cultist in an otherwise cut-throat city. After that, he left his old job as a school janitor and landed a dream position as a fitness instructor. It allowed him to grind the dollars by day and at night train in the gym for his own gains. The humble one-story facility in the city's heart was unremarkable except for its affordable membership fee, great for someone who wanted available machines at any hour and non-judgmental eyes.

While he had not grown up to be the hulking monster he had aspired to be, still a short, lean, and fairly unassuming guy, he never stopped telling himself one day it would be him climbing the Hill.

Too bad his coworkers had less-inspiring words.

"King, you dang rusthead. You could be doubling your paycheck if you started doing night classes. Aren't you always complaining about not having enough money? Just take my shift." His coworker Jeremy blocked his way as King tried to use the timeclock to end his workday.

King's afternoon had been long. The free weights were calling. He wanted to tell Jeremy off, but Jeremy was the first major Mauler fan he met in the city and the one who helped him land this job. Jeremy was the only person King considered to have Maul enthusiasm that came close to rivaling his own. Even better, this saint often volunteered his time to train King utilizing supposed formal routines. King could not muster a nasty word to this great guy. Also, Jeremy was older than him. Not as old as his dad, but King looked up to him.

"Come on, Jeremy. You know I stick to a strict schedule. I gotta get my muscle mass up another couple percent if I'm gonna stay competitive in the spring season tryouts. I wanna, you know…" he diverted his eyes up and away, "be ripped like you one day." King did not embarrass easily. But pointing out his insufficiencies and how much he wanted to be like Jeremy made him feel incredibly vulnerable.

Jeremy chuckled. "Yeah, I know."

King perked up and tried changing the subject. "How about instead of either of us working, you and I do a little joint lifting? I'm always saying you could be a Mauler if you tried. Why don't we squeeze out a few more gains together and you come with me to the tryouts next week?"

"Yeah, that kind of stuff isn't for me anymore." Jeremy seemed a little uncomfortable with the compliment.

Jeremy often reminded him the chances of being drafted by a pro team were slim to none, yet he pushed King anyway to the specifications befitting of a Mauler. The routines were as excruciating as warned. Where Jeremy learned all these drills was beyond him. King just attributed Jeremy's deep Mauler knowledge to the years of watching the matches in-person he had missed out on as a kid. He could be a Mauler if he just tried.

Assuming they had seen enough of each other for the evening, King moved his timecard toward the clock.

Jeremy pretended to flex for no reason, which made King laugh, and he snatched the timecard just before it slipped in.

"Hey, come on, man." King grabbed at it but could not connect.

Jeremy waved it around and evaded King's every grasp. "Why are you standing in the way of a debonair, desirable, eligible bachelor who has a date with one of the most handsome men in the city? There is already hardly enough time for me to grace every person with my presence."

Jeremy kept the card expertly out of reach. His reflexes were sharper than King expected, but that did not stop King from getting in his face and continuing to attack.

"Look, King!" Jeremy was smiling but his patience surely waned. "I didn't want to say anything because I hoped you would just do this for me, but you should know my next shift has some local celebrities in it. Don't you have a desire to get your face more out there?"

King paused. "Yeah, in Mauler territory, not in gossip circles. Who are we talking about? Some city council members who I gotta basically babysit? I reckon my time is better spent grinding." He faked left but grabbed right and reclaimed his card.

Jeremy clapped. "Okay. You're really busting my chops here. Final offer: how about I personally buff your pay, double an hour out of my pocket, for the rest of the night?"

King did the math. His proposal was certainly generous. Who exactly was Jeremy meeting with? A movie star? King would have no problem making rent and would even have a little extra towards that new pair of powergloves he had been saving up for.

Pleased with his unintentional negotiation skills, he said, "Deal. But this time don't pay me in sandwiches. I need hard credits. And come on, tell me who I'm spotting."

Jeremy chuckled and somehow snatched the card back and slipped it into the wall holder. "I don't have time for that. The schedule is right there, rusthead!"

King checked the schedule on the wall as Jeremy bolted off. He had been bamboozled. Did Jeremy even have a date or did he just want to get out of an almost guaranteed difficult and annoying session? Irritation filled King. He was the unlucky sap next to serve the Caldarado Killers, their local professional pariahs. Sure, they put on a good show, but no one would ever want to have a conversation with them.

Inside his head, a little Jeremy voice said, "King, you dang rusthead! This is exactly the kind of opportunity you were talking about. It just fell into your lap." This faux-Jeremy was certainly not his friend. Caldarado's significantly less successful franchise was well known for being utter braggarts. They lose every cross-town bout against the Glo-town Mowdowns but boast about their tenacity and ferociousness as if they were supreme. True, nobody became a Mauler without breaking a few bones, most of the time their own, but that did not mean you automatically earned the credentials to treat other people like less than.

King groaned. A deal was a deal. Since no one qualified remained to help him suit up manually, he stepped into the automated equipment machine. Standing as still as he could upon a buzzing metal plate, a robotic arm swirled around him and clamped metal boots and greaves around his legs. His extended arms bore the gauntlets and vambraces combined weight which he trained tirelessly in. A dense cuirass encased his torso while a tornado of delicate mechanical arms precisely placed metal patches between every remaining gap. His helmet remained but he stopped the machine short so he could breathe comfortably for the time being.

He looked like a tin can and moved about as fast as one would expect, but this suit kept athletes safe during the brutal sport. He turned on the powermat in the Hill training room and waited for the team to arrive.

In the interim period, he looked out the enormous window that stretched the facility's front end. The city street bustled with early evening traffic. He could un-suit and disappear among the passing cars. Forget credits. He just wanted to avoid being yelled at for the rest of the night. He recalled the train car heading back to his hometown. The line could still be running. He could hop home for a surprise visit, kiss his siblings on the head, and catch up with dear Tillie Sue if she were available. What had become of her adult life, he wondered? The dream tempted him something fierce.

He shook off the silly thoughts and took a deep breath when the team walked in with over fifteen people. He regretted his lack of boldness when they immediately expressed their displeasure with him.

"Hey. Who the heck is this little guy? Where's Jeremy?" said a woman leading the crowd.

King thought he would be starstruck when Bethlam Ross, better known by her player name, The Dixon Chixon, pointed at every part of his body, but instead it just made him self-conscious.

King fathomed himself a capable athlete who could lift a powerhelmet as high as the pros, but Bethlam was a beast among monsters. The Killers' lead climber, known for using every ounce of her bulging biceps to claw her way to the top of the Hill, made a short blond haircut work during a time such a do was out of fashion. Seeing her looming above her compatriots in the flesh made King almost believe the rumors that the team's other members were strategically smaller so she could chuck them like weapons at the other climbers.

She had a little bit of an accent not totally different than his old one. He wondered where she was from. This endeared him a little to her intimidating presence, and after a few false starts he extended a hesitant, welcoming hand.

"Hello, ma'am. The name's King Cunningham and I'll be covering for Jeremy today. If you could all suit up…"

"Hold on," Doug Jalls, The Ravenous Raptor, said. He stepped forward and placed his face just barely hovering in front of King's. Those iconic twin scars across his cheek did all the coercion necessary to shut him up for a moment. "We paid for Jeremy to run us through the routine. We ain't sticking around for Jeremy-lite. Go get him or we're outta here."

King did not want to upset The Ravenous Raptor when he was within eviscerating distance, with or without his signature tire iron in hand. But he made a promise to Jeremy and, for better or worse, he was not afraid of a challenge.

"Mr. Raptor, sir, let me assure you I know the routine in full and I am fully equipped with the hardware and strength to…"

"You call that hardware?" Bethlam laughed. The other players chuckled along. "Look, it's not the clothes that make the man, but sometimes they can help when you're scrawnier than a twig. Your dollar-bin armor isn't exactly pullin' enough weight to convince us." The team hollered. Bethlam seemed in good spirits and shrugged her shoulders when a few of them goaded her on. "You know what? The team could use a good laugh. Since you're so adamant, I'll give you a shot. Show me what you got."

King had no idea what would impress these folks but he had to try. He tried to hype himself with the thought, *if they like what they see, I could turn this into my own personal tryout!*

"Yeah, okay! Just keep your eyes on me and check out these moves." He checked all the levels on his suit and used all his strength to stomp onto the powermat.

With both feet conducting, the suit powered on. The signature blue glow of vibrant steel's power seeped out of the flexible joints. He moved effortlessly across the room. To give them a show, he first performed a grueling deadlift. He did a standard wall run followed by a short demonstration with the katanas that got his heart pumping.

He stepped off the mat and his suit went dark. A player helped him remove armor pieces as he huffed out of breath. "Well, what do you think? I got the stuff, right?"

As if the clouds parted and a ray of divine light cast a miracle, Bethlam nodded. "That was a hefty lift. Solid leg and arm components too." King's face beamed until she added, "But you handle weapons like an amateur."

He stepped out of the suit and threw his hands up. "Come on. What're you expecting? We're a gym for amateurs!" He gestured across the building. The facility was not state-of-the-art. He pointed to an old woman struggling to lift a single weight. She noticed him and he was embarrassed for calling attention to her. He rushed over to spot her briefly.

"Jeremy's a retired pro, kid. We trust him."

That revelation caught King by surprise. Jeremy had never mentioned that. Apparently, they did have valid reasons to be concerned about him and his lack of pedigree. Their attention was waning fast so his last strategy was not his proudest moment, but they left him no choice.

He jogged back to Bethlam and fell to his knees. "Okay! I admit I'm no Jeremy. But look, do I have to beg? I still gotta make money if I'm gonna afford a new pair of powergloves. So, if you would just let me lead this one session…"

"Powergloves?" Bethlam grinned from ear to ear. "Whatcha need those for, little King?"

"Oh…uh, just to up my workout routine for the tryout season."

She roared and slapped his back so hard he thought his eyeballs would pop out. "You hear that, folks? Little King here fancies himself a part of the team already!" They all laughed in a chorus that would have left a more timid person shrunken inside, but he puffed out his chest and stepped back into his powerboots.

"You and me, Bethlam! Right now, o-on the floor! If you want to see what I've *really* got, I'll show you!" He thought he was inviting her to come out and inspect him up close, but the way he said it came across very differently.

She heard that loud and clear. She did not hesitate donning on the second set of gear. "You win, little King. You want to know how you stack up? I'll measure you right here and now. You better be ready for a fight!"

The other players hooted and hollered as she suited up and jumped onto the mat before he even had his helmet on. He thought Doug was kind to help him secure his latches, but he could have been eager to witness the massacre.

"N-now, Ms. Ross, I didn't mean to…"

"Don't bother yourself over manners, kid! Surviving this duel should be your only concern."

His first boot hit the floor and his suit became lighter. His second slammed down and every one of his limbs tingled. Electricity surged through his right hand. Tillie Sue's rings clamped together and his fist felt like a ball of lightning. He knew the basics of a duel: first person off the mat loses. Keep your two feet on the ground to draw the most power. And, most importantly, never let your opponent lift you up or your suit would rattle you like a car crash when you hit the ground.

Bethlam, always the professional, did not put on the kid gloves for him. She grabbed his legs immediately and flipped him into the air. He jutted his arm out to redirect his fall and pivoted like a windmill on the rock that was his ringed fist. True to their nature, the power of the rings did not yield and so neither did he.

"Whoa!" Bethlam said after he landed safely on his feet. "Call me stunned, kid. I thought you were too tiny of a thing to support the weight of an entire suit on your arm like that."

Surprise overcame him as well. The rings were even more useful than he imagined.

He winked. "Ah. Well, it seems I've got a few tricks up my sleeve."

She charged at him again. "I look forward to seeing the rest!"

He regrettably did not have anything handy left to give. He scrambled around on the ground for about seventy percent of the match and did everything he could to block her blows the remaining time. But he ignored every jeer from their audience telling him to give up and, most important for his pride, he stayed on the mat.

He did not remember the rest of the night, just that he had bruises in places he did not even know could bruise and that he had to be carried to the hospital by the team for a medical gel bath. The next morning, he opened his mail. A letter instructed him in no uncertain words to report to practice the following Monday as the Caldarado Killers' latest bench warmer. Enclosed was a small allowance to buy his first set of pro gear.

ROVER ENTRY #1025

This is it!" announcer Chad's voice broadcasted over the radio. He and his compatriot called the game from inside the press box high above the Hill overlooking the savage action. The intimidating silver Hill jutted out of the domed facility's center. It was encircled by vertigo-inducing rows of spectator bleachers. All eyes pointed toward the Hill and that's just what the sport wanted. "The Dixon Chixon is attempting her final ascent with the Killers' first-string blockers right behind her. She has had a terrible season so far and has just not been able to find a groove."

"That's right," assistant Shad said. "She hasn't even been within a stone's throw from the summit let alone been a real contender to holding it for any type of score today." Yellow and black caution tape circled the sideline around the Hill. The warnings prevented non-athletes from stepping into harm's way. Coaches, photographers, and support staff ran along the outer track to constantly readjust their view for the best angle of this three-hundred-and-sixty-degree phenomenon. "The team needs to draw every last watt out of the Hill if they want to save face. But to what end exactly? Their hopes for the post-season are long gone, but it's possible they're just hoping to avoid a zero-and-thirty season that would tie them for most losses in this league's history."

Chad chuckled. "Now wouldn't that be a shame? If we look at the match so far, the Tartar Titans seem determined to make their own permanent mark by being the footnote to that fact."

The constant buzzing of electricity. The crowd's roar with every score on the clock. These sounds had become the soundtrack to King's life over the past few months. He adored the flashing lights and glowing cameras. He only wished he were admiring them from the hilltop instead of on the bench. Not naive to think he would lead the pack within his first season, he at least had hoped to experience some field time before they were disqualified for the playoffs.

Regardless of his unrequited desires, he had a responsibility to follow the game closely just in case today he would be invited to fill in to finally grasp at the glory he so longed for. At least in the big city a man could dream freely.

King listened to a small radio accompanying him on the sideline bench. He spat on the ground. What did those gawking yahoos know about what it took to claw one's way up the Hill? Sure, he did not know either, but he was so close he could reach out and touch the opportunity!

The radio droned on. "Let's get back to the action! Dixon Chixon has *somehow* made it to the summit and now possesses the flagpole. Her team has surrounded her to keep her there. But, despite this bold play, the Titan's top breakers are wedging her defense apart. Still, I must hand it to The Ravenous Raptor and Vicious Victoria. Those two on the western front are channeling some amazing synergy as they repel the would-be kingmakers desperate to topple Dixon."

"But, Chad, their score clock has just begun counting up as the match's timer continues to count down. At this point, she needs the entire remaining time to tie."

The microphone muffled with excitement. "That may be all but impossible! The blockers are holding steady but…my word!" A chair tumbled onto the ground. "The Titan's climber Toothy McGee almost knocked The Raptor clear off the Hill with a strike from a bone club! Victoria is unable to hold the Titan's attack all by herself and Toothy slips past her to make his way up to the summit! Just a few more meters to pause the score clock and…what am I seeing?"

Shad's feet thumped onto the floor and his chair was heard flying across the room. "Folks, I can't believe it! Dixon's charged up the flag by pounding it repeatedly upon the Hill. I haven't seen the notoriously difficult Razzle Dazzle Rod maneuver in my lifetime! The pole is absolutely teeming with electricity! She's thrusting it like a lance repeatedly at Toothy and…unbelievable! She's managed to stab Toothy through a gap in his suit! He's convulsed himself off the summit's perimeter! Talk about deferred maintenance biting you in the behind! That's it! The Killers' are going into overtime! Their first win of the season is within reach!"

The stadium overflowed with enthusiasm. Nothing like a good stroke of luck swelled the hope inside a Caldarado Killer fan's bruised, disappointed heart. Banners of red and gold fluttered in the stands. The boos of Titan fans were lost in the celebration.

As the Killers descended the Hill and made their way into the darkened sidelines, King jumped off his butt and waited at the base. He felt obligated to congratulate every single one of them for giving it their all even for a shot at a win that did not matter.

"Way to go, Chuck!" King patted his back. "Victoria, you're a wall!" She graced him by obliging his palm slap, but quickly pulled away.

Bethlam stepped off the Hill last. She yanked her helmet off. Sweat dripped from her hair and a scowl painted her face.

"Bethlam…" he started.

She pushed past him. "Save it, kid. Keep thankin' the real heroes." She disappeared into the locker room.

He did not hold her shortness against her. Precious little time remained before their final round. The team's climber carried an enormous amount of pressure on their back. She had earned a break.

He followed her advice and ran over to Doug who rested upon a stretcher. A medical team attended to his head which took the brunt of that bone club attack.

"Hey, great defense out there. You really put your head in the game."

"Very funny kid." Doug spat into a bucket a medic kept shaking in front of his face.

Were those teeth, King wondered? "I'm sorry. I didn't mean to make a joke about it. You're obviously trying and I respect that." King walked away flushed but swung back determined to be a good teammate. "Are you okay otherwise? Do you need a sling? Some wraps?"

"Don't get in the way of the professionals, kid. Just get me a cold drink!"

King was not more than a few steps away when Doug howled.

A medic shouted, "He's taking a dive! We need to get him downtown fast!"

Doug resisted with a string of profanities while trying to climb off the stretcher. "I can do it! Put me back in there! I'm not going and you can't make me!"

This was bad. King ran into the locker room and found Bethlam soaking her hair under a leaking, sputtering showerhead.

"They're wheeling Doug away!" he hollered.

She twisted the shower handle shut. "Why? What's wrong with him?"

"I don't know. The medical folks are trying to load him onto an ambulance but he's putting up a fight. Should he be doing that?"

She swung her head, water spraying onto the walls, and followed him back onto the sideline. They watched the ambulance exit the stadium with Doug nowhere in sight.

"Absolutely great…" She kicked the air and glared at the Hill. "Well, I guess that means you're filling in, kid."

King's skin tingled, his heart stopped, and a surge of excitement bubbled up from his stomach. "Are you serious? My first match?"

"Yeah. You're the only one who can hold their ground like me, even if it's just a passin' resemblance. Come on, let's get this sorted." She made her way toward the team who were already huddling and scooped up fresh pieces of armor resting on the bench.

He followed her. "Wait. What do you mean *like you*? I'm filling in for Doug, right? I'm blocking?"

She turned back quickly. "Afraid not, kid." The huddle parted for her. She stepped into the center.

King stood sheepishly on the outside and listened in.

Bethlam paced a few steps, eyes toward the ground and her fingers on her chin. Inspirational speeches were the stuff of movies. No one expected anything special. After everyone patiently waited, she slipped on her gauntlets and slammed her fist into her palm.

"Listen up, Killers! You probably saw Doug just get dragged out of here kickin' and screamin' to stay in the game. I expect every single one of you to do the same if we lose."

There were mumbles and coughs.

She stomped around the circle. "But that ain't how it's gonna go down, is it? No! Because we flipped this once and we're gonna flip it again! We're gonna hit 'em with some surprises this time around so that's why I'm fillin' in for Doug on blocker and our little King is gonna be our climber."

King grew anxious. Nobody perked up or nodded at that idea. He could not blame them. He had dreamed his entire life about his professional Mauler debut, but it did not look like this. Climbers had years of experience brawling and grappling. He had an amateur style grown entirely out of television matches, hodgepodge lessons, and hardly a season's worth of trainers. How would he be able to fill her shoes?

Jerky Mike from the back shouted, "Oi, ain't that the trainee? He's like a tiny, little mouse." Grumbling among the team agreed.

Bethlam clanged her fists together until she reclaimed their attention. "Settle down! The kid's got stayin' power. You couldn't scrape him off your shoe if he were gum. But really, climbin' requires the least amount of talent and I would know. We're gonna create a wall that nothin', not even the Mauler gods themselves, could get past. And I'm gonna be right up there with you sorry lot puttin' my limbs on the line! You got that?"

"Yeah," a few said flatly.

"Did you get that?" she hollered. "Don't make me murder you all and have to fight the whole scrappin' team myself!"

"Yes!" they belted.

Bethlam lobbed her gauntlet into the circle's center. "One fist is power. Five are a storm. This whole darn team? We're about to become an unstoppable force of nature! Now, give it up!"

The team piled their gloves on top. Clashing metal flung sparks onto the floor.

King smiled but did not dare to join their ritualistic bond.

One of them noticed him staring. "Come on, kid. You're one of us."

Without hesitation, he fitted a gauntlet and slapped the stack. Their hands exploded like thunder and the anticipation filled King's insides with bottled lightning.

He could have exploded with joy.

ROVER ENTRY #1026

The team finished suiting up well before King. Struggling away on the bench as the others walked off, his nerves slowed him down. He knew the problem was in his head. He had donned the equipment countless times and had never been sluggish. Numerous latches along his arms and legs of this gray warrior suit, embellished with jagged splashes of red streaks, required his attention. He checked them two or three times to be safe. No mistakes. Amateur hour was over.

He trudged to the sideline. Despite training in full armor, the unpowered suit's weight stunned him. Rather than his struggle stemming from the metal, his confidence was rattled more likely by the expectations of quadrillions of spectators from across the televised galaxy.

King joined the team spread out along the Hill's base. Bethlam stood on his right and Mike kneeled to his left. They were his personal guard escorting him to the top. Half a dozen Titans eyeing him like a juicy roast on either side were their enemies.

Already sweating, he caught a glare from Mike and wondered what the Jerk thought about all this. It only made him drip more. Being cooked under the stadium's yellow lights, he found the heat in the suit almost unbearable. He tried to dispel all doubt from his mind, but the torridity kept breaking his focus.

"H-hey." He turned to Bethlam. "Is it normally this hot? Boy, I'm having trouble concentrating."

"Actually, now that you mention it, no. Somethin' must be wrong with the ventilation in here." She looked above toward the stadium's rafters and pointed at enormous, stalled fans. "Those dang things are overheatin' again. Dang it. Our stadium is a junkyard. You gotta win to earn but you can't earn if…"

She kept on complaining as King's mind drifted somewhere less stressful. He knew after lining up that there were only thirty seconds until the clock started. The world stood still during the last few moments. He kept worrying about being knocked down right at the get go. He trembled at the thought of all the hecklers in the stands. They would love nothing more than to see him fall in his first game. The odds were mounted against him.

"Hey!" Bethlam startled him by grabbing his elbow. "Listen to me. Stay focused. I'm gonna shout directions at you. You're gonna pay attention, right?"

He managed a quick nod. To identify his only goal, his eyes scaled the mountain and experienced a brief bout of vertigo. The yellow flag of the summit beckoned him up. The rotating stadium lights blinded him and, for one fleeting moment, he remembered Tillie Sue and wondered if she still watched from home like she promised to do.

The loudspeakers echoed. "Match start!"

King threw himself onto the hillside and scurried up like an animal. The famous smooth vibrant steel of a professional Mauler Hill under his boots made him think this was too good to be true. He could never have guessed he would be the one leading the charge in his first game. The steel hummed loudly and static filled the air so thick it monopolized his senses. He almost lost himself in the moment until the scraping metal of hunter boots brought him back. Snarling Titans closed in.

"Don't look back!" Bethlam scolded, hovering just behind him. "Lesson number one: keep your eyes on the flag!"

The fluttering target high above caught his attention. He charged ahead.

"Contact!" Mike announced. He grabbed hold of two hunters in pursuit and tried to wrestle them away.

King turned. Would they need his help?

"Don't!" Bethlam screamed. "What did I just tell you?"

Her ferocity drove him away and he continued his mission. Grunts echoed from the Hill's opposite side where their own hunters tried their best to stop the Titans' climber, Toothy McGee, from reaching the summit before him. He knew he wanted to be first as it had its advantages like having the higher ground, but it would be him against a constant onslaught from every angle. It did not look easy on television. The defense was probably magnitudes of degrees harder in person.

All this worrying meant King lost track of how far he had climbed. As soon as he realized they had reached the halfway point, a hunter grabbed his leg and he fell on his face. The gray luster of a steel beam shone brightly mere centimeters from his eyes. With the soles of his boots off the ground, in addition to being crushed by his own disappointment, he felt the increasing weight of his suit. He kicked his foot furiously and escaped the hunter's grip, but he failed to right himself. He focused his mind solely, to a fault, on the flag. On his hands and knees, he crawled forward with his suit cycling on and off as his feet scraped the ground. His muscles strained from the inefficient effort.

In a startling sensation, he felt himself lifted off the ground. "What the rust?"

"Get up!" Bethlam growled. She had him by a handle on his back and plopped him back upright. "Lesson number two: always get on your feet! It's your strongest position of advantage." She shoved him forward.

He still had a lot to learn. Feeling lighter and determined to pay better attention to the conditions on the field, he focused on the team's Spotters and the messages they relayed from the Hill's other side. Spotters, observant players that stayed out of the fray and fed information to the team, were trying to communicate with him. But the carnival of noises in a live stadium meant trouble filtering their voices out.

"Three block left, target ten meters! Three blockers zoning in from your left, Toothy is ten meters from the summit!" Bethlam shouted into his ear. "Lesson number three: know the signs!"

"I know the signs!" King spat. "I just can't hear them."

"The Hill doesn't care about your excuses! If you can't hear them, get the rest of the team to relay the calls to you. We're a single wire and we're connected from the bottom to the top in a flash."

"Right." He listened for more indistinct shouting. He pointed at a blocker a far way down the Hill. "Relay the call!"

"Target eight meters! Hurry!"

Toothy was almost there. Time was running out.

"Oh scrap!" Mike collided with a group of hunters to King's right before being shoved off a cliff. The blood-thirsty Titans surrounded Bethlam and King next.

"Rust! I can't find an opening!" King cried.

"Never let a little roadblock take your eyes off the objective. The way I see it, anyone stupid enough to stand in between you and the summit is just fodder for your *rage*!"

Bethlam lunged at a hunter and lifted him into the air. Titan and King alike gasped at the feat. She hurled the man like a cannonball through their blockade and cleared King a way. "Run while I hold them off!"

King slipped past the line and hustled straight to the summit. Pulling himself onto the top, he found the yellow flag wavering alone in the artificial wind. He had won the first contest and now had to keep the flag safe. Euphoria lifted his soul outside of his body as he drew the pole from the black pedestal.

It seemed impossible, holding an official Mauler flag in between his fingers on his first active game. The crowd must have agreed, their roar exhibiting their surprise. He imagined all those rustheads back home who might catch a glimpse of his face on the news during the evening's sports segment. What would their mugs look like?

With King alone on the summit, the game had changed. Yet his mind, filled with exhilaration, dangerously struggled to stay grounded. His teammates were switching tactics and forming an impenetrable wall around him. Even the Titan's blockers became hunters and would remain so until King was replaced by Toothy. King had to pay attention or risk being vulnerable.

"Now's the easy part!" Bethlam shouted from just below. She and the others linked arms around the platform. "Hold still while we do all the work!"

The Titans threw themselves at the line attempting to rend any weak link from the chain. The team held better than anyone expected. King wondered if the Killers were about to pull their first seasonal win out of thin air. In hindsight, sports historians would determine Bethlam was a terrible climber and that blocking was her real talent, but no one could tell her that without hurting her pride.

"The Killers take first count with…who's that?" Chad on the loudspeaker asked. From the Hill's summit, the speakers were closer and louder than ever. Their words penetrated King's helmet. "This is a surprise. It appears they've enlisted their rookie, Killer King Cunningham, to fill in their roster."

"Chad, did you say his alias is Killer King? Thinking he can name himself after the team is a bold flex."

"I reckon you're right, Shad. He looks more like a Little King from up here, so I'm gonna go with that. Little King's started the clock."

The score clock emitted a small beep and cages above the Hill swung open. Brutal melee weapons rained down onto the Hill. A peculiar hallmark of the sport, fans unsheathed their own homemade armaments and hurled them onto the field. Spotters from both teams inspected the best of them, checking for regulation compliance, and tossed them up the Hill to their team.

King never anticipated the frustration of standing on top and not assisting his comrades as they protected him. He knew instead that watching the game carefully was his responsibility. Any holes in the line could jeopardize their lead and he had to be ready to grapple for dominance at a moment's notice. But that offered little comfort as he witnessed Victoria get clobbered repeatedly with a pipe wrench wrapped in bandages and bulging with stones.

"Chad, it's important for us to remind everyone watching from our new markets that in overtime the clock counts up. Victory goes to the first with thirty seconds of controlled summit time. Can the Little King hold on long enough or will his success during his professional debut slip from his fingers?"

The announcer's chatter steeled King's nerves with an armor of defiance. He took stock of his surroundings. Below, the Titans' climber, Toothy, fought among the blockers. His comrades were performing well and were earning him precious seconds. On his other side, Bethlam wrestled three would-be problems. Her smile heralded her immense enjoyment in the act.

The scene turned when the hunters collectively managed to hoist her up into the air. Her suit drained of power and she flailed erratically.

"Bethlam!" King shouted, his arm stretching far out of reach.

This distraction took his eyes off the perimeter for only a moment, but it was long enough for Toothy to burst through the defensive line and catch him off guard. Toothy pulled himself onto the summit and straightened his spine in a never-ending rise above King.

Looming over him, Toothy seemed twice his size. His opponent's black and blue armor reflected the lights revealing scrapes and dents across every piece. Through his grated helmet, scars along his forehead screamed of years of experience.

King froze. Every internal instinct in his gut battled each other and not a single limb responded. His brain fooled him into thinking he was staring at a televised match playing out before him. Seemingly he had no agency of his own as Toothy drew his arm back for a blow that would surely send him reeling.

ROVER ENTRY #1027

Golden rule!" Bethlam cried after she astonishingly regained control and juggled two hunters in a headlock keeping the third at bay with her foot. "You're a rock! Act like it!"

The Hill's power coursed through King's suit. It had been doing so all this time, but for some reason now he could feel it. He cracked his fist out like a lightning bolt and collided with Toothy's gauntlet plummeting toward him.

His glove glowed. A blinding cobalt flash radiated out and faded.

It was a wonder his arm was able to hold its own. Sparks flew as their metals grinded against each other. The stadium's gasps and rupturing applause indicated they were as astonished as him. He figured the world was witnessing the game's greatest recent miracle and it made his chest swell with pride. All he had to do now was hold his ground until his teammates could grab Toothy by the legs and drag him off.

"What's this?" Toothy snarled. He leaned closer, hovering centimeters from King's face. Spittle sprinkled through the grate and rained onto King.

King growled right back, but Toothy just bellowed with laughter.

"So you've got a few surprises, short stack?"

"That's right! You'd better watch out!"

The shrill buzzer indicating The Killers required just *one more* exclusive second startled King. He did not see Toothy's other fist propelling through his shoulder.

King lost his grip on the flag and tumbled off the summit's edge.

His suit's power cycled wildly as he rolled several meters down. This hunk of metal, meant to protect him, rattled him like a pack of loose sardines flopping in an empty can. When his body came to rest, his shoulder seethed with pain. His mind swirled. Cries of his teammates straining to grab a hold of Toothy while being pulled away by the rival blockers permeated his helmet. King felt afraid for the first time in his life while wearing the armor he so glorified.

Bethlam rushed to his side and pulled him back onto his feet. She jabbed her finger toward the summit. "Get back up there!"

"I-I can't! My arm! He's too big!" He could not believe the worrywart words coming out of his mouth, but in that moment, he truly doubted himself.

She had no patience for his complaints. She grabbed his arm and yanked his shoulder into place.

"Oh scrap! Sweet harmony!"

She took ahold of him by his shoulders and shoved him back up. "There's nothin' wrong with you! You're perfect! You're the rock! You won't let victory be stolen from you just when you were holdin' it in your hands!" she wailed. "Now climb up there and *take it back*!"

Rust! She was right. He could not let it end like this. He would not be able to look himself in the mirror if he backed down in his first game while still being able to stand. She knelt on one knee and offered her cupped hands. He stepped into them. Using every watt of her augmented powersuit strength, she launched him like a rocket onto the summit. An opportunist Titan tried to surprise her from behind. Her fist was too quick.

Like a meteor crashing down, he pounded the peak on his hands and knees. In the literal shadow of a superior climber, the score counting up for the Titans and no idea how he would recapture the flag, he stood defiantly on his two aching legs and glared at Toothy's broad grin.

Toothy squeezed the pole and waved the flag in King's face. King grasped but could not take it. "You've come back for more, eh? Not a smart move, friend." Toothy hurled his fist again.

This time King threw out his grasping palm and intercepted the punch. Not as defiant as his first go, but thankfully just as effective.

There were no dramatic fireworks this go around, but a pulsating light granted a sudden revelation. Tillie Sue's rings were glowing clear through King's gauntlet with an amber brilliance. Their latent power was blossoming as they absorbed a critical mass of energy from the Hill.

Toothy drew his other arm back. "Same old trick again, friend? I reckon you know what comes next. Get ready for part two."

The buzzer blared. The Titan's score had caught up.

The announcers broadcasted over the speakers. "Folks, we're in the last second here for *both* teams and the clock has stopped."

"That's right, Chad. During overtime, one side must occupy the summit with the flag in hand uncontested for the entirety of their last second. Toothy McGee will need to unseat Little King or vice versa."

King shut his eyes and braced for impact. Taking blows was his only real talent so he decided to face it like a pro. He waited for the strike, his insides filling with fear, the anticipation of disappointment, and the understanding that even after his best effort he simply lacked first-string material.

But after a painful number of seconds, nothing came. Wondering if the adrenaline running through his body had distorted his sense of time, he cracked one eye open.

With his flag arm still drawn back, Toothy squinted over King's head. "Huh? What's this now?"

Silence befell the crowd.

King craned his neck back. A pulsating glow from far down in the front row seats captivated the audience. Whatever was happening, the details from this distance were impossible to discern. A dizzying scene on the large play-by-play screen overhead provided a better angle. Sky cameras zoomed in on a lone woman frantically waving her arms. The orange illumination originated from one of her hands and it grew brighter obscuring her face.

King watched with morbid curiosity as security personnel closed in around her. A journalist approached the woman and put a microphone in front of her. "What do you have there in your hand?" he yelled. "Are you aware it's disrupting the game?"

She grabbed the mic and drew it near. "I gotta get these to King! He needs these! I can't…I can't throw that far! Let me through! King, I'm comin'!"

The woman revealed a small box in her palm and opened it. Everyone nearby stumbled back from a blinding ray of light. She climbed the game floor barriers and ran onto the play area.

The bounce of her silver hair, the orchid color of her country clothes, and that undeniable accent. King recognized her. It was Tillie Sue!

The sight of her poured fuel over his muscles now burning with a chaotic energy. His calves and biceps seethed, but most importantly his heart scorched ablaze. Whatever fear resided within was gone. This transformation imparted a revelation. It was not the television crews, the billions of viewers, nor the petty doubters back home he was striving to impress. For years it had been only one person and it would forever be so from this day forward: his biggest fan.

Tillie Sue rushed the field and half a dozen security personnel darted after her. The ones behind her were left in the dust but the people ahead positioned themselves squarely between her and the Hill. With little effort, she yelped and plowed through the blockade with a swing of her fist and a flash of bright amber light. Two more personnel tried to converge on her, but she zig-zagged from their grasps and jumped a small barrier onto the sidelines.

"King! King!" she shouted from the Hill's base. She slipped the five rings and glove from her fingers and waved them above her head.

"Whozit whatzit?" Toothy grimaced. "You can't just walk-up charity to the base like that! It's unsafe!"

"It's just another weapon! Don't know any rules against that," Bethlam shouted. She hollered down the Hill. "Get whatever she's got up to King!"

A spotter at the base took the set and placed them back inside the box. She chucked them up to the next spotter and the set made its way up the hillside. All the Titans abandoned their battle for the summit and fanned out for an interception.

"Grab that box!" Bethlam and Toothy screamed in chorus.

The box soared up the final ascent. A sea of hands stretched to reach it. It brushed the fingertips of friend and foe alike. Bethlam grabbed Victoria by the waist and hurled her like a bomb at the mob. After a thunderous crash, Victoria burst from the metal entanglement victorious and rushed to the summit.

King turned back to Toothy, locked together by the fist, and wrestled himself free. He shuffled toward Victoria just as she fell to her knees at the edge. She shoved the box into his hands.

"We're all behind you, Killer King!" she said.

King ripped off his gauntlet. The chainmail glove squeezed his hand a little tight, but the five remaining rings felt just fine on.

He faced toothy once again and clanked his fists together. An immaculate glow emanated from his fingers. A shimmering curtain of cerulean light materialized before him like nothing anyone had ever seen. King found it awe inspiring but this was no time for idle admiration.

Toothy chuckled. "Nice light show, friend. Unfortunately, I don't know any light bulb that can't be smashed!" Toothy threw a barrage of punches. Every blow deflected off the glistening wall of mysterious power. An alien sensation tingled King's fingertips as if tiny hands were gripping him, pulling him, but in what direction he could not determine.

A momentary look of desperation on Toothy's face curled into a wry smile when his beady eyes shifted to the flagpole in his hand.

"Send my regards to Dixon for this move!"

He scraped its base along the ground. Sparks shot out like a struck match. The rod slammed into the summit and radiated with a yellow aura. Toothy leapt back and stabbed the flag toward King's chest with imperceptible speed.

King wanted to dodge but remembered agility was not his forte. Instead, he put all his bets on what he was best at and leaned forward. The shaft met his shield with a crack. A brilliant navy light bathed the entirety of his vision. Every piece of his suit rattled just before his helmet, cuirass, and remaining armor blew clean off. A hurricane of unexplained wind blasted his mostly exposed body cutting through even his bones. Yet he stood his ground.

The gust subsided and his surroundings reappeared. The stadium was drained of every light except for one. He was alone with the flagpole on the ground illuminated by a wispy blue portal floating in front of him. All he could make out was some animal-like creature inside the window-like circle. Not Toothy, but rather a disgusting, oozing black monster in a cage. He stepped toward it but the portal blurred out of existence. He wondered if the unrecognizable place was real or if his eyes, having difficulty readjusting, were playing tricks on him.

The crowd's murmurs grew louder somewhere beyond his sight before the stadium beams bathed him again. He realized where he was and what he needed to achieve.

He lunged for the flag.

He pumped it in the air.

The buzzer sounded, the crowd erupted, and his team lifted his scantily clad body into the sky.

He hardly remembered how he climbed back down to the floor, what Bethlam said to him when they talked candidly in the locker room, or even the press conference after. His first clear memory was walking back out onto the dim, empty stadium floor and seeing Tillie Sue waiting for him with her hands clasped behind her back and her feet tapping.

"Wait up, you rusthead!" she said.

"You're the rusthead. I was walking right at you. Where did you reckon I was going?"

"I don't know. I suppose you were just on your way to some fancy after-party or somethin'. Isn't that what you big city pros do after a win?" She snickered.

He swore her smile shone brighter than all the game's flashes.

"Why the heck did security let you go? I was sure they were gonna haul a troublemaker like you away."

She chuckled. "They did! Took one of your big lady friends to come into that little security room and throw a fit to have them let me out. She brought me straight here to wait for you." Her eyes searched his own.

He understood she was there for him. Not the game, nor the city, or any of the reasons he left their hometown for. No. She had just as a determined goal as him except, instead of Mauler glory, it had something to do with him.

He opened his arms for her.

She leapt up to kiss him.

It was unexpected. His face must have said as much.

She drew away before their lips could connect. "I'm so sorry! I-I thought maybe you'd be glad to see me and…"

King grabbed her by the shoulders and pulled her into his chest. They kissed in the empty stadium without a single witness. This was one victory he preferred to celebrate alone.

He slowly stepped back and laughed nervously. "So, yeah. I suppose this is a thing now. Right?"

She giggled. "This is my first night in the big city. I couldn't miss your last game of the season just in case it was finally the one for you. How lucky of me. Care to show me around?"

"Actually, you were right about those fancy afterparties. I got invited to one. Gotta make my way over there soon, being the MVP and all." He pounded his chest and strutted toward the field's exit. "But, you know, being the MVP means I could probably sneak you in with me. Who's gonna tell me no?"

She ran after him and latched onto his arm. "Well, I sure wouldn't want to be the one. I've heard you're the scrappiest, aim-for-the-mooniest person anyone's ever seen so I suppose you're gonna get what you want."

"I suppose that's what I'm known for, ain't it?"

ROVER ENTRY #1028

King found himself back in the gym a few days later, forced to return to his reliable revenue stream. The ledger of the team's pitiful overall season left no place for them in the playoffs even though they had won. Their manager did say they scored a tremendous amount of press buzz from that last incredible game so at least they could be proud of that.

Why Bethlam made that crazy call and put him in the lead as climber that game gnawed at his mind. She revealed she did not think they had anything to lose, so why not take a risk? They were a relatively young team, she assured, and experimentation would help them find their flow. There was always next season and, with a wave of new sponsorships because everyone loved an up-and-coming underdog, they would be better than ever.

With a mop in his hand, he felt restless. He had just spent a season fighting in a tank built for the human body. The most exciting thing that happened today was an unexplained power surge that flooded the city and turned it into a temporary light bulb. There had been several of these recently and equipment going on the fritz was a real pain.

However, possible excitement loomed for him later that night. He and Tillie Sue were meeting up in just an hour for a major milestone. She would arrive on the train for another coffee date and he toted a little surprise in her old ring box. She had become a security officer back home and hoped to hear about a transfer to the city in a few days. They were quickly making a lot of plans.

In addition to that, one other thing distracted him all day. His eyes kept wandering toward the ball launcher in the corner of the room. He could not stop thinking about that swirly portal that appeared before him during the game. He had not read any reports of it in the news so either the portal was not bright enough to have been seen from the stands or it truly was here and gone in an instant.

That moment was the height of his power. He was the rock, an immovable mountain just like the Hill. We wanted to recapture that and become stronger. Not just for the team, but to keep making her proud of him.

To replicate that singular experience, his only idea was to stage another epic impact. Yet he could not very well do that while clients were still present. As soon as the nice old lady from the borough hung up her towel and walked out the door, he slipped on his ten rings and powered up the automated equipment machine to dress him in a powersuit.

"What do I got, what do I have here…" he muttered as he rummaged through a supply closet. Dumbbells, soft mats, and pieces of armor were not explosive enough. He needed an object which harbored a thunder cloud inside. Unfortunately, anything electronic in the nearby staff office was too expensive to just load into a launcher and decimate with impunity.

He almost turned off the facility's lights and called it a night before he had the genius idea to check the dumpster behind the building. He extracted from the trash a truck battery he believed was exactly what he needed. He brought it inside and tossed it into the launcher without a second thought. This was an incredibly stupid decision.

Only after standing in front of the whirring machine did he remember truck batteries contained a concerning amount of dangerously volatile raw vibrant steel under extreme pressure, not like the relaxed open beams of the Hill he climbed upon.

The launcher hurtled the payload like a bomb. Having no time to dodge, he threw up his shimmering shield and leaned into it just like before. Searing flames from the mighty impact and a bright flash preceded darkness.

Electricity filled the air but curiously no longer where it mattered. The facility's electronics were out. Every hair on his body stood up. It was happening!

A blue spark grew into that curious wispy portal. It materialized in front of him, hovering above the smoldering workout mats and singed wallpaper.

Confusion set in when a person in the weirdest red getup walked across the opening. He had no idea what he was gazing into, but the idea of someone being on the other side surprised him.

This person called out, "You're all in danger!" She said several other things in languages he did not recognize.

King wanted to reach out and wave to her, but his suit had no power and his limbs were locked in place. Worse now, he realized the unpowered automated equipment machine could not uncouple his suit. Without assistance, he was trapped inside a coffin.

He did not intend to dive in, but the angle to which he leaned forward like a statue was not stable. He wobbled back and forth before careening toward the portal. A thousand tiny hands felt like they gripped his body and yanked him the rest of the way.

He wailed. His insides were reversed while he tumbled through a nauseating tunnel of streaking light. His suit repeatedly warped, crushed, and pierced his body despite it appearing to remain intact. Cries echoed off the flashing walls in a chorus of anguish that did not all sound like his voice. However, with what little he could make out, he did not see anyone with him.

Unsure about the length of the trip, it ended with that red person standing over him as the pain quickly subsided. She spoke gibberish and uncoupled his suit with a grateful smile, tears streaming down her face.

The Marbles

File Under: childhood, worthiness, trust

Location(s): Tenocolis

Executive Summary: My interviews with Adiquis taught me much about the galactic-political climate with which the people of Abeona-2 have been completely absent from. This information, in addition to the technical understanding of the most valuable material in the galaxy, vibrant steel, has the potential to launch our planet onto the galactic playing field among the rest of humanity. I recommend this entry for any Abeona-2 statesperson who seeks to better understand one of the many antagonistic factions that await our diplomatic efforts in the near future.

ROVER ENTRY #1031

You've forgotten what's important once again, Adiquis," Father Hannon said with a stern look in his eye. The young orphan across his desk seemed determined to test every patient strand of his amethyst Divine chaplain frocks.

Adiquis looked at Father's metallic desk, out the foggy plastic window, and at a stone bookshelf. His gaze wandered anywhere in the sparsely furnished office of the Orphan House #178 except at Father. His leg bounced as he awaited the next word of admonishment. He had been pulled away from the others during breakfast because of another defensive outburst. The children were teasing him with more vitriol than normal. What was a vulnerable child to do?

He did not fear Father. No, that was not what prompted his nervousness. The older man was kind and generous. He would never hurt Adiquis. Instead, what made Adiquis anxious was failing to grasp how to make Father accept him for who he was. That was all Adiquis wanted, for someone he respected to tell him he was enough.

Father, caretaker of all the youth under his roof, stepped next to the window with hands clasped tightly behind his back. "Questioning a marble's authority to reflect a person's worth threatens the very pillars to which our society is built upon," he stated confidently as fact. "I control the world within these walls."

He pointed out toward their city's neon skyline. It glowed like a gem in front of the new day's emerging rays.

"But beyond? The city expects much from its citizens and you are not ready yet to adopt that responsibility. And still further, past the noble walls which keep us safe from the wilds, there is nothing of value. Just a civilization desert."

"And further than that? Among the stars?" Adiquis asked, a hopeful light growing inside him.

Father shook his head. "Excess, pride, and violence. Nothing compares to the flawless design of the Autocracy."

Adiquis slumped in his chair.

Father drew his hand back. As if he grinded his frustrations with Adiquis into dust, he squeezed his fist and sighed with serenity. "Adiquis, I know you've experienced a great amount of trauma prior to joining us here, seeing more of how this world works than any child should have. It pains me greatly just acknowledging it."

"It's okay," Adiquis said. He watched the morning sun climb over the horizon. It looked like a marble. "I don't remember anything about my parents even though I try."

Father returned to his iron desk chair. Its legs scraped across the gray stone floor. Neither was bothered. The screeching of metal was just a part of their world. "And perhaps that cruelty is actually a blessing in disguise. These walls have come to be your only home and I your only teacher. I hope you have had a good life since arriving. Food in your belly, a dry roof over your head, and an education."

Adiquis nodded. Grateful for everything Father provided while he was watching, it was what happened when Father was not that troubled him.

Father opened a notebook lying on his desk. The pages were made of thin metal. "Your academic scores are highly competitive, you possess a sharpness of mind, and you have a future laid out before you. You'll begin your Autocratic Societal Education modules within the year and I know you have the knowledge to pass the ordinance portions. However, giving the *right* answers in the rest of it, and not the ones festering in your heart, may be your greatest challenge."

That hurt Adiquis' pride. "I can pass the tests," he protested. "I study enough."

"Again, I don't doubt that. But these modules are meant to identify your feelings and not just your knowledge." He lowered his voice to a whisper. "They can detect future *dissidents*."

That word was dirty and it was not just the adults who said so. Adiquis knew being called as such meant you were *worthless*. "I'm not a…"

"No, not yet," he spoke normally again. "But these ideas you keep spouting in the presence of your peers are the seeds of rebellion. Without order, there is no Autocracy. And without the Autocracy, there is no safety. The powers that be will respond to that threat."

Adiquis held his head low. He did not want to be cast out onto the streets again or worse, deemed worthless. "I'm sorry, Father. You're right." But his deep-seeded need to belong bloomed again. "Wait. Who's to say I gotta be judged by what's inside my marble pouch?"

Father sighed. "What did I just say about these radical ideas?" He carefully drew the brown pouch hanging off his hip. He pulled apart the drawstrings with delicate fingers and marbles rolled across the desk.

Juxtaposed to the unremarkable marbles inside the pouch on Adiquis' hip, Father's collection had several colorful swirlies that reminded Adiquis of planetary bodies from his schooling's science texts. Adiquis reached out to catch one as it neared the edge, but Father snatched it up just in time and passed it under a beam of morning light. Violet and teal colors cast along the floor and wall. The room sparkled with wonder. The glass orb astonished him.

"No matter where one finds themselves in the Autocracy's planetary empire, this is the most important measurement of worth. And you will earn a set of respectable starter marbles if you pass your ASE modules. This is an imperative first step along your stringent path to full citizenship. How many times must I impress this upon you? What you see as a restriction is in truth a manicured pathway toward your better self. The *system* relentlessly guides us toward improving our deeply flawed selves, blemished from birth, and it is marbles that signify our progress."

Adiquis grasped the marble when Father dropped it into his eager palm. He had never held one so prestigious before. This tiny ball of hard and clear material bestowed popularity, wealth, power, and so much more. How did it work? His inquisitive little mind desperately wanted to know. He could have dashed out of the room that moment and taken with him the permission to be admired, provided for, and, most desired, accepted. But no, he was not that kind of person.

"But, Father, I don't understand. What's inside the marbles?" He rubbed it between his forefinger and thumb and tried to squeeze out whatever magic resided within. Could this truly be the path to acceptance? "What makes them so valuable?"

The wrinkles around Father eyes smiled as he did. "Ever the curious student. It's not the material. It's what you do to earn them that matters."

The moment for Adiquis was too brief. Father beckoned the marble's return. He handed it over.

"Glass, the rarest resource in the Autocracy, merely denotes the value of the one who possesses it. But you already know that. You must be asking about why that is and how that is enforced."

Adiquis nodded, wiggling in his chair. Finally, a topic he wanted to talk about.

"You'll get these answers during your modules, but there's no harm in getting ahead." Father arose from his chair and pulled a fraying, ancient paper book off his shelf. "Well, for starters, any resource can be rare. Take this paper manuscript for example. In our city, paper products must be imported. That makes them valuable."

"But not metal! Metal is everywhere." He pointed around the room quickly. The walls, furniture, and even the sliding drapes across the window were derivatives of the element. "Why, even my clothing has interwoven threads of steel." Adiquis tugged at his monotoned government-issued attire. A low electrical charge coursed through the fibers. This allowed the fabric to perform general functions like regulating his body temperature and auto dry if a spill occurred, helpful for children.

"Yes, even metal could be rare. But not in our city. Despite it being ubiquitous in our society, the Autocracy chose it to be this way because of its ability to integrate with vibrant steel. Glass, too, could be plentiful if it was chosen to be so, but how would we function as a people without some honest, incorruptible measure of our fellow person?"

"People will tell you if they're honest." Adiquis said, innocent hope shining from his heart. "That's what it means to be honest!"

"Right you are, my sweet child." Father reciprocated a broad smile. The purity of children seemed to energize him. "But no. That isn't how the real world works. The *real* world is dangerous and filled with illusions. The marbles are the only way to begin to gauge and trust your neighbors, associates, and others."

Adiquis failed to understand the mechanism that granted marbles power over his life, but he figured the day would come when he was older and it would all make sense. He was smart enough to trust in that.

Father stood from his desk and walked to his office door. "Your place outside these walls is waiting for you, my dear boy. Your peers are thinking about their future. They all consider their marbles." He opened the door and waved Adiquis back to the dining room. "Oh, and try to play nice with them from now on. Kindness goes farther than scorn. You should understand that most of anyone."

As Adiquis left, Father did not pat him on the back. He knew Adiquis did not like to be touched.

Adiquis thought about his safety as he wandered through the church complex's cold hallways. Adults who challenged the system, like his parents he was told, led to orphans. If their children were lucky, a House would claim them like the one he currently resided in. Here they would be cared for and educated until they could grow into worthwhile members of society. Father's warning implied that if he did not start focusing on his flaws, figuring out what to do about them, and earning himself better marbles, then he could share the same fate as his dissident parents. Once cast out of the city's walls, the dangers of the wilds left him with little hope as he had been told all his life. Fighting others for survival, striving every day to prove oneself anew to gain reentry into the Autocracy sounded like a miserable existence. And that was just the punishment for challenging the Autocracy.

Worse still, if he were ever deemed worthless, determined to be incapable of contributing *any* benefit to the human species, then he would be made to disappear forever. How the government accomplished this, he did not know. But he had heard imaginative stories on the playground of towering cages of isolated individuals held temporarily until they were disintegrated into dust.

Dwelling on scary futures made his stomach knot. His thoughts were complicated further by a slight streak of anger at the unjust system. Just how exactly did harshly judging every little thing about himself make him any happier if, from the few adults he knew, there was no end to this ritual? There was no acceptance at the end of a tunnel like that. A person would never be deemed enough and that meant this was not a system for him.

He returned to the breakfast table and picked up his now cold bowl of oatmeal. He knew the other children, in matching gray jumpsuits, were speculating about the talking-to he had received. Among the orphans sitting with him, there was Sanjah and her beautiful set of gold and brown cat eye marbles, Terrence whose set consisted of solid pastels, and Jannifer with twenty-four orbs that were twice the average size.

Like all the other children, they brought with them their recently departed parents' marbles. These sets were physical indicators of their worth and some children could practically venture out on their own as soon as they came of age. But others had a longer path in order to reintegrate into society. They had to earn themselves marbles of any worth first. Adiquis was one of those children, left with a pouch of oddly shaped clearies. His blank glass orbs with no patterns or colors would make it impossible for him to get a respectable job or to live on his own. He needed to prove himself to the Autocracy to be allowed to belong.

Across the table, Sanjah avoided eye contact with him and spoke to the others. She was the one who called him a worthless rat and slapped him on the head. Perhaps she felt guilty.

"When I grow up," she said, "I'm gonna earn twelve pearly whites just like Rebecca Hudges. I want to have the most beautiful set so people will look at me and say, 'Oh that Sanjah. She's finally beautiful too.'"

Jannifer scowled. "I don't like Rebecca Hudges. I think she's an unfashionable troll and I don't think she deserves all the attention she gets." She and Sanjah slapped each other. Their antics shook the table.

"Watch it!" Adiquis said as his bowl bounced off the table and into his hands. He tried to steady it, but what remained of his breakfast spilled onto the table.

Terrence momentarily glared at Adiquis with disdainful eyes. He turned back to the others and said, "I don't want to get married. But maybe one day, if I have to, I hope to marry into marbles. I probably don't deserve to, but I dream that one day I'll be respected." He faced Adiquis and flung a spoonful of gruel across the table. It splatted partially onto Adiquis' arm. "I can think of one person who *desperately* needs to marry into marbles."

Everyone directed their attention to Adiquis to see what he would do or say next. His last outburst was fresh.

He wiped the gruel from his arm with his other sleeve. He tried to imagine Father watching at that moment when he said, "I think it's romantic Mrs. Hudges married for love. I don't think there's anything wrong with that. And I think her marbles are fine. They're enough and I suppose they do what they're intended to do."

He knew they just wanted to tease him and cared not for his unpopular opinion. He tired of trying to fit in somewhere he felt he would never belong, but he desperately wanted to.

"We shouldn't have to do anything more to feel good about ourselves. I think each one of you is lovely today just the way you are."

Disgust grew on Sanjah's face. "Why would you say that? That's so mean. I'm like an ugly rock. I don't want to be stuck like this."

The others jeered. "Oh Adiquis. Love is all you could get with your pouch of garbage!"

"I hope love keeps you warm when you're exiled!"

The children continued to shout until Father stormed into the room.

"That's enough! For the sake of the Divine, leave him alone!"

He shooed them away and cleared the table. "And I want every one of you to recite the Divine prayer thirty times as a penance!" he yelled to the last few exiting into the hallway. "Adiquis, help me with the dishes, please."

Adiquis followed into the small stone kitchen where he silently scraped what remained back into the pot for lunch. Had he said the right thing and did Father hear any of it? Being pulled between encouraging the Autocracy's improvement system and treating his peers with respect was a delicate dance he had not yet learned.

After a time, Father broke the silence. "You are enough as you are, my sweet, intelligent boy, and the Divine accepts you for who you are."

"I know, Father."

"And yet...their comments are not without merit. No doubt your marbles have some semblance of worth, like you. You're very smart and you could continue to flourish with a proper Autocratic education." Father shelved the last bowl. He knelt down to Adiquis' level. He beckoned the boy near and almost placed a hand on his shoulder, but he demurred. "But we need to consider our actual place in this very real world and all the terrible inadequacies we are born with. You should earn a new set of marbles that accurately represents your true worth."

Adiquis did not want to do any of that. Whereas his mouth was wiser, the frown upon his face spoke too clearly and beckoned Father's continued lecture.

"Don't you want to be better than your parents, better than you are today? Don't you want to grow up, look back at this time in your life, and realize how improved your marbles have become because you focused on never being complacent?"

Father cared about him, but he did not accept him. "How do I know what needs improving," Adiquis asked, "when I'm content as I am now? I feel that I am enough."

Father pointed out the window above the sink. Adiquis joined him in watching the dying leaves begin to fall from the trees. Foliage littered the city. "As we grow, our knowledge and opinions change like the seasons. I hope you will come to understand that settling for how things are today is like pausing forever in a single season. It is like giving up on this joyous cycle called *life* the Divine has gifted us. That is your challenge to overcome. The Divine teaches us we are never complete and the Autocracy gives us marbles to help us signify our progress. To do that, you must prove yourself to others, primarily to the Autocracy."

ROVER ENTRY #1032

Late in the afternoon, Adiquis waited with the other children his age in the annex's classroom. Jannifer sat in front of him and carved the finishing touches of some letters with a sharp piece of wire into the desk. These ancient but respected antique desktops were made of wood. Her actions insulted him on so many levels.

"Don't do that," Adiquis said. "Don't you know you shouldn't deface government property?"

She giggled and continued scraping harder. "I know that, stupid. But you don't."

Before he could figure out what she meant, Father walked into the room. Jannifer leapt up and ran to the front.

"Father, look! I found Adiquis' name carved into my desk!"

"You found what?" An irritated Father followed Jannifer to the carving. He inspected it with his fingers.

Devious glee dripped from Jannifer's face.

"I didn't do it! Please don't believe her!" Adiquis pleaded.

It must have been clear to Father because he simply shook his head and walked away. The lack of artistry might have proved it so. Adiquis was known for his intellect, not his dexterity.

At the classroom's front, his brow twitching, Father said, "Please excuse this momentary departure from our conventional morning prayer. Can anyone remind me of the general history of our Autocracy?"

Jannifer shot up an energetic hand. "The Autocracy is the safest, richest, and fanciest place in the galaxy. When the home world got too stupid to deal with anymore, our founders trashed their rules and formed an empire that would take charge of the wild space frontier we live in today. The home world is still stupid and we're still the best." She smiled.

"That's right, Jannifer. Very good. Although, you should brush up on your Schism Conflict details during your next study session. We didn't break off from Earth because they were just stupid. Can anyone tell me in more detail why we declared independence?"

"Because they were holding us back," Terrence said quietly.

"Speak up!"

Terrence stepped out of his chair and placed both hands on his heart, the Autocracy's traditional salute. "Because they were holding us back! There were a lot of laws that didn't let us protect our people out here on the frontier. It's more dangerous here than back in the Sol system. They didn't understand that and wanted us to fight for our lives with one hand tied behind our back. That's why we pledge our lives with both hands forward. Today, everything is structured and safe. It takes strong leadership to keep the dangers away." Terrence returned to his seat.

"Very good. And I like the respect you displayed there. Excellent form." Father paced the front of the classroom and scanned the children. "Can anyone tell me the dangers the Autocracy protects us from?"

Several raised their energetic hands. Father pointed toward them and slowly panned over the wiggling lot. His finger paused upon Adiquis whose hand was not raised. "Can you tell everyone what it is that we are safe from by being a part of their society?"

This prodding quite annoyed Adiquis. Father wanted to hammer home their earlier lesson and Adiquis did not care to be quizzed. "Oh, um...there are many dangers on our frontier. Just beyond our walls, the desolate wilds and their lack of resources. Astrological ones like killer asteroids and solar storms, the people-caused ones like terrorists and Earth sympathizers, and the existential ones like…like…"

Adiquis trailed off just as Father perked up. Father raised his hands as if to clap. "Go on. And the existential ones like…"

Adiquis turned away and stared out the window onto the bleak city streets. Now with the sun hanging high in the sky, the inspiring beauty of the dawn was gone. Smog, gray upon gray, and undesirable homeless folks reared their ugly heads. A bug crawled upwards on the transparent plastic surface. It had never occurred to him until that moment, but windows could be made out of marbles. Glass was clear just like plastic. There would be no more material left for marbles. That would be lovely.

"Adiquis. Adiquis!" Father hollered.

"…like failing to fulfill one's purpose for the greater good of the Autocracy!" Adiquis finished in a fright.

Father nodded seriously and continued to pace the room. "That's right. A failure to have the opportunity to fulfill one's purpose. I want to remind all of you that lying and general foolishness could lead you down the dark path of rebellion." He cast an open hand toward the children. His dramatic stance made them shiver. "Unless any of you would rather tangle with these dangers, I expect you to behave in the future!"

Adiquis did not want to be molded into an Autocratic drone, but what was there to done about it?

ROVER ENTRY #1033

A few of the older children with equally dismal futures did not take Father's words to heart. The spirit of rebellion must have infiltrated their minds one wintry night. Adiquis awoke to cries of agony. Flames were consuming everything and almost everyone in the complex.

Leaping from his bed, he fled into the glowing red corridors behind a few others who pushed ahead of him. His mind and his lungs were both filled with smoke as he leapt through a flaming doorway onto the front porch. Those who were out first exiled themselves into the city's dark streets without looking back. He collapsed near the cobblestone street with his meager pouch in one hand. He turned back but did not see any more of his housemates behind him.

The bitter winter wind pushed him crawling back toward the blaze. He inched as close as he could and his fingertips thanked him. Crumbling rafters sprayed embers onto the street. He clumsily scooted back to avoid a burn, but not every glowing chunk rolling forward was on fire. It seemed unlikely, even impossible, but several marbles neared his feet and tumbled into a pothole. He hesitantly reached down for the handful of his comrades' pristine specimens. To take them, marbles that he had not personally earned, was a high crime. Yet, he believed he knew what this meant for their owners. Surely, he hoped, some exception existed for marbles that no longer had an owner.

He pondered at the warm flame's edge until the sirens approached. Father could not protect him any longer and he knew what the Autocracy did to orphans deemed worthless. A boy with no module education, no orphanage to train him, and a questionable mismatch of marbles with no history? It felt wrong as he scooped up three of the most unique orbs, but his world was on fire. He escaped into the alleys clutching his scant belongings in search of a new home.

Everyone knew the Autocracy raided the homeless shelters often for people of too little worth and the abandoned factories were already teeming with criminals and terrorists. He spotted a wide sewer entrance at the end of a drainage canal. A nearby staircase allowed him to descend and slink slowly toward the black cave. Dripping water echoed out. Voices of Autocratic officers neared from above. Flashlight beams scanned the area. He dashed into the sewer just as the intermittent freezing rain and snowflakes fell.

He splashed his good shoes into puddles and ran until no more light reached this far deep. He had to stop out of fear of colliding or tripping over the unknown. The scent of wet garbage permeated his nostrils. Yet, for the near future these tunnels would keep him warm.

The snow turned into rain and then summer heat. Adiquis learned the maze-like passageways hid all varieties of strangeness. He was certainly not alone and he met many other fellow sewer rats looking for a world free of the judgment up above just like him.

As months became years, Adiquis found it bizarre that in a place where marbles were not required by an authoritative body, people still proved the worth in their pouch before every shady transaction. He barely considered himself safe around these characters and he certainly did not find that feeling of acceptance he longed for in his heart.

One of the first people he actually got close to in the sewers was a woman named Ms. Petras. They first met after he spotted her from around a slimy-walled corner early one morning. Adults in the sewers were less like Father and more like the other children who tortured him so he usually kept his distance.

Rummaging through a pile of trash, this seemingly eccentric woman with her huge unkempt hair, speckled, long white coat and ginormous golden-rimmed glasses was eager to find something in particular. He knew what because he had seen her searching before.

From his lower-to-the-ground angle, he noticed a collection of cogs and gears under a dilapidated box. He could step forward and point them out for her, but he might have been placing himself at considerable risk. She could try to scoop him up for sale topside like other orphans he knew for a time down there, or she would beat him and steal his only possession of value: his marble sack.

However, keeping to himself had yet to quell his hungering stomach and chattering teeth. He had been watching her from a distance for several weeks and she appeared to be different than the other vagabonds. Ms. Petras was responsible for many creature comforts one would never expect underground. She produced and distributed soap made from fat runoff to anyone willing to approach her. A few families received makeshift cooking stations that burned captured methane from the putrid air. Despite these gifts, the other adults treated her with suspicion and disdain. Adiquis wondered if they knew things about her that he did not. To be fair, he knew nothing about her except what he had spied recently.

Peeking out from a purse hanging from her arm, he spotted a bag of vegetable candies. His stomach ached and he licked his lips. Hoping to gain her favor in exchange for a morsel, he stepped into the light and pointed under the heap of garbage.

"Down there."

Ms. Petras turned, eyes wide with surprise, and clutched her coat defensively. "Oh!" She relaxed. "It's just you, kid."

"Do you know me?" Adiquis asked.

"Well, I wouldn't say I *know* you, but I have noticed you following me around the last few weeks. You're a cleverer-than-average one from what I can tell."

Adiquis frowned. This interaction was going poorly. She already knew more about him than he of her.

"Well? What is it then?" she coaxed. "What are you pointing out?"

"Mechanical gears under the box. You collect those to build things, right?"

She pushed the box away and snatched up the materials with glee. "Excellent! These are exactly what I needed."

She plucked something from her coat pocket. Adiquis flinched not knowing what she was doing.

She opened her palm offering it to him. "Care for a candy? You look famished."

He shuffled near her, extended his shaking hand, and took it.

"Thank you…uh, Adee, is it?" she asked.

"Adiquis," he replied, sucking on the nutrient-rich tidbit.

She laughed. Her flowing white coat flapped with gusto. "My sincerest apologies! I won't make that mistake again. I think it's particularly important to call people what they want to be called. We're all worth at least that type of respect, don't you agree?"

Ms. Petras was the first person since Father that had acknowledged his worth, but she did it differently. There were no conditions. This is what drew him under her wing.

From that day forth, she provided warm blankets and palpable scraps to fight off starvation. She kept him safe, being quick with her fist but ended up using her intellect nine times out of ten. Her knowledge of the world and of things he barely understood constantly amazed him and she shared it all with enthusiasm. She became like a mother to him, or so he believed. He had never known his mother so it was plausible Ms. Petras acted nothing like the sort, but her persistent kindness fed his perennial desperation. This, if nothing else, kept him close to her throughout the seasons.

Another chilly spring in the sewers descended on the undeserving. Adiquis, now a little older and quite a bit wiser, found a quiet tunnel away from all the other vermin. The green, tessellated stone walls and archways of the corridors were covered in slime and mildew. He arranged wood scraps on the ground for him and Ms. Petras. It became a tradition between them to meet up for various things early in the evening such as eating or conversing.

Ms. Petras plopped down with her numerous bags and long, filthy coat. She leaned over the cooking site.

"Please, Ms. Petras! Can I watch this time?" He inched close to her, eager to enjoy the warm fire since his government-issued clothing had fallen into disrepair. He had to start patching spots with whatever the two of them could scrounge up. This made him feel barely dressed above an animal.

"You know the rules. No peeking!"

He covered his eyes but strained his ears for a hint at what magic she used to light the fire. Her coat rustled, but no clues were gleaned. He could not take it any longer, so he barely parted his hands and witnessed a spontaneous spark grow into a flame.

Her secrecy about many things sometimes concerned him. What was she hiding? It never seemed to bring any danger upon him, but Father did tell him that deception was the natural state of bad people. He hoped she was not a bad person.

"Okay. You can look again."

He shut his fingers and lowered his hands with the most innocent smile he could muster. "Is this the magic of the Divine?"

She rolled her eyes. "I keep telling you there's no such thing. All you need to believe down here is reality." She stared at him but then shrugged. "Eh, whatever they drilled into you at that assimilation facility is probably too ingrained. Forget about it. Now, show me what you were able to scrounge up from the surface."

He showed her two apples and a couple of coins he had lifted out of a dumpster only a few blocks away from the old orphanage.

She examined an apple. "Hmm…malus domestica. Juicy, nutritious, and portable. Nice find." She took the coins as well and slipped them into her purse. "And that's for my breakfast tomorrow while I'm topside. Good job, kid."

Adiquis smiled. Validation was nice. He felt like his contributions, although meager, were enough. He was enough. The remaining apple in his palm looked mighty tasty. Before he took his first bite, Ms. Petras perked up.

"Hold on. You know what? Today is the anniversary of your descent into this cesspool. Isn't it? Here." She handed the other apple back to him.

"Oh, thank you!" Adiquis snatched the treat and devoured them both with a hunger yet to be satiated.

She watched him lick his fingers. She smiled and placed a hand on her stomach. "I'm starting to feel hungry as well." A loud pop echoing through the tunnels sent their two sets of ears darting about. Once sure there was nothing to fear, she stared into the flames.

"Hey, kid. You're still keeping your marbles hidden, right?"

He nodded. "I get asked to show them a lot, but I never do. Is that rude? Instead of checking my worth, they just work with me based on unchecked trust."

"That's positively sweet of you to worry, but no, it's not rude. They're being nice to you because they know I'll stop fixing stuff around here if you're not taken care of. Let's enjoy it while it lasts." She blew into the fire. It roared. "The only way you're gonna stay safe down here is by playing it smart. There's a lot of people who'll swindle you if you give them the chance. Surie's always looking for cat eyes, that stabby kid of Luiz's would jump you for anything large, and I know for sure the Flesky brothers are about one pastel away from getting out of here and going *legit* up above."

"I don't blame them. I don't want to be here either. Maybe one day we can all get out together."

She shook her head and smiled. "Kid, you deserve so much better than down here. You've got a soft heart and a bright mind. You understand that what you have in your pouch has nothing to do with what you're worth. Frankly, it takes a genius these days to understand that and that's what makes you special."

She stared at the flames and heaved a heavy sigh.

ROVER ENTRY #1034

Listen. Do me a favor and don't trust anyone down here. If something were to happen to you…" Ms. Petras pulled a deceased animal out of her purse and prepared it quickly. They usually did not eat meat until the weekend, but perhaps she was dizzy or could not resist any longer. "Well, who would I share a proper meal with?"

"What's that?"

Skewered pieces roasted over the fire. "Beats me. Bought it from Surie and, in my experience, if it costs less than a dollar, it tastes better if you don't know."

She turned their meal often and Adiquis watched the flames dance across her huge glasses. Scratches and chips twinkled on her curved, plastic discs. They made her look absolutely disheveled, but he could tell by the largeness of her eyes peering through them she needed them to survive. The glowing fire's shadows accentuated the furrowing of her brow. She thought deeply.

"I've been hiding down here for years," she said, "and I'm so tired of it. I don't need all that pomp I used to have. I'd just settle for clean air at this point." She pulled a skewer off the open flame and took a bite. She passed the second one to him.

He handled the skewer with excited fingers but waited for her to swallow the first bit. Best to let her test for any spoilage. He did not fancy being the experimental subject like last time. "But how would you survive up top? You don't have any real marbles."

"I know." She patted her pouch. The unusual clanking of non-glass orbs would have made any other person feel compelled to get their hearing checked, but Adiquis had seen them a handful of times with his own eyes. "My twelve steely rollers won't even get me the time of day in the city. Metal is everywhere and glass is rare. I get it. But all those doofuses up there just don't know what I got."

Her marbles were different like him in a way. "I think your marbles are great."

Adiquis watched her open her pouch as she peered inside with disappointed eyes. She once told him her pouch held secrets. It took some begging, but she confessed that years ago she found those steelys deep in the noxious depths of the sewer's lowest level. A place of great danger, she claimed she found piles of vibrant steel at the bottom of a pool of electrified water. How she managed to salvage through that, she never explained. From this valuable resource, she made herself a set of custom marbles which she claimed were the most valuable in the world. However, this made no sense to Adiquis because everyone knew vibrant steel could not be compressed, only cut. The material was simply too volatile. Adiquis interpreted this story mostly to be untrue. It meant she did not want to share the truth at present.

Her shoulders slumped and she quickly tucked her pouch deep into her coat. "I shouldn't be frivolously exposing these out in the open when there could be spies lurking about down here." Her eyes darted about.

"Do you really think that?" he asked as he finished his food. A few of her idiosyncrasies puzzled him. They did not seem to match her otherwise collected demeanor. Of what he had learned of psychology in the last year, she may have benefited from professional medical attention.

"Well, of course I do! That's the reason I'm down here. It's the last place they'd look for me, what with my background and all. And this is all only temporary. One day, when I figure things out, I'll return to the surface and stick it back to those Autocratic no-gooders!"

"I'd like that! Take me with you."

She nodded and smiled softly. "Of course. But first, you need to catch up to me if you're going to be able to hold your own by my side when the time comes." She revealed a set of books from her purse. "I picked these new ones off of Doc Sermupets' porch. Seems the old geezer still has a soft spot for me."

Adiquis took the corroding texts of bounded aluminum pages. He flipped through a few rusting sections and understood the etchings were of an advanced math.

"Isn't the doctor putting himself in danger by helping you? Didn't you say everybody you used to know had to stay away?"

"Yeah, I did say that, but the doc is smart. He wouldn't keep it up if he thought they were watching." She took a text back and opened it up to a specific page. She turned it toward Adiquis and pointed inside. "I suppose now's as good of a time as any to introduce you to reverse quantum mechanics. I want you to read about Hiedemon's Law of Faster than Light Travel and recite it from memory ten times. No reference materials when you're ready!"

He groaned.

"Hey! None of that pouting business. I know you love this. You've made so much progress these last few years. I dare say you're a little genius of sorts. If only someone had gotten to fostering your talent sooner."

He smiled mischievously. In truth, he enjoyed schooling ten times over with Ms. Petras as his teacher. Parts of his mind, not stimulated since his school days, tickled to life whenever she spoke of science, technology, and all the machinations behind the world that grinded in secret around him. He felt like she recited fairy tales, but she swore these concepts were real and they governed their world and beyond. Even the Autocracy, she claimed, could not change the immutable rules of science. That lesson alone was revolutionary to him.

"Come on now. Get started. Your continued education is important. You're still young and the city hasn't spoiled you yet. You must arm your mind with the most powerful weapon in the galaxy."

Once they concluded the science portion, he could dictate the next topic at hand before she returned him to her syllabus. He had many favorite pet topics including learning about the talents of individuals all across the city. Some people, he learned, could train to lift impossible weights. Others could lift the spirits of their fellow people with only their voice. While still others could destroy an entire civilization with nothing more than a stroke of a pen. He learned repeatedly what he long suspected: a person's worth was not determined by their marbles. He learned a great many things. Yet today he wanted to delve deeper into a little dream location beyond the city walls.

"For my personal pick, I want to learn more about the tunnel to the countryside outside the wilds, please!"

"This again?" She reached into her coat for her own notes. She mumbled, "What is your obsession with this place?" She pulled out her notebook. "Ah, fine. Remind me where we left off."

His enthusiasm left no time for breaths. "The countryside past the wilds is a land far outside the city that's a beautiful place where people can be free, there is enough space for everyone, and everyone is truly equal in the Divine's eye and a magic tunnel can take you there!"

"That's…close enough." She flipped through the pages and turned the notebook toward him. Complicated scrawls and drawings of the language of science covered the page. At the bottom, she had drawn an illustration of a grassy mound with houses and trees on top. The sun shone high above and little people shook hands and wore strange, colorful clothing. Swirly shaped blue stars churned from the page's edges and in toward the center. They were strange given the scene took place midday.

"The tunnel to the countryside" she continued, "is sort of an analogy for something my old colleagues and I used to dream about."

"What's an analogy?"

She tapped her chin. "It's sort of like a synonym."

"A cinnamon roll?" He smacked his lips.

She laughed. "No, no. *Synonym*. The tunnel is an idea. Or it could be real, I don't know. I never got to find out."

The sparkles were fading from Adiquis' face. His smile partially receded. Ms. Petras took notice. Perhaps she struggled with particularly sullen emotions that day, but she could not endure his gleam waning.

"Uh…what I meant to say was that the tunnel is out somewhere among the outer wilds far away, very far away. It's…hidden, sort of."

"Like a secret passageway? Like the looking glass in *Alice in Wonderland*?" he perked up, recalling his studies.

She slowly nodded. "Actually, maybe it is a little like that. In whatever way you find it, it leads to all kinds of unusual places. The countryside, a land free from the strict expectations of the Empire's aristocrats, could be one of them. Their society is completely without marble judgment. Your pouch is worth what it's really worth: a thin sack filled with mineral orbs of no practical value. In the countryside, you're judged by the content of your character and not the glitz of your globes. There's enough land and resources for everyone and no need to filter out people by classifying them as…undesirables. There are more friends and allies than you could ever want. It's a place people like you and me would want to be."

"It sounds like a fantasy," he said hoping to hear more. "Can you imagine a place where we could feel accepted? At peace with ourselves without the pressure of more, more, more?"

"Well, I wouldn't get your hopes up. The Autocracy keeps people like us from moving about the sprawling city pretty effectively. And besides, I don't even know if this tunnel really exists. It's just something I guessed at as a way of escaping this planet." She looked toward her marble pouch. "I never got all the data concerning…"

Adiquis did not want to hear that. He jumped from the ground. "We should go! I've been dreaming of the countryside for so long. I don't want to wait another day. Can we?"

"What? Come on, kid!" She laughed. "I just told you how difficult it is escaping the city when you're not bound and gagged inside of a sack! Believe me. I know because I've tried. That was my first plan when my life got turned upside down." She followed up under her breath, "Sewer was definitely a distant second."

"Why's it so hard? We could start walking right now."

She flipped through her notebook with a circling finger. "Let me tally the ways for you. For starters, I've never had the privilege of seeing the city's edge, but I've heard it's farther than you'd think. We'd need to procure enough food for up to five days when we're already scraping by day to day. We'd need to pay for some type of transportation. We couldn't take public transit since neither of us have formal documents anymore." She paused and looked at him with a skeptical eye. "That is unless you're holding out on me."

He shook his head vigorously.

She almost reached to ruffle his hair but pointed her finger playfully instead and chuckled. "I'm just teasing you! So, we'd have to buy a ride out of town and lastly, we'd need some security on our hips. Do you understand what I'm saying?"

He had no idea and could not figure it out by the time she continued.

"I'm talking about a weapon. A crowbar or something like that. Once we're on the road, anyone could take advantage of us. We'd have nowhere to run and hide like we do down here. We'd be in the Autocracy's territory and surrounded by all their barriers again."

She reached inside her purse and pulled out her pouch. "Dang. Some of these challenges would require miracles given what I have to my name." She pushed her marbles around. "I have a few glass left, but not many." She scoffed. "Wow. I hadn't taken stock of myself like this in a long time. Maybe I *am* just a sewer rat. An undesirable steely in a world of glass beauties."

Adiquis could tell she was in pain. He slowly placed a brave hand upon hers. He felt her quiver with surprise. "That's not true! You're not a rat! We're both worth something wonderful, just nobody sees it yet." He did not know how they would overcome the obstacles but talking about them regardless made his hopes seem closer than ever.

She looked up through a grate sprinkling freezing rain onto the cement barely missing them both. She heaved a great sigh. "Why am I assessing my worth again? I suppose I haven't broken the habit of what people do when they need to make a big decision. Then again, it's more likely I understand our reality." She looked down at Adiquis. She smiled gently. "I almost got used to living free of their influence. But I guess I'll never get out of here without playing their game. You're pushing me to do it."

She tucked her purse back into her coat. "Now, let's just say we did want to get out of here. How exactly would we do that?" She hummed to herself. "Too bad we can't pay people in good vibes. Nobody down here is gonna do anything for us just because we're wonderful. I hate to admit it, but the only things that get people's attention *are* marbles."

Of course, Adiquis thought. Marbles! They were the cause and possibly solution to all their problems. Without hesitation, he examined the contents of his own pouch. Lacking any valuable sets, and individuals typically having little value on their own, his enthusiasm started to wane. But he considered that only down here could these singles be worth a fortune to the right person.

He had never shown his marbles to Ms. Petras nor had she ever asked to see them. This dynamic endeared her to him during their first days together.

He tried to abandon all the other concerns he had about her. She was good. Now was the time.

"What about mine?" he looked up.

Her eyes squinted softly. "Aw, come on. You're sweet, but I don't think whatever you have in that little raggedy bag is going to help us. Just keep them to yourself and..."

He took out Jannifer's big one. "What if I traded this to the brothers? Don't they have scooters and stuff?"

She plucked the marble out of his hand. "Holy baloney! W-w-where'd you find this? It's enormous!" She drew it near and turned it slowly. The fire's glow pierced through the clear parts and cast a beam of light upon her eye.

"I've had it for a while."

"Did you steal it?" she said with a skeptical tilt of her head.

"No!"

She nodded slowly. "Okay. If you say so."

After a moment of thought, she jumped and propelled the marble towards the ceiling. "Yeah! This could work!" She paced and mumbled. "We're onto something here, but what're we gonna do about food and protection?"

He rummaged in his pouch and pulled out Terrence's pastel. "What about Jonathan? He and his dad have all those knives."

Ms. Petras clicked her heels and took the pastel too. "Right, stabby kid." She rolled the pastel in her palm. "Remarkable. This is in fantastic condition. Where'd you get these from again? Oh right. You *didn't* steal them." She waved dismissively. "Never mind."

"And I think Ms. Surie probably has more meat where this came from. She likes cat eyes, right?" He took out Sanjah's marble. This orb was his favorite of his non-original bunch. Sanjah's memory did not add any emotion to this transaction, but the flame-like design inside the marble reminded him of the heat and fire the day he stumbled from the orphanage. He survived. This trinket had reminded him for years since.

When she reached out for it, he instinctively drew back slightly. He was not sure he could part with it.

Surprise spread across her face. "Whoa! Sorry, kid. Do you not want me to take these?" She offered the two others back. "Listen. I'm not going to do any of this if you don't want me to. I just thought you were making a plan with these wonderful finds. I understand if you think we should find another way, but how..."

He placed the cat eye in her palm and pushed the lot toward her. "No, you're right. It's a good plan. Do you really think you can make these trades?"

Without hesitation, she picked up her purse and stuffed the marbles inside. "Absolutely! Over the last few years, I've learned how to hustle a good game down here." She checked her watch and brushed the filth off her clothes. "Okay. Let me go talk to some people and see what kind of inventory is out there. I can make some requests for their next supply run topside if they're a little low at the moment so we shouldn't have any problems."

"Be quick. Can we please leave tonight?" he asked as she took two steps away.

She stopped dead. "Tonight?" She ran her hands through the rat nest on her head and hummed a stressed tune. "Well, I thought I'd sort of see what's out there. You know, start buttering people up tonight. But...but I could rush them with what else I got." She peered inside her purse and mulled over several items. "I can't promise you anything, but I'm gonna try my best."

She darted back and forth before deciding to run. "Stay right here and continue your studies! I'll be right back!"

She ran through a trail of puddles and disappeared.

ROVER ENTRY #1035

The roasting fire continued to burn brightly. Ms. Petras' footsteps faded until all that remained were Adiquis' shallow breathing and the crackling flames. Staring into the fire, a memory, or rather a vision, crept up from the recess of his mind and gripped his heart. Air expelled from his lungs. The flames were jumping higher, overtaking him, licking the tips of his shoes as it filled the sewer with smoke.

He dropped his skewer. The clink upon the ground startled him back to reality where the small flame remained respectfully in place. Visions of fears he had not yet come to terms with haunted him. He could not stay in the sewer any longer. This was an extension of that calamity and he desperately needed a place to feel safe again.

He could not risk their plan failing. They should be tackling this together especially if he would one day become her partner in the future like she promised. She might find more marbles were necessary. Or she would have a tough time getting a fair deal among her detractors. He snuffed out the flame hastily and gathered his paltry possessions.

Adiquis strained for any echo of her footsteps ahead. As expected from Ms. Petras' long legs, he heard nothing. Navigating through the tunnels, he passed the shivering homeless and heartbroken huddled together along the damp, black and brown walls. Many of his fellow sewer rats were suffering from the season's coldest temperatures. He rounded a dark corner and an old man, who once chased him halfway through the sewer for a piece of his lunch, flashed him a deranged smile. Adiquis recoiled out of habit, but today it appeared the man was too weak to give him a hard time. That broad smile surfaced a memory from his earlier literary nod. *Alice's* Cheshire Cat.

The profile of a trickster. A terrible feeling arose from his gut. Ms. Petras claimed the text contained cautionary tales for him to help identify swindlers and opportunists. Every lesson she had taught him started to seem relevant, but in the most regretful way. Was the question of whether Ms. Petras had fooled him into handing over his marbles now being entertained? She had never asked about them before, but was that just to lower his defenses? It was he who brought up going to the outer wilds, or was that an eventuality once tutoring planted the seed in his mind? She taught him these were the tools of the predator. Ms. Petras knew them well. Perhaps too well.

He hastened his pace and diverted his search away from Ms. Petras. Instead, he would find the Flesky brothers, Mr. Luiz, or Ms. Surie first. If he found her targets, she would come to him. Sprinting as fast as he could, he first came upon Ms. Surie illuminated by the moon shining through a missing manhole cover and standing over her open-air cooking pot. She mumbled words he could not understand. It sounded erratic. It gave him pause.

He approached cautiously and tried to get a glance at what she was doing. "Excuse me," he said. "Did Ms. Petras come by?"

By the motion of her arms it looked like she was stirring a soup, but no flame shone underneath and the water produced no steam. She did not respond so he scooted a little closer.

"Um, Ms. Surie?"

"Oh!" She spun around holding his cat eye in a wet towel. Water splashed onto his shirt. She scrubbed the marble and drew it close to her chest. Her skeptical eye looked him up and down as if she were assessing his trustworthiness. "Adiquis?" Realizing who he was, a soft expression returned to her face and she resumed waxing. "What can I do for you?"

He felt a chill from the drafty tunnels upon his chest. He stared at his wet spots, but no apology came.

"Did Ms. Petras already ask you about food?"

"She did. Completely cleaned me out and had the nerve to say I was in riches now. Three cat eyes are hardly a set, but I do think I'll be able to crawl back topside and get into a rehabilitation program. I've got credentials now."

Her tooth and gap smile made Adiquis happy, but he had little time to congratulate her.

She stared into the marble. "Looking for her, eh?"

"Yeah. If she's not here, then I gotta go." He turned to leave.

"Wait!" She grabbed his arm.

Startled at first, she held firmly but not aggressively. "What is it?" he asked as he tried to tug his arm away.

"Look. You seem like a nice kid, but I got a bad feeling about that woman's intentions."

"I don't understand." He wiggled free. He took a couple of steps back.

"That woman. She's not really trusted around here, you know? I've always seen you hanging around her which is why you should know it's because she…well, there are a lot of folks that remember all the science and junk she's done." She scrubbed the marble vigorously and peeked inside the towel. "She has a reputation in the city, you know. You're young, so it's understandable you don't, but anybody who's been pushed out of the society knows it was, in part, because of the things *she's* done."

Ms. Surie stared deeply into her marble. Her fingers squeezed the towel increasingly tighter as the drops of water turned into a steady drip. Adiquis sensed a madness in her eyes boiling over from a wrong in her past. He thanked her for the advice and scampered off.

He found Mr. Luiz right away dipping his feet on the other side of a nearby pool of run-off rainwater. His son, Jonathan, sat next to him. Jonathan fiddled with a small knife. Fellow rats found this a popular spot to swim and bathe in. The deep, dark water was the cleanest in the sewer, but Adiquis had always been too scared to dive in. He had read too many creature-feature novels during his free time. What lurked below that shadowy pool was probably hungry for children who were not as well equipped as Jonathan.

"Hello, Mr. Luiz." Adiquis shouted and waved from across the pool.

"Hi there, kid. I don't remember your name." Mr. Luiz waved politely and returned his attention to the stagnant water soaking his feet.

"I'm Adiquis."

"Adiquis, right. Is that supposed to mean something?" Mr. Luiz kicked his legs a little and splashed the icy water about.

"That's a stupid name," Jonathan said.

Adiquis shot Jonathan a nasty look.

Mr. Luiz noticed and shook Jonathan by the arm. "Come on now, son. That isn't right to say. Apologize to him."

Jonathan pouted and hopped up. "I don't need to do anything."

Mr. Luiz shrugged.

Adiquis spotted a box of knives at Mr. Luiz' side. Mr. Luiz was a collector first and a businessman second. Knives were in high demand among the defensively minded, but he was usually reluctant to sell unless the deal heavily slanted in his favor. Adiquis recalled a text Ms. Petras once shared with him called *The Psychology of Persuasion*. If Ms. Petras traded for a knife tonight, she would have needed to be incredibly crafty with him. Adiquis too needed to be cunning to get the information he desired considering he had nothing valuable to trade anymore.

"Ms. Petras told me she was going to come around here. Have you seen her?"

Mr. Luiz cast a curious gaze upon Adiquis. His eyes squinted. "Are you asking if I've seen Ms. Petras? Why? Are you lost? Do you need my help with directions?"

"I just want to know if you've seen her."

Mr. Luiz rubbed his chin. "Well, I don't recall exactly. What's that information worth to you?"

Jonathan repeatedly stabbed a slimy creature that had the unfortunate luck of crawling out of the water at the wrong time. The knife clanked against the stone floor over and over again. Mr. Luiz liked to sell good knives. This might become a problem for him. Adiquis could recall a thing or two about metalwork from his studies, standard nationalist curriculum for Autocratic orphans.

"Would you consider trading information for information?" he asked Mr. Luiz.

"Depends. What are you offering?"

He pointed at Jonathan. "He's really abusing your hardware. Do you know how to sharpen those?"

Mr. Luiz raised an eyebrow. "Of course, kid. Do I look stupid?"

"But do you know how to sharpen them *well*? Scraping the blade against a whetstone is all fine and good, but you need to keep the blade straight, free of minor irregularities that sharpening doesn't correct."

Mr. Luiz leaned forward. It seemed his interest was piqued. "What are you talking about?"

Adiquis stepped next to Mr. Luiz. "One of your knives, please."

Mr. Luiz hesitated before handing one over. "That's not for keeps. Just show me what you're going on about."

Adiquis nodded. "Look closely at the blade." He held it steadily and they both leaned in. Adiquis pointed to the cutting edge. "Sharpening removes part of the metal. It makes the blade sharper, but that sharpness may not be aligned in the same direction. This seriously reduces the quality of the cut. Any good purveyor of knives will be able to tell just by a quick look. You need to hone your knives as well. You can do that with a special tool that I'm sure anyone can find topside."

Adiquis handed the knife back.

This claim was a bluff. While it was true that sharpening and honing was an important part of maintaining sharp objects, such microscopic imperfections were not visible with the naked eye. However, Mr. Luiz did not know that.

"Hmph. Well I'll be. I can't say that doesn't sound a little familiar; it's been a lot of years since I was in school. But I'm not too big of a man to admit I had plumb forgot about it. I'll have to get that tool next time I'm out. Thank you, kid. So, you want to know if I saw Ms. Petras? Yeah, I did." He patted his marble pouch. "I gave her one of my discounted ones in exchange for a huge, sparkly fella."

"That doesn't seem very fair," Adiquis said.

Mr. Luiz lowered his head and shook it slowly. "Fair? That *woman* has a lot to answer for down here. She's taken so much from us. But you wouldn't know anything about that being a young kid now, would you?"

Ms. Petras was moving incredibly fast and possibly bartering or swindling people at an expert's pace. Adiquis left them without a word and ran as fast as he could toward the sewer's entrance.

He came upon the two Flesky brothers sifting through their marbles sprawled across the concrete.

"That makes eight, brother!" the youngest said.

"That's it! I'm gonna go back to school!" said the eldest.

"Whaddya mean? You're not the one who made the trade! I'm gonna elevate our game and start selling our motors up top!"

Adiquis recalled his lessons regarding the Autocracy's system of business. Any hope that these two could sell property they did not construct with their own hands would never come to pass.

"Give 'em here!" They wildly grasped at the marbles and a few scattered about.

Terrence's pastel rolled to Adiquis' feet. He picked it up.

"Hey, boy! Give that back!"

Grime covered the marble. The beautiful swirls Terrence was so proud of were barely visible. It made him sad. "It's not going to work."

"What's that?"

"Your plan to have a business selling used motors. You can't do that. It's illegal."

The eldest grabbed Adiquis' wrist. "What do *you* know?" He shook Adiquis' hand until the marble dropped to the floor.

Adiquis pulled back, crossed his arms, and stepped away.

The brother scooped up the marble. "Can you believe this place? Can't make an honest trade around here without somebody trying to take it from you."

"That's usually our schtick, hee hee" the other said. "First, we get fleeced by that woman for our greatest hog, as if she hadn't already done *enough* to us, and now this kid…"

"Ms. Petras came through here?" Adiquis asked.

"Who?"

"Tall! Long, white coat! Gave you that pastel!" he demanded.

"Oh, the scientist. Yeah, just missed her. She climbed up topside. If you hurry, you might be able to yell good riddance before she takes off. Seemed like she was in a real hurry."

Adiquis darted out of the sewer and into the city's open air within the dumping canals. A slushy light rain fell over him and he desperately wanted to enjoy the clean water dripping down his face. The delightful moment was short lived when goosebumps covered his skin and his wet clothes froze in the icy air. He floundered up a slick staircase when an engine revved and sputtered out repeatedly somewhere above. He prayed to the Divine he was not too late.

"Ms. Petras! Wait! Don't leave me!"

ROVER ENTRY #1036

Kid? Where are you?" Ms. Petras' voice echoed from above. A crack of thunder followed.

He reached the street shivering and gasping for breath. She stood next to a fancy motorcycle. She rubbed her palm upon the bike. The headlights grew brighter until he had to direct his gaze away. The engine came to life and the lights dimmed.

"Adiquis! What're you doing topside? I told you to wait! You could get snatched up out here by a roving paddy wagon!"

"I followed you! I didn't want you to leave me behind, to take my marbles and…and…" A few tears mixed with the raindrops. They blurred his vision. He stumbled forward and fell to the ground. Scrapes covered his hands and knees. His clothes were turning to ice.

Ms. Petras tucked a tiny item from her hand into her coat and ran towards him. She stopped just shy, her hands reaching out, and froze. "I'm sorry. You don't like to be touched…"

He spared no words, instead bursting into tears. His hands opened and clasped for her presence.

"Kid! Oh my gosh!" She scooped him up.

He squeezed her and sobbed.

"Adiquis, you're freezing!" She slipped off one of her two coats and threw it around him. "Hold still. I picked up a little treat on my way here that I had a feeling you'd need."

She revealed two small fabric patches that contained functioning smart machines to jump-start his ragged clothing's nano functions. She slapped them on his sleeve and pant leg. His clothes emitted a cloud of steam. Once dry again, she zipped up the jacket. She padded him ensuring the coat's snug fit.

"Of course I was coming back for you. I did exactly what you said and got everybody to give us what we wanted tonight. My purse may be significantly lighter, but we did it. You made it possible!"

"But the bike and you were going and…"

"No, kid! I was just making sure this rust bucket actually worked! I can't let those Flesky brothers sell me a bad ride and disappear tomorrow! Come on, what did I teach you?"

"Don't trust anybody," he said through sniffles.

She squeezed him. "Okay. I guess I see where you're coming from." She knelt and grasped his arms. She looked him straight in the eyes. "There's no way I could leave you behind. You're a little genius like me! We have to stick together. Oh, I can't believe this is how I'd find out you were ready, but there's no doubt you can hack it out here on your own a little."

The curl of a smile formed on his cheek.

"I gotta be honest," she tugged at her collar. "I wasn't planning on taking us to the countryside."

"What?" Alarm bells went off inside. "Y-you were lying to me?"

"N-n-no! It's not like that! It's just not that easy getting to a place so… uh, unknown! I was just going to get us out of the city and see what came next. But now…" She rose, pressing her palm against her aching spine. "I see that you indeed learned from me. With both of our heads combined, it may finally be possible to find the tunnel there."

She slipped on a helmet and threw him a pair of goggles. "Come on. Let's get out of here." Both saddled on the bike, she pulled his hands around her waist. "Hold on tight. You can't fall off because we don't have enough fuel to muck around. We need a straight shot to the city limits. Are you ready?"

"Yeah!" he said while wiping his last tear away.

Ms. Petras twisted the throttle and they slowly lurched forward. Once on a main street, they picked up speed. They drove through the dirty city's underbelly. They were above the sewers but still in undesirable territory. They passed the ruins of the old House.

These few blocks had been Adiquis' whole life and he would never again have to sleep on the cold ground or be judged by his marbles. As they passed by glowing buildings and statues he had never seen before, he read billboards plastered high upon the sides of buildings for marbles and their related accessories.

Be the talk of the town with Aero-glass

Luxury pouches for people of luxury

A loud train rattled along the tracks alongside them. Graffiti covered a car.

Food > marbles
Eat your marbles

It took them many days, barely sleeping under overpasses and in ditches, until they approached their final obstacle: the spectacle that was the city wall. Adiquis did not know what he expected, maybe a thick black line painted on concrete, but an imposing wall stretching above the clouds was not it.

No other vehicles were in line this late at night so they drove up to a gate next to a small building. Adiquis leaned past Ms. Petras to peer through the long, narrow tunnel carved out of the dense wall. A glimpse of the other side revealed no buildings, no metal. Just green grass and open sky. His hands shook with excitement.

"Is this it? Is this the tunnel to the countryside?"

"No, kid. That out there is just the wilds. We need to go even further beyond to find a place safe enough to start searching."

Ms. Petras leaned the bike and deployed the kickstand. "Adiquis, I know this might be a difficult thing to do but pour your marbles into my pouch." She passed her pouch discreetly back to him.

He wondered if he should. Was this her final ploy to fleece him? No. After everything she had done for him, that simply could not be true. He poured what little he had left. One by one, his misshapen glass clearies became hers. He now had nothing to his name, but he felt hope swelling in his heart promising him it would shortly no longer matter.

A stout man in uniform exited the small building and approached them. Tall, thick boots thumped on the pavement. His marbles, inside a clear sack, hung from his belt. Adiquis could see from this distance he had several different sets. But as the man neared within a few paces, Adiquis' eyes widened at the sight of a single steely.

"Quickly!" Ms. Petras warned. "Hand it back!"

Adiquis finished pouring and pushed her bag into her grasping hand.

She shoved her pouch back into her coat. The man stopped at their side and she took off her helmet. "Hello, officer."

"Hello, miss. Please turn off your vehicle and hand me your documents."

She silenced the bike. "Ah, just a second." She pulled out her purse and rifled through it. "You don't need documents to go outside the walls, isn't that right?"

He scratched his head. "Well, technically no. But you'll need them to get back inside, so…"

She paused and placed a palm on her cheek. Her face scrunched up. She looked exhausted. "Well, can we just be on our way? I'm sure they're just somewhere in all this mess." She chuckled. "I can't seem to find them at the moment."

"It's in your best interest if…"

She rolled her eyes. "I don't understand what this is all about anyway."

"Ma'am…" He reached a stiff hand toward his belt.

Her eyes followed his movement. She eked out a meek smile and said softly, "I'm just taking my son for a ride around the outer wilds to see the unpolluted night sky. You know, you can't see the stars like that from inside the city."

"Pollution?" he replied tersely. "There's no such thing in the Autocracy's realm. I assure you it won't be any better out there."

"O-oh! I meant just the incredibly dense cloud cover."

The man raised tilted his head. He reciprocated her slight smile. His arm relaxed to his side. "Is that so? Yeah, I can see that. But are you really in that much of a hurry? You'd be taking an unnecessary risk."

A heavy sigh flowed from her lungs. "Do you have any kids of your own, officer?"

"No, ma'am. Can't say the opportunity has exactly presented itself."

"Well, you wouldn't understand I suppose. But see, I never gave my son the time he deserved growing up." She twisted back and gently ran her hand over Adiquis' cheek.

This surprised Adiquis, but he tried not to show it. If anything, he delighted in it. He felt wanted. He felt enough.

It was like they were acting in the performance written by the ancient playwright William Shakespeare in which Romeo made a tasty hamlet for his loving father, Lear, and they lived happily ever after. At least, that is what he thought that piece meant. His interpretation of theater was always riddled with errors.

"I cashed out all of my vacation days and for the first time I can show him whatever he wants. This precious boy said over dinner, 'Mother, I'd like to see the stars in the night sky.'" She gestured up into the hazy atmosphere. "So I said, 'You know what? Let's go right now!' We jumped on my bike and drove straight out here as fast as we could. I decided I'm not going to waste another minute of our time together."

The officer shook his head and shrugged. "If you say so." He wrote on a clipboard.

"Thank you so much, officer. We'll be back before you know it and I'm sure I'll have my documents at that time." Ms. Petras turned back and smiled at Adiquis.

Anxiety and joy both buzzed in his stomach. He tried his best to follow her lead. With a reciprocated smile, he said, "Thanks, m-mom."

Her eyes grew as large as her glasses.

The officer cleared his throat. "I don't mean to interrupt your touching moment, but ma'am I'm going to need you to open your pouch so I can inspect your marbles."

Ms. Petras' body stiffened. "Excuse me? I've never had to do that before. That isn't regulation, is it?"

He signed the bottom of his page and glanced up. "I don't know what you're talking about. It's been standard procedure for as long as I've been working the border. Now, could you please?"

She shrugged. "If you think that's entirely necessary, officer. I mean, they're just all worthless anyway. Barely have enough to make ends meet most days." She pulled her pouch out slowly and opened it ever so slightly. She glanced inside first before offering him a look.

"Thank you for your cooperation, ma'am."

She watched as his eyes scanned her contents. "See? Nothing to talk about. Just a poor woman's heirlooms."

He took several notes on his clipboard. "Uh huh. A poor workaholic with a nice bike and a child permit." Mid-scribble, his pen paused. His neck slowly craned up and he asked, "Wait. Do I know you?"

She shook her head quickly. "Can't say I recognize you. So probably not." She flashed a toothy grin.

He stared for a moment, his pupils brushing over every facet of her face. "Eh, you're probably right. Okay, just hold on for a minute." He walked back toward his little building.

Adiquis recalled a lesson in which one could tell if someone was attempting to conceal information by listening to artifacts in their voice. *Principles of Suggestion* maybe the text was called. This man sounded nervous and suspicious. Adiquis watched the man enter his hut and pick up a telephone.

"I don't like the whole feel of this," Ms. Petras said. She glanced about every way surveying the barren street and vertigo-inducing building tops.

Adiquis thought she seemed overly paranoid, but he too felt uneasy. Certainly, suspicion was healthy given their fragile situation. She should know what he knew just in case.

"I saw a steely in his pouch. He had one like you."

"What?" She whipped back toward him. Her eyes flashed with disbelief. "How many?"

"J-just the one. Should we be worried…"

"That's impossible! Unless…" She moved her hand to the ignition key. "Hold on, kid. We might have to make a run for it."

Standing near a window, the officer shook his head vigorously and slammed his fists upon a table. Adiquis made out he was laughing. The officer completed his call and walked back outside.

He called out with a broad smile as he approached. "Good news, miss. You're clear to pass."

Ms. Petras whispered, "We might be okay after all." She let go of the key.

The officer's boots clattered to a stop near them. He tapped his clipboard for her. "Before you go, please sign this temporary identity pass and take the below copy with you just in case you don't find your documents."

She provided her signature. She tore the bottom and stuffed it into her purse. It was only open for a second, but he pointed at her pouch.

"Oh, and I need to confiscate those marbles. You know the ones."

"Excuse me?" her voice shuddered.

"I'm not stupid. I know like half of those are phony. You *are* aware counterfeiting is a Level 1 class offense, right?" He took off his hat and fidgeted along the brim. "Look, miss. You seem like a nice, if not complicated, lady. I don't want to make a big deal out of this. I'm just doing my job. I'm not going to tell anyone and I'm not calling the Autocratic Guard. Simply hand them over and I'll dispose of them properly. You can go on with your night and give your kid as much black sky as he wants."

She pushed her pouch deeper into her purse and lifted her helmet to her head. "No. I'm not doing that. You file whatever report you have to, but I'm gonna go and you're not gonna stop me."

"Now miss…" he said as he reached toward her. "*Dr. Petras…*"

From inside her purse, she wielded a knife with one swift motion.

The officer cursed and stumbled back. He reached into his pouch. "Don't move!" He pulled the steely out and pointed it at them.

Adiquis thought this action was beyond peculiar. He knew firearms existed to enforce the Autocratic will, but a person pointing a marble at you certainly was not that. He did not flinch, but Ms. Petras leapt off the bike and yanked him behind it as well.

"Keep your head down!" she cried. A flash of light cast a long shadow from the bike. A chaotic line of surging electricity hovered over their heads faster than the eye could process before a brick wall in the distance exploded. Debris flew toward them and scattered along the street. They were lucky not to be pelted by errant stones.

Ms. Petras opened her pouch and pulled out several steelys intertwined between her fingers. "Cover your ears!" she screamed as she emerged from behind the bike.

Adiquis did so and a sonic boom pushed him and the bike onto the ground. He thought the officer had shot at her a second time so he swung around to witness the carnage. But only she stood triumphantly, her white coat and dirty hair flapping in the wind when the smoke cleared. The officer was no more, just a blemish on the ground covered in pieces of fabric and marbles.

She ran to the grave and ignored all the other glass. It was the single steely she was after. She shoved it into her pouch and righted the bike. A rumbling in the sky, high above the gray clouds of city smog meant a threat loomed above. But neither of them wanted to wait long enough to find out of what variety.

"Come on, kid! We gotta go!"

He could not comprehend what had just occurred. He stood catatonically while she beckoned him forward. She had to grab him by the hand before he regained control of his limbs. He climbed aboard the bike. They shattered through the security gate and delved into the long tunnel.

ROVER ENTRY #1037

Whew, that was close!" Ms. Petras shouted above the vehicle's reverberations echoing through the tunnel. "Look, things are going to be different on the other side so I want you to keep your wits about you. I never told you the truth about my steelys, but now that you've seen it for yourself, I think it's time you knew. *This* is what I've been talking about. This is the work we're going to do."

Adiquis shook his head. "I don't understand. I know your steelys are secret, they're special, but what was that? I thought you made them out of that sewer metal." He struggled with confusion. "Why did that officer have one too?"

"Ah, that sewer thing was a lie. Sorry, I didn't know if I could trust you, so I came up with that little yarn until I knew whether you were the right one."

"The *right one*?" Adiquis' eyes widened despite the wind punishing him for it. Deception yet again? But for what purpose? Was it time for her to reveal her manipulation? And now he could not escape aboard her bike at such an incredible speed. They were about to leave the safety of the city and into the wilds where no one could stop her.

"What do you want with me?" he spoke agitatedly. "People in the sewer told me not to trust you! Why did they keep saying that? What did you do to them? What are you going to do to me? Are you going to steal what *few* marbles *I have left?*" he screamed.

His fear echoed farther and louder than the engine.

Instead of a devilish smile befitting a mastermind thief, her brow furrowed with anger. "What? Who said that about me?" She turned intermittently while keeping her eyes on the road. "Oh, for goodness' sake. Were people badmouthing me down there?"

She let her head hang and shook it softly. "No. I suppose I deserve that, but they didn't have to go and do it behind my back. Listen, Adiquis. I've done some things that I'm not proud of, but you have nothing to do with that."

She reached her arm back and grasped his small hand on her waist. "This is about your worth as a person! Just like I've always taught you, everyone has worth and it's got nothing to do with what's in their pouch. Listen. When I said you were *right*, I meant that you understood that. That's not exactly common knowledge around here if you haven't noticed!"

A deep rumbling had them scouring for the source. Behind, Adiquis made out that the tunnel had closed.

Ms. Petras reached into her pouch and took out a steely. She rolled it across the bike and the lights shone brighter. "Hold on!"

The exit up ahead quickly shrank by the second. They picked up tremendous speed and shot forward. Adiquis squinted and made out two blurry dots who formed into people pulling the exit doors shut. He held his breath and closed his eyes dreading what came next.

But they did not crash. Instead, a rush of cool air blew through his hair. He opened up to a grassy plain split in half by a single road under a brilliant, twinkling night sky. Just as she described!

"Ah! Ah ha! Ha, ha, ha!" he cried.

Jagged strips of electricity cracked over their heads from somewhere far behind. Ms. Petras pushed him down and commanded the bike forward and out of range.

"I did it!" she squealed when the attacks subsided. She turned and smiled with tears smearing over her face. "*We* did it! We're finally free for a moment!"

He glanced across the plains. They were devoid of any buildings. Not a single advertisement in sight. The menacing wall behind them grew smaller by the second and would soon disappear beyond the horizon. He expected to see evidence of the countryside's free people, buildings, lights, or just their physical presence, but there were no signs of anyone beyond the walls. This confused him. Part of what Ms. Petras said was true, there was freedom from the Autocracy beyond the walls. But also the old words of Father Hannon rang with justification: beyond the wall lied only a rural plain devoid of civilization.

A rumbling from the sky made the hair on the back of his neck stand up, but a patient pause for anything more sinister failed to materialize. He wrote it off as thunder and relaxed. He asked what he could not vacate from his mind.

"Ms. Petras, what are those steelys really? Who are you?"

She laughed. "Okay, no more secrets. I gotta be honest, nobody's asked me that in a really long time. For a while I just assumed I was the Autocracy's number one fugitive and they made sure everybody knew that. I suppose a detached kid like you wouldn't know anything about it though, right? Well, how about this. All you need to know is I was once an inventor and researcher for the government. I created some things that made the Autocracy stronger across the frontier, but they definitely made the lives of a lot of people worse. I regret that. The truth about the steelys is they're like no marble that's ever existed because I invented them!"

She stared dreamily into the night sky. "Before I went into hiding, oh those were the days. But it all crumbled when an Autocracy trade mission to a frontier planet returned with a sample of vibrant steel that had undergone some type of unknown chemical reaction. For the first time, the material had become inert just enough to be pliable using methods we couldn't use before." She patted her marble pouch. "It took a little while for me to discover the right chemicals to replicate the phenomenon, but eventually *I did.* For my last and greatest project, I made it so vibrant steel could now be compressed to marble-specifications without exploding in our hands. And let me tell you, a lot of people tried and failed before!"

"But I thought glass was the only thing the Empire allowed marbles to be made from."

She nodded. "Sounds like someone's remembering their Autocratic history. For too long, incredibly rare glass had been the only material authorized for marbles. I always thought this was stupid. When I received the authorization to begin making vibrant steel into official marbles, I envisioned this as the start of the material blockade's end. One day there could be enough marbles for everyone, of all kinds and types. I knew such goals were against the Autocracy's covenants, but I angled for it anyway. I don't know. Maybe that was just my inner guilt trying to atone for the societal damage I had done. Regardless, if I hadn't taken the project, I probably wouldn't be running for my life right now."

"What did you do that made people so sad?" Adiquis asked.

Ms. Petras scowled and turned her face away from him. "I know I've been telling you everything, but please forgive me. I can't talk about that right now. Perhaps another time."

One more concerning rumble from the clouds hinted at snow or rain. At their speed, they were at risk of freezing alive.

"Don't worry," she said. "It doesn't precipitate unpredictably in the wilds like it does in the city. Not so much pollution mucking everything up. Anyway, with the marbles, it turns out I should have trusted my gut. The Autocracy discovered my plans to create a leak in the eventual supply chain. They were planning to only distribute these to the elites. On the other hand, I was hoping to gradually diversify the general material pool for the rest of society."

"But it wouldn't have been safe to give everybody the steelys. They shoot lightning!"

"Relax, kid! There was more to my process. I could turn them inert before they went out. But the Autocracy found out about that too!" She slammed her fist against the bike. "I had no idea their only goal was for me to invent the pliability process so they could create weapons! They knew they could be the most powerful weapon in the Autocracy. You saw a taste of that back there and it just gets worse when you get more marbles together. When I found out they were planning on transferring my research elsewhere and reassigning me to an isolated desk job, I destroyed my research and took all the prototypes into hiding with me."

"But that guy at the hut…"

"I know. It appears they've finally figured out how to replicate my process. Everyone is in danger now and we need to get every last one of those steelys out of the wrong hands."

Adiquis could tell she was being painfully honest. Despite this being difficult for her, she was laying bare almost all of her secrets. A mutual respect was forming. He had been deemed enough in her eyes. She trusted him. He would now trust her.

An unexpected bright light bathed them. Behind them breaching over the city's wall, the rumbling they had heard before was in truth a massive hovercopter in quick pursuit. The approaching black vehicle filled Adiquis with dread.

"Dr. Petras," the chopper announced as it neared, "you know who we are and to what lengths we are prepared to go. Hand over the steelys and this tragedy will end. Refuse and we will take you into custody for judgment regarding treason against the Autocracy."

"No! This is too soon! He's not ready!" she screamed to herself. She sped forward and tried to outrun them. When it became clear they could not escape, she turned to Adiquis and shoved her pouch into his pocket.

"Kid, don't take those marbles out! Don't show them to anyone! They still think I have them and so it's me they're after. I thought we'd have more time, that I'd be able to teach you everything we knew about them, but it looks like I'm being involuntarily summoned elsewhere."

The copter hovered near. "You have twenty seconds to pull over or we will forcibly engage."

She fiddled with the bike's control panel and fastened her helmet onto him. "Out here, there's one last thing I need you to do for me, no, for everyone in the city, no, for all the *worthless* in the Empire. I know you came all this way to find people who will accept you, but I need you to put that on pause."

"What?" He adjusted the strap on his helmet. "What are you saying? Why aren't you coming with me?"

"No, listen please! Find a secret place, somewhere no one will find, and pool all the marbles together on the ground. You'll need to initiate a forceful, energetic strike and…"

"Ten seconds, Dr. Petras. You're an asset to the Autocracy. Don't throw it away again."

"and…I suppose use whatever you can find. Once you do, stand back because you may theoretically be creating a small rip in time space which *may* allow you to call for help through *the tunnel*. Remember your education. You'll be experimenting with a crude form of reverse quantum mechanics. We don't…"

"Five seconds, doctor. Don't make us lock you up. You'll never work again."

She tapped her chin in search of the right words. "No one's ever conducted a controlled trial to find out how vibrant steel marbles, already modified by my process, will react under those conditions. But my theoretical calculations allude to a possible way for us to create tunnels to other places. *Just take the steelys and…*"

A net engulfed Ms. Petras and yanked her into the air. Adiquis lunged forward and grabbed the bike's handlebars, but they seemed to have a life of their own. His feet could not reach the footrests he witnessed her constantly kicking, but it did not matter.

"Go, kid!" she shouted from her hovering entanglement. "Hide! Find the tunnel, get help, and find me at Undesirable Holdings! M-may the Divine guide your hand, or whatever!"

ROVER ENTRY #1038

The bike revved and shot toward the horizon leaving the hovercopter far behind. The sky became dark once more. Adiquis determined nothing he did affected the bike so he laid his head down to rest in exhaustion. He drifted off into periodic restless sleep. He rode all night to the end of the concrete road, over dirt, and grass until coming to a stuttering stop on a green hill near a sprawling mountain range.

Adiquis opened his eyes. The morning sun just crested over the peaks. He tried, but he could not turn the vehicle back on. His head hurt and his vision blurred from a lack of restful sleep. He pushed himself to survey the horizon for any sign of civilization. As much as he hoped to see other people, he knew Ms. Petras would prefer he did not. He had not seen a single person during his long journey outside the wall. Where were all these free people among the countryside, deep in the outer wilds, which she spoke of?

Before he left the bike behind, he recalled Ms. Petras' advice regarding a forceful, energetic strike. He did not have anything on him that produced energy, but the bike's engine surely did. Drained or not, it was at least worth a shot. From what meager automotive knowledge he had, a self-conscious shortcoming because every little boy his age was supposed to be into cars and trucks or so he was told, he at least knew where the battery was. About the size of a sandwich, he unplugged the white rectangle filled with vibrant steel and brought it with him. Now he had to walk.

The midday sun would fry him without the protective clouds of the capital's engineered stratosphere. As the morning began to fade, he neared the mountain range's base and spotted a small cave entrance. Slowly, with little remaining energy and a rumbling stomach, he climbed inside.

Adiquis did not venture far before he sat down on a wet rock and realized, with much disappointment, that he was back in the sewer again. The walls were just as damp and it was twice as dark to boot. He wondered if the absence of other people was better, but he was not sure. Regardless, he could not stand to live like this again. He needed to call for help, as she had said.

He poured the steelys onto the floor and gripped the battery between his hands. After a quick visual check of their positioning, the Rashaan Principle of Electrical Chain Reactions guided him to arrange them in a circle.

"I hope you're right about this. May the Divine lead my hand." He chucked the battery onto the marbles and a single spark grew into a blinding flash. The explosion blasted him out through the cave's entrance. The sky spun below him and the ground above as he flew through the air. With an abrupt thud, he lost consciousness.

Adiquis awoke in the grass with the sun high among the clouds, but a strange blue hue bathing everything around him as far as he could see confused him. What was wrong with the yellow sun? He climbed to his feet and did not feel any worse for wear. He worried he had destroyed the steelys so he climbed back inside the cave. The immense aqua light came from a wispy blue portal floating in front of him. He had found the tunnel.

He had to shield his eyes and squint from the glaring glow as he neared the swirling disc. A strange sensation like tiny hands gripped his clothes and pulled him toward it. A startling black figure on the other side of the seemingly transparent portal darted inside the cave. He dived for a steely and rushed behind it.

Nothing was there. He turned around and that hulking shape was now on the other side, or so he thought. In fact, he realized it was like looking into *Alice's* mirror. This black, dripping blob of a creature was somehow inside another plane of existence. Although frightening, this creature was the only thing he could ask for help from at that moment. He trusted Ms. Petras' instructions so he gave it a shot.

"Hello? Can you hear me in there?" he asked.

A guttural growl made his blood run cold. Was this a new Autocratic weapon in the same vein of marbles? Had they even infiltrated the sanctity of the countryside? Before he could fire the marble, which he had no idea how to do, the beast leapt out of view. After what sounded like an intense scuffle, a man in strangely colored garments appeared, wiping his hands clean of a black goo.

"You want more? I got more where that came from! Yeah, get out of here!" the man shouted. He noticed Adiquis. "Hey, Red! Someone's in this super bright one! Oh scrap! This gate's beam is blinding. This is definitely going to attract attention. Wait, can you hear me in there? Are you just a kid?"

Adiquis smirked as he knelt and scooped all the steelys into his pouch. "Yeah. But I still got a lot of worth in me. Are you from the countryside?"

"Sorry, kid. I didn't mean to imply anything else. Here, let me start over. My name's King and I guess you can sort of say yeah, I'm from the countryside. But it's been a long time since I've been back there." He smiled and pressed his thumb to his chest. "I'm definitely a city boy now! Your turn, little man. What should I call you, other than kid?"

"Adiquis."

"Nice meeting you, Adiquis. If you're brave enough to approach a gate, then I guess you're worthy enough to join the fight. Come on and jump on through. It'll hurt like the worst but only for a second."

Ms. Petras was right. There were others like them in these outer wilds, but the nature of these people and the tunnel to the countryside was nothing like he imagined. He would need all his knowledge to understand his potential allies and convince them to fight the Autocracy. It threatened to subdue everyone and he did not know what to do.

He jumped into what he desperately wanted to believe was the answer and Ms. Petras' only hope.

The Hiders and Seekers

File Under: fear, responsibility, perseverance

Location(s): Earth

Executive Summary: The people of Abeona-2 have long believed the home world was lost forever. The discovery of its persistence, and subsequently its grandeur, has brought hope for many of us that a better future for ourselves was within our generation. My connection with my associate, Minnie, will be key during this new era. The following entry, adapted from my interviews with her, sheds light on the worst casualties from the Great Answer Crisis and what humanity should work towards actively to counteract.

ROVER ENTRY #1041

An oozing, blackened monstrosity stalked the soulless hospital hallway. It scraped the claws of its six limbs over the long unsterile tile floor.

Barely a dozen dark treatment rooms away, Minnie lifted the lid of a hibernation tube. A motionless woman laid with arms tucked to her sides. Was she alive? Minnie had little hope given the state of the several others she had already checked. Her failures thus far pained her.

Minnie placed a wary hand on the woman's cheek. Her skin was warm. Minnie noticed snowflakes colliding and melting against the room's window. Something was keeping the freezing winter at bay. A light bulb overhead blinked and faded again. Curiously, power lingered inside this room despite the collapse of the global energy grid over three weeks prior. Perhaps the vibrant steel components within the rare life-maintaining machinery leaked enough residual electricity to keep it running but she was not sure. She had yet to take Vibrant Steel Principles in high school and she was certain she never would.

Minnie let out a relieved sigh. Her hands trembled as she released the woman's leg and arm restraints. She felt weak for reasons she preferred not to acknowledge at the moment.

Needles slipped out of the woman's wrists and her eyes shot open. Coughs and wheezing echoed down the lonely hospital hallways unheard by anyone except the one inhuman terror.

Minnie shut the room's door. She examined a nearby medical chart. The woman's name made her heart heavy. It was the same as her mother's.

"I'm so sorry, Sara," she said with a quivering voice. "I need you to be as quiet as you can, please."

In the hallway, a metal gurney crashed onto the ground and shattering glass heightened Minnie's fear. The creature likely hastened its pace. Minnie summoned an inner courage and steadied her breath. With a firm hand on Sara's arm, she said, "Come with me. We have to go."

Sara pushed herself up. Her bare feet slapped on the floor. The chilly tile recoiled her toes. Her first step was a stumble. She grabbed Minnie's shoulder for support. Her face became flush when she noticed her nudity.

Minnie considered giving Sara her mauve sweatshirt, but her exhausted state already wreaked havoc on her body's ability to keep warm. Instead, she snatched a simple gown from a chair and draped it over Sara.

"You're experiencing hibernation sickness. It'll wear off eventually."

"W-what was that sound out there?" Sara tied the gown behind her. She followed Minnie to the door. "Is it dangerous?"

Minnie carefully pulled the doorknob and peeked into the hallway. The sight of the nearby Seeker monster made her chest tighten. Clouds of choking black smoke radiated from the beast's body as it poked its head into every room. It knew its prey were near.

"Yes," Minnie whispered. "It hasn't detected us yet, but we're gonna book it in a few seconds." She turned toward Sara, concerned about her ability to keep up. Sara's face was pale, muscles thin, and eyes sunken. "Can you run?"

"I-I think so." Sara stared at her shaking arms. "I have a lot of adrenaline flowing through me right now, but no promises. Why don't we hide? What's going to happen?"

Minnie leaned out again. The beast entered the room she waited for. She grabbed Sara's hand. They took one step into the hallway and a loud pop, followed by a bellowing roar, sent them both sprinting.

"Oh Divine! What on Earth was that?" Sara cried.

"A distraction! Run!"

The Seeker trashed the room and galloped out. Its rows of eyes searched the corridor with efficient speed. It perceived their motion, but it could not decide what scurried before it. Its nostrils inhaled their musk emitted in part because of fear. This and the pitter-pattering of their feet swelled a primal hunger within it. The instinct to devour and grow was all-encompassing. If it did not soon, it would begin to waste away.

Minnie rammed the stairwell door with her shoulder and swore when her aching arm protested. She ushered Sara inside and barricaded the door with a nearby fire axe. They descended a staircase while the Seeker tried to force its way through. Flights of stairs toward the hospital lobby were little obstacle in the face of Minnie's resolve to save this woman. Yet, every hard landing tested her remaining energy.

Sara pushed open the door at the bottom. A smaller Seeker scraped against the glass of a massive fish tank in the high-ceilinged lobby. She pointed with fright. "Look out! It's another one!"

The Seeker whipped around and screeched.

"You can't keep yelling!" Minnie shouted despite her message. "Just get out of the building while I distract it. Meet up near the red truck."

Sara ran toward the front entrance and right through a noxious cloud of Seeker-emitted smoke. She coughed. The Seeker bore its fangs. It took an inquisitive step after her.

"Oh, for Divine's sake." Minnie quickly prayed, "Please watch over me." She waved her arms at the demon. "Hey! Over here, slowpoke!"

She knew this was risky, but she had outmaneuvered them before. She charged the beast. It snarled. Black drool dripped out of its massive maw. Anticipating its pounce, she darted to the side, leapt over the reception desk, and slipped into a waiting room. She slammed the door and jammed it with a chair.

The Seeker pursued and drove its claws through the pathetic wooden door. She crawled under a desk and waited as the door splintered open. Its shapeshifting head violently drove through a widening hole. Its eyes swiveled back and forth in search of its target.

Watching through a glass wall, Minnie witnessed Sara exiting the building. She emerged from the desk, grabbed a chair, and threw it at the glass. The panel cracked, but it did not shatter. She lifted the chair and slammed it repeatedly as the Seeker ripped the door apart and pulled itself into the room. Its jaws, lined with teeth like jagged glass, snapped in her direction. With one last waning swing, the chair burst through and fell out the other side. Even with her muscles protesting, she deftly leapt through the gap and sprinted toward the entrance.

Just meters away from safety, her feet hesitated to a halt. Behind her, the Seeker had attempted to pursue her but it became caught in the narrow glass hole and tore gashes in itself in a frenzy to get loose.

An opportunity was presenting itself. The beast had something she wanted, although whether this was the best time to get it could be up for debate. She gripped the Divine charm around her neck, golden rays of light interlaced through her fingers, and said another prayer.

She hustled back toward the writhing horror. It sensed her presence and spun its arms, furiously rending fissures with its claws into the floor. Its body was too wide to strike directly below itself in the center. This was her path. She laid on her back and carefully slithered below it. From her pocket, she retrieved a small plastic vial. A paw swiped just above her head. Sweat dripped from her forehead and things seemed blurry for a moment. She may have pushed herself too far.

Attempting to steady the vial with all her concentration, her trembling fingers betrayed her. Coupled with double vision, she failed securing a sample of its ooze several times. A deluge of fluid spilled on the floor around her. Several drops splashed upon her face. The sticky tar irritated her skin and threatened to distract her last remaining brain cell devoted to this task. Almost at her physical limit, a drop fell into the vial. Swirling and smoking as she corked it, her stomach growled, a piercing headache descended upon her, and the vial and her hand continued to blur.

Smoke gushed from the Seeker's smoldering wounds and billowed around her. Dreading she had made her final mistake, she held her breath, scooted out, and climbed to her feet. No more than two steps toward the exit, the ceiling above cracked and crumbled. The Seeker from upstairs crashed down. It crumpled into a massive unconscious body sprawled out on broken tile and pieces of metal and ceiling. Only a mere arm's length away, its muscular hindquarters were even larger now, no doubt due to a consumed victim or two she failed to rescue. The beast had begun to grow.

She knew a fall like that would never silence these seemingly undying nightmares. Four of its six limbs swayed independently as it pushed itself up with its two remaining working forearms. As if it felt no pain, it pivoted toward her and opened its foul mandible. She stood stunned, unable to process. Was it fright? Was it exhaustion? Why would her feet not move? Her mind was steeped in confusion.

Rolling smoke covered the floor. Their relentless hunting tool brushed past her ankles and crept up her legs. Minnie closed her eyes, grasped her charm, and whispered, "Mom, please..."

A cup bounced off the larger Seeker's back and shattered on the ground. "Leave her alone!" Sara screeched. The crippled creature growled and twisted itself back around.

Seeing Sara in danger cleared Minnie's mind. She bolted around the beast just as the smaller Seeker disentangled itself from the glass. Both whipped in a fury, they dragged themselves with whatever limbs still worked toward the escaping women.

Minnie stumbled across the wintry parking lot and climbed into her truck's driver's seat after Sara. It was already running. Welcome warm air heated Minnie's icy fingers.

"I hope it's okay I started it up. My feet were cold," Sara said, wiggling her naked toes.

"Of course." Minnie pulled out a map from the glove box and handed it to Sara. She pointed with a wavering hand. "We're here and...and we need to get there as fast as possible. Give...give me directions..." She touched her temple. "Oh, my head."

She slumped onto the steering wheel and blared the horn.

Sara grabbed Minnie by the arm. "Oh my! Are you okay?"

The Seekers fought among themselves as they tried to fit through the single exit. Drool sloshed from their orifices and evaporated the snow below upon impact. The horn drove them into an even more fervent frenzy.

Sara pulled Minnie into the passenger's seat and took the wheel. She recognized the locations on the map and raced out of the parking lot mumbling wishes of safe passage to any deity willing to listen.

ROVER ENTRY #1042

Minnie regained consciousness in the safety of her own bed surrounded by the stone walls and dirt floor of the underground. She sat herself up and shuffled into her kitchen area.

Dad sat at the table eating dinner. He wore his frocks so he must have just finished the evening prayer service. The exposed light bulbs hanging from wires flickered occasionally. There were tissues piled underneath the table beside him. He had been crying profusely and did not try to hide it. It was not about her anyway.

"Bimini. Thank the Divine you're awake." He sounded worried but he would have been more so if this had not become a habit for her.

"Dad? What happened?" Had she only been out for a few hours or an entire day?

He shook his head with thin lips. "One of your lost souls dragged you into the church's infirmary. The nurses patched you up and brought you back down here. I can't believe it. You pushed yourself too far this time."

"Sara…" Minnie sat at the dining table.

"I'm sorry, what?" he asked, hands shaking.

"Huh?" She heard prayer beads in his pocket rattling from his jittery leg. "Oh. No. I'm sorry. I didn't mean to make you feel…" She placed her moist palms upon the table. Her heart was racing like before, but this was a different kind of fear and disappointment. "I…i-it was just a woman with the same name."

"Ah." His eyes fell slowly. "That's…okay."

A bowl sat already filled for her. She hardly cared to eat but her stomach forced her to think differently for the moment. She dived in ravenously and only took a breath long enough to say, "Thank goodness she's safe. She was the only one I could wake up on that trip. I'll do my rounds around here and I think the cover of night will let me…"

Her dad waggled his spoon at her. "I really don't want to hear this, Bimini! I'm thankful the Divine was with you and kept you safe, but it's unwise to continue challenging such angelic grace!" His spoon slipped and rattled across the table just out of reach. He tried to stretch himself, but Minnie picked it up and handed it to him. "Thank you. Oh Divine. If something were to happen to you, I'd have no one left."

Minnie pushed herself away from the table and pointed toward the ceiling. "She's…mom's still out there!" If only for a moment, she felt weak for releasing her pent-up emotions. A daughter of the Divine should be known for her composure. She touched her Divine charm around her neck and took a deep breath. "She's alive," she said softly. "But even if she wasn't, we both have our respective congregations. I, the people out there that need this church, and you, these new parishioners I bring back. You've no shortage of people to care for."

"Bimini, you know that's not what I mean."

She crammed down her last morsels of ham and beans. With a little sleep and now a full stomach, she felt ready to head out again. A knock on their dilapidated, wooden corridor door interrupted them. She eagerly stepped away from the table to find her friend Kyle on the other side.

"Minnie, the new girl's asking to see you. You got the energy?"

Kyle looked well. Save for the dirt-caked soles of his shoes, no doubt he had less on his mind than she. And that was good. He was a junior scientist now with his lab coat and pocket full of datapads. High school chemistry and the natural sciences were always his strongest subjects. Fortune shined upon him when the science wing announced they were seeking additional assistants. If by some Divine miracle everything turned out to be okay, this would be one heck of an internship to write about on his college applications.

"Of course. I was just about to head over there. Is she all right?"

Minnie kissed her grumbling dad goodbye and followed Kyle into the catacomb corridors. The earthen hallways sprawled beneath the church was where they hid from the numerous dangers outside.

"I think she's fine. Maybe she hit her head or something. Asking a lot of questions about the city and the Seekers. Has she been living under a rock?"

"Sort of. I pulled her out of a hibernation tube."

"Oh. I guess that would do it. Well, could you just lend her an ear and calm her down a bit? She's driving the nurses nuts."

They ascended to the street-level and walked into the chapel's central nave. The cathedral ceiling made the room feel larger than reality. Most pews were stacked against the walls to make room for sick and injured folks. Minnie looked up and felt sorrow for the beautiful stained-glass windows not being able to shine at night. Yet even the daylight could not penetrate the wood barricades they constructed on their outside. The elegant chandeliers were not powered in order to divert their meager vibrant steel generators to other pursuits below. Instead, candles and lanterns laid scattered about.

Refugees slept on cots across the hall. Volunteer nurses cared for them until they were well enough to join the others underground. Despite almost a month of monstrous carnage, survivors knew little about the long-term health effects of inhaling the Seeker's smoke or the infection that festered after being slashed by their claws. People feared it was contagious while symptoms showed, but no evidence supported that. Still, everyone there practiced an abundance of caution. Quarantine up top may be protecting those down below. A boy coughed profusely as they passed and Kyle covered his nose and mouth with his shirt.

Minnie's heart felt heavier every time she walked by a person or family who she brought into these squalor conditions. Each one waved or nodded and she returned gentle smiles. The chapel was frigid but warmth did exist below. She hoped they would not freeze to death before being well enough to migrate. Otherwise, would they curse her name and have wished they had taken their chances outside on their own?

She found Sara sitting up and nibbling on a piece of bread while she coughed. Speckles of ash sprinkled the white loaf. She had yet to expunge the sticky smoke residue plaguing her lungs. If its purpose was to make a person easier to find, it was effective.

"How are you feeling?" Minnie knelt by Sara's side and examined her eyes. She looked weak. Takes one to know one, she thought. Minnie guessed she was somewhere between fifteen and seventeen, about her own age, and must have gone into hibernation sometime before the Seekers appeared.

"I'm better. Mmm…why does this bread taste like the best bread I've ever had?"

"Probably because they don't serve you solid food in the tubes," Kyle said.

Minnie kicked his shin.

"Ow!"

"Please excuse my sarcastic friend. He's not exactly sensitive. Tell me how I can help you."

"Bimini, right? That's what a priest called you when I dragged you in here. But everyone else seems to know you as Minnie."

"Yeah, that's my nickname. Either is fine."

"Okay. So Minnie, you're the one who rescued me, right? What the heck is going on here? While I was driving, the city looked like a disaster movie and those monsters were poking their head out of every nook. What did you call them? Seekers? I almost hit one with the truck trying to outrun another. I swerved out of the way and barely avoided crashing. Those walking ooze buckets are relentless."

"Excuse me!" Minnie called after a passing nurse. "Can I get her a glass of electrolyte juice?" She felt lightheaded after twisting her neck so quickly. She wondered when she last drank enough water. "I'm sorry, but can I get one for myself too?"

"Hydrate so you don't die-drate," Kyle laughed.

"Of course!" the nurse said. "Anything for you, Minnie. And by the way, thank you for those new bandages yesterday. I was losing my mind ripping up our remaining clean bed sheets."

Minnie smiled. She refocused on Sara. "So, I'm gonna need you to take what I say at face value. Can you do that?"

Sara shrugged. "I mean, I've already seen the Seekers. Anything is possible, right?"

"Thank goodness they haven't figured out how to burrow underground yet," Kyle said.

Sara pressed her back into the bed. "Should we be worried?"

"Again, ignore him," Minnie said with another smack to Kyle's shins. "All you need to know is you've been in hibernation for about a month according to your bed chart."

"Oh. Did they figure out how to treat the black smoke cough? I really expected to have that taken care of when I woke up."

Kyle glanced toward the ground. "Um, it turns out the cough wasn't so much a disease as it was a symptom."

Minnie gently took Sara's hand. "The Seekers. They cause the smoke that makes people sick. And no, they don't yet have an immediate cure. Although, I can gladly say people seem to recover just fine if they're away from it long enough. You end up coughing out whatever gets inside you."

Sara exhaled. "Thank goodness. But what are these Seekers and what do they want?"

"All we know is that Seekers are out to find us, gobble us up, and grow bigger. We need to run and hide until they're gone."

"How long is that gonna take?"

"We don't know."

"Where did they come from?"

"Nobody knows. They just appeared."

"Why don't we leave the city?"

"It's like this everywhere."

"What about the police? The military? The government?"

Minnie ran an unsteady hand through her hair. There were loose strands between her fingers. She shook them off. "I'm sorry. Everything is in shambles all over the world. From Washington to Neo-Tokyo, I saw the entire world burning before world-wide media crashed. My dad and I are trying to provide shelter for people here, but we've been having a difficult time lately."

She did not want Sara to share in her burden so she intentionally failed to elaborate on their numerous other challenges. Instead, she pointed toward the chapel's altar where a nurse's station operated. "For you, we have good, caring people with clothes, food, and medicine so feel free to take your time recovering from the smoke. When you're cleared to join the general population below, come find me and I'll help you get sorted into the community."

"Okay. I have an idea of what you're going to say, but can I ask if you think my family is still alive?"

Minnie and Kyle exchanged concerned glances.

Minnie said, "Well, there are a lot of people down below. It's possible…"

"We're going to do everything we can to help you find them," Kyle said. "There's a chance they're already here. But if they're not, we'll post a note up here for when they do find their way. There's a bulletin board by the door. Does that sound good?"

"O-okay." Sara looked confused, but she laid down and rolled away from them.

"I'll pray for them," Minnie said as she left Sara's side. Prayers were good, but she longed to do something more to make up for the many more she left behind.

ROVER ENTRY #1043

Minnie made her way to a small room behind the altar and pulled a ladder down for the church's steeple. She climbed with Kyle in tow.

"So, what do you make of her? Think she'll be okay?" he asked.

"Absolutely. She only breathed a little bit of smoke and she's still got all her limbs."

"No. I mean about transitioning into all this mess. She's been asleep for the entire attack. It's gotta be jarring to go to sleep and wake up in the middle of this."

"You're probably right. I'll keep an eye on her."

He scoffed. "You say that about everyone that comes in. How are you going to find the time?"

"The Divine helps those who help themselves. You know that. We just need to trust in the plan and actively walk the path like we always do. There will be time if you have faith."

She reached the belfry, a snug little room just below the open-air upper tower, and slipped into a stashed winter jacket. She made sure to zip it to the top so her charm would not reflect any light and broadcast their hideout. To reach the upper tower, she stepped on Kyle's shoulders, pushed open the trap door, and hoisted herself outside. The shutters creaked as she pushed them open to survey the city.

In the distance, half submerged in the ocean, the red setting sun mirrored off the hull of Earth's final colony ark. She believed Seekers even found their way inside that last lifeboat and devoured everyone aboard. All the others like herself that remained would surely be forgotten in time by the hundreds of colonies among the stars. The thought made her a little bitter. She would give anything to be lightyears away from the home world right now.

Like how the sun painted the sky, fires continued to rage across New York for an eleventh consecutive night. The turf war between the two apocalyptic gangs, the Survivalists and the Posse, saw no end in sight. This opportunistic violence made it a matter of life and death anytime she emerged from hiding and it had nothing to do with the Seekers. She thought about how stupid humanity was to fight among itself in the middle of their common enemy's hunting grounds. And for what? Control of an infested death trap?

"For your information," Kyle shouted from below, "I was trying to give Sara some hope by pointing out one of the Seeker's limitations."

Minnie rolled her eyes. "She wasn't asking for that. Whether or not Seekers are teeming underneath us is now just another fear of hers. We don't need people worrying any more than they already are. I have a lot on my mind right now. Everyone is asking me to grab something when I'm out there and the Corp keeps asking for more of my time. I don't need you stirring the pot too. Can you do *that much* for me?"

He stood silent for a moment. "Ah. I didn't mean to make it more complicated for you. I was just trying to lighten things up."

She wondered if she had been too harsh. "Hey, how about you? We haven't really talked recently, but how are you holding up?"

"Thanks for asking. I'm a little frazzled at the lab with loads of new survey reports coming in from the Corp. My mom's been on my case about forgetting to bring my brother to lunch yesterday. But other than that, I'd say I have it peachy compared to you. So that keeps me grounded."

She managed a slight smile. "I don't know what you're talking about."

"Minnie. Seriously. Have you considered cooling it down just a notch? You should be grieving, not saying yes to every person who asks you for help. You don't owe these people anything. In fact, it's *them* who owe you a great deal."

Her smile melted into a grimace. "You sound like my dad. This isn't about me owing anybody anything. I do this because I'm young, I got the time and energy, and…" She stared at the supermarket across town where her mom last traversed. "These things that I do? *That*, I can control."

Mirrors they had placed in the windows of nearby buildings reflected no light leaking out from within. Checking for leaks was important in this new reality when any creature comfort was in danger of being fleeced. Minnie introduced the idea to board up the chapel and hide their sanctuary. Dad perceived this as a pivot away from the open-door policy their faith espoused. The Divine's will was not to conceal themselves from those seeking refuge. But he came around after mom disappeared during a food run.

With nothing to fix tonight, she hopped back down. They descended and returned to the catacombs where they walked the corridors of the massive necropolis that had always hid beneath their feet. Not until the Seekers invaded their neighborhood did Dad pry open the boarded stone archway in the basement and find possibly the last remaining entrance into the ancient tunnels. As the days passed and more soldiers, scientists, leaders, and common folk joined them, they probed deeper into the unexplored zones.

Minnie found news regarding the darkest depths fascinating. Rumor had it the Survey Corp discovered a vast cavern no one had seemingly stepped foot in for hundreds of thousands of years. This captured her imagination during a time when any distraction was welcomed. She was hungry for new information, but everyone was patient not to expand into this strange area too quickly and risk stumbling upon a new challenge that would make their lives more difficult.

Minnie and Kyle stopped at the intersection between general housing and the science quarters. Kyle looked down the hall and back at her. "Please. Just know that I'm getting on your case because I'm worried about you. You don't see me being the personal quest runner around the clock for every person alive."

Minnie turned her back toward him. "Hmph."

He yawned and wagged his finger. "I'm not done with you. It's just getting late and I want to check in on some notes in the lab before bed."

"Now who's overworking?"

"Just give what I said some thought." Kyle walked away.

Minnie watched him and did not relax her annoyed expression until he was out of sight. He had no idea. She was not weighed down by these tasks. Instead, they gave her great satisfaction. Her next stop would be a reminder of that.

She knocked on the orphanage. Tara opened the door.

"Minnie! Come in, please. During your last run, did you have a chance to look for those things I asked about?"

Minnie revealed three datapads from her pocket. "I did. Just like you requested, some light children's literature."

Tara clutched them and tapped through the content.

Minnie smiled, amused. "Fresh from the pediatrics wing. I hope they're age appropriate. I'm not sure how to check for that sort of thing."

"Oh, no, these are wonderful!" Tara closed her eyes and squeezed them to her chest. "Thank you, thank you, thank you! You have no idea what this will mean to the children. They could use any distraction we can give them and stories are the best way to usher them to a different place."

"I suppose you're right." Peering through the doorway, she noticed all the children were already asleep. Those poor kids, she thought. Almost every single one of them witnessed their parents being consumed by a Seeker. If a book could help in any way, then she was glad she could deliver that unto them.

Tara pointed to Minnie's neck. "Is that a Divine charm? I didn't know you were so devout." She looked up pensively. "Although aren't you the preacher's daughter? Oh. I suppose that makes perfect sense. Silly me!"

"Oh." Minnie squeezed the charm between her fingers. "It was my mom's. I don't really believe in the practice of jewelry being necessary to maintain your connection to the Divine. But there are other reasons in the scripture to wear it." She stared into the golden rays. "She gave it to me a few years ago for my birthday. I only recently started carrying it."

"I see. Well, nice jewelry like that is becoming a real rarity these days. Thank the Divine for your mother's foresight."

Minnie thanked Tara for her kind words and left the orphanage. She stopped next at the research corridor where anyone with even the tiniest amount of lab experience studied the Seekers for any signs of weakness. They had been at it for weeks but had uncovered little of tactical value. Minnie aimed to change that as long as she had the energy to roam the surface.

The scientists did their best to keep a clean area. She tapped her shoes at the entrance to shake off any stuck dirt. She lifted a white tarp to enter their wing. Although late, activity in the room was high. Tarps draped over the stone walls made this improvised laboratory almost look clean. Metal plates lined the floor to keep the soil from kicking up. Everyone here had a passion for progress and they were willing to put in the time like her, but in their own way. Kyle sat in the back completely absorbed in a stack of datapads.

Dr. Ortaculus noticed Minnie and greeted her with an enthusiastic grin. His bristly, enormous mustache always made her smile, reminding her of a cartoon character.

She had to admit she enjoyed these side jobs. Kyle disapproved of her doing anything more than she really needed to but completing them made her smile.

"Minnie!" He took her hand in with both of his and shook vigorously. "I'm always glad to see you. What brings you back our way? Another field sample I hope?"

"You know me, doc." She handed him the vial of Seeker fluid.

"A new specimen! Fantastic. This just might be enough for our next round of tests. I swear, without you we'd be only dreaming about conducting Seeker research!" He turned to walk the sample to their lab but swiveled back around. "How did you procure it, if you don't mind me asking?"

"Some other time, doc. I gotta run." She waved goodbye, but he stepped after her before she walked out.

"Minnie, just a second."

"Is something wrong, doc?"

"No, nothing like that. It's just that I wanted to say there are a lot of new discoveries coming out of the unexplored zone. Not all of it is physically tangible though. Exciting anthropologic evidence is helping us understand the nature of the area. I think everyone would feel safer if there were fewer mysteries. Your friend Kyle has been a huge help with transcribing the field team's notes into digital."

"Notes on physical paper? That's unusual."

"Yes. It seems there is a certain quality in the deepest depths that affect our electronics when exposed long enough to its environment. We're not sure what that quality is yet, but datapads have proven unreliable. Nevertheless, that's not what I wanted to say to you. It's about Kyle. He's been doing a lot of work and I'm sure that comes with mounting pressure. Thank you, Minnie, because I know it's you who's been keeping his spirits up."

Minnie rubbed her shoulder and glanced away. "Eh. Maybe ask him again. He's sort of been on my case regarding something I'm not exactly up for discussing. I think he thinks I'm stupid or whatever."

"Nonsense. You were the first thing he talked about as soon as he came in and it was only good things, I assure you. Oh! This short delay allowed me to remember that Corporal Jonas asked me to send you his way if I saw you. Says he's got a special mission for you."

"A mission? What kind?"

"He didn't say anything beyond that. He said to look for him near the edge of the unexplored zone."

Minnie thanked Dr. Ortaculus for the message and trekked through the numerous Survey Corp checkpoints to reach the catacomb's furthest depths yet to be mapped. Only because she was summoned did the soldiers permit her to venture this far. A rush of warm air engulfed her as she exited the confined corridor. She walked into a vast cavern that overlooked an ocean of darkness down below. She had only passed this point once before to deliver a lunch box to an old schoolmate, Dee, because her dad asked really nicely. This was fine by her. She found the area unsettling.

The warm air breathed life back into her aching, cold bones. A barely remembered lesson from high school, she understood geothermal heat was the cause. The further down they dug the more insulated from the winters they would become. She wondered whether the rumors of this echoing chamber were true. Had it been intentionally excavated by unknown peoples long before the modern era? She resisted the urge to shout into the void and listen for her own reply. She did not want to be scolded by Corporal Jonas like the first time.

Wall-mounted lanterns, shining with real flames, illuminated her path forward as she carefully watched her step on a catwalk made of questionable wood panels. The Corp found this walkway already constructed. The atmosphere had an aura of an ancient place, like walking into the past. She guessed the brown rock and dirt her fingers touched as she steadied herself against the carved wall had never seen the light of day. If it ever had, it would have been long before recorded history.

She would have continued to ponder, but she spotted Corporal Jonas speaking to a survey team on a stone ledge up ahead.

"Make sure that sample gets to the pocket protectors for a composition analysis. I want a confirmation of our suspicion as soon as possible." He handed Lieutenant Darlyn Tates, his second-in-command, a shiny object. It could have been a piece of metal but Minnie was too far away to discern with confidence.

"Yes, sir!" Dee replied. She waved enthusiastically as she passed Minnie on her way back toward the catacombs.

"Hi, Dee!" Minnie could hardly see Dee's shiny scholar pins she was so proud of clasped to her fraying ROTC uniform from their old school. With the light so low, both would need to carefully watch their step so the interaction was brief. Minnie knew she was supposed to now address Dee by her official title, but Dee was not much older than her and they had known each other all their lives.

Corporal Jonas noticed Minnie approaching and executed a stiff salute. His navy-blue uniform appeared almost ebony in the poor light. It was not the color of the Corp, they did not have a unifying one, but of his last branch before the invasion. At least his perfectly centered chrome buttons flickered when the flames reflected just right. Routine and ritual were sacred to this man. How someone managed to appear so put together in this time of chaos was beyond her. She was comforted knowing he coordinated their defense force.

She returned a salute the best she could, but she had no idea how to position her fingers. It looked complicated.

"Bimini. Finally taking me up on my offer to join the Corp? We could use your energy full-time."

"Not today I'm afraid, sir. I'm just here because Dr. Ortaculus said you asked for me."

"Right. Follow me if you would." He pointed toward a ladder in the distance that descended into the blackness.

"Um..." Minnie did not move.

"I know. You've never been in the deep unexplored zone before. I assure you it's not the least bit scary like the rumors you must hear back at home describe. It's just an abandoned snapshot of the past. Whose exactly, we're still trying to figure out."

ROVER ENTRY #1044

It took them a moment, but Corporal Jonas and Minnie equipped themselves with safety tethers clipped to the ladder.

He started down the ladder first and she followed. They descended so
far that she stopped counting when she realized the rungs did not know
when to quit. The air grew warmer and more comfortable. She contemplated
taking off her sweatshirt, but she had no idea what she would do with it
if she did. The dryness in the air, however, was irritating. A distinct lack
of moisture made the back of her throat scratchy. It reminded her of the
Seeker's smoke and that skipped her heart for a moment. She wanted a drink
to dispel the connection, but she did not have anything on her.

Once at the bottom, she looked up at the twinkling lanterns mimicking
stars in the night sky.

"So, this whole cavern is uncharted?" She took a flashlight from him
and followed behind as he led the way with one of his own. Their beams
kept flickering. She smacked her light a few times.

"Don't bother. Something in the air tends to mess with electronics. They
should last long enough for a short trip."

They stepped onto a dirt pathway leading into the shroud of darkness.
"This area is becoming charted," he said. "After discovering the tunnel that
led us here, the Corp has been exploring around the clock. We've mapped
out promising spaces for more refugees and possible sites for storage

facilities. But nothing has caught our curiosity quite like what we found this afternoon."

"Wow. I wonder if the Divine's light reaches even somewhere as deep and dark as this." Minnie cast her beam around her. Emerging before them, houses with arched doorways and buildings made of mudbrick walls lined what she supposed was a primitive street. The realization the rumors were mostly true bubbled an excitement within her. The unexplored zone was indeed vast and home to an ancient city of some sort.

Corporal Jonas cleared his throat. "I'm sure the good Pastor would say yes. Who's a heathen like me to challenge that?" After a period of silence, he asked, "I don't mean to pry, but how are you and your old man holding up? I heard about what happened to your…um…"

"I'm fine, actually," she said quickly. "I try not to think about her. I mean, what's there to think about? We don't know what actually happened so we're just waiting for information." She smiled to keep up her facade, but for what purpose? It was too dark for him to see. It only masked her anxiety from herself.

"I suppose that's true. Well, I hope she's all right and on her way back home."

"Thanks."

Dry, cracked, but surprisingly well preserved, the buildings around them were reminiscent of how Minnie's school texts described early Mesopotamian civilization architecture. Yet they resided in the wrong hemisphere and the pictograms and inscriptions she noticed carved into the walls seemed out of place. They were not of animals or people but of sharp zigzag lines and swirly, wispy circles.

"Admiring the glyphs? My gut has been telling me those are going to be important to solving the many mysteries down here. I've got the eggheads up top trying to decipher them." He cast his beam upon an arched entryway. "Oh, we're here."

The path met a dead end. The entry appeared almost completely obstructed by loose stone rubble.

"End of the line, huh?" Minnie asked.

"We stumbled on this antechamber that leads to a large ceremony room. We've had trouble getting any heavy equipment down this far so we haven't been able to move the debris and get a solid look. But I figured there was a chance you'd fit inside and tell us what's going on. A lot of the folks under my supervision are of the stocky varicty."

"Of course. I'll do anything to help."

She identified a small opening near the top. If she did fit, it would be tight. With careful footwork, she scaled the stones. She shone her flashlight inside to get a gander. A light shining back startled her before she realized it was her own beam's reflection.

A shiny metallic arch stood in the center of a vast rotunda. The arch was a little worse for wear. Its otherwise seamless exterior was missing a large chunk. Elaborate carvings decorated the walls and ceiling reminiscent of the style she saw on the external buildings.

She carefully climbed back down. "I'm not sure whether everything looks fine or not. How do you gauge a ruin?"

"Yes. I suppose parameters would be helpful. What is the approximate size of the chamber? Are there any other antechambers leading from it indicating alternate ways in? If it's as large as we're estimating, this could be an excellent new home base for us."

Minnie dusted clouds of sand off her clothes. "I'm not sure about all that just yet. I did notice an arch with a piece missing from it. Does that by chance have anything to do with what Dee...er, Officer Tates is running tests on?"

He smirked. "Very perceptive as usual, Bimini. Yes, we were able to get a drone inside to pry a sample off that structure. Now let's see if you can wiggle in too."

"Okay. I'll certainly try." She scaled up again and, with a little effort, slipped through the opening. There was no debris incline on the other side so climbing back up would be a pain but doable. She fell with a modest hop and dust floated into her face. She held her breath until it settled. Her flashlight scanned the chamber.

"What're you seeing in there?"

"It's huge!" her voice echoed. The interior appeared bigger than she expected. "The ceiling is a dome and it's maybe fifteen or twenty meters up. The room itself is about five, about six chapels wide. It's circular and the metal arch is smack in the middle. There are intricate designs all along the floor that lead from the walls into the center."

"Ah! Imagine no more catacomb-living. Instead, we'll have a real city, a Neo New York to call our own and it can all start with this one massive space. What else?"

Minnie walked toward the arch and shone her light against its shiny material. A single spark from the missing piece sprang forth like a shooting star. She dropped her flashlight with a start. Her beam spun around the rotunda. The arch cast an eerie, rotating shadow. The spark faded just as it landed near her foot.

"Uh, I think something's happening," she shouted back nervously without taking her eyes off the arch.

"What is it? Is everything okay?" Rocks shifted on the other side as Corporal Jonas unsuccessfully tried to climb up and peer through.

Minnie picked up her flashlight and illuminated the metallic surface again. The arch stood silently as if intending to make a fool out of her.

She let out a slight chuckle. "Never mind. I thought I saw something, but I think my nerves are just making me see things that don't make any sense."

"There's no such thing as sense anymore, Bimini. Tell me exactly what you saw."

"Well," she replied calmly, "it was the arch. It sparked like it was discharging an electrical pulse, but we're at the bottom of an ancient city inside a stone room in the dark. I mean, it could be vibrant steel, but that would be an almost insane contrast of old and new. Who would secretly build a modern power source under the city where..."

A crackle preceded a single boulder dislodging from the decrepit ceiling and plummeting down, crashing onto the arch. The arch radiated a blinding flash. Minnie threw her hands over her eyes and tripped backward onto the ground. Her flashlight rolled out of her hand again and flickered until it faded. However, she was not plunged into darkness. The arch glowed with the most tremendous, shimmering aqua light. It sputtered a few times and then beamed without further interruption. A swirling, wispy portal appeared in its center and she was equally captivated and terrified.

"What's going on in there? Where's that blue light coming from?" Corporal Jonas shouted. Panic laced his voice.

Minnie jumped to her feet and scanned the area desperately for a source of power she could unplug. There had to be a wire, transformer, or even a wireless fusion drive nearby. Without anything in sight, she suspected the arch was indeed vibrant steel. Even accounting for the metal's strange properties, the phenomenon remained a mystery. She had never heard of such an immaculate light show being associated with the electrical element.

She stopped asking herself questions when a thick, opaque smoke billowed below her knees. She felt a distinct scratch in the back of her throat. This was not the dryness of the cave.

"Th-the arch just powered on! I don't know how, but it's glowing and… and…oh Divine!"

She tried to scream, but no noise passed through her lips as a grotesque limb lurched from the portal followed by another and still several more. The pulsating, shapeshifting head of a Seeker emerged. She did not want it to notice her so she focused her entire attention on carefully backpedaling away.

Halfway toward the antechamber, her foot slipped over her missing flashlight. She stumbled before steadying herself. The beam flickered back to life and grew brighter, gleaming like a blinding beacon before popping and frying out.

The Seeker's four eyes affixed themselves upon her.

ROVER ENTRY #1045

Seeker! It's a Seeker!"

She sprinted for the antechamber and leapt at the high gap in the rubble. Her fingers gripped the ledge. She struggled to pull herself up. Quivering stones preempted a tectonic shift as the Seeker charged. She glanced back and two more Seekers exited the arch. They, too, detected her. Their thunderous stomping brought the obstructing rocks crumbling down and sent her tumbling with it. She laid dazed upon the ground.

Corporal Jonas crawled through the new opening and yanked her up. "Take my hand and follow me!"

They fled into the city street. He passed her another flashlight. Their beams illuminated only mere meters ahead. Pebbles on the ground bounced with each Seeker's stride behind them. They pushed themselves, panting desperately, but the Seekers were glued to their tail. The haunting howls of the hunt frightened Minnie so much she refused to glance over her shoulder. Instead, she said a prayer and kept a hold of the Corporal's hand with all her strength.

"In here!" He pulled her through a mud structure's doorway. No door to shut so they ducked around a stone table. "Turn off your light!"

Although Minnie was winded, they both tried their best not to breathe too loudly. In the absolute dark, the Seeker's sounds were more pronounced in her mind. Surely, the monstrosities listened for them too.

Pounding stomps creeped closer until growling originated from just outside the doorway. Smoke tickled past Minnie's knees and quickly brushed up her arms rising to her nostrils. She wanted to stand and lift her head above it, but she could feel with her hands the table was short and provided little coverage. Did the Seekers have night vision? She feared she was about to learn the answer.

She grabbed her Divine charm and squeezed it until the golden rays felt like they were cutting into her skin. She held her breath in hopes she would not cough. She assumed the Corporal could do the same, but he let out small gasps.

He softly cleared his throat. A stifled cough sprung forth.

The ground trembled and the air thickened.

"It's no good," he whispered through desperate breaths. "I'm going to lead them back to the rotunda and try to get around them in that open space. You go the other way and climb up to the top. Warn everyone and do whatever you can to seal this area off."

Before she could argue, he leapt over the table and out of the building. He shouted at the beasts. The beam of his flashlight flickered through the doorway momentarily and then disappeared. The footsteps of human and Seeker faded. After silence fell, she turned on her flashlight and bolted back to the ladder. She ignored securing the safety tether and accomplished the excruciatingly long climb through pure will of mind.

Two Corp members spotted her as she crested.

"Help! Help me for Divine's sake!"

They reached down and pulled her up. "Where's the Corporal? Wasn't he with you?"

"He might be trapped down there! We were ambushed by Seekers and he distracted them long enough for me to get away. He said to seal this whole area off!"

"Seekers down here? That's not possible. Nobody's reported any breaches in the perimeter..."

"I'm telling you what I saw and what he said!"

Deep below, the sound of a Seeker's roar echoed up and rattled their bones. Goosebumps cascaded over Minnie's skin. Were they surrounded by hundreds of them, stalking them from just beyond their vision? Or were the broad cavern walls just amplifying their triumphant hunt?

One of the men trembled. "I...I...understood! Let's get to it!"

They radioed their comrades a brief message before their handheld receivers puffed out a thin column of smoke and failed. They escorted Minnie over the catwalk, through the checkpoints, and back to the catacombs.

Dee stood in the middle of a bustling junction. She ordered the Corp to the unexplored zone and evacuation route. Minnie noticed explosives in the arms of those rallying forth.

Recognizing Minnie in the group, Dee grabbed her hand.

"Come with me!"

She pulled Minnie inside her nearby office. Two chairs, a desk, and a lone lamp did little to turn her hole in the wall into a professional space, but it appeared she had tried.

Minnie took a seat across from her. Neither uttered a word for a much-needed quiet moment. Minnie let her head fall into her hands. She desperately tried to dispel the pervasive worrying thoughts swirling in her mind. All her loved ones. The others she brought here. She wondered if she should bolt out of this room and warn them all to evacuate. The stress cascaded over her, flowing over her tight shoulders and within her sweaty palms.

"Minnie," Dee said in a perfectly normal tone that felt mismatched given the situation, "I heard what you said to the boys on the radio. But I wanted to hear it from you. Where's the Corporal?"

Minnie scrunched her pants between her fingers. "I don't know. I think he's gone."

"Where has he gone to?"

"He's *gone*. I think he's been *eaten* by a Seeker."

"What?" Dee pushed back her chair and paced the room. "So, I didn't mishear that. What exactly happened down there?"

Minnie described the darkest depths, the pictograms on the walls, the glowing arch, and the Seekers that emerged from it. She spoke as quickly as the words would fall out, taking very few breaths. Her mind spun.

Dee startled Minnie when she pushed her chair impatiently across the floor. She pulled at her cuffs while continuing to pace. "You're telling me all this time the Seekers have been coming out *right under our noses* from that portal made of vibrant steel?"

Minnie fired back. "Hey! I don't know *for sure* if that's what it's made out of!"

Dee's datapad beeped. She checked the notification. "No. That's exactly what it is. The research wing just finished their analysis of that shard. It's one-hundred percent vibrant."

"Well anyway, how would I know if all the Seekers came from the portal?" Minnie protested; her voice wavered with irritation. "I saw three down there, but I don't know if that means they've always been!" She covered her eyes. A few tears leaked out. She fought against a flood of emotion and managed to bury her feelings back inside her. She thought that was what it meant to be strong.

Dee did not push it further. She returned to her seat and said quietly, "No, you're right. I'm sorry. I just want answers."

"Of course. Me too." Minnie wiped her face. "Dee, what is going on? We were supposed to be safe in hiding down here."

Dee let her gaze wander toward the ceiling. She tapped her foot. "You don't think all those little drawings on the walls meant anything important, do you? The Corporal used to devote a lot of resources to documenting them. I want to believe he was on to something."

"I don't know. I guess, maybe. I think Kyle was looking into those."

"Kyle? Is he the guy who's always following you around like a puppy?"

Minnie nodded.

"Okay. I need to talk to him. Maybe the glyphs have a clue as to what hole these Seekers are crawling out of and what we can do to turn it off." A knock came from the door and someone handed Dee a note. "Shoot. I gotta handle this. Can you do me a favor and find out what Kyle knows about those symbols and the arch?"

"Absolutely," Minnie said without hesitation. She grasped for direction, a cause, anything simpler than the intertwined worry she wrestled with in her mind. Yet, the logistics of the retreat fought for her attention and she could not control the priority of her thoughts. Her mind struggled between embracing exhaustion and her insatiable desire to keep going. And the desire was strong.

Among her ideas to feel useful, she could first find Kyle and get the gist of the research. After reporting back to Dee, she would find Dad. Or she could stop by and warn the orphanage on the way and check in on Sara and the rest of the new arrivals in the infirmary. If fast enough, she could run up to the belfry and see if the turf war had calmed down around them. Someone needed to plot a safe route to their predetermined evacuation location.

Half a dozen other tasks needed doing. All these people were her responsibility. This was the congregation she built. The fear of failing to save them weighed heavily on her.

Dee placed a firm hand on Minnie's back. It jolted Minnie back to the present.

"Thank you so much," Dee said.

Minnie nodded.

Dee opened the door. "Come find me on the frontline when you're done."

ROVER ENTRY #1046

Dee and Minnie exited into the panicked corridor. Shoulders rubbing against the walls cast brown dirt into the air. A group of her soldiers waved Dee toward the unexplored zone.

Minnie ran the opposite way. She did not bother to kick her shoes clean while stumbling through the white tarp into the lab space. Her sweaty palms failed to grip a table and she slipped to her knees.

"Kyle!" she cried.

"Minnie, what's wrong?" Kyle dropped his datapad and rushed to her side.

"It's about your research…"

He waved her off and pulled a chair near her. "Are you okay?"

"Listen! I need to talk to you about research…"

"Shh!" He placed a firm finger near her lips.

Her wide eyes crossed in front of his hovering hand.

He retracted his finger. "Sorry! I…I just need you to take a second and stop doing things for everyone else! You've run yourself ragged!"

"That's not true," she pouted.

"Look at yourself." He lifted a mirror from a table and handed it to her.

She took its handle if only to shut him up and glanced at her face.

She did not want to accept that he was right. Bags under her eyes told the tale of all the sleepless nights she spent volunteering with the Corp or out rescuing people on her own. Her chapped lips and sickly skin spoke of her malnutrition due to quick meals. Her thinning hair was no doubt affected by the unimaginable responsibility she carried.

These were the things she could see. Much more disarray existed in her head. She wanted someone to blame, the Seekers, the gangs, or the demands of others, but Kyle had at least partially already discerned the truth. She alone placed this stress upon herself. She could have just been another girl, like Sara, and let the adults handle more.

Had she deluded herself? Were her Samaritan actions a collection of unconscious service penances? Did she hold out hope the Divine would grant her an exclusive miracle as a reward? Such a scheme was sacrilegious.

A voice in her head spoke.

None of it helped bring Mom back. And she's never coming back. But you already knew that.

Minnie dropped the mirror. It shattered on the ground, but she could not muster a single care for it. Several other researchers took notice of their conversation.

"Okay, Kyle. You got me. I'm at the end of my rope. But there are Seekers down here in the catacombs and I need your help."

"Wh…what?" Kyle stepped back. "You can't be serious. There's no way. Seekers?"

Everyone in the room ceased their tasks. They gathered around her. The commotion attracted Dr. Ortaculus. "Seekers? That can't be. The Corp never found another entrance other than through the chapel. How could they have gotten in?"

Minnie looked into his eyes. Her lips trembled. "There's so much more down here than we ever imagined."

Kyle slapped his forehead. "Well, why didn't you just come out and *say* that?"

Minnie glared at him until a Corp member hurried into the room.

"Grab everything you can and evacuate through the chapel. This is not a drill!"

Dr. Ortaculus scooped up a handful of datapads. "Well, that's all the proof I need! Everyone, secure the research immediately. Talemek & Jonathan, wrap our glass-contained experiments for transportation. Kyle, the datapads..."

A faint explosion and a low rumble shook glass instruments to the floor. The room erupted into chaos. Stacks of datapads spilled near Kyle's feet. He picked up a collection, covered in thin smoke, and shoved them into his pockets.

Minnie grabbed his arm. "It's too late! They're here!"

ROVER ENTRY #1047

Minnie pulled Kyle into the stone corridor. They turned left, but another explosion sent them scurrying right. A cloud of dirt wafted behind them. They weaved through crowds of refugees pouring out of rooms. The mob flowed down the narrow hall.

A Corp man pushed passed Minnie with a bundle of explosives.

"Place and arm the charges in sub-corridor B-2!" Dee shouted, directing her people toward the unexplored zone and pointing the evacuating folks to the chapel. "Make time for the evacuees by slowing the enemy advance at any cost!"

Minnie pulled Kyle's hand along and shoved her way next to Dee. "I've got Kyle and his research…"

A Seeker howled alarmingly close. A man screamed. An explosion rattled the tunnels.

"Run!" Dee shrieked.

Minnie and Kyle rammed their way around the nearest corner and barely evaded the blast of another explosion. Black clouds of soot barreled down the hallway. So many crying people instantly silenced.

Dee stumbled out of the smoke coughing and fell at their feet. Her uniform was stained black with tar.

She lifted her head and spotted Minnie staring at her with horror. "Minnie! You're alive! Don't stop, keep running and…oh Divine, no!"

Dee dug her fingers into the ground as an unseen menace dragged her inside the thick smoke advancing toward them.

Minnie threw her arm out too late. She grasped at air and felt her heart crack.

"Up, up, up!" Kyle yanked her to her feet. He tugged her through the horde almost at the chapel.

They stopped as the crowd jammed. The hands of the people behind Minnie pressed against her and the backs of those in front inched in reverse. The space was closing in. Her instinct told her trouble was up ahead.

Fearing they could be trampled in the bottleneck, she pointed at an adjacent dormitory room and she and Kyle slipped inside.

Kyle slammed the door shut. "Oh Divine! How can this be happening? We've never been breached before!"

"Help me!" Minnie waved him across the room. Under a single swinging light bulb, they lifted a dresser to the door and barricaded themselves inside. "They didn't break in. They were already here, underneath us."

"Already? Where?"

"In the unexplored zone. There's an ancient city. I saw three of them come out of a metal arch. A flash of light caused a blue portal to materialize out of nowhere. They must have been hiding inside. And there were carvings on all the walls. Zig zags and swirls."

"Portal technology? That's science fiction. And in a pre-Mesopotamian ruin? No, no." He froze. "Unless…" He pulled out his datapads and swiped his finger across their surfaces. "Electricity, archways, swirls…where are they?"

Snarls and screams in the corridor sent chills through Minnie's body. She placed her ear on the door.

"Oops!" Kyle dumped all his datapads on the floor.

"Shh!" A heavy stomp. Drip, drip, drip. The growling of hunger. Danger lurked just outside. Hiding was their best bet. Kyle sifted through the datapads with quivering fingers. She would need to calm him if they were going to avoid making more noise. She pulled away from the door and grabbed his hand.

"Hey," she said just above a quivering whisper. "Let's focus on what you're doing. What is it? Show me."

"Ah…o-okay." He picked up a screen. "Here it is."

"What is it?" She sat down and scooted next to him. The datapad had pictures of pictograms and inscriptions just like the ones on the city's walls. Notes spanned the screen's margins and more scribbles were written on top of those. It looked like the thoughts of a madman.

"These symbols you described," he said as he zoomed in on a swirl, "they've been seen elsewhere, but they're extremely rare. I believe someone commented about archaeological research in Egypt in one of these notes. Ah, right here." He pointed to a drawing of an archway, lightning bolt zigzags emitting from it and a swirly portal in the center. "This metal arch. Did it look sort of like this?"

She tried to restrain her excitement and managed to exclaim quietly, "Yes! That's it! It had a blue portal just like that."

"Amazing. It seems pictograms like this have been found all over the world in pre-Mesopotamian ruins and…" He zoomed in on a note. "Am I reading this correctly? Sometimes on other planets?"

Minnie pushed her face close to the image. "That doesn't necessarily mean they're related. There are plenty of universal symbols that appear randomly in nature. Like the nautilus, right?"

His shoulders relaxed. "Have you actually been paying attention when I talk about work?"

"Maybe a little," she smiled. "Don't let it go to your head."

"Well, based on your description of that area, this vibrant steel arch is completely out of place in one sense and yet fitting in another."

A flood of screams echoed through the door. Minnie turned her trembling back toward them and shut her eyes. "C-could these Seeker arches really be all over the world?"

The datapad shook in Kyle's hands. "Well, there's no m-mention in these notes that anyone has ever seen a standing, glowing arch matching the pictograms before. The one…"

A thundering Seeker roar shuddered the door.

Kyle gulped. "The one you saw seems to be the first intact artifact. If these structures are as old as their surroundings, then it's plausible most, if not all of them, crumbled, decayed, or were destroyed for a variety of reasons. Maybe you found one just in the right place in the right environment. Perhaps there are a few others deep underground elsewhere. That would help explain the seemingly sudden appearance of Seekers all around the world with no known spawning point."

Minnie smacked her parched lips. When did she last drink enough water? "It was incredibly hot and dry down there. If those ruins have been preserved like the pyramids, could a similar climate, like what they have in the middle east, harbor another glowing arch?"

"That's plausible. Do you remember where the first attacks occurred?"

She thought hard about what she had seen on television before everything went dark. "There was us, of course. I think the other originating sites were the North American Southwest, the Australian outback, and the Middle East's fertile crescent."

They gasped together. "Dry climates!"

"Perfect for preserving artifacts," Kyle concluded.

Unsure how long the corridor had fallen silent, Minnie suddenly became aware of it. She prayed for the carnage to have passed and wanted to check, but she knew better than to poke her head outside. As she debated in her mind, a tickle at her ankles decided for her.

Smoke seeped through the crack under the door and between its loose slats. She leaned her body against the dresser and waved to Kyle to do the same. They pushed the decrepit wooden barrier as flush upon the frame as they could. They managed to slow the flow a little, but the rotting planks only did so much.

Minnie said a prayer for the Seekers to pass by their room. Booming footsteps shook the dresser. She scrambled to silence the rattling drawers. The smoke rose. She locked terrified eyes with Kyle and they both took a deep breath before committing to hold it until the end.

A Seeker bumped against the door. It broke the hinges. Kyle threw his hands onto the fracturing planks and kept them together.

Through a crack, Minnie witnessed the noxious liquid that covered the Seeker's body dribble onto the dirt, its head scraping against the ceiling. Its trunk-like legs splashed through the black, oily pools. For it to have grown so large, this beast must have devoured a disgusting number of people. Of the little information they did discover regarding the creatures, the researchers were confident Seekers had an incredibly rapid metabolism. They grew with each meal in a gradual expansion. She feared that as this monster continued to feed, it would grow too large to fit inside the corridors. In short time, the catacombs would cave in around it and anyone near.

The Seeker emitted a gurgling cough as it passed. Kyle was startled, his hands slipped, and he fell to the ground below the smoke line. Smoke filled his lungs. He coughed violently.

Minnie tried to cover his mouth, but she too failed to suppress her coughs any longer.

"We have to risk it and get out of here!" he gasped. He pushed the dresser to the side.

Minnie grabbed his leg to try and stop him.

He resisted and pulled the door away. Smoke poured in. "Come on!" He grasped her arm and they dashed, coughing into the obscured corridor.

Without vision, the terrifying sound of claws scraping against stone sent them running away from it.

Kyle led the way. Minnie kept a hold of his hand hoping each squeeze would not be their last. They stumbled from the cloud and into clean air. She turned back suspecting to see the jaws of death.

Desperate growls roared forth from within the smoke.

"I think it's stuck?" she said. Stone crumbled out of sight. "But not for long."

"Well great. I'm pretty sure the chapel was in that direction. What're we gonna do now?"

She peered down the path of silence. "We have to go back. There aren't any other exits."

"Go back where?"

"Through the arch. It brought the Seekers here. It must connect to somewhere else."

Kyle blinked, aghast. "Are you crazy? We want to hide from them, not find more of them!"

She threw her hands up and screamed, "What other choice do we have?" The rumbling of a massive shift made her stomach drop. "Let's go!"

Only their two pairs of feet and the stalking Seeker's three echoed through the series of checkpoints leading back to the unexplored zone. The trip was chilling. Weapons, datapads, and torn swatches of clothing were all strewn about. There were no other people.

"The surviving Corp members could have had the same idea and went back toward the arch," she said, picking up a flashlight along the way.

"Then why didn't they take their stuff with them?"

They did not linger to investigate. The Seeker's hungering growls were always not more than a few corridors behind them. When they reached the sprawling cavern's mouth, she pointed her flashlight forward and warned Kyle to watch his step on the rickety catwalk.

He grabbed a lantern off the cave wall. "We gotta hurry up!"

"No! This is old and delicate. I don't want to die falling to my grave while running from a Seeker."

Sure and steady, they made it to the opposite stone ledge. A low grumble behind them signaled the Seeker's entry.

"Do you hear that? It's trying to cross!" Kyle said. The creaking wood straining under the Seeker's weight was too distant to see. "If we're lucky…"

A thunderous crack preceded the entire catwalk splintering apart. The Seeker roared as it fell into the abyss. Its guttural howl echoed further away until a resounding thump silenced it.

Minnie leaned cautiously over the edge, but the blackness hid everything. "Wow. What are the odds?"

Minnie stepped onto the ladder.

"This is gonna seem like it never ends, but you just heard there is a bottom so let's go."

They clipped on the safety tethers and descended as quickly as they could.

Her plan was insane, she thought. Hiding from the Seekers was always their first and best option. To move towards them was suicide. Then again, she did charge one at the hospital and managed to outmaneuver it. In the sprawling city below, she may just be able to leverage her agility against the growing atrocity. But what of Kyle?

Once in the pit, she scanned her flashlight across unfamiliar stone rubble strewn about. "Why are these buildings destroyed? The Seeker didn't fall anywhere near here."

Kyle stretched his lantern forward and revealed a puddle of vile black liquid in the street. "It might not have landed here, but it sure did pass through. It survived."

They darted into a nearby mud structure and peered out a window. Minnie used her flashlight briefly to determine where the puddles led. With a good enough idea, she extinguished the beam.

"It looks like it headed inwards toward the arch."

Kyle dimmed the lantern to a barely visible glow. They emerged into the street and cautiously followed the puddles. Their ears were tuned as sharply as possible as they trailed its copious secretion. Minnie said a silent prayer for them to find the Seeker before it found them.

Halfway to the arch, an object unseen rustled nearby.

Minnie gripped Kyle's arm. He snuffed out his lantern and they were engulfed by the frightening darkness.

"Do you hear that?" she whispered. A pebble rolled into her foot. It took all her courage not to shout. She groped her way to a wall and pulled Kyle through a doorway. She felt for a stone table and hid behind it.

"I think it's close," Kyle said.

Stonework crumbled somewhere behind them. Thin dust, decidedly not Seeker smoke, wafted past her body. A sudden quake lifted her feet off the ground. She fell hard on her back and several more tremors popped her about like a toy.

"What's happening?" Kyle half hollered. "Are those Corp explosives going off?"

Minnie's elation for having been right earlier caused her to shout. "They fled down here! They're fighting back!"

In a moment of calm, she turned on her flashlight and stumbled into the street. She scanned the buildings, alleyways, and the rooftops, but there were no other lights or people. An unnatural darkness stretched overhead. The twinkling lanterns along the ceiling were missing.

Kyle walked to her side. A massive deluge of bile splashed down between them.

She realized the ceiling was actually obscured.

"For Divine's sake, run!"

They sprinted down the street as smoke descended upon them like a fog. Crash after crash of the towering Seeker's feet destroyed the buildings around them. Deadly debris soared overhead.

Another seismic step popped Kyle into the air and his lantern flew out of his hand. He landed on his feet and turned to retrieve it, but Minnie pulled him forward by his shirt.

"Leave it! Stay close to me. I'll show the way!"

She widened her flashlight's beam and took his hand. Within a few more thunderous steps, they got the hang of its gait and hopped in tandem to avoid the upheaval.

The behemoth did not seem to know they flailed right under it, but it knew they were near. She estimated they were approaching the arch's antechamber when one oily trunk came smashing down in front of them. It blew her off her feet before retracting upward.

Kyle's hand slipped away as she hurtled through the air. She fell into the crater the limb vacated. She slid safely down its slope and kept moving forward as she scurried out the other side.

"Minnie, wait!" Kyle cried as he slid inside the pit and struggled to claw out.

She threw her arm out. "Grab my hand!"

Another wayward limb shattered a nearby building to pieces. Rubble collapsed into the crater burying Kyle.

"Nooo!" she shrieked.

After losing Dee, this pain was more than she could carry. An instant of overwhelming grief gave way to stoic survivalism. Her bitter brain convinced her heart that anguish would not serve her here. She needed to run. The consequences of this denial to feel would need to be faced later.

The Seeker erratically stumbled about. A steaming breath blew through her hair. She directed her flashlight above and revealed an eye the size of a truck blinking at her.

Leaving a piece of her soul behind, she sprinted into the antechamber and vaulted over debris to enter the covered rotunda. Sand rained down from the ceiling with every enraged stomp.

The arch sparked randomly but continued to glow brightly as she approached. She pointed her flashlight and inspected the missing piece the drone extracted. There were no perceptible electronics inside. She had no concept of how vibrant steel created a portal or whether this was at all safe, but being buried alive or eaten were her only other alternatives. She was no good to everyone else if she were dead.

She vowed to return for Kyle and all the others. Her eyes closed while her fingers clutched her Divine charm. She leapt toward the gate. A million tiny invisible hands grasped onto her and pulled her through. Her flashlight slipped out of her grasp as every muscle, every part of her being convulsed in pain. A symphony of blood-curdling cries rang out. She was unable to deduce whether it was her vocal cords or someone else's ringing in her ears.

She did not open her eyes until she slammed onto a hard surface. The pain faded away as abruptly as it started. She slowly lifted her head. Blurry, swaying pillars before her made her wonder if she had crossed over to a higher Divine plane. Yet, when her vision came into focus, she found the sight before her unbelievable even coming from a world where every expectation had been shattered.

Beneath an unnatural, hazy orange sky, massive metal pens filled with Seekers were stacked on top of each other tenfold as far as she could see. She, along with her nightmares, were trapped inside a massive walled-in concrete facility. Behind her, countless glowing vibrant steel arches of all sizes lined the horizon. Small ones, like what she had leapt through, spanned the ground and enormous circular spectacles floated magically high in the sky. She barely recalled school texts describing titan-sized vibrant steel rings. However, those were found deep in the mountains of a frontier planet long ago and she had never heard of the steel glowing blue inside.

Even more disorienting, a large spaceship like nothing she had ever seen hovered overhead just in front of a sky gate. This was no Earth colony ship. Where had she been transported to?

A small Seeker rattling inside a cage nearby startled her. It may have detected her invading presence. She jumped to her feet and ran toward the surrounding towering wall in hopes of finding a door or tunnel she could hide in. But, as she neared the encircling barrier, it appeared to be a smooth, flawless block. She twisted her neck back and gasped as the Seeker violently broke out of its cage. It snarled and ejected streams of oil onto the ground.

Was this truly the end? After everything she had lived through, was she about to be devoured alone in this strange place?

"We've got another tourist!" an unfamiliar voice called.

She looked up and spotted a woman in red standing in a newly revealed doorway too high for her to reach.

"Give me something to throw to her! Come on, quickly!"

The woman tossed down a rope and pulled Minnie up and inside just as the beast charged and snapped its filthy jaws out of reach.

The wall sealed behind Minnie operating on some type of automatic door system. All light ceased before the room's lamps illuminated and blinded her momentarily.

"Who are you? Where am I?" she asked, her mind swirling from exhaustion. She slowly reached for anything to rest on and settled for sliding down a wall for a seat on the floor.

Her eyes adjusted. The woman in red, a muscular man, and a child leaned inquisitively toward her.

"Give her some room!" the man said. Everyone backed up.

Minnie surveyed the room. Small, looked like a garage or storage closet. The paint upon the walls were of blue or gray tones. The vibe could be described as muted.

The red woman waved. "I'm Red."

Yes, you are, she thought. This was strange.

"The big brute is King and the smart short-stack is Adiquis. We're all from other planets, like you, and traveled here through the gates."

"Where is here?" Minnie asked. She placed a hand on her forehead. A headache was settling in.

"As far as we've determined, we think this is the alien home world. Or *maybe* an outlying scientific research station? We're not sure, but I'm formulating a plan to hopefully figure it out. And, now that you're here, you can help us!"

"I don't understand. You're telling me I'm not on Earth anymore?"

"Earth?" Adiquis shouted. He pushed past Red and leaned close to Minnie's face. "You're from the home world?"

Minnie nodded slowly. "Uh huh. Why?"

Adiquis laughed. "Oh, never mind. She's just a home world dummy."

"Excuse me?"

Adiquis said something assuredly rude while the last ounce of Minnie's energy drained from her body. She crawled forward, a hand reaching out for anything to grab. King tried to help, but he was too late. She crumpled across the floor. Her Divine charm spilled out of her sweatshirt and slid in front of her eye. An image of Kyle under the debris jolted her back to her feet.

"Oh Divine! I need to go back! My friend, my congregation needs help!"

King grasped her shoulders and slowly pushed her back down. "Whoa there, you dang rusthead! Listen up!"

His grip was firm. She did not feel like he was trying to hurt her, but rather he believed it was for her own good so she let him speak.

"I get it. We all got people we want to go back to, some integral to what we need to do next. But there's no way you're prancing back out there and not immediately getting devoured. Besides, you look a little more than just rattled. What we need to do now is lay low for a while until one of them aliens come around and cages that beast back up. We'll check for any more travelers and consider seeing about helping your folks."

"But, but…" She wanted to struggle, but she had reached her physical and mental limit. Everything spun and her vision went black.

The Capturing of the Flag

File Under: war, originality, tribalism

Location(s): Jangala

Executive Summary: Like Abeona-2, there were other Great Expeditions. Olyana Origo is only a few years older than me but has lived a different life due to her planet. Her culture, like their manner of speech and how her people's names followed strict naming conventions (her tribe's names all start with vowels) shined a light on the diversity of humanity's people all within the same galaxy. My interviews with her created the following entry that serves as a cautionary tale against any type of war or armed conflict within our colony. These are terrible acts which our people have been right to avoid for as long as as we have.

ROVER ENTRY #1051

Olyana sat in her personal quarters high within the Ark of the Endeavor. The room was quiet as she prepared for the many events of the Solstmas festival. Steel blue, seamless walls, and one luxurious window framed her private room. Such luxuries were afforded to the Captain of the Endeavoress. It was her responsibility to ensure the festivities of her people occurred without incident. Besides domestic obligations like the Harvest Reveal and the Witnessing of the Eclipse on her mind, there were also foreign affairs to prepare for.

Despite the simple pleasures of rural galactic frontier life, Olyana was not a simple person. She belonged to a people who were not simple nor did they have simple desires. They had hoped for almost a millennium for peace in the valley that they called home. But to achieve that, they would have to end the Perennial War with the northern people, and war was like the rainy season: it was either happening or being planned for. She and her people were called the Southern Tribe of the Endeavoress and they had always been at war.

Trophies adorned her walls. Weapons and articles of clothing used hundreds of years ago, levitated inside illuminated cases via the power of boxed lightning. Yet one piece drew her attention on this important day. She gently opened a case. With delicate fingers she lifted out a hand-written parchment. This was their oldest artifact although their history on Jangala predated even it.

More than forty generations prior, their enemy, the Northern Tribe of the Divine, broke the Treaty of the Valley at the annual Solstmas Festival. They struck down Captain Josef Attikus of the Endeavoress during the ceremonial Breaking of the Bread. The resulting Thirty-Day Conflict left countless bodies strewn across the lush valley that connected the two tribes. Those that were lost took with them profound knowledge of their combined people's technology and culture from before the Great Expedition, the journey that brought them to Jangala from the ancient home world.

As a child, the mystery of this parchment and ink's essence fascinated her. Several chemical analyses over centuries by their most dedicated doctors only determined that the composition matched no known compound from their small slice of the explorable planet. It must have been from before the Great Expedition. That seemed so ancient. Such a scale of time was unfathomable.

She would recite the words upon the parchment at a ceremony today. She did not want to, but it was her responsibility. As decades became centuries and centuries almost surpassed a thousand years, the question as to *why* anything happened more often was answered with *this is how it had always been* even when no one could confirm it was true. Like her mother, and her mother, and her father, and his father before her for as long as they had lived on Jangala, the Endeavoress was led by the Captain. No one questioned the practice of familial power and why should they? It had served them well. As the latest Captain, it was Olyana's burden to carry the people's fate on her mind like her mother had.

She stared into her vanity mirror as she recited the original Captain's speech. Written on the crumbling yellow piece of parchment, it was for the Airing of Grievances. She wanted to define herself at the ceremony, to wield the old-world words peculiarly adjoined by an apostrophe and of which were crossed out with fading pencil, but she did not know how to pronounce them.

"We canet allow our people to…no. We cantee allow…" She huffed. "Oh, forget it." There were no audio recordings of this vocabulary which she understood to be just shortened versions of full words. Why their distant ancestors selected only a few phrases to abbreviate was lost to time.

She watched her facial expressions as she practiced the rest. She did not like how her mouth just uttered the words as if they were not her own. Granted, they were written by a forebearer, but she wanted to come across as authoritative, fearless, as the seasoned leader she believed she had the knowledge to be but had yet to prove. She had already spoken at the ceremony a few times, but each time she perceived condescension from The Divine and their delegation.

The gleam off one of her lapel pins brought her eyes toward her outfit. She admired it in her reflection. In accordance with Captain tradition, she wore a muted gray and apricot jumpsuit as her everyday attire. She adorned herself with pins and regalia. Her top was comfortably unbuttoned and loose for the time being. On this holiday, she embellished herself with an Endeavor Orange kerchief tied around her neck. Her voluminous, draping ponytail ran down her back.

Advisors constantly implored her to cut it because they said it made her look like a child, but she refused. Her only complaint was how rogue strands would fall into her eyes, but the ponytail kept them mostly in check. This compromise retained her rebellious locks and, she believed, still met the professional expectations of her station. In fact, she knew they met the expectations for it was she who set such standards. Sometimes it was good being the Captain.

She returned her gaze to the mirror. As she tilted her head, there were a few angles in which her style did make her look young. Still of the age in which young women wished to be perceived as older than they were, this irked her. Perhaps she was not such a fan after all, but she could not rectify that on today's busy schedule.

Only in her first few years as Captain, there were many expectations for her to rise to. Her mother's sickness from the plague made her the youngest leader in the entire valley's history. The plague was absolute but also slow.

For ten years under her mother and her advisor's tutelage, she trained tirelessly for the moment she would begin to lead their people. Her mother's last words were of no regrets. Even though she herself did not dare critically examine many of their people's traditions during her lifetime, she believed her daughter was poised to do so in a way that could keep the settlement safe. Her only child had always carved her own path and being a leader would not liberate that out of her.

With Olyana at her bedside when she passed, the former captain shared her only hope that Olyana would temper herself further. The greatest decisions could only be made by those who were prepared to sacrifice the most. And this duty could not be executed by the weak of will.

After several recitations of her speech, Olyana assessed her effort as acceptable. She shifted her focus to the tactical map table in the center of her room. With a wave of her hand over its surface, a shimmering topographical map of the region materialized. She studied the mountains and grassy plains made of wavering light floating above the vision table. As far as they knew, a poisonous gas covered the entirety of this planet except for the two tribes' surrounding areas.

She ran her finger through the long, narrow valley which offered the only safe connection between their two settlements. Her hand came to rest above a structure in its center. The grievance ceremony's rendezvous point always took place at a stone altar. Her studies taught her that a special power resided in this spot, or at least it was believed. It was akin to the controlled lightning that flowed through their ark's metallic hulls.

Hundreds of years ago, both of their peoples constructed this altar. It was during a brief truce when the discovery of its power brought hope for peace and cooperation. Leaders of the day believed it promised a future of unlimited resources, but that dream failed to materialize. The Divine claimed the altar for their god, the Great Divine, and the Perennial War began again. Recalling the history of this place and the thought of returning to it made her chest feel tight.

A knock came from her door. "Captain Origo...I mean Olyana. It is I, your humble advisor."

"Azul, please enter." She waved her hand over the table and the map vanished without explanation. Her mother's most trusted advisor, Azul was now hers. She had known him her entire life and he provided a continuity between her and her mother's tenure that served their people well.

"Thank you, Captain." The doors parted without assistance and he entered dressed in his formal apricot fabrics.

Her nerves felt calmer in his presence. "Ah. Seeing you already dressed for the ceremony gives me confidence that at least one of us is prepared."

Azul raised an eyebrow toward her loose clothing but did not address it further. "Captain, will you not reconsider allowing me to address you properly? Maybe, just for today, we continue to reinforce your authority and again address you by your surname. This may not have been the best month for you to experiment with original, shall we say, less than professional titles."

She flicked her hand. "I do not want that. Captain Origo was my mother. I think the title of Captain denotes sufficient enough power. If anyone believes I am weak just because I connect better with the people with my first name, then I care not for their respect yet."

"Very well, Captain." He handed her a time tablet.

"Thank you." She swiped across its illuminated glass vision surface. It presented several frozen moments of time from within the valley rendezvous point earlier that morning. "Oh, and are the liquid coolant reserves topped off? Are all our lightning cartridges charged and at the ready to... wait. What are they doing?"

Several images disturbed her. The Divine were already positioned and in greater numbers than was traditional for this once-a-year ritual.

"They seem to be preparing an ambush, my Captain."

"That is absurd. Are we not currently under the Solstmas ceasefire? Is my reading of the Lunar Counter incorrect?"

Azul tapped the wall. The Lunar Counter appeared in light upon it. "It is the thirty-fifth of Juleen. No, you are correct. Solstmas is here."

"Do they intend to break our agreement, the agreement of both our ancestors, and leave us with no reprieve from war at all?" She stomped across the room back to her mirror and buttoned up her uniform.

"Our observers have yet to make contact in search of an explanation. Should I send word for them to approach and attempt a dialogue? Or shall I order the lightning shooters to open fire and end this mockery of the ritual? We are at the ready watching over the area from our forward towers."

Olyana considered the consequences as she paced through her quarters. She paused next to her window. Her gaze pierced between the gaps in the metal shades. The dense jungle that surrounded their two tribes was filled with the impenetrable, toxic blue fog. It had kept their two peoples within the proximity of their arks since the Day of Arrival. Her tactical mind hummed, honed by her mentors for complex decisions such as this. If the Divine were to attempt a surprise attack, she hoped their defenses could repel them. But at what cost? If she underestimated them, her people would have nowhere to relocate, forcing them to make a last stand within the ark. She would defend the ark with her life if necessary. The future of her people depended on it.

The ark housed a wondrous machine they did not understand. It resided in a mechanical room on the ship's uppermost floor. Described in their history texts as a terraforming device responsible for keeping the fog at bay, the letters F.L.A.G. were inscribed upon its various glass tubes and metal chambers. They believed harm to the wonder would mean the engulfing of their settlement and almost certain extinction of all living things in their care. Part of being the Captain meant taking an oath to protect it. Thankfully, an attack on either settlement's F.L.A.G. had never occurred. This was unlikely to ever happen since it being on the top floor made its room the most inaccessible location of the ship.

The moment of quiet reflection granted her a decision. "Tell the soldiers to stay alert but to hold their fire. I will speak to Terrinad and see what this is all about."

"Are you sure that is wise? Remember, we do not traditionally permit any contact with the Divine during the week leading up to the ceremony. Doing so may disrupt the already fragile and brief truce, my Captain."

"My duty to protect our people takes precedence. I want answers."

Azul nodded.

ROVER ENTRY #1052

Olyana threw a jacket over her shoulders and waved for Azul to follow her into the hallway. As the heart of the settlement, the ark interior pumped with activity. This floor, then, could be considered the brain.

They walked past the doctor's offices. The tribe bestowed the title of doctor upon those of valuable specialties who managed the complexities of society, culture, and technology. They learned of this respectful naming convention from the ark's ancient archives.

"Hello, my Captain!" Dr. Elaynor Obstent waved from her desk as Olyana stopped in front of her doorway.

"Elaynor. How is the effort of cataloging the people's grievances progressing?"

"That is complete. I am almost done with the finishing touches of your summary. It should be ready within the hour for your review."

"I am glad to hear. Did you consult with the children as I requested?"

Elaynor nodded hesitantly. "Ah, yes. I did speak to a few as you instructed. I did not end up including any of their grievances into the final report, as you might expect, because…"

"Consider your report *not* complete. I am the Captain of *all* the people. That encompasses the youngest of our tribe as well. Include everything they shared and deliver it to the delegation at the wall when it is."

Elaynor nodded.

A young man waved as they crossed paths. "Captain, I am looking forward to your very public bout next week. I know Inieda has odds on you two to one, but I am rooting for you!"

"Thank you," Olyana replied. "Much of what I know I owe to her. But a captain must know how to protect herself in combat. Thus, practice I must. If it entertains the soldiers, then it is a lovely bonus."

"Do not be so coy, Captain. You have bested every soldier in the ranks! Inieda cannot be at the top forever. Good luck!"

Azul and Olyana boarded a moving box with doors that parted and closed by themselves. They descended to the sixteenth level. Olyana exited the box.

Azul remained inside. "I shall speak with the War Council and return to you." The doors closed.

Olyana almost strolled right past the textiles fabricators before pausing. She backstepped and peeked in through the doorway hoping to see but not be seen. She overheard two of the child workers discussing a recent history lesson from school.

"Do you really think the other place where humans came from before Jangala is really up in the clouds, so high that we could never go there?" a little girl asked the boy next to her. They both used their diminutive hands to control a machine that needed human guidance to weave a clothing garment.

"No," the boy replied. "I think that is just a fairy tale, something they tell little kids to make them not want to leave the settlement. I think if you were a chicken and you could fly high enough, you would see the place called Arrth and all the people who still live there. You would see your ancestors, your relatives, and all kinds of people who live on the other side of the fog."

The girl squished her face with a sour expression. "I do not think so. There is nothing outside the fog. I once saw a chicken get loose and run into it. It stopped moving before it took a second step. Nothing can live out there and there is nothing but fog beyond the settlement."

What a curious philosophical discussion between children, Olyana thought. She leaned in closer to hear more, but a group of others spotted her and cried with delight. "Olyana!" The lot ran toward her as she stepped into the large bay filled with machinery.

"My Captain!" Izack, the bay's adult supervisor, powered down the machines and wiped his hands clean. "I-I did not know you were scheduled to visit today of all days. I do not have a demonstration planned for you, but I can show you if…"

"No, Izack," she waved a comforting hand. "I am not here for that. Please, be at ease."

Izack sighed, relieved. "Is your mind not full of the pomp and festivities of the day?" He picked up little Ulissis who paid no attention as to where he ran. Izack's swift arm saved Ulissis from colliding with Olyana. The child noticed her and grasped wildly. "No, Ulissis! We do not grab at the Captain!"

Olyana laughed and took the boy into her arms. "Little one, you have an eye for what you want in life! That is admirable. But also know you must earn what you desire. What have you done recently to earn my affection?" She pulled him away at arm's length and feigned placing him down.

"No, no, Lady Olyana! Today I entered instructions for three upper garments, two metal tool handles, and one bundle of twine."

"Oh! You have been incredibly busy." She drew him in warmly and released him to the others. "Have you all been productive today?"

"Yes, Lady Olyana," they chorused.

"Very well. After the ceremony, I shall return here first to tell you all about what ridiculous things the northern tribe has asked for. But be sure to continue helping our settlement while I am away."

The children erupted in excitement. They rushed back to their machines.

"That is a generous offer," Izack said, stepping to her side and observing the children at work, "but you do not need to spend your evening with the young ones. Would it not be better to come back tomorrow after you obtain a well-deserved night's sleep? Or spend quality time with your loved ones?"

She smiled. Not a bad idea. "Leave the decisions of what is best for the tribe to me, Izack."

He bowed as she returned to the corridor.

ROVER ENTRY #1053

After a short walk, Olyana entered the Communications bay and approached their master distance talk engineer.

"Good morning, Dr. Adonus. I wish to make a face talk with Terrinad of the Divine regarding the ceremony site. Can you see if he is available?"

"My Captain. Yes, right away." He tapped the wall and their face talk window appeared in light upon it. "Let us see if these treacherous snakes remember how to conduct diplomacy."

"Doctor…" Olyana warned.

He straightened his posture and stared directly at the screen. "I apologize, Captain. I am feeling a tad feisty after being present during a conversation filled with lies last week."

The chiming of the bells continued for some time until an image of Father Paul of the Divine appeared before them.

"What is it, heretics? This is highly unusual. Will our people not see each other in person soon enough?"

"Father Paul, this is Dr. Adonus. Captain Olyana requests to speak to Cardinal Terrinad in regard to the disputed valley."

Father Paul leapt up from his desk. His plum robes flapped as he cast a finger toward them. "You speak of the Divine Corridor! You shall use the proper title of that territory or I will entertain you no further!"

As if forgetting Olyana stood at his side, Dr. Adonus responded with a fury in his chest. "After the Thirty-Day Conflict, our two sides agreed to many concessions. Yet the ownership of the shared valley was not one of them, my dear, forgetful colleague! Because of the original crime you committed against our Captain, my ancestors claimed the right to the bounty and wonders of the valley as reasonable restitution!

"Your remorseless ancestors refused to yield that land believing it delivered unto them by holy will. What heresy I do say, my pious friend. Does not your scripture forbid you from divining the unknowable truth of your creator? The Perennial War is *your* fault and I need not acquiesce to any of *your* grating requests."

Dr. Adonus turned to Olyana with derision in his eyes. His sudden rise in volume surprised her only initially. She soon remembered that Dr. Adonus and Father Paul had a storied history together during their long careers as engineers. This was par for the course and required no special attention.

She leaned her head on her hand and shook it with disappointment. Acquiescing to their frivolous demands did not please her, but it was her duty to do whatever was necessary to ensure the tribe's safety.

"Just do what he asks, please."

With an assuredly shared frustration, Dr. Adonus continued. "Very well. We request an audience with Cardinal Terrinad regarding the Divine Corridor. Can it be done?"

Father Paul straightened his frock and returned to his seat. "No, he is not here. His Holiness is personally overseeing the preparations for the Airing of Grievances. The last report I received indicated our delegation will be ready earlier than anticipated. If you desire, you may meet him in the valley at your earliest convenience." He abruptly ended the face talk.

"Why that little…" Dr. Adonus attempted another chiming of the bells, but no one answered.

"Thank you for your help. That is enough." Olyana intended to leave the bay but poked her head back in. "You seem stressed. Please do remember to utilize your recreation hours. We have standby engineers for a reason."

"Absolutely, my Captain."

Olyana left the bay and crossed paths with Azul on her way back to the moving box. They boarded together and he handed her the time tablet again. The frozen moments seemed largely the same. "What am I looking at?"

"Peer beyond the soldiers. Behind them in the brush." He pointed on the glass.

Each tribe traditionally cleared their valley's side of any vegetation making it harder for the enemy to sneak up to their gates. But since she had become Captain, Terrinad stopped clearing his side of the altar. In the frozen moment's rear, lightning shooters of his own attempted to obscure themselves within the brush.

"An ambush indeed, Azul."

"I suppose it is possible that they are merely responding to our own security forces pointed in their direction."

"No, your original intuition appears correct. Our lightning shooters perch upon towers for all to see. We are not employing subterfuge. They wish for us to attend with a comparatively leaner entourage. Strengthen the vanguard to show them we know."

"Yes, my Captain."

They exited onto the ground floor. The main hangar led them out the ark's bay door and into the open air of the community. The humid wind felt wonderful and the sun and the moon were high in the sky preparing for their meeting later that afternoon. Azul hustled toward the wall protecting the settlement. Olyana crossed the dirt and grass field to enter the nearby stables and check on the livestock. She opened the wooden door to the coop. An electric lock clicked open. Their buildings were made primarily of the natural resources imbued with technology from the ark.

The chickens were happy and healthy. Like all their animals, these descended from the first settlers. She picked up a particularly friendly one. It overflowed in her arms. The avian beast had a few eggs yet to lay so she placed her gently back into the nest and patted her colorful plumage.

As she passed through the central market, citizens waved and tried to hand her holiday delicacies to try, but she politely demurred. Her stomach was too filled with anxiety to invite in any rogue elements. Apricot and white colors adorned the vendor stalls and clothing of her people. A man opened his window and unfurled a rust-colored banner. The good folk clapped when they noticed the orange kerchief around her neck.

She left the lively town center and made her way toward the settlement outskirts. Some believed the Experimental Wonders warehouse was too close to the fog, but this arrangement dissuaded snoopers from the secret work conducted and was therefore desired. The more traditional of her tribe would never approve of artifact destruction. This occurred largely in secret within, but Olyana deemed it worthwhile.

The warehouse's metal retracting door stood wide open so she quietly sneaked inside. She spotted and approached her project manager, Emillee, undetected.

Emillee sat hunched over a table of hopeful wonders in the making with small metal tools in her hands. Her plain umber jumpsuit was entirely practical, no festive frills to speak of, but Olyana also liked how it fit. Olyana tapped her shoulder with bubbling anticipation.

"Oh goodness!" Emillee jumped. She turned and curled her lips into a beautiful smile. "My Captain!"

Olyana placed a hand on Emillee's wrist. "None of that formality, please."

"Very well, my Olyana." Emillee gave her a kiss. "Do you have time to waste here when you should be preparing for the ceremony?" She picked up a magnifying glass and returned to her work. "I am not trying to turn you away, but this is an important and busy day for you."

On Emillee's table laid a Wings of Fire backpack. These ancient flight devices, classified as wonders, were few and irreplaceable. It was dissected into pieces. The many internal widgets sprawled out and labeled across the table were curious.

Some on the Council doubted any of the amazing wonders were within their ability to understand. Much of the old-world artifacts had proven thus far beyond their comprehension. However, Emilee had solved a centuries-old problem no more than a year ago. Their lightning rifles tended to wear down and explode unexpectedly. With how ancient everything was, every shot was a gamble. She discovered the flaw in their original design and drafted new schematics for replacement parts.

Olyana convinced the War Council to sacrifice one wing pack for research with assurance that if they could only unravel the secrets that gave their warriors who wore it the power of flight, they could replicate the pieces and build their own. She hoped for the best and she believed the amazing Emillee could do it.

"Is coming to see you not of the utmost importance?" Olyana leaned on the table and observed Emillee's precise dexterity with the small electronics. "Well, you are right. I am here for a reason. It seems the Divine are up to something. I wanted to know if you had made any progress on the orb."

"Ah!" She twirled on her heels. "I am so excited you asked!" Emillee placed her tools down. "I have at last discovered the proper fuel recipe the orb requires. Come, see it for yourself!"

She took Olyana by the hand. They giggled together as Emillee led her outside behind the warehouse and onto the empty lot. The glass-like white orb sat on a concrete slab in the center of the secluded yard. The mysterious device's back hung open. Emillee climbed the ramp and pulled Olyana inside.

"So many lost technologies," Olyana said, running her hand across a white table in front of a chair. "A wonder like this, discovered in the armory, and dormant for centuries. What is your function?"

Emillee picked up a long, clear canister with both hands. A navy liquid the same color as the fog splashed around inside. "So, I believe I have enough of this fuel for a series of initial test flights, but I am not entirely sure how to control the vehicle."

"So, you have determined it *is* a vehicle?" Olyana sat in the chair. The blank wall in front of her seemed curiously placed. Why stare at a wall? Could it be a far talk window or something like it?

"I am confident." Emillee pointed to a small hatch on the floor. "See right here?" She kicked the cover open and revealed a hole. "This is where we pour the fuel. As I suspected, it is liquid, not cartridges of lightning like our other wonders. I believe it gains the power of lightning after it consumes compatible liquid."

"And this in our hands is the distilled fuel?"

Emillee twisted open its cap and poured a small amount into the hole. She sealed the canister and hopped outside. "Follow me, quickly. We should give it some room."

They left the orb and stepped behind a metal barrier just a few meters away. Olyana hesitantly neared the corner wondering if she could see the craft.

"It is okay," Emillee said. "You can peek."

Olyana leaned out and witnessed the orb emit a light from the inside. A barely perceptible hum joined the swish of the wind in her ear. To her surprise, the orb hovered ever so slightly off the ground.

"My goodness! We should get a better look. Why are we hiding?" She took one step out before Emillee grabbed her arm.

"Careful! I have only tested this a few times and…" The lights within the craft flashed and the hull shuddered. "This usually happens." With a loud pop, the orb crashed onto the ground and rolled about slightly until settling into its upright position. It went silent and dark.

Olyana ran to the craft and climbed inside first. A table of light faded. She noticed many buttons for a second before its glow ceased.

"It has controls like the ark's bridge room!" Olyana said. "This is a flight control table!"

"That is right. That was my clue to it being a vehicle." Emillee leaned around her. "Did you get a good look? I have not understood any of the symbols or words."

Olyana ran her hand over the now blank table. "I have read the Captain manuals hundreds of times and I recognized several of the words I saw here. There was *viewer* and *altitude* to name a few. The orb is indeed capable of controlled flight like you guessed." She swiveled toward Emillee. "This will be an amazing tool for protecting the Endeavoress!"

"Perhaps." Emillee repeatedly tapped the table, but nothing sparked to life. "But I have yet to test the fuel enough to feel confident there will be no problems." She frowned. "With my current knowledge, I am afraid we are still weeks away from such a feat."

Olyana rubbed her palm in circles upon Emillee's back. "No worries, my dear. You have achieved considerable progress and I am proud of you."

Emillee smiled.

"I will bring the War Council word of this development. I am confident they will be much more willing to provide you with the resources you need to continue your other work. And seeing you happy and engrossed in your projects brings me the most immense joy."

Emillee drew Olyana into a hug before she shooed her toward the exit. "Now get back to work! It is almost noon and you have a ceremony to attend, my lovely Captain."

ROVER ENTRY #1054

The settlement wall bordering the valley grew taller as Olyana neared it. Salvaged metal from the ark's lower decks had stood for centuries due to their ardent maintenance. Its looming, dependable presence was comforting. She spotted Azul speaking with one of her war commanders. He was already dressed for combat like the soldiers. She joined him at his side.

"My Captain." He handed her the awaited grievance report. He spoke as she flipped through the summary. "As you requested, we have bolstered the military arm of our delegation. The Divine appear to have noticed. Their soldiers in hiding have emerged and we do not detect any other trickery."

"Very good. Is the rest of our delegation ready?"

"Yes. Everyone is armed and suited. I just equipped my armor myself. Shall you don your suit as well so we may begin?"

Olyana headed for her private field tent. "Watch the entrance, please," she directed.

She drew back the fabric and stepped inside. Laid out on a bench for her was her warrior suit. She sat down and removed her garments. She cleansed her skin using a basin of water and cloth and dried herself with a freshly fabricated towel. As she slipped into the steel blue suit, she treated every piece with reverence.

Her people's most valuable wonder would protect her. Filled with power enabling a person to survive a strike of lightning to the chest, she could also summon the strength to lift a boulder if necessary. Their armory numbers dwindled over the years due to wear and their inability to understand how they worked yet. That was Emillee's task. Olyana's responsibility was to not take advantage of her position and reserve a suit exclusively for her daily use. She rarely placed herself in a position to have to wear one. She designated the entire supply for active military circulation. It was her duty to ensure the bravest of her tribe were protected. This was not always the policy of the Captain, but it was hers.

Once fitted inside the loose garment, she squeezed the back of her neck collar and the suit expelled air. The fabric tightened around her body. She emerged from her tent discreetly tugging at all the creases to achieve comfort inside its adaptable form. She did not typically put much thought into her appearance but her nerves were clearly getting the best of her.

"Looking confident, Captain," Azul said with an honest smile.

"Thank you. Let us get this over with. And please remind everyone to keep their senses sharp."

Her delegation of over a hundred soldiers, administrators, and historians stood inside the settlement's tall metal gates. Operators pushed the doors open and the representatives marched into the valley joining an already sizable military force keeping watch. This was the unusual time of year when the grass beamed green and not grim, stained red from their endless conflict. While many generations ago the wholesale loss of life gradually became less common, small invasion battalions regularly probed for weakness and lives were still lost annually.

Olyana passed under several wooden defensive towers worked by long-range lightning shooters. These snipers watched the advance carefully and would cover the delegation's retreat if anything were to go awry. Never in the ceremony's hundreds of years was this ever necessary. Yet no Captain was foolish enough to show any weakness during such a vulnerable excursion.

Olyana could finally make out the shape of the stone alter. Once again, she was the farthest she had ever crossed into inhospitable territory. While curious about the other side, she had never visited it herself nor had any Captain in recorded history. The only peaceful cross-contact occurred during this ceremony and amid the brief Trade Days in the month of Desembra.

Her curiosity peaked as a child during a phase of high optimism. She believed she could devise a violence-free diplomatic visit with the goal of cultural exchange. As she matured, she understood a hard truth. Their enemies could interpret such a program as a softening of determination. Perhaps she had lost the resolve to defend her tribe with force. She held onto that dream inside a small corner of her heart and hoped to one day find a way to execute it safely.

The delegation approached the altar's short staircase. Olyana located Terrinad and his advisors standing on the other side. Just as the observers relayed, he had a significant force stationed before them. The Divine people's garments were ablaze with the colors of their god, plum and white. Flowing capes and metal plates were undeniably attractive to look at, but she questioned whether they provided the same protection as her stoic combat suit. Banners painted with their religious symbols waved in the wind. The chanting warrior monks echoed off the cliff sides. She was aware of several prayers dedicated to ushering about miracles in times of need, but she had never seen any of these actually work. The monk's presence seemed to just lead to deceased monks on the battlefield.

Stepping up to the stair's base, she noticed most of the Divine had their eyes closed in prayer. She waited out of respect for their ritual to end, but minutes passed and it became apparent this would not happen without her action. She caught Terrinad's gaze, one of the few Divine with their eyes open, and nodded to begin their ascent. He returned a terse acknowledgment.

Her foot touched the first step and she recognized the otherworldly feeling of this sacred site's power. Although nothing to behold with the naked eye, the sense of a thousand invisible children gripped her suit and pulled her subtly toward the ground. The unique sensation did not hinder her, but it was an awkward annual reminder that everything to come would be uncomfortable.

Azul and Olyana met Terrinad and his advisor across the grand stone table on the summit. Terrinad was an old man of similar age to her late mother and was described as a traditionalist. Recent intelligence reports painted him as more of a revolutionary. Every few months he made claims of having divined a new revelation. Even an immutable belief system had its way of pivoting it appeared.

"Captain Origo," Terrinad greeted. "I would say it is a pleasure to see you on this anniversary, but then again the Great Divine instructs us not to lie."

"You will call me Captain Olyana from this day forth and I am only here to air our grievances, not participate in your tit for tat."

"Olyana?" He seemed disgusted. "No, I do not think I will. I do not like the informality which that implies and you and I are anything but informal." He smiled wryly. "I too am here to state our grievances and this time you shall listen and take heed of our demands unless you wish for the destruction of your tribe to finally come to pass!"

He seemed irked when his threat failed to elicit any response. However, this type of talk was typical at the ceremony so it lacked any earnestness. Terrinad unfurled a parchment from within his thick robe. "Well then. I shall begin with..."

"No. You were first last year so I am going to begin this time." She reached back and Azul placed her speech and the grievance report in her hand.

She cleared her throat and did her best to project to the hundreds of observers. "I am Captain Olyana of the Endeavoress and I am speaking to the Northern Tribe of the Divine on this day, the thirty-fifth of Juleen. As a symbol of our shared desire to bring peace to our two tribes and the valley, I present a list of this year's grievances that I humbly request your consideration in addressing. It is in this action that I hope we may come closer to understanding each other and begin to engage in a productive dialogue for both of our peoples. We cannot allow the whole of Jangala to fall to our disagreement."

She slipped her ceremonial speech into a random spot of the report. Flipping open to the first pages, she placed her finger on the grievance she was most eager to recite. Ah, one of children's. Yes, she was right to include them. Their imagination and hope knew no bounds.

"Our first grievance: a child requests that the absolute restriction of our common folk to communicate with each other via face talk be lifted for the youth to meet one another. This is in hopes that one day a cultural exchange program could…"

The page grew dark from what she presumed was an errant cloud. Yet it was too dim for a normal cloud. This made her wonder. Raising her eyes, she witnessed a peculiarity. The moon began crossing over the sun. This was incorrect. Many hours remained before this celestial event was scheduled to occur. She returned her attention to Terrinad whose emerging bold grin disappeared under the retreating light. The valley fell into impenetrable darkness.

He bellowed, "Behold! The Great Divine has answered our prayers and engulfed our enemies in righteous judgment! Now open your eyes and see them with the *vision* of the Divine!"

"Captain!" Azul cried as he grabbed Olyana's arm and yanked her backward.

For only a few moments, there was nothing to see. But then flashes of lightning shot across the valley. For the first time, blood spilled during the ceremony.

ROVER ENTRY #1055

Splashes of light struck Olyana's soldiers with deadly accuracy. Her people fired back, but the likelihood anyone could see the enemy, the cliff side, the ground, or anything at all was small. Without time for their pupils to adjust, they were functionally blind.

Olyana stumbled toward the stairs when her suit absorbed an immense blast upon her shoulder. The powerful blow pushed her tumbling down the stone steps.

Lying at the base, Azul's hand desperately pulled at her to rise. "Are you injured? Can you walk?"

"Yes, I am fine! The armor did its job."

Her shoulder pounded, but thankfully she felt no burn. She stood and gazed upon the moon a second time. From the slightest glow of its corona, she was puzzled by the presence of more spherical moon-like objects floating near it.

Azul tugged her arm and they ran toward the back of the battalion amid the screams and chaos of war. Her vision was just starting to adjust when the moon inexplicably moved with haste and flooded the valley with light.

Sight hindered again and the cries of more soldiers falling at the hands of their enemies brought her to the edge of despair. In the sky, dozens of spheres slowly floated from the northern settlement. She squinted to examine the closest sphere. A basket hung from beneath. While she believed a person stood inside the basket, fanning navy flames upward into the sphere, the concept did not make sense to her.

"Captain! Come with us!" A war commander placed his hand on her back and escorted her and Azul to the wall. "Here! Take this in case." He handed his pocket lightning sidearm to her. Their forces were in full retreat as they passed through the gate with the roar of the Divine mob not too far behind.

Olyana and Azul ducked inside her field tent. Azul spoke into his far talk box.

"Evacuate all civilians into the ark and open the armory for all volunteers to arm themselves. Rally them toward the wall and instruct them to report to any commander for further orders!" He pocketed the far talk. "Captain, we need to get you into the ark and at the helm of the war council. Are you prepared to fire the Lightning Tunnels to protect the F.L.A.G. at any cost?"

Fear dominated Olyana's thoughts. Her eyes looked far beyond that which was in front of her. A thousand worries paraded through her mind but halted with disorienting urgency when Azul mentioned the F.L.A.G. She turned to him with sweat dripping down her forehead.

"They have never been fired in recorded history. A-are we sure they even work?"

Azul nodded, eyes stern. "The engineers performed their preventative maintenance just a month ago. My reports indicate yes, they should fire."

"G…good." Torn between her duty and what executing it meant, she denied showing her true feelings. Instead, she publicly exhibited resolve. This was the Captain's burden.

The tunnels were doomsday weapons equipped to the hull of the ark. Both arks had identical sets and these were regarded as the final decision should the war ever end in force. Neither side's tunnels could point cleanly through the valley to hit the other, but that did not mean they were useless. If necessary, they could fire into the valley cutting off their only connection to each other with rubble. Or a direct blast into their own settlement could decimate any invaders in it and the unlucky few who failed to evacuate into the ark.

In the absolute worst-case scenario, both tunnels firing into the valley repeatedly would carve the cliff sides away and reveal the other's ark. In this instance, an exchange of shots would surely affect the functioning of the F.L.A.G.s and mean mutually assured destruction.

Never had a Captain ever wanted to fire the tunnels, but they knew it always needed to be a possibility. Knowing the other side believed in their resolve to do anything mostly gave the Captain comfort. But now having to consider the feasibility of such a reality, could she order these ancient weapons to awaken and fire?

A great pounding echoed through the settlement. She and Azul stepped out from the tent and observed the valley's sealed wall trembling. The lightning shooters defended from the parapets firing hopelessly against a surging tide. The Divine were pushing her to reveal her hand. Perhaps they hoped her limited experience would prevent her from acting with utmost boldness. That, she reasoned, was a gambit the Divine were betting would succeed. It was her responsibility to ensure it failed.

"The massive cartridges are on standby and ready to load, correct?" she asked.

"Yes, Captain. I will far talk and confirm." A smoke pillar rising from the settlement's edge caught Azul's attention. "Have you seen Emillee today? Was she already inside the ship or..."

"Oh my goodness!" Olyana dashed away while shouting back, "Meet me in the war room! You are to make the decisions until I return!"

No one may have approached the remote warehouse to relay the evacuation order. She entered the town and wedged herself into the throngs of citizens retreating through the main thoroughfare. Traffic leading toward the ark pushed back against her ill-advised direction.

"It is the Captain!" an old woman shouted. "Let her through! Make way!"

The crowd parted around Olyana like a boulder in a raging river and she quickly passed. Out of breath when the warehouse became visible, her suit lent her its great stamina powered by artificial muscles woven into its threads.

She did not see Emillee as she stepped into the building. "Where are you, my heart?" she hollered. She stumbled hastily through the front entrance, anxiety welling up in her stomach.

"Olyana? I am over here by the distiller." Emillee emerged behind a massive gurgling machine wearing gloves and goggles. "What is the matter?"

"Oh goodness! You are safe!" Olyana ran to her. Tears wicked out from the tips of her lashes. She scooped Emillee into her arms. Olyana squeezed Emillee tightly and infused her everlasting love for the woman through her sheer will of force.

"Ooo! A little tight, dear! What is it?" Emillee asked amused, but her expression turned concerned. "What happened at the ceremony?"

Olyana released her. "I thought a group could have infiltrated and made its way here first and…" Olyana shook her head and unclouded her mind. "We just need to go. The Divine violated the ceasefire and the wall will be breached any moment now." She bumbled around and picked up various pieces of Emilee's research. Her hands were full in an instant, several metal doodads falling to the floor.

"Careful!" Emillee said. She grabbed for them but let them lie and rubbed Olyana's back in little circles instead. "I understand. You can put those down; they are not that important. Just let me finish this quickly and we will head to the ark." She pointed to a table for the items and poured the last of a bucket into a canister. She placed it into a crate with several others.

"Use more haste, dear!" Olyana waggled her outstretched hand for Emillee to take. "I may have to employ the Lightning Tunnels."

"What?" Emillee lifted her goggles. Her eyes were wide. "You are not being serious." She searched Olyana's face for intention. "You are. It is happening." Her hesitant hand waffled between reaching for Olyana and grasping a stack of crates filled with dozens of canisters.

"What are you waiting for? We must go!"

"Wait! If we leave all these canisters, an attack of that magnitude may cause a chain reaction. Blowback may even damage the ark. If firing the tunnels is even a possibility, we need to secure these crates."

"There is not enough time!"

A distant boom, likely signaling the breaching of the wall, meant it was now or never.

"We must take the risk!"

Emillee shook her head. "You do not understand what we are dealing with. This substance, while benign now, can become volatile again under the wrong conditions…"

"Then…then," Olyana hastily lifted two crates, "we take it all with us!"

"This is not possible! We could not possibly carry all of these unless…wait! There is another way." Emillee hoisted a crate. "Follow me!" They waddled behind the warehouse. Emillee pointed at the orb. "We can load them and fly it all to the ark."

"But you said it was untested."

A series of disturbing explosions resounded nearby.

"True, but in theory it should be fine. We have more than enough fuel, I think. You can pilot it, correct?"

Olyana gazed upon her love. She was confident of Emillee's plan while doubtful of her own abilities. Her heart wanted Emillee to be right, but reality did not usually take her desires into account. "I…maybe? I mean, I have read about flight controls but I have never flown anything."

"That is enough assurance for me. Hurry, enemy soldiers may be nearby soon!"

They loaded all the crates into the orb and climbed inside.

Emillee opened the floor hatch and poured more than half of the canisters worth of fuel.

"I do not believe in this," she shouted, "but I pray to the Divine, the stars above, to the blue fog for goodness' sake if it will get us out of here!"

ROVER ENTRY #1056

The white walls of the orb's cabin reflected the table's emanating blue glow. Olyana stood above the illuminated command table and reviewed the many buttons and sliders. Her feet felt unsteady. The craft shuddered. Her stomach was anxious. The ground outside the still ajar back gate was no longer visible.

"Okay, let me see. Can I close the gate?" She tapped the table and the gate retracted. The door sealed and additional artificial light brightened the interior. "Now, I need the altitude controls."

She swiped her finger along a slider. A frightening sensation caused their legs to stumble. Muffled wind preceded a sudden stop. The soles of Olyana's feet popped into the air ever so slightly. She aced her landing but Emilee floundered onto her back.

"Ooof!" A canister escaped Emillee's grasp. Fuel spilled all over the floor. Her hands and legs dripped with the liquid.

Olyana rushed to her side. "We must wipe the poison off quickly!"

"It is okay!" Emillee waved assuredly. "The distilled version of the fog is not poisonous. Try not to slip on it, but do not worry if you get a little on yourself."

Olyana sighed and returned to the controls. "I need the viewer…the viewer…where is it?"

She found the button and a shimmering window appeared on the wall before them.

The view above the cliffs awed them, a sight unseen by the people of Jangala for almost a thousand years. From such a tremendous height, the two arks seemed smaller than the impression she had in her mind. The fog-infested jungle stretched far. Her studies claimed it was extensive, but the reality dwarfed her imagination. Rippling waves traversing a vast body of water in the distance struck her like a revelation. The Captain manual alleged of an endless pond on the horizon. She had never believed it. The truth was more amazing than the rumor.

"Look! What are those?" Emillee pointed to the enemy spheres floating nearby. They were dropping explosives upon the settlement. "Fascinating. It appears they have employed a similar principle using the fog as a lifting medium for their cloth-like spheres. Why have I not thought of that?"

"Those need to go." Olyana took her place in the pilot chair and tried to remember her theoretical studies. She turned each dial. "Yaw, pitch, acceleratiooooon!" They zoomed forward and stopped effortlessly above the once distant pond.

"What did you do?" Emillee asked, her arms trying to hold several crates steady.

"It appears I need to be much more sensitive." She gently handled the table and managed to turn the orb around and navigate back to the valley. She spotted the spheres ahead and searched the table for armaments. "I do not see any weapon controls. I do not think we have the means to destroy them."

"Nonsense. They are assuredly made of a textile of inferior tensile strength. Just ram through them."

"But they are filled with fog, are they not? It is volatile, yes?"

"I think the small craft's size could not hold enough to be dangerous. Our hull *should* be fine."

Emillee did not sound resoundingly confident, but Olyana trusted her. She directed the orb into the closet sphere at a moderate speed. They collided. The enemy vehicle exploded in a tremendous blue blaze. The cabin shook fiercely and the window filled with haze until they emerged seemingly undaunted on the other side.

"It worked!" Olyana reoriented the orb toward the next target. One by one, she destroyed them all.

A blinking warning icon accompanied a number upon the command table. Emillee brought it to Olyana's attention. "Hull integrity is at fifty-six percent. Hmm. That is a little less than I predicted, but we seem to be through the worst of what the sky has to offer."

They were grinning with relief when inexplicably the window crackled with distortion. She turned the orb toward the Divine's Ark. Its Lightning Tunnels were glowing with power. A gauge on the table measured an immense energy spike in the atmosphere. This would cause wonders all over the two settlements to act strangely. No doubt the Endeavoress War Council would soon notice.

Emillee rushed to the window and pressed her face against the illuminated glass surface. "This is insanity! They must know we will arm and fire our own if they shoot first! We have to stop this nonsensical escalation before it is too late!" She turned to Olyana. "But what can possibly be done?"

A bright number upon the command table drew Olyana's eye: the orb's current altitude. This sparked an idea. She was hesitant to speak it into words because its mere acknowledgment could further convince her of its viability. It would be a horrific act she may never forgive herself for. Scores of people, families, and children would suffer excruciating deaths if she were to cross the taboo line she had vowed her life to prevent. But if she did not act first, then her people would suffer in another way.

Could she justify ushering in a calamity against those that wished to exterminate her?

Olyana's own face betrayed her. Emillee examined the struggle within her eyes. "What is it?" Emillee asked. "You are planning something, right? Tell me what it is."

"I…I do not want to say," Olyana whispered, "but I think I should. We only have a few minutes before they are capable of firing. We…oh goodness." She paused one last time to stop herself from speaking the truth if she so wished to. "After all these years of promising to protect our people, do you think I have the fortitude to do absolutely anything, whatever necessary, to save them from this disaster?"

"Of course!" Emillee replied easily. She took Olyana's hands. "You are…"

Tears dripped down from Olyana's cheeks. "Even if it meant betraying the values within my heart? I am not a killer! And if I do this, I will become a force who devours all, soldier and innocent alike! I will be like the fog!"

"What are you talking about? What is this plan?" Emillee squeezed Olyana's fingers. "Tell me! Allow me to share this hardship!"

The decision was the Captain's duty. Burdening another to also wrestle with the moral quandary could be considered by some cowardly or weak. But if anyone knew her heart well enough to assure her she would not lose her conscience on the other side, then her beloved would be the one.

"We…" she choked through the tears. "Aboard this flying wonder, we can reach the top of their ark and board it from the hatch near the observatory."

"Boarding? How do you suppose we would fight our way into their war room and subdue their leaders?"

"We do not need to. We need only gain access to their F.L.A.G."

After a moment, Emillee gasped. "That would mean the poisoning of everyone in the Divine settlement." Not nearly as tormented as Olyana, Emilee nodded. "But have they presented us with a choice? If we are unable to stop them, it may mean the end for both of our peoples regardless."

An invisible force pressed against Olyana's chest. She struggled for every breath. This was the true weight of responsibility the Captain was always meant to bear. To decide such a thing, without the consultation of her advisors, was terrifying. Yet, Emillee's reasoning was fair and the Captain's highest order was to lead her people to victory. As a child, she never imagined triumph to take this form, but it was the clearest path before her and the Divine had obstructed all her preferred roads.

"And so it will be."

ROVER ENTRY #1057

Olyana's fingers slipped from Emillee's hand and reoriented the orb. Their craft hurtled through the valley, over the Divine settlement, and came to a rest on top of the enemy ark. The exit ramp clanged against the roof's usually unseen metal. They walked out onto the hull where the wind almost wrestled Olyana's ponytail out of compliance. As recently as that morning, she would have been curious to analyze the mysterious tribe from above. However, not even the strength of a hundred soldiers could turn her head now to look upon the ones she intended to doom.

Olyana brandished her sidearm and fired at the access hatch's bolts. It took their combined strength to twist it open. "Stay behind me and watch our tail."

Emillee nodded, eyes full of trust.

Olyana hopped down into the observatory first. Several gawkers immediately spotted her. She remembered her stale firearms training, opened fire, and haphazardly sent each one to the floor.

"Catch!" Emillee fell into Olyana's open arms and jumped to her feet. She appeared disheartened by the lifeless bodies. If Emillee had anything to say in protest, she did not make it known.

They ran through the nearest corridor and entered the room of the F.L.A.G. They found it easily because, as they were noticing, their arks were laid out identically. Massive, luminous tanks of bubbling chemicals surrounded the humming machine. Pipes, thin tubes, and spinning dials looked like an engineering nightmare.

Emillee immediately took to the wonder as she stepped inside. The shimmering colors reflected off her enchanted face. She examined a flickering gauge with her nose mere millimeters away from its glass housing. She had never been allowed to see their own F.L.A.G. although she had inquired many times.

"This technology...it is beyond anything I have ever seen. I understand the core principles of the device, the flow of fluids, the mechanics, chemistry that leads to reaction, but how exactly does it do what it does?"

"We are not here to dawdle. Please watch the hallway."

"But no one is guarding it."

"Of course not," Olyana said as she sized up the machine. "In this conflict, they are the invaders. They would not suspect us here. But regular patrols could still be ongoing."

Emillee stepped back and peeked into the hallway. It remained empty. "If we deactivate their F.L.A.G., will that stop the Lightning Tunnels?"

Olyana shot open a maintenance flap and ripped out wires. "I doubt it, but they may not fire if the operators abandon their post when they realize what is happening. Or they fire, but Azul and the others will see the fog pouring into the valley and will not fire back causing more senseless damage."

"Or," Emillee added with a pointed finger, "seeing they have been bested, their operators decide to fire recklessly, endlessly in an attempt to destroy us as well."

Olyana used the bottom of her weapon to bash a control panel and several walls of light into pieces. "I do not think so. Terrinad is likely still with the invasion force. Whatever they are preparing for is a calculated play. The operators would not want to harm their Cardinal and most of their warriors."

"Are you sure of that? Is there not something we should be doing just in case?"

"Please. Just keep watch."

Olyana was too far along to begin considering the many ways this could go wrong. The humming in the room sputtered and stopped. She stepped back and fired at the chemical tanks. The glass resisted at first, but repeated shots cracked the reservoirs before shattering. Fluid gushed and splashed upon the floor. Olyana leapt away as a precaution. It was wise that she did. When the chemicals mingled together, the floor sizzled and melted beneath the concoction.

"Curious how life-saving materials could be so dangerous," Emillee said.

"Back to the orb!"

They returned to the observatory with the bodies strewn about. The massive window beckoned Olyana toward it. She tried to resist the need to gaze out and confirm success. Certainly, diligence at this stage was prudent. Yet she wanted to pretend she had not designated uninvolved people as collateral for her war. As if Azul and her mother were watching her to make the right decision, she understood that it was the duty of the Captain to be sure. She stepped toward the scene.

Behind her, Emillee stacked furniture to reach the hatch on the ceiling. Shouting echoed from down the corridor. "Hurry!" Emillee warned. "Whatever you are doing, do it fast!"

Time felt sluggish as the settlement far below came slowly into view. The fog, as tall as the ark, cascaded onto the buildings with an unforgiving haste. She knew it impossible to hear the fleeing dots, but she perceived their cries of desperation and anguish. The sight of almost everyone disappearing into the haze wounded her heart in an irreparable way.

Emillee wrested Olyana from the window and pulled her toward the furniture tower. Just as they climbed out, weapon fire erupted in the observatory.

"Quick, get inside!" Emillee had to pull a semi-catatonic Olyana into the orb and push her out of the way to sit herself at the controls. Drawing on what she witnessed Olyana doing, she managed to lift off and begin accelerating toward home.

Through the orb's window, Olyana beheld the tunnels still flush with power, yet they erratically rotated on their bases. She broke from her trance.

"Something is wrong. I think they have lost control, but the tunnels still hum with devastation."

The window inside turned white. A thunderous crackle rang their ears and the orb's interior jostled them. If the Divine gods themselves had grabbed ahold of the craft and shaken it like a toy, she would have believed it.

"Oh my goodness!" Emillee slid fingers across the control table in a desperate attempt to steady the orb. When the outside became visible again, the tunnels were teeming with sparks and pointing toward the sky.

Olyana waved Emillee from the chair and rotated the orb. She scanned the valley for the impact crater hoping with all her heart nothing permanent had been destroyed.

She exhaled. "It must have fired directly into the clouds, right? There is no damage."

Emillee closed her eyes. She let herself relax and placed a comforting hand upon Olyana's back. "I guess this all sort of worked."

A beeping sound accompanied a new flashing light on the control table. Olyana tapped to silence it. "Additional fuel is desperately needed. Please, can you pour another canister…"

A second resounding shot occurred. A mighty eruption sent stone debris streaking past the window.

"Hold on!" Olyana slid her fingers over the controls, but massive boulders pounded the orb from above. An array of blinking lights colored the cabin. "The hull integrity is too low! We are losing…!"

Olyana grasped for Emillee, but they tumbled about like dolls. The Ark of the Endeavor spiraled outside the window as they plummeted toward it.

ROVER ENTRY #1058

There are two…" Visions of plum and white.

"Detain them both…" An incredible soreness.

Olyana awoke lying upon cold dirt with a chicken looming over her.

"Ah!" She tried to scramble to her feet, but great pain stabbed her limbs. Her arm rested in a sling and one of her legs was wrapped in a splint. She examined the hay-filled coop she resided within and dragged herself to the door. Locked. She looked around and noticed Emillee sprawled upon a pile of hay with two chickens on top of her.

"Shoo!" She found the strength to stumble forward and push the fowls off her. She held Emillee in her arms. "Can you hear me? Are you okay?"

"Oh…what?" Emillee awoke. She touched Olyana's face. "We are alive. Where are we?"

"We appear to be back home in the settlement. We are in the community coop, but it is locked from the outside."

A soldier of the Divine approached the door. "Hey! Their Captain is awake."

Olyana gawked in bewilderment as a pair of soldiers unlocked the entry. "What is happening?" she asked.

They entered the coop and stepped tentatively toward Emilee.

"Stay away from her!" Olyana staggered to her feet and placed herself in between.

"She's the one," the soldier outside said. They seized Olyana and dragged her out.

"Let go of me!" She struggled, but she did not have the strength to wriggle free.

"Leave her alone!" Emillee cried as they locked the coop with her remaining inside.

They propped Olyana up in the street and backed away. Just outside of town near the stables, her ark stood before her with new black scars speckled across its hull. She identified a large depression above the orb, which laid upside down in the grass, where it must have impacted.

"What is going on? Who is in charge?" she asked the unsettling number of Divine soldiers in her immediate area. If her limbs were not screaming in pain, she estimated she could have taken about half of her captors down and attempted an escape.

A soldier stepped away from the group. Intricate patterns and regalia adorned his plum armor. He appeared seasoned, tired, and standing on his last ounce of strength like her. The others gave him deference as he approached her.

"I apologize for your treatment, Captain Origo," he said.

She leaned forward. Sternly, she commanded, "You shall address me as Captain Olyana."

He responded absent of the disrespect Cardinal Terrinad was known for. "Very well, Captain Olyana. My name is Lawrends Murcario and I am Archbishop of the Divine Tribe."

"I seem to have hit my head recently. Explain to me why I am being detained in my own settlement and why you are not all in my custody."

His lungs vacated a lengthy sigh. "That is why I am eager to speak with you. It has been three days since the Divine settlement was engulfed in fog. We have no home to return to. You have won the war."

She blinked in disbelief. Was this news a deception or the truth? If her fragmented memory was to be trusted, she suspected it to be true. But there was no telling what ruses the Divine may have employed since she had been incapacitated. If this indeed had occurred, then she had succeeded where her ancestors had failed and this revelation would come with mixed emotions.

"Possible subterfuge! Prove it, Divine trickster!" she demanded.

He turned slowly, face sullen, and pointed toward the valley. The cliff walls were crumbling and littering the grass below with boulders. The horizon through the valley should have been peppered with tiny Divine buildings, but now a towering pile of rocks enclosed the path. A thin fog shimmered between her and the debris. Fog had never been in the valley before. Whatever remained on the other side was almost assuredly lost.

"Oh my…"

Her legs wavered. She placed one hand over her eyes and reached out her other for what she did not know. The Archbishop offered his arm and she hesitantly steadied herself with it. Either his side or hers, she repeated in her head. His side. Her side. Two sides locked in a mortal war for generations. As the Captain, she was supposed to celebrate, feel at ease and fulfilled upon achieving her charge. Why did surprise and disgust linger like a bad taste on her tongue? She could not stave off the wave of grief filling her soul. She felt her throat choking. It took the wanton destruction of thousands of innocent lives by her hand to achieve possible peace. But only for some on this planet. Frustratingly, she did not know if she had done the right thing and was uncertain if she would ever know.

"If…um," she said with a mouth that would not cooperate, competing emotions vying for a moment all their own to cry out, "if that is truly true, then…then it further begs the question, does it not? Why am I being detained in my own settlement?"

"Cardinal Terrinad was not willing to surrender when the fog claimed our home nor when our Lightning Tunnels blasted the valley. Instead, he ordered us to lay siege to your ark and take this land as our own. Your people sequestered themselves inside and have maintained limited, brief contact with us. During our offensive, you fell from the sky and we detained you without resistance.

"We spent the first day attempting to breach the hull, but none of our weapons could. On the second day, I executed Cardinal Terrinad for leading us into this state of affairs. I have been trying to negotiate a peace treaty with your ark, but they will not entertain prolonged talks unless I assure them you are alive. Now that I have proof, I intend to use you as a bargaining tool to secure my people, what is left of them at least, a living space here in your settlement."

He spoke boldly and without pomp. Olyana admired that. But what intrigued her more was his willingness to negotiate, a rare trait in the valley. "Very well, Archbishop. I am willing to advocate for your plan. I saw...first-hand…"

She squeezed her eyes shut. For a moment, she was unconvinced she could continue. The memory in her mind felt too fresh. Her heart ached as if a deep fissure was being filled with acid. She strained her eyes open. The Archbishop waited patiently. She respected that. "I apologize. I was saying that I saw what your people went through when the fog engulfed them and I had no pleasure in personally making that happen."

She intentionally implicated herself in the destruction of his tribe. She paused for a reaction. Was he truly a leader in control of himself? The arch of his eyebrows contorted slightly and returned to a restful state. This pleased her.

"Archbishop, show my people a sign of goodwill to initiate negotiations. Release me back to them and I will speak for you on the inside."

He smirked. "Absolutely not. Once you return, you will have no reason to reach back out to us. You will have all the power and you could simply wait for us to freeze in the coming winter."

His mental aptitude was respectable. "Very well. Then release *her.*" She pointed to Emillee. "She is a high-ranking official with a value rivaling my own. She will not be able to negotiate like I, but she will be an appropriate sign of goodwill."

The Archbishop stepped away and conferred with his colleagues. When he returned, he unlocked the coop and ordered Emillee to return to the ark.

"Olyana! I am not leaving you here!" she cried in the arms of soldiers escorting her away.

"Go. Tell them what you have seen. When they are ready to negotiate, send Azul."

Emillee sobbed and slowly made her way to the ark. In the distance, they witnessed her entering through the wide main port.

Good, Olyana thought. *She's safe. They're all safe inside. Whatever happens to me, I have fulfilled my duty.*

She stepped next to the Archbishop as they both stared at the ark. His soldiers raised their weapons, but he waved them down.

"You know," she said, "there is no guarantee they will agree to your terms. My people are resourceful. They could carry on without me."

"I am aware of that possibility."

"Then why risk weakening your position, even slightly, just now?"

He turned back toward the valley. "During countless generations of conflict, never has an unwavering resistance to compromise ever led to the peace or prosperity of the valley. I suppose at a certain age one becomes truly tired of it. I believe we are at the precipice of an opportunity to show earnest intentions of peace. It may be a result of our own desperation, but what other choice do I have? I have inherited the responsibility of ensuring my people's survival."

A reluctant steward. In some ways they were alike. Neither lusted for power or glory. If the situation somehow resolved, perhaps he and her could finally begin healing the deep ideological valley between their two peoples.

A soldier handed the Archbishop a far talk box. Olyana made out the voice on the other side. It was Azul.

"Yes, that is correct," the Archbishop replied. "Yes, we are agreeable to those terms. Well, no. We will not forfeit our weapons." He argued for a moment further and placed the talk box into a pocket. "It seems negotiations have temporarily stalled. He said he would chime the bells again soon. This is a good first step indeed."

Olyana detected a strange noise from somewhere in the valley. Like a machine rousing awake, it was steady and powerful. The Archbishop heard it as well and, with his help supporting her with his arm, he and Olyana both made their way toward what remained of the settlement wall. Many of his people accompanied them with their weapons drawn. An otherworldly, shimmering blue light beamed into the sky from about where the ceremonial altar should have been. The ray was glorious, albeit worrying.

Olyana strained her vision. The altar was no more, shattered into fragments. A crater, presumably from a tunnel blast, laid in its wake. A cloud of black smoke spilled out from the fracture and covered the valley's ground like nothing she had ever seen. Akin to the fog but thicker. A peculiar rhythm echoed which she recognized as the stomping of hooves. There were no known native animals on Jangala, but her school texts had hinted at the existence of the majestic horse creature elsewhere in the galaxy. She surmised this tempo mimicked their own gaits but became aghast when a nightmarish beast emerged from the miasma. The monster stood about as tall as a person on six legs, with four eyes, hide as black and as flowing as oil, and a maw like a gaping chasm.

She twisted toward the Archbishop. "Is this one of your last remaining creations? How did it survive the fog?"

Equal repulsion upon his face only frightened her more. He answered without the need for words.

He drew his pistol and waved to his soldiers. "Paladins! Form a defensive line and stop that creature from reaching the wall!"

The soldiers rushed into the valley and opened fire. The creature absorbed many shots before it burst into pieces. Black goo spurted out. It stumbled and crashed lifelessly onto the ground. A small group ventured forward to investigate the beast, but they never made it. The crater shone even brighter like the brilliance of a blue sun and black smoke overflowed into the valley.

Thunder reverberated off the cliff sides. Stones bounced in the dirt. The sound of a stampede frightened Olyana and she grabbed the Archbishop's arm.

"We need to retreat!"

"No! We were able to slay that welp. We may have fallen to your crafty tactics, but we will not be bested by these monstrosities!"

A herd of beasts manifested from within the smoke and charged the remaining warriors. Accurate shots wounded some terrors, but every person was devoured in a grotesque display of gluttony. Those remaining upon the wall rained down righteous fury upon the beasts. Yet for every creature they cut down, two more pushed forward and took their place.

"Full retreat toward the ark!" the Archbishop ordered to Olyana's relief.

As they fled, he chimed Azul using the far talk. "We are in mortal danger! We are being pursued by an unknown horde of creatures and they have eaten some of our soldiers! We have your Captain and wish to return her safely if you will allow us into your ark immediately! Please respond!"

"We will not abide by those terms," Olyana heard Azul reply. "You are not permitted to enter the ark under any circumstances."

Betraying her ingrained sense of duty, a pledge to give her life for the tribe, a profound fear drove her to grab at the far talk. The Archbishop handed it over and turned around to fire at the beasts breaching the battered wall.

"Azul, this is serious! I have seen the creatures and they are not of this world. Reconsider with the War Council and let us in!"

"Negative, Captain. It pains me with all my heart, but your sense of responsibility must understand that we are in too delicate of a state to introduce a rogue element like the Divine inside the ark's walls without a clear plan."

Of course he was right, but she was desperate. "Then what would you have me do? Everyone will die out here, myself included!"

"Hold strong, Captain. Help is on the way."

The main port's swinging whoosh brought her hope. Her soldiers poured out armed with their greatest wonders from the Vault of Champions. Several soared into the sky with the Wings of Fire strapped to their backs. Others secured the Distance Explosive Tossers to the ground with stakes. A small unit ran past her each carrying Lances of Light and wearing their most wondrous warrior suits.

The Archbishop's soldiers drew back and formed a tunnel for her people to charge through as they collided with the beasts. Smoke and black liquid soaked the valley. They won the battle quickly with minor injuries.

ROVER ENTRY #1059

Many days had passed. The beasts continued to appear in waves. Their bodies were only becoming larger with each attack. While the two tribes had come together to build a new, secure wall along the valley, Olyana recognized that defending would not buy them unlimited time. She and the now Cardinal Murcario adorned their most precious equipment and soared over the wall and into the valley to survey the altar's remains themselves.

She scanned the area with the instruments equipped on her gleaming helmet made of light. Once confident there were no beasts present, she came to a rest at the edge of the altar's ruins first. Her rough landing with the Wings of Fire aggravated her limb injuries not yet fully healed, but her combat suit held her together enough. Her helmet dispelled into sparkles with the tap of her shoulder. She crouched down to inspect an artifact on the ground.

"Murcario, come and look at this."

He descended next to her and knelt to pick up a piece of pulsating metal. Hundreds of pieces of this teeming metal on the ground surrounded a sprawling wispy blue pool of water like neither had ever seen. This was the bright, grand beacon's source shooting up into the sky.

"I believe the beasts are emerging from this small pond," he said.

"The shoreline is about the right size for some of the big ones we have been seeing. However, does it not look like the water's edge has expanded? Look at these drag marks." Olyana pointed to the ground where the metal pieces had pushed outward from the pool's center. "I do not think this will limit the size of them in the future as this pond grows."

"You are right. If we do not come to understand this source, their increasing size may come to overwhelm us."

While the Cardinal examined the stone of what little remained of the altar, Olyana reached hesitantly toward the pool. What sort of water was this, seemingly so shallow but capable of hiding countless enemies just below the surface?

Her hand neared the water's edge when the altar's familiar but uncomfortable power once again embraced her. A thousand tiny tugs took hold of her hand and drew her nearer to the water's edge. She wondered if she should fight it, but it had never hurt her before so she decided to see what she could learn from it.

The force intensified and pulled her forward.

"Ah!" she cried.

The Cardinal ran toward her but he was not fast enough.

She fell into the pool and the pain of a hundred lightning bolts struck her body repeatedly. Her ears were accosted with screeching she imagined were the sounds of the Divine she had exterminated. Her body twirled through a tunnel before coming to rest abruptly upon a stone surface.

Her sore arms and legs were pulsating with pain as she climbed to her feet. She took in her surroundings. She was no longer on Jangala. This intriguingly smooth-stoned valley housed a concerning number of beasts of all sizes. They were confined to cages under an unfamiliar orange sky. This was their source. Now she could do something to stop it.

One of the nearby cages rattled violently and burst open. A group of three oozing fiends charged toward her with clear ravenous intent.

"You!" she pointed at one. "Bring me to your master, foul monster!"

An unseen voice called out to her. "What are you doing? You can't talk to those animals! Hurry, this way!"

She ignored it.

She uncoupled from her back her Lance of Light. The first beast lunged and she impaled it through the mouth. It exploded into a shower of pieces. Black smoke filled the area. She activated her helmet and waded undaunted through the cloud. Her vision was compromised, but her hearing was amplified.

The second beast pounced from the haze immediately to her left, but she gripped one of its teeth and ripped it out of its jaw. She skewered that monster too and it ceased living.

As the smoke cleared, the third beast watched her from a distance. It spit a deluge of bile into the sky and it rained down onto her. The viscous substance restricted her ability to move. She activated her Wings of Fire, burning off much of the slime, and flew into the sky. She chucked her lance, barreling it through the beast below, and descended to retrieve it from its remains.

Olyana searched for the earlier voice's source. A strange person in red poked out of a hole in the impressively smooth perimeter cliff.

"Hello there. Are you friend or foe?" Olyana asked.

"Friend! Friend!" the red person said. "We're humans like you! At least I think you're human."

Olyana flew over and came to a rest within the tunnel. There was a small boy, a man, and second young woman inside as well. "What do any of you know of these creatures?"

"Lady," the man said, "you've got a mighty impressive set of armor. You gotta let me get a closer look sometime. But, as to your question, we're here to stop these Seekers from devouring all of humanity."

"Is that so? Then why are you cowering in this hole?"

The man scratched his head. "We, uh, just haven't had the firepower that you're packing. Nor the combat experience, to be honest. I'm more of a brawler myself and my suit is sort of out of range of my power source."

As the man continued to talk, she looked these people over. She was a good judge of character and she believed these hiding folk were as disturbed by the beasts as she was. What they said could be true, but she needed to speak to them with her advisors present to be sure.

"It is not safe here," she interrupted. "Come back with me to my settlement and we will talk further."

"Of course," the red one said, pushing the babbling man out of the way. "I'm very ready to tell you everything. I really hope you'll be the key to ending this galactic nightmare!"

The Hidden Cards

File Under: revelations, ethnography, perspective

Location(s): Abeona-2, Creare

Executive Summary: The following entry is again written from my personal perspective. My entrance into the Omega settlement's gate is well known. The story of what happened next has been a topic of much interest. This is documented in the following entries using Rover-compliant narrative style. Please note for clarity's sake that this entry picks up precisely after my first entry when I still stood on Abeona-2, which is prior to the ending of the last entry in which I first met my associate, Olyana Origo.

ROVER ENTRY #1061

Thousands of people gathered from across the dusty settlements of Abeona-2 to witness the overactive arch within the Red Rover's home. Dressed in storm-protective gear, the wall of tan chanted with their hands linked in solidarity.

"Red Rover, oh Red Rover! Send our questions on over! Red Rover, oh Red Rover! Bring answers back over!"

Red clutched her small sack of supplies and kicked up sand with a running start. The portal shimmered as her foot breeched its surface ever so slightly. The sensation of a million children's hands yanked her inside.

An immediate pain tormented her unimaginably. Magnitudes worse than when her hand was plunged through as a child, her body tossed, twisted, and stretched in countless directions as she sped through a swirling tunnel of blue and white. Her fingertips were as far from her toes as the canyons of the Lonely Basin stretched. Silver, aqua, auburn, and ruby trails of what she believed were starlight streaked past her along the confining walls.

She wailed but did not hear herself. Instead, distant horrific cries of children echoed throughout the tunnel.

"Why! Why! Why!" was the word in her language that repeatedly resounded.

She clasped her ears to dull out the gut-wrenching howls, but that had no effect. The sound was coming from inside her head.

The tiny hands returned. From the soles of her feet to the loosening strands of her hair escaping from her hood, blue disembodied appendages with trailing wispy tails tugged her body around. She shrieked at the sensation of being torn apart by a crowd of children trying to take their due in flesh. She had never believed in an afterlife, and she was not sure this qualified as such, but there was no denying these children were not at peace.

The nightmare abruptly ceased. She collapsed face-first onto an uneven, solid surface. The otherworldly pain dissipated, but she struggled to lift herself. Her mind was in a daze. Her vision came into focus. She recognized what appeared to be human bones laying between her fingers.

Blood felt as if it drained from her body. Underneath her knees were coarse white powder, bones she had smashed with her landing. Could this be all that remained of the children sacrificed over the ages in the Divine's name? Piling up inside a portal that had nowhere to empty to until now?

She rolled away from the bones. Surely every creature on the planet heard her scream.

Lying on the ground, staring at the amber sky with peculiarly shaped clouds, she noticed the air was not dry like her home hemisphere. Instead, a thickness in her mouth was foreign to her. She placed a hand on her chest and felt an uncomfortable pressure inside her lungs. Like the time she was stranded in the Desolate Plains during a settlement-crushing terrornado with only a small cave to hide herself, every breath was pumping anxiety through her body.

She tried to remember her Rover training regarding how to calm oneself whenever one lost control of their environment. Not trying hard enough, her breath quickened. Her vision blurred. Her mind lifted away from her head and looked down at her body below. She counted down from twenty and aligned each gasp to a single second. She placed a hand on her chest, following the rise and fall of her struggle. She gradually took command of herself.

With her consciousness anchored again and her eyes readjusted, she committed to continuing the expedition if at least to fill her mind with anything but the horror she had experienced. She was trained to live through this. She certainly had not over committed herself like her mother, she tried to convince herself.

Red took stock of her surroundings. Turning her head about, she laid at the edge of a massive concrete fort that dwarfed any of her settlement's city centers. She gasped. Behind her spanned a horizon of arches and rings. There were a variety of sizes, shining suns as numerous and varied like an arm of a clear galactic night sky, and so many shimmered brightly. Modest ones, like what she had just jumped through, stretched along the ground. Colossal metal rings high in the sky floated with what she could only guess was some type of unknown levitation technology.

"The arches are…pockets? No, I can't still be inside it because you don't put more pockets inside of pockets. No, no. Are they…" She considered what she knew of technology. "They are gateways?" Just like how radio translated audio into waves and transported it across the colony, so too could the arch be sending objects to another location.

In the facility's center, large rectangular crates sat stacked low and high. While some were constructed of solid metal walls, others sported cage-like bars. She noticed mounds of black material piled irregularly inside the cages, but they did not appear remarkable from her vantage point.

She surveyed the sky. Only a single remaining setting sun cast an atmospheric hue similar to her home hemisphere. The familiarity was short lived when she made out hovering objects that were not clouds. She slipped on her telescopic goggles and peered above. These objects were spaceships. Flying, operating vessels! Where on the planet had she been transported to? It had been almost a thousand years since the last ship flew. Furthermore, she did not recognize any of the ship designs from her school texts.

She sighed. Nothing could be done about flying mysteries at the moment. She prepared for the work she came to complete.

Red reached into her sack and placed her Impulse Encoding Transmitter next to her gate. She attached a wire and it hummed with power. Her jittering hands slipped headphones over her head and turned a dial to the mysterious frequency she first heard with Green and Purple months ago. She scribbled with her pencil recording her observations in her Journal. The indecipherable wailing was just as strong at this end. She, Green, and Purple thought these scream-like distortions were just space radiation. She now interpreted it with a graver perspective.

It was undeniable that these ghastly, howling shrieks were from a chorus of young lungs. They had been vehemently wronged for a lie that spanned centuries. How many children were cast into limbo only to endure the rest of their meager lives in loneliness and agony? She did not want to bear the thought, but she had to document her conclusions. She had vowed to Green, and especially to Purple for her brother, that this would be the first Great Answer she would unravel.

A distant booming electronic horn pierced her headphones. A rumbling beneath her feet placed her on high alert. Even through the alarm, a guttural growl rumbled from an unknown sinister source behind her. Fear plummeted into her stomach and gripped her body.

Red twirled around to the sight of a foul, shape-shifting creature stalking in her direction. She had failed to notice this mutant, but there was a good chance it was the caged black mound from before. Behind its morphing head with four eyes, a swinging gate with a broken lock confirmed her hypothesis.

As her breathing grew shallow and her feet struggled to move, she realized more animalistic monstrosities were contained inside the countless cages stacked upon each other. They looked savage, like the rare canidaurochs of her frontier, but these were thrice as horrid. Black oil and smoke seeped from their bodies and onto their barren enclosure's floors.

The horn stopped and the beast charged. She threw off her headphones and ran toward her gate. The vision of her people on the other side was so close. A great whoosh of air followed an unexpected calm. Concentrating on placing one foot before the other, she dared not take her eyes off the gate to see what the monster was doing.

The beast made itself known when it descended in her way from a mighty leap. It decimated the pile of bones in front of her. So startled, she fell to her knees. Red shed tears of remorse as the creature devoured the innocent children's remnants. Flashes of light and popping sounds from the top of the vast perimeter wall frightened her more. Was not a rabid, grotesque horror enough?

She searched for anything to crawl and hide inside when several projectiles impacted the monster's body. It bellowed before flopping onto the ground.

Slender tubes pounded upon her jacket piercing her expedition suit.

"Oh my gosh! I've been shot!" she screamed to no one. But the projectiles were not lethal. Upon her arm, chest, and leg were syringes filled with a yellow liquid. Her eyelids felt heavy. She crumpled to the ground.

ROVER ENTRY #1062

Visions of swirling portals.

Tunnels of children, all those lost children.

Their bones, all their tiny bones.

Who did this? Who? The Divine. Not her people. Other people.

Superstition did this!

Red awoke screaming. She shot up lying on a blanket cast upon an otherwise cold and naked metal floor. She panted while noticing the steel bars that imprisoned her. The cage stood somewhere outdoors in the middle of the facility. She could not tell how long she had been unconscious, but a single sun shone from elsewhere than where she last remembered. Where was the second? Why was it still not visible?

The hunger pains in her stomach and the filth on her body suggested she may have been out for several days. Around her were empty cages thankfully not filled with the monsters she had seen before. Upon a second glance, all were indeed vacant except for one.

Only about a stone's throw away, what could only be described as an extraterrestrial, a genuine alien, gripped the rusted bars of their cell with their four spotted green and black hands. This being stared at her with their four eyes. They were tall, their skin smooth and shimmery, and they wore a tattered garment that barely covered whatever reproductive organs their species had to hide. Pools of an oily liquid speckled their floor. Perhaps they had been locked up for a long time. The conditions seemed inhumane.

This all was startling, but she had already exhausted so much of her energy at novel things she just accepted this as it was. Her jail mate stood out of arm's reach, but close enough she believed she could talk to them.

Red scooched toward her bars and waved at the alien. "He-hello? Where am I? Am I still on Abeona-2?"

The creature stared at her without response. She wondered if they did not speak her language. She tried using the old-world tongues. First in Mandarin, then Arabic, and finally Orderlish.

"You...speak...us?" the alien replied, barely understandable. It was as if they spoke with sand in their mouth. They pointed to themself. "No. I... speak...you...a little." Black liquid sprinkled the bars as they clutched their chest and coughed. The oily substance clung to the bars momentarily before loosening its grip and oozing down the rods fizzling and smoking until too thin to be seen anymore.

"Oh! So you do know a little. Does that mean your people are the ones who are sending the messages through the gates?"

"My...people. Not...my people."

Red had trouble deciphering the alien message. There were so many reasons this first encounter could be difficult. She wondered how productive their conversation could be. She decided to make it as simple as possible to gather the information she needed.

"Where are we?"

"Creare."

Red did know of any documented planet named Creare. In addition, that did not fit the naming convention the Rover Order used when designating planets. Could they be referring to Abeona-2 by another name? She may have to navigate a different language for describing the same things.

"What is your name?"

"Denish. I..." They rubbed their stomach as if a pain were rising. "Oh. Denish el Zulack."

It was common among the decoded gate messages for speakers to identify themselves by name and community of origin whether that was a planet,
ship, or colony. Her people introduced themselves using their name and then
profession. She was at least familiar enough with the message's convention
to believe Denish was of a place called Zulack. Curiously, Red was not aware
of that location ever being documented in a Rover report.

She wished to match his custom. "Hello, Denish. I am Red of Abeona-2,
a planet of the Milky Way galaxy."

"You...Red. You creature of C-94."

C-94, she wondered. Was this what their people called the Milky Way? If
the alien said she was *of* C-94, did that mean they no longer resided within it?
How many galaxies were their people aware of? At least 94! The knowledge
and scope of their people must be incredible. She indulged in a moment of
exciting thought.

The alien pointed at her. "You...first resource. Will want...information
from you."

"Resource?" She considered whether the alien's translation was off. "Do
you mean roamer? My profession is as a Rover. Are you expecting others like
me? Or perhaps you mean child? The message I received through the gate was
children levels are not yet appropriate for the size of the garden. Are we your children?"
What a strange thought.

"No. Resource. You...misunderstand children...or perhaps we misuse
your...word."

Machinery grinded somewhere too far to see. Marching footsteps put
Red on edge. She jumped to her feet and scanned the area. Around a corner
of cages came a group of creatures like Denish. The one in the lead crossed
their four arms along their chest and wore sparkling, thinly draped clothing.
Their skin was vivid, what could be described as a healthy green devoid of
black spots like her imprisoned compatriot. Behind this alien were several

others dressed in similar beautiful clothing. Brutish ones in rigid black armor, carrying stick-like weapons, followed several paces behind them all.

The lead alien approached her cage and pointed back and forth between her and Denish. They asked Denish a question in a foreign tongue. The two hotly conversed. Denish sounded irritated yet passionate. Red did not believe the lead alien cared about Denish much.

An armored brute neared Denish's cage and shot them with projectile syringes. Unlike the yellow liquid she reccived, he suffered a black, oily, goo that seeped out of a wound on Denish's side. Denish screamed and chucked the vials back at their captors. They seemed to pay Denish no mind and, causing her much fright, they turned their weapons toward her.

"Oh my gosh! Please! Don't shoot!" she exclaimed in as many languages as she could muster in the fraction of a second.

"Oh good!" the lead alien said in respectable Orderlish. "This specimen already speaks our devised common tongue for its species. Someone, please make note of that!"

ROVER ENTRY #1063

The brutes lowered their weapons. An alien scribbled on a device. Despite all the craziness thus far, it was awkwardly comforting to witness their respect for documentation like a Rover. Perhaps this started as a misunderstanding. She may have been called to share information between their people and this entire captivity situation would be resolved shortly.

"Hello," the lead alien said. "I am Ulmaids el Songead. I am your ambassador and will be at your disposal during your stay with us. I do want to apologize for the rough welcome you received. The nature of our work necessitates a culture of shoot first and ask questions later."

Ulmaids pointed to her cage and a brute unlocked the gate.

"We've been waiting so long to hear from your galaxy. Now that we've met, let's get started right away. Please, follow me." Ulmaids gestured vaguely and the entire group walked toward the wall. "Someone please grab its expedition gear, wherever that's lying around."

"My what?" Red asked.

"Your space suit, dimensional stabilization equipment, or whatever it is you wore to travel here."

"I-I don't have anything else. I just wore this," Red said, tugging at her jacket.

Ulmaids stopped and turned. They blinked twice, technically four times if you accounted for their four eyes. "You…you traveled through the portal in the raw?"

"Well, again no. I was wearing what I am now, but…"

Ulmaids drew their lips back. "Yikes. What hearty material is your species made out of? Well, that's not important. Let's stay on schedule." They continued walking.

Red cautiously stepped out of her cage grasping her supply sack. She figured she was meant to follow them. However, she had many questions. For the first time in a long time, fear accompanied her walk toward the unknown. This was despite her entire professional career being built upon exuding the brave soul of discovery.

"Wait! I mean, h-hello. My name is Red. I'm sorry, but where am I? Who are you exactly?"

Ulmaids spun around again and frowned. "This creature seems to not understand the task at hand. Perhaps it even misunderstood my previous response. Is my common tongue insufficient?"

Others around Ulmaids shrugged.

"Well, there shouldn't be any travel distortion of the mind, unless the LIT system is malfunctioning." Ulmaids consulted a device in their hands and shook their head. "Never mind that now. Let's get this Red to the examination room."

An armored brute grabbed Red's arm and dragged her along. She struggled out of its grasp, no simple feat considering how the brute could have wrestled her back with three other arms. In her desperation, she dropped her sack. A few glass vials inside shattered. The brutes drew their weapons again.

Red threw up her hands. "Wait! I understand you fine! I just want answers before I follow. What planet am I on and what are you? Are you aliens? Some sort of evolved animal? What are all these creatures in cages? Why do you have functioning ships? What is this facility used for? How do I get back home?"

Ulmaids' eyes narrowed and a thin smile stretched across their face. "It seems your mind is still intact, but your cooperation continues to lack."

Ulmaids waved over a compatriot and whispered into their ear. They shook hands. Ulmaids turned back to Red. "While unorthodox, if a little out-of-order explanation will encourage your participation, I can answer a few of those quickly. Then we must get back on schedule. Again, I am Ulmaids and you are on the planet Creare. I suppose to you, yes, we are aliens as we are not of your home galaxy. I come from the Tau Noi galaxy which is approximately 600 million light years from your own, C-94."

She lifted her goggles to her forehead. "600? 600 *million?*" She gritted her teeth, pulled back her hood, and ran her fingers through her hair. She always wondered if the gates were of alien origin. The prevailing Rover hypothesis claimed gates were the ancient tech of a long-deceased civilization, but the Order had no substantiating proof of alien life in or out of our galaxy.

There was a fringe theory among the citizens that the gates were a long-forgotten technology from within the colony arks. Their true purpose was supposedly obfuscated by the Order due to a grand conspiracy. Red knew this was implausible for many reasons. But even that idea seemed more plausible than this.

"Oh." Ulmaids hurriedly waved over an attendant. "It's happening. Look at its face. It's freaking out. See?" The aliens groaned and waved several hands toward Red. "This is why I always encourage the examination before explanations."

"Shall I inject it with the mood levelers?" the attendant asked, handling a bottle in their hands.

"Inject? No, please! No more injections!" Red pleaded.

Ulmaids blinked slowly at Red. "I suppose it still has the wit to converse so we can leave it be for now. But do keep the levelers handy."

The brute grabbed Red's arm. She lunged for her sack and clasped it close to her body this time.

As they neared the great encircling wall, she felt panicked while taking mental notes of her surroundings just in case she had to flee. It did not help that everything looked so similar. The location of her own gate was a complete mystery.

Uncertainty filled her regarding whether these aliens were more foe or friend. She had never trained for anything even resembling combat. The best comparable skillset she had was how to elude a starving canidauroch hot on your desert trail.

Their version of the canidauroch was already massively more terrible. What level of despicableness may these aliens turn out to be?

Red and the aliens neared the skyscraping wall. A door materialized upon it where there certainly was not one before. It slid open and they walked inside.

The interior shone blindingly bright. White walls with rounded edges, where the floor met the wall and again where the wall met the ceiling, made a setting she found unsettling. They were trapped inside of an egg, or so it seemed. A pair of simple chairs and a table sat in the middle of the room along with shelves of instruments and computer-like devices along the back wall.

Two brutes positioned themselves at the door. This led her to believe she was not free to go at will. The brute holding her arm rather politely asked her to sit. She complied. The chair had four armrests, presumably for the alien's two sets of arms. She chose to use the first pair instead of stretching herself to the outer ones. She examined the walls. She was familiar enough with research spaces to suspect one or more of the walls were probably made of opaque one-way glass. She wondered if more aliens watched her in secret. What were they hoping to gain from her?

An alien wheeled a machine behind her with a metal cap that hovered just above her head. The cap hummed to life and its rim blinked with a peculiar display of lights. Ulmaids sat in the other chair and looked at a device about the size of a Journal in their hands.

"Am I correct that you call yourself Red?" Ulmaids asked.

She tried to speak but found it difficult. Her tongue felt dry, breath shallow from apprehension. She nodded instead.

"Nodding one's head. Is that an affirmation in your culture?"

"Y-yes, that's affirmative," she squeaked out.

"Okay. Thank you for confirming." He looked up from his device. "We're like that too, by the way, but you never want to assume these things. I can't count the number of times I've been wrong for doing so and, well, since I have so many fingers and toes, you can infer that it's been a great many times."

Ulmaids chuckled slightly as did several others in the room.

She politely smiled. The situation's perceived levity confused her sense of it all. Was she not in danger? Had she put up her walls prematurely? On the one hand, their first inclination upon detecting her was to shoot and imprison her. Then again, they did say they carefully protected themselves from other threats, so perhaps they were actually scared of her. This seemed silly considering the aliens stood on average almost twice her size. Was there any logic left indicating this continued to be a big misunderstanding?

Red closed her eyes and imagined the last time she felt the most unsure. It was at her mother's passing ceremony. Her future and that of her grandpa's was unknown. What would become of a colony without a Rover to bring it knowledge and glory? And how could an old man or a child hope to carry that burden so suddenly? Yet, she did. She learned, studied, and persevered despite her doubts.

Furthermore, here she was on her latest expedition smoothly communicating with strange aliens. She was equipped to rise to this occasion, a freak storm in its own way like the one that took her mother. Possibly she had failed to give her mother enough credit for leaving her the linguistic tools to shine in her own right. Maybe. She would have to ponder that another time.

"Mmhm," she muttered as a calm cascaded over her body. She pointed to the cap above her head. "Listen. You're not going to dissect me or something like that, are you? I have a lot of people waiting for me back on the other side of the gate and they're going to be curious if I don't return.

I don't want to come across as an aggressive representative of my species, but I think it's important I make myself clear when I say we are capable of defending ourselves."

This was a bluff. There had not been a military conflict on Abeona-2, or plentiful weapons to wage one for that matter, since before the Order. She did read in her school texts about a few scuffles between settlements, but those were mostly political posturing. The planet was their collective enemy and the people could not turn their attention away from it for long. Nature would remind them of that time and time again.

Ulmaids placed several hands upon their cheeks. "My dear Red, goodness no! You are a very valuable specimen indeed, but you're worth so much more than your anatomy. No, that type of knowledge doesn't interest us." Ulmaids pointed toward the other alien operating the cap machine. "What are you seeing? Are you getting a clear picture?"

"Yes, it's coming through just fine," the other alien said. "Although, it seems to be rather limited. The specimen may be cut off from the rest of its species."

"Let me see." Ulmaids walked behind Red and handled the machine. "A barren planet. Yes, that much is clear. But where are images of the rest of the genus?"

Red cleared her throat. "May I suggest you…"

Ulmaids poked their head around. "Quiet, please. Keep still." They returned to the device. "Does this one not have access to their intergalactic media?"

She did not like being shushed. And besides, they were wasting time. "Just ask me your question directly. I could tell you."

Ulmaids emerged again. "Being stubborn again, are we? Alright. I suppose I could use your anecdotal claims for now, but that'll be hardly valid enough to file my report."

Ulmaids returned to their seat across from her. "Please, Red of C-94. Tell me what you know of your species' prevalence among the stars, their ability to harness their natural resources, and the age, size, and approximate number of planets and suns in your galaxy."

She had hoped for a more micro question, but now that she promised competence, she had to try.

"Well, I know a little about that," Red said to the expectant aliens. "We call ourselves humans and we're from the Milky Way galaxy, known as C-94 of course."

Ulmaids nodded gently.

"We originated from a planet named Earth in the Sol system and sent colony arks elsewhere probably over a millennium ago. I don't know a lot about our home world or any other planet for that matter because my colony didn't have the technology to establish communication with them after we settled. We're actually not sure they're still out there. We may be the last of our kind."

The aliens exchanged what Red supposed were worried glances.

"Um…oh wait! I brought an archive just for this occasion."

She could tell the aliens' interests were piqued when she reached into her sack and pulled out a data stick.

Ulmaids accepted it and inspected it closely. He waved her off the chair. "Let me use this for a moment."

She stepped away and tucked her hands into her pockets to appear less threatening. Ulmaids placed her data stick on the seat and nodded to the one controlling the cap machine. The machine hummed and many aliens gathered around the other side in front of a monitor. Colored light flashed upon their reflective, moist faces.

"Oh, look at that," one said.

"Hmm…rudimentary. A clever way about it, but unrefined," said another.

"Oh," Red peeped up. "Th-that's incredibly old file footage…"

"That's not very efficient."

"Look! They're still puttering around in those!"

"Again," Red tried to interject, "this is mostly archival footage from prior to my colony's home world departure. If we wait just a little longer, current details regarding Abeona-2 will…"

"What do you make of this, Chlorian?"

One particularly lively alien chortled. "That's it? They're barely into stage three," They wore a silky pink garment and operated several devices in their hands and pockets. All the others paid attention when they spoke. "This specimen said they have no contact with the species' home world. Could it be that this information is grossly out of date?"

"As I was trying to add, it's the latest compendium of humanity I have to offer. I'm proud to report it does include the last thousand years of developments from my own planet."

"Well, that's certainly nothing to report *at all*." Chlorian chuckled. "We only invited you here because you were the first of your species to interface with the Longitudinal Intergalactic Transit System."

"The gates?" She carved the shape of an arc in front of her with her hands. "The blue glowy arches that emit unlimited power?" She felt stupid wording it so simply, but Ulmaids was probably right in that there was no sense in assuming they were referring to the same thing.

"Glowy power arches!" Chlorian crooned with a roll of the eyes. "Sure, we'll call them gates. It *was* you who sent the signal using our constructed common tongue on behalf of your people seeking additional information from us, correct?"

"That's right!" She almost jumped with childlike joy, but she dared not appear too animated and make people nervous. She did not know if bouncing excitedly was universal. Still, they had received her message after all and this filled her heart with pride. She was also concerned they assumed she could speak for her entire species. "I deciphered the wavelength signature of the messages you were sending us and I used pretty standard equipment to send back one of my own. But it wasn't on behalf of all of humanity. I was just sort of messing around and figured it out."

"You did this alone as a sole individual?" Chlorian turned to their colleagues. Their brows arched in possibly the universal expression for surprise. Fingers tapped across their arms. "And messages? Is anyone aware of any active messaging campaign to this garden?"

Several shook their heads and shrugged.

Ulmaids consulted several computer-like devices. "I don't have any record of a communication campaign currently running. That would be blatantly against standard cultivation procedure."

Chlorian paced the room. "No. That doesn't seem right."

A comrade to their left chimed in. "Well, consider that it's been a few billion years past the traditional benchmark for ripening and we haven't serviced the LITS in this garden during the last few cycles. It's possible the hardware has become brittle, breaking down, and leaking erroneous signals."

Chlorian nodded. "Possible." They pointed at Red again. "Specimen, if what your data stick contains is true, coupled with your species' inability to seamlessly connect your worlds, wouldn't that imply that your people are in a rather juvenile stage of galactic industrialization?"

Red had no idea how to respond to that. She was not a galactic politician or an ambassador herself. How should someone even react when accused of being more primitive than one thought? She entertained a brief non-sequitur in which her appreciation for the Rover Order leaders grew if this was the type of pressure they endured during their politically-hot annual results conferences.

Her loss of words apparently sent the room into a tizzy. Seemingly forgetting her presence, they argued among themselves. It was also possible they deemed her too simple to understand the following details which she found disturbing.

"Why would you ask it that? How would it know?"

"This garden is not anywhere near harvestable levels. What a shame."

"We've been practicing this common tongue for eons and for what?"

"This is all a wash. It's been too long. We should just weed the whole thing and start over."

"Restart now? We'll be hundreds of billions of years behind schedule!"

Chlorian stomped their feet. "But what do we have to show for it? A bunch of planet-hopping explorers that haven't even started refining solarite? No. This seed was a dud. The next seed will do better. The soil is still fertile. However, the LITS system *will* need considerable refurbishment."

Ulmaids emerged from behind the cap machine. They sighed. "I agree with Chlorian. The children should weed the garden." They waved another alien closer. "Accelerate children production by four-hundred percent. Connect all LITS waypoints. Begin prepping the first wave. Follow the first stage of our typical harvest protocol starting with the home world."

Ulmaids checked a device in their hand. "Do we have the location of that so-called Earth somewhere on file?"

"We do," a comrade said. "We'll be ready to execute the first stage in a little under three weeks."

Red understood enough to know the settlements, no, all of humanity were in danger and only she could warn them.

ROVER ENTRY #1065

Red had to warn her people. Her eyes darted around the sterile room, but there were no other exits besides the crease in the wall she had entered through. What could she use as a weapon? She was kidding herself. She was no fighter. How could anyone grapple against a four-armed brute?

The loud cranking of machinery parted the crease and revealed the way outside. Someone entered in a hurry.

"Blasted rusting cages! Another one got loose. Can I get some help corralling it back in?"

The brutes near the door followed the messenger out. The rest hotly contested each other. As soon as the doorway was clear, Red grabbed her sack and ran.

She almost tripped over her feet during her mad dash to freedom. She was already outside by the time Ulmaids shouted, "Wait! Where'd it go?"

The facility's mighty sprawl made her next move difficult to discern. There were many alleyways to run down created by the stacks of crates, but hardly any nooks to hide in. At a loss for good options, she darted behind the largest red crate hoping to blend in. Several aliens exited the room nearby and split in their pursuit. The crate along her back shook slightly. From within came a ferocious growl.

She was not keen on the mystery inside giving her hiding spot away, so she slinked between other crates, along the wall, and creeped ever closer to the horizon made of gates. Her warning about the ripening, harvesting, and weeding had to make it back home. But would she be able to locate her way out of this labyrinth?

When she stumbled upon the cage she was detained within, hope bubbled up inside. She wanted information from Denish. She neared Denish's cage but jumped back in horror. Inside, only a grotesque monstrosity remained. Jet black spots and oozing oil across its charcoal body made her wonder: was this Denish?

The beast twisted itself. Sharp teeth snapped at Red from behind the bars. She screamed. Smoke emitted from the monster. Had the aliens injected Denish with some type of poison? How could they do that to their own people?

She ran until she reached the gates without stopping for a further breath. To her left and right, glowing options stretched endlessly. She picked the side she was most confident with and into the portals she peered as she ran alongside them. A handful of them had images now appearing clearly, unlike the abstract swirls she was used to. Some were terrestrial, like the inside of caves, while others presented a window into the emptiness of space. She hoped to recognize her people gathered on the other side, but how long had she been missing? Days? A week? Was anyone even waiting or had they designated her a lost cause to a foolish expedition?

Inside one gate, a small group of people whom she believed to be spiritual folk won her attention. They knelt before the gate. They waved their arms dressed in exotic tangerine robes and occasionally bowed toward her end. They worshiped from within a stone temple, ceilings as high as the Alpha capital building and white stone walls that had not seen a speck of dirt since they were quarried from the ground. Pillars with black and white swirled patterns stretched far beyond, back towards an entryway that struck her as curious. A soft yellow light shone inward, perhaps through an exterior exit, but the color was not the orange sun she was used to.

Her Rover mind burst with wonder. This did not look like any place she had ever visited. Was this finally proof that humanity still existed elsewhere among the stars? Oh, how she wanted to leap through this gate and converse with the temple dwellers! What wonders could she learn about the remnants of humanity? Was their home like hers, a wayward colony living out their meager lives upon an inhospitable mistake?

Red resisted the powerful urge to document these people and instead refocused on the task at hand. Despite their misplaced beliefs, warning others of the impending doom seemed like the right thing to do.

Into the gate, she shouted, "Can anyone hear me? You're in danger!"

The stranger's elated smiles raised the question of whether they could understand each other. If these gates truly were connected across her galaxy, there was no telling what language these people spoke. With no time to dawdle, she resumed running and yelling into each gate she passed.

The image of a menacing hunk of metal caused her to pause again. It looked like a robot. Could this device be a weapon? Unimaginable technology like this did not exist on Abeona-2. The evidence that humanity existed elsewhere among the stars grew stronger. Regardless of where in the galaxy it hailed from, protection was exactly what she needed.

"Hey, robot! Can you see me? Jump in here!"

It seemed to hesitate before lunging through the gate. The robot emerged and was twice the size she anticipated. To avoid becoming a part of the crater it pounded into the ground, she skipped back and shielded her head from the flying concrete. To her surprise, she noticed a man inside the armor. Latches on the suit's sides locked him within. Was he trapped?

She knelt and uncoupled his helmet to lift it off his head. The man was young, but older than her. His thick hair was black, unlike the people on Abeona-2. Slight scars across his face looked sort of scary. His dazed but fierce eyes told a tale different from her own.

She reached for other couplings on his suit and said with delight, "I'm so glad you came through. I could really use your help."

The man blinked and shook his head. "What happened? Where am I?"

He spoke the old-world English. Red adapted. "Listen, calm down. You're okay. You're safe. I know you probably took a real beating traveling through that gate, but you made it to the other side so no more pain. What's your name, friend?"

His eyes fluttered over the facility and came to rest upon her. "I'm King! Who the heck are you? And what are you doing touching my suit?"

Before she could answer, a snarl behind them made her heart stop. She turned to see an oozing beast lurking between a pair of crates. Black oil seeped from its skin and formed puddles on the ground. Smoke emanated outward from the widening pool. Barely visible spots of green dotted its underside.

"Denish? Denish el Zulack! It's me, Red!" she pleaded. She climbed to her feet and threw her hands cautiously out. "Denish! Snap out of it! They've done something to you!"

Denish bared their teeth. With each encroaching step, their smoke cloud rolled closer to her until covering her shoes and climbing up her legs like a creature possessed. A slight whiff made her cough. She cupped her sand scarf over her mouth, but it did little to help.

"Oh gosh!" King screamed. "That thing is going to eat us alive!" He struggled and coughed inside his metal prison as the smoke overcame him. "I've still got no power! I'm going to need a little help!"

The smoke rose above their heads. The beast howled incessantly. Other monsters out of sight joined in a frightful chorus. If the aliens were smart, they would investigate the epicenter of this disturbance. Red would have to find her home another time. She believed their best option was to retreat through this man's gate. But the thick, billowing smoke disoriented her and she could no longer locate it. Rather than blindly search and accidentally fall prey to the beast prowling nearby, she set her sights on the only remaining visible point of reference: the tall wall.

"We're going to be fine!" she said partially for him but mostly for herself. "I know you don't know where you are, and frankly I barely know myself, but we're going to figure this out. Right now, I need your help finding somewhere to hide because some really bad aliens are looking for us."

Thick feet stomped just beyond her vision. With jittery fingers, she managed to uncouple King's remaining latches and yank him out.

"Come on! Get moving!" she demanded. Hand in hand, she pulled him toward the nearest part of the wall.

He coughed. "But my suit! I can't leave that behind!"

"If we stay, we're going to suffocate, get eaten, or worse!"

King ripped his hand through her fingertips. He hustled back and lifted the leg of his suit. Dragging it behind them, he grunted. The veins on his neck looked ready to burst.

"I can't believe this!" Red ran back and lifted the other foot. "Oof!" It was heavier than she expected and she already suspected a challenge. "I don't think I'm helping at all."

"No, you are! Come on. Pull on one, and two, and one…"

They stumbled out from the haze and spotted the wall's edge straight ahead. Red let the suit drop and frantically pounded the wall's uniform surface in hopes of finding one of those hidden doors.

"There's got to be an entrance along here somewhere. I've seen them open before. Help me look!"

"What, like a secret passageway?"

"Yeah, I suppose!"

"Move over. I got it."

King dragged his suit into a tight hiding space between two crates and took the pair of gauntlets with him. He placed his ear upon the wall. He pounded against it with his heavy fist. "No…not here." He reached up higher. "Wait. There's something up there! Lift me up. Wait, reverse that."

Red climbed onto his shoulders. Once steady, King handed her a gauntlet. It was a struggle to lift it, slip it over her hand, and pound along the wall. King slowly shimmied down the perimeter.

"More to the left. No, more," she said.

A growl from the smoke nearby made King's body stiffen.

"Whoa!" Red almost toppled over. "Hold steady!"

"I think that thing is still on our tail! Find the door already!"

Red pounded until a section of concrete slid back to reveal an entryway upon a ledge. She climbed inside.

Denish emerged from the smoke and galloped toward King. "Give me your hand! I'll pull you up!" Red shouted.

King winked and waved her back. After giving himself a runway, he charged the wall, ravenous jaws at his heels, ran vertically up the smooth stone, and lifted himself onto the ledge.

Red grabbed his arm and tugged him inward away from further danger. "What were you thinking? That was completely unnecessary showboating!"

He glanced back, chuckling. Denish paced the wall's base until running off elsewhere. "I'm used to buzzer-beating performances. You'll get used to it."

His bravado did not comfort her. She shoved his gauntlet into his stomach and faced the dark passageway before them. She figured it had to be less dangerous than staying outside.

He must have thought the same thing.

They cautiously entered the darkness.

ROVER ENTRY #1066

King followed Red further inside the wall's interior. The entryway groaned behind them, scraping concrete until it slammed flush. They were plunged into obscurity.

"H-hey, you got a light?" King asked. "We didn't just walk into our own tomb, did we?"

"Hold on." Red poked at the darkness but could not find a wall.

"Don't go thinking a big guy like me is afraid of the dark…I'm just used to being around the bright light is all."

"Uh huh."

Red opened her sack and drew an illumination stick. She cracked its casing. A low, red glow defined a wall annoyingly close given her fingertips must have just missed it. A single switch looked easy enough to operate. She flipped it. The walls themselves illuminated, growing bright with light.

Shelving units with little boxes lined the walls. Suspended countertops and numerous cabinets hung above them. No other door was at once apparent. If you solely considered the room's size, it was sort of cozy.

"I think we'll be safe in here for now. Thank you, King."

"Don't mention it. Hey, how about you? What's your name?"

"Red. What was with your getup out there?" She pointed at his gauntlets, the last remaining piece of the metal suit that had hid his whole body. Now he stood before her in a thin white top and shorts. His shirt was closely knit. It looked soft yet dense, resistant to sand squiggling through, but it was not of a leather which was the only textile she knew of to be so impervious. His blue and gray shorts were of a similarly comfortable but impermeable material. Compared to her cactus fiber pajamas, the only truly soft materials she owned and even those itched, these looked cloud-like in nature. Her eyes gravitated toward his muscular and toned arms. She had not seen a lot of men this closely before nor with as little clothing. He absentmindedly gawked around the room, picking at a scab on his knuckles. Several feelings collided inside her. It was sort of embarrassing to be in his presence. She would never find herself so underdressed unless she were preparing for bed. There was also intrigue.

King noticed her staring. "A getup? I could ask you the same thing. What are you supposed to be, a post-apocalyptic desert warrior?" He looped fingers around his eyes to mimic her goggles.

She huffed and turned toward the shelves. "Watch it. Going back for your stupid suit almost got us shredded."

King chuckled. "Yeah. It *was* a risky play. But that was a premium power-suit you were trying to get me to ditch. Like, you recognize what that was, right? Pro Mauler Hill equipment?"

"A what-hill?" she shrugged.

His mouth fell agape, but he smirked and brushed it away. "I'm just gonna take that as a no."

Unlike her, Red noticed he seemed to take things in stride. If they were going to survive in this room for an undetermined amount of time, then someone would have to be serious and start assessing their situation. There were many nooks in the room. She opened several drawers filled with strange glowing instruments. She observed them from above and at different angles to attempt to ascertain the risk of touching one of them. Being unsure overall, she gently pushed the drawers shut.

King paced the room. "Growling monsters, hidey-hole walls, and did I hear you say something about aliens back there? I'm pretty sure we're not in the city anymore. Right?"

"I don't even think we're on either of our planets anymore."

King scratched his head. "Well, which planet are we on then?"

She expected more surprise at the insinuation of off-world travel, but perhaps his colony had retained the means of spaceflight. This scant evidence that other living colonies existed once again ignited her Rover curiosity. Later, when survival was not the most pressing concern, she would hound him with a thousand questions and record every answer in her Journal.

He gradually walked past a row of cabinets and swung compartments open. "Hey, do you think they got anything to eat up in this closet?" He picked up a rubbery doodad and squeezed it gently.

"Don't touch that!" She skipped over. "We don't know what it does!"

Startled by her scream, he flung it back inside. It shot black bubbles out of one end. Red wafted them into a wall. They sizzled, scarring the stone with pocked craters, until fully dissipated.

Red slammed that drawer shut. She waved her hands until she locked in King's attention. "Hey! We're probably on an alien world surrounded by unknown technology. Look. I'm as curious as you are, but we need to proceed carefully!"

"Sorry. I don't know about you, but I got somewhere to be. I can't stalk around this dump oohing and aahing at every little thing. Let's just find an explosive, chuck it at that beast, and get back out there to the portal I fell through."

"Zero chance. That monster is only one of many obstacles in our way. Believe me, we're going to be here for a while."

"You've gotta be kidding me. Really?" His feet continued to thump as he paced the room. He threw up a finger. "Say, what's the deal with that blue waterslide that brought me here? Scrap. I felt like I was being pulled apart. And the screeching. It was awful."

Red quickly diverted her eyes. She never had a hand in the atrocities that created them, but she felt an unfair guilt knowing her people did. "I...I-I didn't hear anything like that. Weird."

"Really? It was the only thing I could..."

"You're talking about a gate, right? Did you not see an electric metal archway where you came from? Wispy blue portal in the middle? Probably powers your entire city?"

"Uh, no. Things around me make electricity from the usual sources. You know, solar, water, vibrant steel?" He tilted his head curiously. "Is that not normal for you? Where are you from exactly?"

"Vibrant steel? What's that?" Still investigating, Red opened a closet and clapped happily. What appeared to be boxes of dried protein-like foodstuffs filled the shelves. She had no idea what the writing on the packages said, but she recognized food and would analyze it with her chemistry field kit to be sure.

"Power metal. Electric alloy. Don't tell me you don't know about conductive metal. It's only the number one export in the galaxy."

"Conductive metal...yes. That is what the gates are made of. You call it vibrant steel? Huh." She plucked out her Journal and jotted this revealing linguistic discovery down. "Does this mean it's human-made?"

"Nope. We mine it out of the ground."

She paused mid-note. "That doesn't make sense. The gates were on my planet before we arrived. Who would have uncovered them prior to..." Her eyes grew wide. "They were here before us?"

"What are you talking about?"

Red flipped through her Journal. She opened her mother's side by side. The best chemical dating of the gates placed them well over several billion years old and beyond the test's reliability. Academics mostly regarded that as an error. How could a metal structure be that old and still stand? Yet, what if the tests were right? What if their captors constructed them galactic eons ago? What if the gates once glowed as clearly as they do now? Could humanity have stumbled upon dysfunctional relics and dismantled them not knowing they were dormant alien structures?

She squeezed her pencil and placed its tip upon a fresh page. "I need to know everything about where you're from! Tell me, now!"

"Whoa! I like the enthusiasm! I'm glad to talk up everything going on back home, but there's something about you that tells me I need to start at the beginning. Like *the* beginning. Are you ready for a galactic history lesson?"

"Yes!"

King shared all about the galaxy beyond Abeona-2. He confirmed what she knew, her colony was one of a handful of early expeditions to the galaxy's edge. These parties were lost to the history books, never heard from again. As a result of those perceived initial tragedies, the home world ceased further ventures of that distance. Instead, humanity settled on fully colonizing several portions of their immediate galactic neighborhood. King was from this reigned in frontier.

Red finally learned why no one ever reached out to her colony. Everyone thought they were all long departed.

Next, he revealed what she did not know. The home world, Earth, was a planet she only knew from long-believed dead broadcasts. These radio messages that slowly crossed the stars, often mistaken as signs toward the Great Answer, were indeed from centuries long passed. Yet this did not mean their origin was from an extinct culture. No. A civilization still lived and thrived in the birthplace of her people.

Her hand trembled as she recorded that fact. This knowledge would change everything.

"I can't believe it. This is an incredible revelation." Red whispered.

She closed her eyes. Tears welled up near the edge. Colonies across the stars were out there and they were overwhelmingly more successful than her home. Her heart swelled with immense hope. She could return with aid for Abeona-2! Food, raw resources, perhaps modern terraforming power to calm the terrornadoes.

But more importantly, she needed to recruit help to counter the alien's plans. Somehow, she needed to speak to the colonists of one of these connected worlds. She knew this would be no simple task. Schooling had taught her just enough about history and politics to wonder if anyone would believe her. She was a sole traveler from an unknown world with an almost unbelievable story. This made finding her home gate even more imperative. They would believe her. They could help her make others listen.

King threw a gauntlet on the ground. "This is so frustrating!"

Red opened her eyes with a start. "Ah! What's wrong?"

"Um, sorry. I'm just tired of talking. I'm ready to make my move. We need a plan. How are we going to get ourselves home?"

With her chemistry kit bubbling next to her, Red flipped through her Journal with a declared-safe protein bar in her mouth. "We're going to have to observe everything we can. This facility, the aliens, those cages, the gates, anything we can catch a glimpse of from our little doorway. We need to witness it and come to understand it. This is the safest, most reliable approach."

He tapped his fingers across his distractingly broad chest. "I'd rather punch things, but you *did* save my life and somehow survived here before me. I'm not stupid enough to not know a tactician when they're sitting in front of me."

Red smiled. "When it comes to discovering and studying the unknown, I'm your gal."

He slapped his massive bicep with a grin. "Well, if you need something smashed, then count me in. I'm a professional and, I don't mean to brag, but my team's expected to rank among the top sixty-six percent of seed place-ments for the next season."

She rolled her eyes playfully. "Sixty-six percent isn't exactly something to brag about, unless you're touting your results as being barely statistically significant."

"Hmph! Well, I'm just saying. I'll punch anyone in the face that tries to get in here. You come up with the plan and I'll watch our backs."

"Fair enough."

King watched her flip through endless pages of scrawl and scratch. "Say, what is that you got there? That little book?"

She pointed to her Journal. "This? It's a complete record of my trav-els, discoveries, and musings. It's basically my job if I had to describe it succinctly."

"Your job is to be an explorer? Like a kid's cartoon character?" He stifled a snicker. "I suppose there's all kinds of ways to spend your life."

Red gently placed her Journal down. She tried to restrain her brewing indignation. Was this guy she barely knew trying to diminish her life's work?

"What is that supposed to mean?"

He shook his head and waved politely. "Sorry. I didn't mean to sound rude. I just meant that I *personally* wouldn't want to do that. I'm more of a work-with-my-hands kind of guy. I also like to stay in one place and just settle in. It took me a while to find my home, but recently my life has finally started to make sense. That's why I gotta make it back no matter what."

There was nothing like pulling into the Omega settlement and putting her feet up on her grandpa's chair. She, too, just wanted to get home, but she was now burdened with the knowledge of the aliens' plan and no closer to locating her home gate. Large challenges loomed ahead of her. Did she have the savvy to unravel this great disaster?

And what if she were stopped? Would he return to Abeona-2 to deliver the message alone? Could he risk everything to deliver the final expedition discovery of her career?

"King, can I ask you a serious question?"

"Sure. I've got nothing to hide."

"What if I told you it was imperative that we tell humanity what's happening here? Like, our lives were insignificant compared to the delivery of this information. If we get this warning into the hands of my people, they'd believe us. They know I'm here and they're expecting something, anything about life on the other side of the gate."

She waved her Journal. "I'm not saying we don't find your gate and get you home, but it's absolutely necessary for me to get *this message* to my people. Whether I do it myself, or something happens to me and I ask you to..." Memories of her mother invaded her mind. A traffic jam of words formed in her throat. Her eyes were burning. "To...to..."

"Whoa, wait a minute." King scooted to her side. He threw an arm around her shoulders.

Her sadness broke like a fever. Her face continued warming but for another not fully understood reason. King's closeness felt foreign. They were not both working on a machine in close quarters. Nor were they each other's life mates. Where he was from, did people who were not a bonded pair get this close to each other more often?

She committed to talking through her confusing feelings. "I-it's just that I don't know what's going to happen and I don't have a plan *quite* yet and..."

He squeezed her in closer. It was alarming, exciting, but most of all it felt like safety. "Nothing's going to happen to you, lady. Don't talk like we've already lost the game. We haven't even started the first round. We're safe in here with plenty of supplies." He pointed to her Journal. "You're cooking up a plan. If I hadn't seen all this crazy stuff myself, I wouldn't have believed it. But I can tell that what you're doing here is really important and that it threatens the people I care about back home too. I want to get back, I do. But I have a feeling you're going to need help and what kind of team player would I be if I didn't stand at your side?"

He gestured around the bare room with a goofy smirk. "I'm afraid I'm the only one you've got right now."

Red warmly nodded. His resolve stirred a ball of confidence in her gut. It grew larger. Given how little she knew about this person, it may have been illogical but for some reason she was willing to believe in him.

"You're going to tell your people yourself. I guarantee it." He threw out his palm.

"It appears the handshake is a universal gesture, huh?" She grasped it tightly.

They both laughed.

He was sweet. Equal parts confident and ignorant, the grin across his face made her not want to push the logistics any further. But she had no idea what she was doing. At this point, either of them could be right. It was a real toss up and Rovers were never supposed to risk their lives with these types of odds.

The Right Play

File Under: patience, camaraderie, recruitment

Location(s): Creare, Jangala, Tenocolis

Executive Summary: My personal account created from my notes continues. I believed it important to introduce all my known associates prior to presenting the challenges we faced and how we navigated them together. I could never have predicted I would ever travel off-world, let alone across the galaxy. And yet, Creare was only the beginning.

ROVER ENTRY #1071

Red used a datapad from her sack to track their three Abeona-2 weeks in hiding. They observed their captors and recorded their every move. Poking out from the wall was dangerous and there were a few times patrolling guards almost noticed them. It pained Red to peep and do nothing as aliens released many groups of those ghastly, smoking creatures into the gates. She feared for her people and had yet to act. However, new recruits stumbled through the gates. Their lives were filled with immediate danger. Rescue missions served as much needed distractions.

Red noticed Adiquis' bright gate first, beaming like a beacon unlike any other, but King was the one who bravely insisted they investigate. This ended with him running from a monster because he had no talent for stealth, and Red venturing out to grab the boy.

"What was that tunnel?" Adiquis asked as they ran through corridors of tall containers. "It hurt my body and my ears!"

Red held his hand and aggressively led him back toward the wall. His writhing hand proved difficult to hold. A snarl made her sweat. Heavy footsteps shook the ground beneath their feet. She whipped him about and yanked him behind a crate.

Adiquis tried to pull away from her. "Ow! Be careful!"

"Be quiet!" she stressed softly while placing a gentle hand over his mouth. "We're being followed."

Dripping liquid splashed on the ground just around a corner. Smoke drifted over Red's shoe. King whistled foolishly somewhere in the distance. Hooves thumped away from their position. She towed Adiquis toward the wall again.

Adiquis gawked as they retreated. "The countryside looks nothing like I expected."

"Okay, here is the short version of what you need to know," she said as she swung a rope with a solid box of protein bars tied to the end against the wall above. "We're on some alien planet and the aliens are going to weed us all like plants." The entryway appeared. She threw the rope back up and grappled it around a chair she had secured to the floor. "Quickly! Up, up!"

Adiquis scurried up first followed by Red. From the entrance, she spotted King running circles around a beast, even managing to slap it on the behind. Maybe he was not so foolish after all. Big maybe.

Once the facility horns wailed again, as it did several times a day when beasts broke loose, King hustled back and climbed into their hideout.

"Whew! Now *that* got my heart pumping!"

"King, meet Adiquis. Adiquis, King," Red said while catching her breath.

"Yeah, we met through the gate. Had ourselves a little chat." King approached small Adiquis with a broad, extended palm. "Hey, welcome aboard, kid...I mean Adiquis. By the way, what kind of name is that? Your parents couldn't think of any normal names?"

Adiquis looked uncomfortable. He did not shake King's hand. "As an orphan who has never met his parents, I've wondered that myself my whole life."

The color drained from King's face. "I...uh...oh boy. I'm sorry. I'm just going to shut up in the corner over there." He shuffled away.

Red granted Adiquis a polite wave. "He means well. He's just not super tactful. I'm glad you're here, Adiquis. My name's Red. Are you okay after traveling through that gate? I know you said it hurt quite a bit."

She offered him a protein bar. He tore it open. When was the last time he ate, she wondered?

"Thanks. Jumping through that portal sure did hurt. And those screams."

Red looked away. "Oh…? What about them?"

"They were awful. It reminded me of the orphanage fire."

They both stood silent. Each recalled a bitter memory.

Adiquis shook his head and pumped his fists. "But I did it to save my friend, Ms. Petras! She has a plan!"

"Who is that?" Red crouched down.

"She's a scientist. She wants to dismantle the Autocracy."

King, listening patiently from a distance, jumped back in letting out raucous laughter. "*Dismantle* the Autocracy? That's a good one! Her and what army?"

"Well…um," He pointed at the two of them. "I guess whoever I can find on this side of the portal." He shrugged. "She had a plan to recruit fighters and reclaim her marbles."

"Eh…" King scratched his head. "That doesn't exactly inspire confidence."

"Marbles? What are those?" Red asked. "Are they some type of weapon for fighting?"

Red thought she was wrong because King looked befuddled, but Adiquis said, "Yes! They shoot intensified electric bolts! Although, I'm not sure how. I bet Ms. Petras understands."

"Hold on," Red said. "Your friend is a scientist with a plan who has access to super weapons? She sounds like someone I'd like to meet. I could use another egghead in here." She winked toward King.

King rolled his eyes. "No offense taken. Just don't forget about me. I wouldn't want either of you to bruise a brain cell. If we ignore for a moment that marbles are toys, these particular one's sound pretty hardcore. I say we get them."

Red almost patted Adiquis' head, but she drew back when his eyes narrowed. Instead, she smiled gently. "Don't worry. We'll help you rescue your friend. We're going to need all the help we can get."

Adiquis stared up and smiled. He looked so pure. "Thank you. Thank you so much. I really want to get back to her. She makes me feel…safe."

"I'm glad to hear."

He nodded slowly. "But to do that we're going to need to take on the government."

Red flipped through her Journal. "King, I recall you mentioning this Autocracy briefly before. What exactly are we looking at here? Are they part of the alien's forces?"

King shook his head. "Affiliated with these monster ranching clowns? What would make you think that? No, they're definitely human."

"Well, I supposed if they were the enemies of humanity, then…"

He sighed. "Things aren't so black and white out there, Red. Look. I'm not the closest follower of politics, but just know that in the rest of the galaxy humans are just as much of a threat to each other as the aliens. If you're thinking of helping him and taking on the Autocracy after we get out of this prison, know that you're going to need an entire army."

A military, Red pondered. A combat organizational structure she had only read about in her school texts. Abeona-2 had never had a need for one. She would have to leave such matters entirely in the hands of others if the time came for her to advocate for Adiquis.

"I don't know much about that," she said, "but I do think we need someone from a powerful planet."

"Like Earth?" King suggested.

She smirked. "From what I've heard, that'd be a real boon to our efforts. But what are the odds…"

King jumped up and ran to the room's still ajar entryway. "Red! We've got another tourist!"

Red joined at his side and spotted a young woman running erratically through the facility. A monster stalked closely behind.

They pulled Minnie into their hideout and barely had a conversation before she passed out.

When she awoke, she surprised everyone by saying there was little a good night's sleep and nutritious food could not remedy. She and Adiquis immediately did not get along. Apparently Adiquis had a prejudice against people from the home world. Minnie avoided devoting much energy arguing with him.

After playing mediator for a short time, Red shared what she knew about the gate's origins, vibrant steel, and the interesting properties the material exhibited. King, Adiquis, and Minnie all shared as well. Each had witnessed the element display an even greater diversity of power. This enlightening conversation led to many new pages in Red's Journal.

No more than half a day passed when Olyana joined them, an inspiring individual to Red. Their new leader acted swiftly. Olyana used the small crater King's suit pounded into the ground as a reference point to determine which gate belonged to whom. All except Red's. No one had seen her emerge from it and she could not remember where it was.

Olyana led them to her own gate. Red was awed when she carried King's stashed suit with ease. No one was completely sure if people could go back through the gates yet. Olyana bravely tested it and returned to escort each one of them back to her planet.

Red was not eager to travel through again. She did not want to hear the cries. She believed she was the only one who knew the truth about the wailing. It continued to rack her with guilt. She let Adiquis, King, and Minnie be chaperoned ahead of her.

With Red tugging at her jacket and standing last, Olyana must have read her mind.

"Red person, it is time for you to go through. Take my hand and it will be fine."

"M-my name is Red and yes, I know. I just don't want to feel like my insides are being pulled to the outside, you know?"

"I do."

"You've been through the gate eleven times! That must be agonizing."

"It is."

"Well, you could have just asked us to go through on our own. You didn't have to escort us all back."

"No, it is best I do it this way. If someone or something were to return without me, my comrades would destroy it on sight."

"Oh!" Red was surprised at the overwhelming response. "I'm glad things are safe on the other side."

"Not safe, but rather controlled. My people have participated in war for hundreds of years. We are used to this."

A colony gripped by war? That gave Red some pause.

Olyana outstretched her palm. "Please. Take my hand and have peace in your heart that I will take care of you."

Red decided to trust this woman. She certainly exuded a confidence that was convincing. Besides, Red had already crossed one too many Rover boundaries so she might as well seek solutions in the same way. Together they neared the shimmering wall. But just as they were about to step through, Olyana's grip quivered like hers. As amazing as this warrior woman was, she too was human. Red hoped she had not placed too tremendous a burden upon Olyana.

ROVER ENTRY #1072

The cries of the children continued to disturb Red, but travel felt quicker the second time. On the other side, a massive armed force greeted them. Soldiers wore garments she was unfamiliar with and there were so many weapons.

The four young travelers followed Olyana through a wide, verdant valley. A large settlement waited for them at the end. This place confused Red. The lack of metallic walls made it appear primitive, although she could not discern what the buildings were actually constructed with. Perhaps this dark, textured material, which had a passing resemblance to the thick fauna growing out of the ground, was the result of a hyper advanced process. Accounting for grasses and the cacti farms, there were not a lot of plants on Abeona-2 for her to draw conclusions from.

Contradicting her first impression, she started to notice glowing technology intertwined within the settlement. Electronic doors, elaborate clothing, and bright lights upon every street corner hinted at a stable, safe society. What truly took her breath away was the magnificent colony ark that overlooked it all. The beautiful and bright hull looked just as her school texts described the ancient ships to be. It existed in stark contrast to the salvaged, decaying husks she was familiar with.

"Wow! That's a vintage Colony Star Cruiser!" Minnie said, running toward the vessel. "What a funny thing to see!"

"You aren't still flying around in steel cans on the home world?" Adiquis quipped.

"I'll have you know Earth is an incredibly progressive place. Much of our technology is exported across the galaxy."

Adiquis stuck out his tongue and ran ahead.

Minnie sighed. She turned to Red. "As I was saying, I think it's neat seeing a classic starship like this in person. My dad is a real spaceship nut, believe it or not." She pointed toward the ship's wings. "The M-700's on Earth were the last to be built. They sure look different than this. Although there is something to be said about the whole retro aesthetic with the fins up top and the mounted energy turret."

"Those are our Lightning Tunnels," Olyana said behind them. "They are a devastating weapon that recently almost destroyed us all."

To her disbelief, Red perceived no exaggeration in her voice.

Olyana pointed behind them at the giant boulders inside the valley. Red thought the rocks alone kept the strange blue fog, swelling just beyond the barrier, at bay. But perhaps they had no relation to it. Instead, the landslide could be the scar of a disastrous event.

"Oh. That makes sense," Minnie said. "I hear those things are used to clear away asteroids. Definitely shouldn't fire one at point-blank range."

King trailed behind, constantly being distracted by all the native folks staring at him, until he picked up his pace and strolled beside Olyana. "Say, those were some pretty fancy moves you pulled back there on the monsters. Where'd you learn to fight like that?"

Olyana's eyes stayed focused toward the ship ahead. "As the Captain, I underwent years of close-quarter combat training to protect myself from any threat. If I were to become incapacitated without an heir to take my place, my people would be gravely vulnerable."

"Do you have a kid? You can't be that much older than me and I sure as scrap couldn't raise a littler version of myself."

"I have no heir nor have I begun planning on adopting one either. But that time may soon come." She turned her head toward King. Her face was soft. "Why do you ask?"

"I mean…" He felt his cheeks flush. "Hey, listen! I'm sorry! I didn't mean to imply anything. I'm definitely not interested, lady." He smiled sheepishly and let Olyana get ahead of him a few paces.

After a moment, Olyana waved him back forward with a small smirk upon her face.

"Hey, sorry again about that," he said. "Sounded like a sensitive subject."

"There is no need to apologize. The topic is merely factual. I have no shame or worries relating to it. Did I hear you say you are interested in my fighting style?"

He laughed and clasped his fist in his palm. "Exactly! Whew! I'm so glad we're talking about something I'm comfortable with. So, can you show me any of your metal moves?"

Olyana glanced at his arms. "From the looks of you, perhaps. After we settle in, ask me again and I will see if I can set up a sparring session in the armory." She smiled. "I could use fresh meat."

King jumped. "Excuse me?"

ROVER ENTRY #1073

Olyana led the four travelers inside the ark and up an elevator to a spacious hall she called the war room. Tall white pillars encircled an elegant, long table in the center of a circular set of short stairs leading downward. A wall covered in computer screens displayed what Red presumed was live footage from around the ship. Scenes of the settlement outside and charts overflowing with data also played. On the entrance's far opposite side, a gorgeous sprawling window overlooked the valley below.

A group of adults greeted them and introduced themselves as members of the War Council. They wore garments of two notably distinct colors and styles. There were those in apricot that Red noticed Olyana spoke with warmly. The others in plum were purely formal with her. The language they spoke sounded like a waypoint between the old-world English and her own derivative. It was fascinating and thankfully coherent.

Olyana instructed Red's group to sit at one end of the table together. Servers treated them to drinks and light snacks upon trays. Red politely accepted a glass of stunningly clear water unlike the liquid of her home. The grain-like snacks were a welcome change of taste from the protein bars she had survived on during their hiding. She had failed to identify the bar's strange flavor, slightly familiar yet mostly foreign.

Folks rushed to each other from across the room and whispered in pairs. This type of gathering reminded her of formal affairs akin to the Rover annual research conference. At that familiar function, patrons shook hands, presented their latest research findings desperately wanting to attract interest, and tried their best not to offend anyone. She hoped the others knew this as well because they were about to make their vital first impression.

Olyana took her seat and every remaining person in the room did the same except for a stoic older man in orange standing to her right. Red could tell Olyana respected him by the way she watched as he spoke.

"Hello, travelers," the man waved warmly. "My name is Azul Irinelly and I am the advisor to Captain Olyana."

Another man in an intricate set of plum armor stood next. Numerous medals embellishing his metallic uniform clanked as he rose. It distracted Red a little.

"Hello and well met, prophets. I am Cardinal Murcario and I am the leader of the Tribe of the Divine. Our scriptures foretold the visit of our brothers and sisters from across the stars. News of your impending audience has brought my people a great renewal of faith. I hope we can learn much from your tales and in what ways the Divine has touched your lives." The Cardinal returned to his seat.

Azul smiled despite a twitching eye. "Thank you, Cardinal. I am sure if any of our travelers would like to discuss the Divine further, they will seek you out."

He waved toward his guests. "As I understand it, the four of you are in search of assistance for a grand conflict. We must get to know each other, trust each other before we may discuss anything you desire of us. We are navigating a time of great turmoil ourselves and must be selective with our resources. Tell us, from where across the galaxy exactly do each of you hail from?"

Red was about to raise her hand when King blurted out, "I'll go first!" He jumped out of his chair and onto the table. There were more than a few gasps from the room. He flexed and said, "The name's King Lee Cunningham of the planet Balamanda, but you can just call me Killer King!" He squeezed his fists. Rings upon his fingers illuminated. Eyebrows raised and a few guards tightened their grips on their weapons.

Red worried he would blow their entire greeting. She placed a steady hand on King's arm and mustered a laugh she hoped did not sound completely fake. "You're such a kidder. I thought you told me a story about how they call you *Little* King."

A few people smirked and the tension loosened significantly. King took his seat with his head hung low and his fists faded. "You didn't need to go and tell them all that."

"I'm trying to make a good first impression!" Red whispered with a smile plastered on her face.

"I know! I thought we needed a dramatic entrance!" he muttered back, patting her shoulder while grinning.

Azul responded with amusement. "I am glad to see you remain in good spirits, young man. And you, little one?"

Adiquis stood and bowed his head.

Red leaned in closer to him. She whispered, "You don't need to go, little guy. I know all this politicizing might seem intimidating."

Adiquis smirked. "Actually, I've studied a thing or two about diplomatic engagements." He gestured warmly with one arm behind his back and his other open, raised palm to the room. "My name is Adiquis and I am from the planet Tenocolis, the capital of the Autocratic empire. It is a pleasure to meet each and every one of you. I notice that you do not speak in contractions. Is that a cultural value of yours?"

Azul leaned close to one of his colleagues who spoke into his ear. "Ah. Are you referring to the shortening of the language using the apostrophe? We have read such a manner of speaking in a few of our archives. However, none of our ancient video materials ever enunciated it for us. Therefore, we do not use them."

"I can understand how that could be possible if all of your references were of a military, scientific, or technical nature. I do not think I ever came across a contraction in any of my school texts. Well, I hope our first impression upon you is favorable and my effort to avoid contractions in this moment demonstrates our respect for your customs and eagerness to work together. I have a friend in danger on my home planet. I want to get back to her. Hopefully, we will earn your trust and prove ourselves as being worthy of your help."

Red's mouth fell slightly at his response. It seemed Adiquis was quite learned.

"Young one," Azul smiled, "you certainly have left an impression upon me. I am grateful we have met and look forward to learning more about you. Feel free to return to the style of speech you find most agreeable."

Red nodded warmly as Adiquis took his seat. She raised her hand and stood slowly. "Hello. My name's Red. I come from the harsh desert world Abeona-2. It's a planet on the edge of the galaxy. Like your ancestors over a millennium ago, my people established one of the first colonies during the Great Expedition. Despite our similar origins, I can tell our settlements have taken different paths. I'm excited and eager to learn as much as I can about you for my inevitable return."

"Thank you," Cardinal Murcario said. "It appears that our people have been greatly blessed by the Divine. To have lasted this long despite our planets being seemingly inhospitable is a demonstration of mercy. Have your people heard of the Great Divine as well?"

Red looked up toward the ceiling. She traveled all this way only to be subjected to the Divine once again. Was this some type of supernatural punishment? "Um, yes. We have a faction of settlements that worship the Divine. Although, I'm not sure if their practice and rituals would be recognizable to you."

Cardinal Murcario chuckled. "The Divine speaks to us all in different ways. I am sure your settlements are hearing exactly what they need."

Despite her discomfort, she nodded out of respect. "Secondly, I have grave news about the aliens on the other side of your gate. I'd like to speak with your leadership as soon as possible. Thank you." She took her seat.

Measured, cool, and short. She regarded her appeal as professional, a speech to be proud of. She questioned whether King's dramatic approach had value considering the gravity of it all. Yet, she recalled how these bureaucratic events usually went. It was important to plant the seed of cooperation early. Waiting for leadership to reach back out was always best. Political relationships were born out of respect and patience.

Last to speak, Minnie pushed against the table and let the chair roll. Her feet thumped the floor and she took a slow stand. She gazed above and around the room, anywhere but upon the curious audience.

"Hi everyone," she said with a soft voice. "My name's Minnie and I come from the home world, Earth. I'm...King had a cool title so I suppose I should say that I'm also the daughter of a Priest of the Divine."

Many of the unfamiliar faces leaned forward eagerly. Cardinal Murcario nodded. "It is an honor to be in the presence of a *Divine Princess*." Several folks nodded and murmured in agreement. "Please continue, my dear daughter."

"Oh wow." Her face flushed. "I haven't been called one of those in a long time. I suppose I do know the rites and rituals, but I'm not sure any of that will help us right now." She lowered her head. Nothing on the floor, but anyone could have been forgiven for thinking there was by the way she was staring at it. "I'm afraid it's possible the Divine has left us to our own fates."

"Nonsense," Cardinal Murcario said. "Keep the faith and you will be rewarded."

Minnie raised her chin. She smiled politely. "Thank you. I'll try to remember that. While I wait for Divine intervention, I suppose it's important for me to explain what's going on. I've seen up close the horrible acts these monsters, the Seekers, are committing. I've witnessed the chaos that humanity can cast itself in when all hope seems lost. Before my eyes, the beasts ravaged people I've grown to care for..."

She paused and choked back tears.

Cardinal Murcario rose from his chair. Azul eyed him suspiciously but did not interject as the Cardinal crossed the room. He stopped at Minnie's side and placed a soft hand on her shoulder.

"My Princess, I too have lost those most dear to me in a recent conflict. My family and life-long comrades, gone to the great plane beyond. Yet, remember your teachings. Scripture promises of the Divine afterlife where all souls await us when our time ends."

Minnie nodded. She delicately pulled away from the Cardinal's touch. "Yes, sir. I'm familiar with the Word. Scripture also promises those who help themselves will then be helped by the Divine. So, I..." She closed her eyes.

After a deep breath, she stared at the tops of the room's looming pillars. "What were we doing wrong? On Earth, I mean. First there was the initial attack on my church during a blood drive. Was that wrong? And then the city burned. Was my dad not supposed to open the church to all those refugees? Then my mom..."

Side conversations around the room fell silent.

The hum from the ship's systems grew louder with every passing second. Red wanted to say something wise just to break the stillness, but she did not know what would be appropriate. Much that was happening was outside her comfort zone. Minnie shared vulnerable personal thoughts out loud and about her struggles with things that Red herself would not dare discuss with strangers. Minnie's heart stood curiously open. Would such an emotional appeal resonate with the leadership? Red had her doubts.

Minnie ended the silence by sobbing quietly into her sweatshirt. She wiped her tears away. She straightened her face and said, "I mean, what's the point of coming here and talking about the Divine? Taking matters into my own hands and praying didn't help me back on Earth so perhaps that wasn't how I was supposed to help myself. I've been thinking about it since I left. Maybe I need to take a more pragmatic approach. Instead of just prayer and myself, I must now ask for your help. I can't do this alone. I simply don't have the energy anymore. I hate the thought that my future may be out of my control, but I don't know what else to do."

Olyana cleared her throat. The entire room turned. She slouched in her chair. Her eyes looked exhausted.

"Minnie, Princess of Earth. While I am not yet convinced these other-worldly problems should necessarily be my people's priorities, I am willing to listen to any proposed solution. The beasts you describe are likely the same we fight today. If so, we may yet share a common goal in their extermination."

Minnie drew a piece of paper from her pocket. "Absolutely they are. But you have to understand the monsters are not the true threat. I've learned from Red that they are merely tools of the aliens. What I have here is a plan to defeat them."

She handed it to Cardinal Murcario.

"Let me see," he said, unfurling the paper. "Step one: Rescue Ms. Petras. Step two: Repair the Galactic Communication Relay. Step three: Counterattack."

A rumbling of low voices spoke among themselves.

Red turned to King with surprise. He shrugged.

She did not know Minnie had already devised a plan of her own. This irked Red because she had fashioned herself as the de facto leader among them. She had a few plans of her own that took into consideration all the observations she had made since arriving on Creare. She knew the alien's patrol schedules, their spaceship numbers, an approximate size of their staff, and a rough understanding of the type of weapons they carried. To her knowledge, Minnie had none of that, just all the stories the group shared during their long talks in the hideout.

"Hey!" Adiquis yelled. He hopped out of his chair and thrusted a finger at Minnie. "Who said *you* could save Ms. Petras? Getting the rescue party is *my* job!"

Many people around the table lobbed other questions at Minnie all at once. She began to answer one, but then diverted to another. "Yes, but… well, you see…I'm not sure about that…" She seemed overwhelmed by it all. "I have more to it. There's more to my plan."

Olyana waved her hand until the room quieted down. "Princess, what intelligence is this plan based on? And who is this Ms. Petras?"

Minnie pointed at Adiquis. "I've overheard him exalt the amazing genius of his mentor, Ms. Petras, a researcher of vibrant steel technology. I've also learned that vibrant steel is of alien origins. It's crazy, but I've seen crazier these days. We may be able to use the alien's technology against them."

Olyana beckoned Azul close and they whispered to each other. Olyana shrugged and Azul waved his fingers haphazardly in circles. Perhaps, like Red, they were unfamiliar with vibrant steel and its history. Red raised her hand.

Azul pointed to her.

"Excuse me, but vibrant steel is the glowing electrical metal's official name which the gates are made of. The gates are the swirly portals which we traveled through. This material emanates unlimited energy."

Olyana closed her eyes. "The altar. Those resonating metal pieces along the valley soil." She pointed toward Cardinal Murcario. "You have seen the metal as well."

Cardinal Murcario nodded and walked the piece of paper to her. "Yes. What they say could be true."

"And what is the nature of this research, young one?" Olyana asked.

Adiquis' eyes shot daggers at Minnie, but he turned to Olyana and smiled. "Ms. Petras has been studying this exotic metal for years. I don't like to admit a home worlder could come up with such a smart plan, but I agree. Ms. Petras can help us use the power of the steel, but she's gonna need time. We should definitely get her first so she'll have an invention ready by the time we're ready to do something big."

"I don't know," King said. "This sounds a lot like a personal rescue mission. Do we have time for that? Wouldn't it be better to recruit more allies that know how to fight?" He gripped his rings until they glowed. "Follow me home and I'll get my whole team to join us. Maybe more! We'll punch those Seeker monsters into piles of goo!"

"No," Minnie spat back. "The Seekers aren't the *only* threat. This is the way to go. Besides, with my plan, we'll get recruits a hundred times over."

"There's no promise in that!" King snapped.

"I give you my word!"

Minnie and King continued to bicker until Olyana raised her hand. She pointed at Cardinal Murcario.

"Thank you, Captain," he said. "And what is this Galactic Relay? Is it a Divine weapon?"

"A wonder perhaps?" Azul asked.

"It's no weapon," Minnie replied. "Rather, it allows us to communicate with all the modern planets. Everybody knows it has two parts: the control complex in New York and the signal station in orbit. The control complex is probably abandoned so we'll need to bring it back online before calling for more help. My plan assumes the signal station is unharmed, but I have little evidence one way or the other, I'm afraid."

"It appears to be an interplanetary far talk device," Azul said to Olyana.

Olyana read Minnie's plan carefully. "Princess, if we send this call, do you genuinely believe others will come to our aid? My experience advises me that the heart of humanity does not always move toward reason."

Minnie's face was stern. Defiant even. "They *have* to. Despite my shaken faith, I am hoping I just haven't found the Divine's true path for me yet. My way may still lie before me. Once others across the stars hear about what happened to Earth, and that it can happen to them next, they'll have to respond and I'll be there to help."

She turned and pinned her serious eyes on Red.

Red lacked a reply. Why was Minnie looking at her for moral support? The content of her words seemed logical enough, but Minnie was putting just as much trust in her faith as she did in her plan; a plan not based on reliable research. This seemed like an irrational error and Red had seen enough of that behavior committed by her planet's own Divine. Did she want to reinforce this type of conduct?

Minnie might have deciphered Red's feelings. She continued loudly for the room to hear. But her words seemed to be intended for Red. "I mean, of course we're gonna attempt everything we're capable of. And Red has a wealth of information to share with us concerning the aliens and their base of operations. I believe in us just as much as I believe in the Divine. I am *not* making a leap of faith. This is a solid plan."

The room was quiet. Cardinal Murcario even looked skeptical.

Minnie scanned the indifferent faces and said, "Anyone? Will none among you answer the call of the home world?"

Silence still.

For a moment, a flash of her friend Purple stood before Red. Her dear colleague back home hoped in the less than reliable as well, but she managed to follow the Rover path with success. Somehow, Red accepted Purple despite her flaws, and Purple would say the same about her. Minnie's hope and courage reminded her that people were complex. Would Minnie show her yet another human side of the fanatics?

Red decided to give her this one chance buoyed by her personal research.

"Oh, forget formality." Red stepped to Minnie's side and took her new partner's hand into her own.

Minnie squeezed back, surprised for sure, and thankful for the blessing she was receiving.

"I...I think she's right," Red said to the room. "I saw parts of what she described with my own eyes. With those oily monsters already going through the gates, the weeding has already started. This planet, among others, is already seeing the process unfolding. We're too far behind to waste any more time."

Red faced Minnie. "I know we don't have a lot to go on and the path forward is somewhat unclear, but I'm not afraid to attempt the unknown with a good enough plan." She turned back toward Olyana, Azul, and Cardinal Murcario. "I'm volunteering to venture forth and attempt this solution with your people's help or alone if we must. I hate to admit it, but frankly all other options I've tried to work out myself just seem worse."

Adiquis skipped to their side and slapped his hand on top of theirs. "I came here to rescue Ms. Petras and get help for all the ones considered worthless in the Autocracy's eyes. If I gotta team up with a home worlder to do it, I guess I can stomach it."

King rolled his eyes and firmly encased all their hands in his palm. He looked at his fellow travelers. "Listen. I can tell you've already made up your minds. You're not gonna be able to do this alone so I'll go with you and make sure nobody sneaks up on you all. This way I can be sure those I care about back home will be safe."

The atmosphere in the room felt frozen. Red worried if it was disrespectful to ask for help then commit in front of everyone to do it themselves.

Olyana rose. The entire council did the same. She walked past the length of the table, her echoing footsteps building tension as she strode.

She stopped in front of the four. Olyana was tall. Red felt her eyes judging her.

Olyana's gaze surveyed the others.

Red squeezed Minnie's hand.

The others did the same.

"Together you have the bravery of explorers, the determination of warriors, the confidence of the worthy, and the energy of the faithful. You will no longer need to prove your trustworthiness to me. I hereby order that we execute the first step of your plan to recruit a tactical mind and see if it comes to fruition. I hope we can discuss the rest when you return triumphantly."

ROVER ENTRY #1074

Soldiers escorted Red to her own personal resting quarters. The others were assigned similar accommodations although she did not know where aboard the ship. She wondered if unsupervised intermingling was being discouraged since they were strangers during an uncertain time, but perhaps that was only her skeptical mind being paranoid.

After her room's automatic door closed behind her and she was alone, she examined her furnishings. A one-person bed, a bath facility, and a desk, mirror, and drawer for her things. This ship was old, older even than anything she owned at home on Abeona-2. However, strenuous upkeep and plentiful resources hid that fact by the looks of the fresh linens upon the bed and shiny walls devoid of holes.

Such luxury was not taken for granted. She immediately threw herself onto the bed and delighted in the soft bounce juxtaposed to the hard floor of the storage room she slept on for the last two weeks.

Blissful comfort was instantly interrupted by the gross feeling of her soiled clothing against her skin. Even on Abeona-2 she would not have gone longer than a week without a bath during the busiest of travel seasons. She scurried out of bed and made sense of the strange water basin. One rejuvenating cleanse and the softest towel of her life later, she sat at the desk with her Journal and started documenting the incredible journey she had experienced thus far.

Early the next day, Olyana proved the earnestness of her trust. Red, King, Adiquis, and Minnie spent the morning on a factory floor within the ark. Children measured them for clothing described as impenetrable warrior suits of wonder. A frazzled man named Izack supervised the operation. He was constantly in motion trying to entertain the children who did not have a task assigned to them.

A workshop doubling as a daycare was like nothing Red had ever seen. She jotted the concept down in her Journal. Whether this was an idea worth integrating into her society was questionable, but research was research.

"Your physiques are just slightly different from ours," Izack said to Red with one child in his arms and an electronic scanning device in the other. He hovered the buzzing rectangle across her body. After consulting the device, he handed it to a girl who ran off toward a churning textile contraption. "It should not be a problem as these armors adapt to each person's individual form. But they do fit best if we alter them to be at least close to your dimensions."

"You're all significantly taller than me," Red said to the group as a child panned a measuring laser down her leg. "Well, all except the children."

"That's strange. We're all humans, aren't we?" Minnie paused for a reply. "Of course we are! Come on, laugh! That was a joke!" She giggled and tapped her chin. "Although, I do wonder why that is."

Red was happy Minnie seemed in higher spirits after the previous day's dour mood. As the children ran by, Minnie smiled and waved.

"Living in different biomes for hundreds of years may have something to do with that, dummy," Adiquis said from across the room. "Everybody where I'm from learns the basics. *Beasts, Biology, and Backgrounds: Biomes of the Galaxy*. Do they not have that text in the home world nurseries?"

A furrowed brow across Minnie's face. Adiquis' constant disrespect caused palpable tension anytime they were together.

"Come on, knock it off, Adiquis," King said from the other side of the room. He was surrounded by children poking at his flexed biceps. "People from the home world are as smart as anyone else."

As if King had just spoken gibberish, Adiquis appeared bewildered. "Who told you that?"

"Why would anyone think people from specifically the home world are dumb?"

"Because they are. They made a mess out of Autocratic space."

Minnie let out a single, brief laugh. "Wait. Wasn't it you who said the Autocracy are the bad guys where you're from?"

"Well, yeah. But…but…" He froze.

Red watched curiously, quietly. She wondered if Minnie had broken him.

"Hey, watch the threads, little one!" Minnie yelped. A child tugged her baggy top garment, pulling and stretching the cloth between his fingers.

"What is your fabric made of?" the child asked. "Our fabricators do not make anything as soft as this!" He rubbed his face all over it.

Minnie giggled softly. "It's a cotton sweatshirt. It comes from a plant which…I'm beginning to guess you don't have here in the jungle."

King lifted two children on each arm. He swung them around as they giggled and kicked their legs about. "Olyana calls this the twirling whirl wheel defense! What do you think, kids? Am I as good as her yet?"

"Picking some things up from her already?" Red asked. She was glad he found a goal worthwhile to pursue. He risked everything by following her when he could have just returned home.

"Barely! I joined her on the mat this morning and she threw me around like a toy! She said she was trying to 'appropriately gauge my skill level'," he said wistfully. "I tell you, Red. I thought I was better than that. I've got some bona fide experience blocking punches from people twice my size, but none of that seems to matter much when you're toe to toe with someone who's seen some real bad stuff."

He lowered the children and they ran off much to Izack's displeasure.

"I'm sure if you keep at it, you'll pick up a few moves. New skills require research and patience."

"Oh, I've got no doubt. We're meeting up again tonight and she's gonna actually teach me something this time. She promised!"

King noticed the child tugging at Minnie's sweatshirt. "Say, is there any way you can get me a pack of those hoodies? It'd cost me like two paychecks to snag sweet home world gear like that back on Balamanda."

"Wow," Minnie said. "I had no idea how popular my fashion choices were going to be. Had I known, I would have worn an actually luxurious piece like wool. Now *that* would have blown your minds."

Adiquis popped his head through the neck hole of his altered suit. He timidly glanced at Minnie's curious clothes. "Is…isn't that the textile harvested from the agrarian livestock known as the sheep?"

"Yeah," she replied, unamused. "Why are you saying it like that? So textbook. Do you think I don't know what a sheep is? They go *bah bah bah*, don't they? Yeah, Earth people know that."

"No…" He carefully searched for his words. "I mean, it's just that we don't have sheep on Tenocolis. The Autocracy tried a bunch of times but failed to raise livestock within the city. They, uh, did a lot of things wrong. They're still doing a lot of things wrong…" he trailed off.

Minnie's eyes floated toward Red. She smirked and shrugged. "Yeah, that's what you said. Well, I hope you don't mind me helping you fix that."

The beginning of a tiny smile began to form. "Okay," he whispered.

Red sighed, relieved. Adiquis may have been brilliant, but he was just a kid that wanted to get back to his mother…or older friend. She picked up that their relationship was complicated.

She too curiously admired Minnie's strange top. As Minnie tugged and adjusted it, a glint near her neck drew Red's attention. A Divine charm. This might have surprised her if not for Minnie's religious display at the meeting.

Despite that, she wanted to build a trustworthy, working relationship with Minnie just like the others. When survival was on the line, you needed your colonists beside you.

"Um, that's a nice piece of jewelry you have there," Red said as she pointed toward the charm. "We have the Divine Church on Abeona-2 as well."

"Oh, this?" Minnie tugged at it, bringing it into full view. "My mom gave it to me."

"Oh? My mother left me this glove." Red waved her other hand. "I guess it's sort of like a charm too."

"That's interesting. Does it have any Divine significance?"

"Oh, no. Nothing like that."

"Well, perhaps it's a blessed artifact that connects you to her no matter the distance?"

Red was not savvy on Divine details, but she was aware that believers treasured and retained artifacts to connect them to the dear of heart or departed. Despite having no supernatural fear in faking a supposed commonality under the eye of gods, respect looked the same regardless of belief. It was not worth it to debase a sacred belief.

"Oh no. It's just a glove. It was *her* glove actually. But I don't think of it in that kind of way."

Minnie tucked her charm away. "I see. Well then it isn't really like a Divine charm at all."

Red was irked. Minnie's tone sounded fine, but Red felt compelled to read between the lines. "Hm. I should get going. I have a lot to write in my Journal."

Minnie nodded and approached King instead. They struck up a boisterous conversation.

Red considered it silly of her to try to befriend a devout believer. They were colleagues by chance, nothing more.

"Hey!" Minnie yelled as she playfully punched King on the bicep. "Did I hear you right? You're gonna fight Olyana?"

"Yeah, at some point. What of it?"

She punched him again. "I'd be down for watching you two spar if you don't mind. I follow wrestling back home."

Red perked up. "M-me too. Can I come?" she asked from afar.

"Sure," King smiled. "I always do better with an audience."

Minnie crossed her arms. "Didn't you say you had a lot of writing to do, Red?"

"I-I do. But I'm sure I can record and watch at the same time. Maybe there'd be something noteworthy to witness there too."

King laughed heartily. "Oh, believe me. You're going to want to remember my moves!"

ROVER ENTRY #1075

The four travelers returned with their suits to their individual resting quarters. Red held hers in front of her and frowned at the absence of her designated color. Steel blue from neck to toe. She knew eventually she would have to acclimate to her new host's customs. She just wished it was not happening so fast.

She placed her Rover uniform back into a drawer that had cleansed it the previous day. What a wonderful machine that she absolutely needed to learn more about. She pulled off her mother's glove and placed it inside as well. Azul instructed them not to wear anything underneath the suit to ensure its functionality. She had not worn the glove long, but it already felt like the warmest part of her went missing. The suit's cold fabric brushed over her skin as she slipped inside. It gave her chills. The desert heat was much more her style.

She checked herself in a mirror and shrugged. The suit appeared baggy. It did not seem to fit her as seamlessly as promised. Staring at her exposed head, no hood to cover her hair, she realized at least one part of her uniform could accompany her. She strapped her Rover goggles on. It was not just for fashion, she told herself. It kept her hair out of her eyes.

Red joined everyone outside the ship on the beautiful, luscious, green grass. The blades parted with every gentle kick of her boots. No trudging through sand, nor a single surprise buried rock waiting to stub her toe. She started to see the charm of this world, the second to which she had traveled now. Visiting others just as beautiful seemed like a prospect she was going to enjoy.

Minnie conversed with Olyana until she noticed Red approaching. She waved Red over.

"You know, they call these suits Augmented Strength Combat Armor back on Earth," Minnie said, tugging at her suit. "I've only seen army folks wearing them on television, although these particular outfits are prehistoric. I think I've seen these markings only in history texts."

"Yeah, well I'm not super crazy about the color. Do they all look the same?" Red glanced around. Every soldier contributed to a sea of blue.

Olyana stepped beside Red. They stared at the same sea. "I knew it. I could just tell. Red one, you are a woman of habit. I had a feeling you might not take to the look." She pointed at Red's goggles.

Red felt a little embarrassed, but she smiled. "I hope it's okay. I don't exactly know all the regulations surrounding your uniform policy."

Olyana drew a red kerchief from her back pocket and tied it gently around Red's neck. "Care to have a look?" On a screen made of light emanating from her wrist she projected Red's reflection.

Red touched the fabric while admiring her image. Soft and bright. Simply that it was new, unlike anything she owned, delighted her the most.

"It's beautiful! I don't know what to say."

"Stay true to your values and words. That is all I ask."

King walked toward them picking at the loose edges of his suit. "This thin cloth doesn't exactly feel indestructible. As soon as I figure out how to power my armor again, I'm definitely switching back."

"Yeah. It's a little loose on me too." Red tugged at the spots dangling around her wrist. Olyana stepped behind her and pressed a button near her neck. Startling at first, the fabric expelled air from the inside and vacuum-fitted her body. It was interesting, like being hugged all over.

"Good," Olyana said. "It appears the measurements were exact. And despite their age, I have seen these wonders save many lives from the greatest of threats." She tapped each traveler's neck.

"Oh! These things are now a little too tight, don't you think?" Minnie tugged uncomfortably at the corners. "Nobody look until I'm done!"

Olyana chuckled. "You never do get used to that."

Two soldiers approached the group. Olyana said, "Very well. I leave you all in the capable hands of our warriors. I wish you much success and a safe return." She walked back to the ark.

Red was one of a team of six. She accompanied King, Minnie, Adiquis, and the two other soldiers. Missionary Sarenth looked excited and young. He was assigned by Cardinal Murcario. Commander Inieda appeared seasoned. Wrinkles on her face and a scowl discouraged chit-chat. She was assigned by Olyana.

"Greetings, travelers," Inieda said, pacing stiffly before the group. "The two of us are your security escorts for today's mission. It is our job to get you to the target, Ms. Petras, and extract you all safely. It will be your job to show us the way, tell us what may threaten us, and otherwise do as I say. Is that understood?"

Red nodded seriously.

Adiquis placed both fists on his chest and yelled, "Sir, yes sir!"

Inieda leaned in and glared at Adiquis. "Boy, are you mocking me?"

"Not at all, sir! You remind me of another adult I know, but I've never met anyone quite as scary as you! I'm just trying to fit in, sir!"

Her hardened veneer cracked, revealing a sudden smirk. "I like your style, kid." She ruffled his hair and picked him up, throwing him up onto her shoulders before he knew what happened. "You earned yourself one free ride."

"I'm equal parts excited and terrified!" he screamed and gripped her hair.

The team walked together through town and to the massive portal's edge swirling in the valley dirt. One after another, they leapt in.

This time Red was a little more confident. She was returning to the other side with allies!

ROVER ENTRY #1076

Red rolled out the other side.

Minnie stumbled forward and flailed toward the bars of a beast's cage. It snarled and snapped its jaws almost turning her hands into snacks, but Sarenth threw his arm around her waist and hauled her safely to the side. She yelped with surprise.

"Be careful not to get too close," he said as he released her. "Some of their claws are quite long."

"Trust me. I know." She followed his lead toward the others.

The group darted carefully between crates on their way toward Adiquis' gate. Red's documented observations provided the path and timing needed to avoid detection.

"How long have you been a soldier?" Minnie asked Sarenth.

"I have served as a holy soldier of the Divine for a few years. My father was a farmer and he thought I was going to follow him. But when I heard of young Captain Olyana's ascension across the valley, I felt strongly the Divine needed more youth like us to serve for a greater purpose. I applied and was accepted into the academy that same year."

"I did the same thing to my dad. I went to a public school instead of seminary. I think he's still waiting for me to say I made a mistake and he was right. Us youngsters have a lot to prove, don't we?"

Sarenth's steps slowed. "You have a remarkable story, Divine Princess Minnie. Yes. I believe…"

"Sarenth!" Inieda snarled quietly. "I am confident there are no dawdle doctrines in your religion. Pick up the pace!" She pointed at a gate glowing far more intensely than the rest. "Everyone is waiting to jump. Hurry along with the spunky one."

Minnie shrugged delightfully and rushed ahead, leaping through first. Everyone followed and tumbled into a cave on the other side.

Red picked herself up off the ground. She was learning that the pain of travel reliably left the body immediately upon arrival. The gate's blinding blue glow puzzled her. It illuminated the stone as bright as day. No other gate shone as brilliantly.

Adiquis waved them forward. "I think the exit is this way." He neared the cave entrance around a sharp bend and peeked out hesitantly before climbing out.

He appeared afraid. What was the Autocracy he had run from, Red wondered? Would it now seek to find *them*?

Red stepped out of the cave to a breathtaking sight. A single sun emerged from the morning's horizon. A wave of greenery unveiled across the landscape with every new ray of light. The sky looked scarlet at first, but it shifted to a hue of blue which she struggled to find the words to describe. Clean, sand-free air filled her body. She never wanted to forget the feeling.

"I will survey the area." Inieda blasted off with the power of a curious device on her back. After circling the sky a few times, she landed and handed Adiquis a datapad. She pointed to a photo on the screen. "Is this the city we are looking for?"

Red caught a glimpse of it. A distant, blurry walled structure stretched across the entire scene.

"That's the capital city. Ms. Petras is somewhere inside."

"We now have a direction. Let us begin walking."

Red kept her nose in her Journal and sketched the oasis around them. A small Rover analysis device in her pocket recorded temperature and air chemical composition datapoints. Its lights blinked and caught King's attention.

"What are you doing?" he asked. "Nobody's gonna quiz you on the Tenocolis capital."

"It's my job to record everything about the gates. But lately I've been thinking that what's on the other side counts too. I'm quite sure everything I've seen this last week is going to change my home forever. I need precise, descriptive notes."

He pointed to a sketch of the sun. "You got a note about there being only one. Why is that?"

"Where I come from, we have two."

"Two? Whoa. That'd be too hot for my taste. I'd probably roast like an oven chicken inside my suit."

Red laughed. "No one would ever wear something that crazy back home."

King stretched his arms and yawned. "How far exactly is this city? Does anyone know?"

Red watched the gentle breeze flow through his dark hair. A scene like this was uncommon on her planet. To be anywhere with the wind blowing, you would have to be stupid to take your gear off. Nothing about him had changed, but she found him more handsome.

"Maybe a day's walk," Adiquis answered him. "I think I drove it in just under six hours."

"Wait. You drive?" Minnie asked. "I just got my license a year ago."

King grumbled. "That's too far! We gotta hitch a ride or find a better way."

"That would be ideal," Inieda said at the head of the group. "If we can find any type of transport vehicle, we should commandeer it. It will also serve as a much-needed disguise for when we infiltrate their fortress."

Minnie and Sarenth walked alongside each other at the rear.

"Wow," she said. "Inieda knows her war stuff, huh?"

"Yes. She has been an Endeavoress soldier for many years. I was fortunate enough to have never faced her on the battlefield. She told me she was first a lookout over the valley before becoming a lightning shooter. Now she is a Commander Specialist."

"What's she a specialist about?"

"Special Operations. I do not know the details, but she is of the Endeavoress' elite and this mission is perfectly suited to her talents. Other more experienced soldiers have told me to trust her judgment..."

A twinkle among the clouds caught his attention. He jogged ahead and tapped Inieda's shoulder. "Look! A flying craft."

High in the sky, they spied a floating dot.

"What is that, Earth girl?" Inieda asked.

"*Earth girl*," Minnie muttered, then replied, "Are you serious? It's a hovercopter. Good for carrying people over long distances."

Inieda spat into the grass. "Your tone is unwarranted. We have not had any operating flying craft until very recently." She directed everyone to hide themselves in the grass and wait for further instructions. She waited for the hovercopter to fly overhead before she blasted into the sky after it. The craft landed near them shortly after.

Inieda shouted from within. "Get in!"

The team climbed into the back of the noisy vehicle. An unknown woman sat behind the cockpit controls. The pilot kept her head facing forward. Red noticed that fear had made a home in her eyes.

Inieda had a pistol pointed at her. "Bring us to the city."

Everyone took a seat, but Red failed to do so by the time the craft made a loud noise. Her feet scattered beneath her like there was a quake. She grabbed onto anything not moving and caught a glimpse of the ground out the window. It darted in complete disorder. Her stomach churned as they rose and dropped repeatedly.

"Careful!" King said. He gripped her arm and pulled her onto the seat next to him. "Haven't flown in a hovercopter before, have you?"

She was shaking. "I've never flown in *anything*!"

He laughed and pulled her closer. "Relax. I won't let you fall out."

Red's stomach was aflutter.

They flew over the vast green plains until a menacing black edifice rose up from the soil. It stretched left and right as far as they could see.

"There it is," Adiquis said. His body shivered at the sight of it. "Ms. Petras is somewhere inside the capital city, but I don't know exactly where. She said they were taking her to Undesirable Holdings."

"That could be like a complex for prisoners," Inieda said. She pushed her pistol against the woman's helmet. "Take us to this place!"

"You're crazy! Why would rebels want to go there?"

"That is of no concern to you. Bring us there or I will have no use for you."

They crested over the great wall and soared above an enormous and dense city. Red felt conflicted because she wanted to document the sight but could not will herself to release her grip on the seat. Civilization here easily dwarfed the largest settlement of Abeona-2. The buildings breached the clouds. She spotted no sign of decay. Like a bastion against the elements, the city was plated in pristine metal. Even in the daylight, illuminated buildings and spotlights bathed the area in a seemingly infinite source of electricity. This appeared to be a place of prosperity. Why any conflict transpired here seemed beyond her understanding.

The craft ascended up through the clouds and approached the roof of one of the tallest buildings. Red did her best to not let her gaze wander over the edge. She guessed she would only feel sick if she looked down.

Adventure did not always agree with her, it seemed.

ROVER ENTRY #1077

The hovercopter landed softly on the top of the structure that scraped the sky. Sarenth remained in the craft and took responsibility for the hostage.

"Be quick," he said to Red, the last to hop out. "By the Divine's will, we will be ready to depart as soon as you return."

Inieda pointed at the rest. "Follow behind me in a single file. Make no noise and listen to my every instruction."

Minnie idled behind her. "I can't believe I'm standing on the rooftop of an Autocratic jail. For Divine's sake, I've spelunked inside hospitals and caves, but this? This gives me the shivers!"

"Stay with me and this will be no different, Earth princess." She knelt near Adiquis, "Genius boy, what does Ms. Petras look like?"

His eyes went from concern to joy. "She's tall, big, messy hair, wears a long, dirty, white coat, and big glasses!" He used his hands to make circles around his eyes. Defying expectations, his fingers spread farther and farther apart. The glasses grew comically large.

There was no way they were that big, Red thought.

Inieda's emotions were unmoved. She nodded. "That is a fairly general description. I will rely heavily on your ability to identify her."

The team followed her down a plunging stairwell. At the bottom, she slowly pried open a heavy metal door and waved everyone inside. They entered a long, narrow hallway. An eerie red light bathed the walls and countless doors lining each side. Moans and cries of madness came from inside the rooms as they passed by.

Inieda huffed. "This facility is massive. To locate Ms. Petras promptly, I am afraid we will need to find a prisoner manifest."

She rounded a corner alone and shot her hand back, waving for them to stop. Out of sight, a yelp preceded a thud. She returned with a datapad in hand. "We are lucky today. Genius boy, do you know how to use your people's records?"

Adiquis typed a few commands and handed it back to her.

"Room 11920. How fortuitous. We are on the correct floor. Quickly, this way."

They retraced their steps and navigated knowingly through the labyrinth. Inieda located the door with the precise numbers etched upon its frame. It had no window or doorknob. How they would open it seemed like a puzzle to Red.

"Stand back!" Inieda pointed her pistol at the door and shot a beam of light. The metal barrier remained unfazed.

King stepped forward and rubbed his hands together. "I got this!" He clenched his fists and his fingers gleamed with light. With a battle cry, he smashed his fists into the door. It left an admirable dent, but the barrier stood defiant. "Well, shoot. Anyone else got any bright ideas?"

"I don't know if this is going to work but let me try." Adiquis opened a pouch hanging from his hip. He held a handful of metal marbles. A particularly shiny one slipped between his fingers. He steadied his feet and pointed it toward the door. "I'm not even sure how I'm supposed to..."

"Little boy," Inieda said, "this is no time for toys…"

A sonic boom shoved everyone onto the floor except the expectant Adiquis.

Red pulled herself up along a wall. When the smoke cleared, she glimpsed through the ruptured hole in the door. A woman sat on a bench inside the dark, otherwise plain, box. Her head hung low. Her big, unkempt hair obscured her face. She wore a long, white coat just like Adiquis said she would.

"Ms. Petras!" he squealed. He squeezed past Red and clamored into the room.

She perked up and embraced him as he hopped onto her lap.

"Adiquis! Is that you? You really did it? You got help?"

He nodded wildly. Tears sprinkled them both as they laughed warmly.

She squeezed him tightly then put him down. After tapping her lower back and muttering something about her old knees, she stood tall like a woman filled with hope. Red noticed her glasses reflecting the small amount of red light seeping into the cell.

They *were* huge.

ROVER ENTRY #1078

Ms. Petras climbed through the door and into the red light. "So, who all did you bring from the countryside?" She scanned the lot of them and pointed at King, grinning. "I like the cut of this young man! Aren't you a rugged, handsome one? Punch any authority figures lately?"

King smirked. "You've got a talent for judging character. Yeah, I'm a bit of a rabble-rouser."

Inieda cleared her throat. "I understand the value of introductions, but we should be evacuating as promptly as possible."

"I agree with the serious one," Ms. Petras said. "I'm going to assume since you all are with the kid that you're not here to execute me. However, I'm sure I'm next on their list. Given my level of value, and that you forcibly breached my door, any second now…"

Sirens blared and their piercing waves drew everyone's hands to their ears.

Ms. Petras shouted. "Full security forces are on their way here! We need to get out! You!" She directed a decisive finger at Inieda. "You look like you can handle yourself! Can you get us out of here?"

Inieda nodded and waved for them to follow.

Two guards in black jackets and helmets came marching around a corner. Their fists extended forward.

Red thought it strange neither brandished a weapon, just a shiny glint of metal in their hands.

Ms. Petras shrieked, "Get down!"

Red crouched against the wall and a jagged bolt of static electricity surged over her head. An errant spark licked her arm and it singed her sleeve. The burned fabric looked nasty but she felt no pain. The special armor had done its job.

Behind them, an explosion erupted that put the sirens to shame. Gray smoke and small metal debris tumbled past their feet.

King stepped in between the action and smashed his fists together. A shield of light absorbed additional bolts.

From behind his cover, Inieda fired her pistol and the two men scattered.

"Follow me! Single file just like before!"

Red and the others formed a tight train behind Inieda and they carefully turned many corners. Inieda occasionally shot at emerging guards. Everyone ducked behind King's shield for protection.

When a pair of datapad-toting administrators bumbled across their path, Adiquis pointed his marble at them in a fright. Inieda quickly pushed his hand down.

"No!" she said. "They are not soldiers and you wield too much power. Also, you might destroy our path forward or a route to retreat. You have much to learn about tactics, brave child." She let them flee.

The hallways were crumbling from the constant exchange of fire and Red thought she saw other prisoners running free, but it was hard to tell through the haze and the chaos.

When they approached the rooftop stairwell, Inieda pointed everyone forward. "Wall man, create a shield and block the doorway!"

King laughed and pounded his fists together.

She stood behind him and pointed her weapon back into the hallway. "Everyone, up to the craft! We will defend your retreat until you ascend halfway!"

Ms. Petras and Adiquis were first. Red grabbed Minnie's hand as they followed. Weapon fire rang out below and strong words were used liberally by their defenders.

Only a quarter of the way up, Minnie said, "We should go back and help them."

"No," Red replied firmly. "Inieda said to go. Come on." She pulled Minnie along.

"No, I want to go back down." Minnie struggled out of Red's grasp.

Red snagged Minnie's sleeve. "What are you doing? Stop it! It's dangerous!"

"Of course I know that! But neither King nor Inieda are followers of the Divine. They could use a little extra luck."

Red pulled frantically. "That's ridiculous! There isn't extra credit for being a follower of anything. Flames, smoke, and lasers are fighting them down there and that's all there is. Now, come," she pulled again, "*on*!"

"No!"

Minnie tried to wrestle herself away while King and Inieda's own argument echoed up the walls.

"Let me take a crack at them! I'll show them what a Mauler can do when faced with a challenge! You escort the bunch and make sure there aren't any surprises up top."

"I told you to go now! This is not a game!"

Another explosion shook the steps under Red's feet and she tripped up the stairs. Smoke rolled into the stairwell followed by a burst of flames. Emerging from the disaster covered in soot, King and Inieda floundered up the steps. Inieda clutched her side. King helped her walk, but her knees buckled. He threw her over his shoulders.

He spotted the two ladies wavering above. "Go, Red! We'll be right behind you!"

Red pulled Minnie harder until she went along. They caught up to Adiquis and Ms. Petras at the top. Ms. Petras kicked open the rooftop door and they ran toward the hovercopter. Red was puzzled that neither Sarenth nor the pilot were inside.

Ms. Petras ripped open the side door and waved urgently. "Come on! We have to go before the air defense system deploys!"

"Wait!" Minnie shouted. She ran back toward the stairwell.

Ms. Petras pointed at Red. "Stop her!"

Red tried to grab her, but Minnie was too fast. Minnie opened the stairwell door and smoke ballooned out. To Red's horror, she dashed inside.

"We might need to forget her!" Ms. Petras said. She hopped into the pilot's seat and operated the controls. "I'm sorry, really I am, but we've got about thirty seconds until this copter is useless. It may be either some of us or none of us."

She pointed at Red standing near the side door. "Are you in or out? Make your choice!"

"Come on!" Adiquis beckoned from the back.

Red looked at the hovercopter and back at the door. She was paralyzed.

King blew the door off its hinges. He and Minnie carried Inieda out of the roaring flames. Red climbed in and assisted pulling Inieda inside. The hovercopter blades whirred. To Red's disbelief, Minnie did not join them.

"But where's Sarenth?" she cried. She surveyed the rooftop.

Ms. Petras pounded the control dashboard. "I don't know who that is, but if we don't take off right now, this copter is going to turn into a metal coffin!"

"Minnie, please!" Red pleaded.

"Get in, you dang rusthead!" King yelled.

Minnie stepped back and forth until she screamed frustratingly into the sky. She climbed in. At the last possible moment, Sarenth came running around the back of a rooftop structure holding his injured arm. Minnie and Red pulled him inside. They lifted off.

"What happened?" Minnie asked as she opened a medical pouch upon a wall and wrapped his arm in a sling.

Every one of Minnie's touches caused him to wince in pain. "The pilot fought me and attempted to escape. Only by the Divine's intervention did she fail to pull me off the edge along with her during our final struggle."

Ms. Petras turned several dials on the control panel. "I hope you two aren't performing surgery back there. My pilot's license isn't exactly up-to-date and we're going to need extreme speed to get far enough away. Everyone, hold tight!" The hovercopter flew across the roof and fell over the edge like a stone.

The building's windows blurred past. Red's stomach jumped to her throat. Sarenth screamed and Minnie wrapped her arms around him to keep him from moving. Inieda coughed concernedly but otherwise barely flinched.

"Whoa! That's not it!" Ms. Petras grabbed at the controls.

Red's body compressed into the seat as gravity suddenly became overwhelming. She reached for King and gripped his hand like a vice.

"I-it's going to be okay, I think!" he shouted.

The glimmering skyline outside gradually leveled out. Red felt normal again.

"Heads up!" Ms. Petras said. "We got some angry prison guards behind us. I've never done this before, but I'm deploying the smoke screen. Let's see…" She slammed a button. The craft's back hatch slowly opened. Cargo boxes and loose items hurtled out.

"Wrong button! Wrong button!" Adiquis cried as a clipboard flew over his head.

Ms. Petras pressed the button and the hatch retracted. "Is it this one?"

Red heard a hiss. The view out the window became as black as night. They traversed through it without incident for a time. When they reemerged into the open sky, the great perimeter wall quickly approached. An unsettling beeping sound started slowly but then grew more frenzied.

Ms. Petras tapped concernedly on a glass sensor. "They're locking missiles on us! No smoke screen is going to obscure us that well." She turned back to the team. "Can any of you shoot straight?"

Inieda, Sarenth, and Adiquis all raised their hands.

She smiled at the two professional soldiers. "You two look like a mess. Look, no offense, but I'm going to go with the kid on this one. At least he knows how to use them." She pointed at his marble pouch. "Adiquis, take out a fistful of marbles, interweave them between your fingers, and get ready to fire out the hatch. I'll reopen it so you can shoot the other copters down."

Adiquis climbed into the cargo area as the hatch opened. King and Minnie held onto his legs as he aimed his fist. Their pursuers emerged from the smoke. There were a series of booms and the hovercopter violently shook. Whatever pursuers remained changed their minds.

The beeping subsided. Ms. Petras sighed. "I believe we're in the clear. We're far enough outside the city limits so they shouldn't be able to track us anymore. Gosh, I think I dumped enough smoke back there to blot out the sun for a week. I guess good luck with that, you Autocratic scumbags!"

Adiquis climbed into the front compartment and slapped celebratory hands with Ms. Petras. They traded several other colorful insults for their enemies, which must have been regional slang because Red had never heard of them, until the hovercopter landed outside the cave.

The blades ceased whirring and King helped Inieda and Sarenth out onto solid ground. With pale faces, they both looked awful.

Inieda pointed a wavering finger toward Ms. Petras. "Please tell me we rescued the right person and that you are indeed Ms. Petras, the resourceful scientist."

Ms. Petras dusted her coat and wiped her glasses with her sleeve. After putting them back on, they were possibly even dirtier. "As of today, I can proudly say I am once again *Doctor* Petras. I would appreciate it if you referred to me as such." She quickly pointed to Adiquis. "But you're a legacy. Keep calling me whatever you'd like."

Adiquis giggled. "It's important we call people what they want to be called."

He stepped next to Minnie, his fingers twiddling away. "Um, I want to say thanks."

"Listen kid. You don't have to say it. This is for me too."

"No, I should. People are amazing. Everyone is worthy of respect. For all the things I learned from schooling, I hung on to a bunch of the wrong stuff. I still have a lot to learn. Thanks for reminding me."

"Okay."

Inieda leaned toward Dr. Petras and frowned. "Doctor is a title indicative of profound respect among my people. Have you studied under the greats or accomplished great feats to earn it?"

Dr. Petras leapt onto a boulder and pointed toward the sky. "Oh yes! And I'm going to do so much more. I can't wait to get started!"

They traveled back through the gates and returned to Jangala just as Inieda lost consciousness and Sarenth collapsed. Soldiers rushed to their aid and carried the two swiftly back to the ark. Red knew undoubtedly by the escorting soldier's scowls that they were not pleased with the cost they had paid for victory.

The Hail Mary

File Under: risk, support, faith

Location(s): Jangala, Earth

Executive Summary: Visiting the home world was a remarkable experience. I am aware of the great opportunity I was bestowed with and do not take it for granted. I hope my documentation serves as a small light into the mystery that is our ancestral planet and the state I found it in because of the Great Answer Crisis.

ROVER ENTRY #1081

Strong, passionate voices echoed from the war room's high ceiling. Dr. Petras followed soldiers somewhere else, much to Adiquis' distress, but she promised him they would see each other again soon. Stepping into the grand hall, Red overheard chatter from several passing aides. Inieda was fighting for her life in the infirmary. Sarenth had suffered wounds but would thankfully heal.

One of the room's massive pillars supported Cardinal Murcario as he leaned against it. He held a hand to his wrinkled forehead. "That young man was one of my rising stars and now he is damaged goods. Had I known we were sending him into a deathtrap, I would never have approved of it! I seriously question our ability to continue this gate-hopping roulette when we have no understanding of the dangers on the other side."

Olyana studied a pair of datapads. "They succeeded, did they not? That is a soldier's purpose, to execute the hard decisions during war. No one ever wants to sacrifice themselves, but…sometimes the greater good must be considered." She pressed a pair of fingers upon her temple and turned away.

Their leader noticed the four travelers approaching. She gestured for them to take their seats at the far end of the table.

"Trouble in paradise?" King whispered to Red.

She sat in the same chair as last time. "I hope not. We're sort of relying on them having it all together."

Olyana patted the Cardinal's arm and sat herself at the table's other end. The War Council also took their places.

Olyana spoke quietly with Azul. Her chest rose and fell in starts. Red felt guilty. She wondered if Olyana struggled with the stress of all this.

"Travelers," Olyana said, "I wish you had not seen that. Please, vacate from your mind any worries regarding our unity. I assure you this is a minor disagreement and we are here to support you."

Cardinal Murcario tapped his fist upon the table and nodded stiffly. "Here, here," he muttered. "As I understand, the extraction team was successful in retrieving the one called Ms. Petras. Is that accurate?"

Red was unsure if she possessed the authority to correct him, but she agreed with what Adiquis said earlier. It was important to call people what they wanted to be called. "I'm sorry, but apparently it's *Doctor* Petras now."

A low mumble filled the room.

"So I have heard," Cardinal Murcario continued. "Have any of Captain Olyana's people explained to you the significance of that title?"

"A little, but I don't fully understand it," Red answered.

"Doctor is a title of great honor bestowed upon those who are an artisan of their craft in her tribe. Most of the Jangalan people will be reluctant to address her as such until she proves her worth."

Adiquis jumped out of his chair. "She's got the worth! She's got more worth than almost anyone I've ever met!"

The room rumbled with a roar of disapproval.

Olyana waved Adiquis down. "The Cardinal did not mean any offense. Although, he is correct. She may be a doctor among your people, but Ms. Petras has yet to earn that title here. If the sacrifice we endured today proves to indeed be worth it, then I feel confident she will."

Adiquis returned to his seat, frazzled.

Red nodded toward him comfortingly. He smiled a little.

Olyana continued. "We will need some time to consider our next step and whether your plan remains viable. Please rest yourselves until we call upon you again. You are all dismissed and free to explore the settlement."

"You'll see!" Adiquis said as the four walked out the door. "She's gonna leave you amazed!"

Red left the meeting worried, but thankfully Dr. Petras turned out to be exactly who Adiquis claimed.

As soon as the good doctor settled in, she worked with Olyana's friend, Emillee, who Red learned was an engineer. Together, they modernized many of the Jangalan people's technologies. They strengthened their combat armor, taught the people about harvesting and manipulating the vibrant steel in the valley, and Dr. Petras helped Emillee design a portable wonder that she claimed would change Jangalan lives on the planet forever. A bold claim.

Even King expressed excitement about all this *science stuff*, as he called it, when the two ladies shared that they were devising a portable power supply for his suit. But Dr. Petras said it would take some time so he should muster whatever patience he had in his body. He complained it was in short supply.

Red was selected to brief Dr. Petras on everything about the alien conflict. As soon as she could, Red joined Dr. Petras at her worksite. The assignment delighted her, eager to see all of these technological advancements in person that were being whispered about.

The corrugated metal warehouse, large and isolated, was next to that ominous blue fog that everyone kept telling her was poisonous. She was hesitant about conducting their business there at first. Adiquis greeted her with a broad grin standing under a tall sliding garage door. Someone she considered smart enough to not be somewhere stupid, his presence eased her concerns.

Red sat on the bare floor near Dr. Petras in the lab. Not as spacious on the inside as she had predicted, most of the interior was cluttered with electronic spare parts upon tables and shelves. The owner of the lab, Emillee, apologized that chairs were in short supply. The site was historically intended for a sole researcher.

Emillee excused herself to work on another project elsewhere in the building. Adiquis idly swung his legs from atop the workbench at Dr. Petras' side. He seemed truly content just watching her.

Dr. Petras tinkered with an enigmatic white tube while Red spoke. Red observed with delightful interest as Dr. Petras used tools, made of what she could only describe as light, to poke and maneuver minuscule components of the machine she had no understanding of. Unlike Rover Order mechanics and their dying machines, Dr. Petras was a creator and she was used to having all of the galaxy's raw materials at her disposal.

Blue sparks would fizzle out of one end on occasion. This concerned Red but she trusted Dr. Petras. If what she heard was to be believed, Dr. Petras was the smartest person on the planet, conceivably the galaxy.

"You know," Red said, pride in her IET device that started this all still fresh in her mind, "I like to think of myself as a bit of a tinkerer too. What exactly are you working on there?"

Dr. Petras' focus did not waver from her work. "What do you know about dark matter energy signatures?"

"Um…dark signatures what?"

"Gravitational space-fabric measurements?"

"I…uh, gravity is a force…"

"Experimental oscillating wavelength weaponry?"

Why did it have to do with weapons? How frustrating. "Guns? Not so much."

Dr. Petras tugged off her goggles. She turned toward Red with a blank face. "What about energy? Do you know anything about electricity?"

Red perked up and pointed a finger in the air. "Yes! I know quite a bit about electrical currents and wiring!"

"Mmhmm. You and every other high schooler in the galaxy."

"What's high school?"

Dr. Petras shook her head slightly and chuckled. "You're a strange one, Red." She returned to her work. "To make it brief, I'm working on a weapon to defeat the aliens."

"Ah." Red looked away to hide her embarrassment. Adiquis still had that cheesy grin on his face. Emillee's whistling resonated throughout the building's rafters. Dr. Petras was swaying to the tune. Red waited for her to elaborate, but the growing silence between them made her uncomfortable. Was Red being a nuisance? She hoped instead to show some personal interest in the doctor's work. People usually liked to talk about themselves.

"Do you make weapons a lot?" Red asked.

Dr. Petras' hands froze. Her shoulders stopped bobbing. The delicate little tools, suspended in time, continued to shimmer in brilliant white. Beeping, from a small console on the tabletop, grew seemingly louder in the vocal void. It appeared Red had gaffed again.

"I…" Dr. Petras paused. Her breathing ceased. The air was still.

Adiquis stared, tilting his head at an almost ninety-degree angle. He too seemed curious as to what would cause such a bold woman to draw back.

"Yes," she continued at last. "I *did* make weapons. But I don't want to do that anymore. At least not like that and for those kinds of people." She cleared her throat. "I've felt this way for a long time. I don't want to hurt people anymore. So many *people…*"

The fact that a weapon sat before her seemed ironic, but maybe there was something Red did not understand.

"I'm a new woman," Dr. Petras said with a dramatic turn of her wrist. "Have been ever since this little guy showed me the way forward." She offered her fist for Adiquis to pound. He reciprocated with a giggle.

"So…" Red decided to move on, "I'm supposed to update you on the alien conflict." She paused for dramatic effect. Her eyes narrowed and a knowing smile grew as she leaned toward Dr. Petras. "Yes, you did hear me correctly. There are *aliens* now."

Dr. Petras just smirked and nodded. "Figures."

Red was caught off guard by the lack of bewilderment. "Oh. Did Adiquis already tell you?"

"Actually, no."

"Oh!" Adiquis perked up. "I forgot to mention that I was chased by alien dogs!"

Red scratched her head. "You seem unsurprised. Maybe even expectant? How can that be? My colony's best researchers have never stumbled upon any signs of extraterrestrial life. Are other colonies the wiser?"

Dr. Petras snorted. A short chuckle trailed off. "No. We've never had any evidence of their existence either. And don't ever go thinking the rest of us are smarter than you all. From what little I've been told by Adiquis of where you come from, your planet has peace at least figured out and that has eluded the rest of humanity for millennia." Sparks flew from her workbench. She wiped her dripping brow. "It's true, I'm not terribly shocked. You see, a good scientist always keeps her mind open to all possibilities. Otherwise, she'll miss the truth sitting right at her side."

Red nodded. She liked that mantra and wrote it in her Journal.

ROVER ENTRY #1082

Dr. Petras and Emillee's advancements restored the War Council's support within a few days. The Council largely agreed the conflict with the Seekers and, subsequently, the aliens could not be won alone. Therefore, the four travelers received the blessing to embark on their plan's second leg: the mission to Earth. Their task was to reestablish the galactic communication signal. This time, they would be accompanied by a larger escort.

Much to Red's dismay, the Council instructed the four to train with Azul in the use of the same pistols the Jangalan soldiers used. Back home, she had never seen more than two firearms in her life and both were in a school text. She never spent any time with the defense forces that protected the settlement's perimeter from the rare canidaurochs and muscle moles. That was true only if you excluded the days she spent staring at that wall-guarding Omega boy who she never managed to start a conversation with. What was he doing now, she wondered? Were he and everyone else on Abeona-2 safe? Would her handling a gun make them any safer?

Standing on a shooting range near the settlement's outskirts, Red examined a weapon in her hand. Holding it was immensely uncomfortable.

Adiquis ran by pointing his pistol erratically. "Pew pew!"

"Stop that this instant!" Azul commanded. He grabbed Adiquis by the collar and lifted the boy off his feet. "That is a lethal weapon you are callously waving around!"

Adiquis wiggled his way out of Azul's grasp and skipped several paces away. He presented a view of the pistol's side. "The safety's on! Everything's okay!" He stuck his tongue out and hopped away.

Azul snarled. "And they call him a genius?"

"He's still just a kid," Red said at his side. She turned the weapon in her hand and located the switch Adiquis brought attention to. Would this make her weapon safer as the name implied? She flipped it. The weapon hummed loudly.

"Do not activate that yet!" Azul snatched the pistol out of her hand and flipped the switch back. "You are not yet trained in even the most basic of handling or…"

"Wahoo!" Minnie kicked her heels up while shooting her weapon repeatedly into the air. "Look at me! I'm a space varmint out on the frontier!"

Azul screamed. "For goodness' sake!"

After several hours of confidence boosting, Red was at least sure she would not shoot a colleague in the back by accident.

Another day of preparations and the team was ready. The four travelers donned their special armor again and walked to the valley. Red spotted Sarenth waiting for them alive and well. She welcomed the sight. He waited patiently with a group of eleven other soldiers. Inieda was notably absent.

Minnie skipped to his side and punched him in the arm. "Look at you, war machine! We showed them what the youth could do, didn't we?"

"Ah." He winced.

"Oh! I'm sorry! Was that your bad arm?"

He laughed. "It is all right. I feel like my entire body is my bad arm. Regardless, I am excited that this time it will just be us young folks. Let us show them what we can achieve."

He waved for everyone to gather close. "I am honored all of you are giving me another chance in this undertaking of immense importance. I am sorry I will not bring the same expertise and talent as Inieda, but I hope you trust the Divine's grand plan in which I have become the lead of this operation. Through the Divine's will, we will triumph!"

His soldiers cheered. Minnie, Adiquis, and King clapped, but Red did not. She disliked his cavalier attitude toward their assured success. His attribution to the Divine regarding their current circumstances also disagreed with her. She believed Inieda's professional experience carried them through their last mission. She was simply injured during a dangerous mission. No mystical plan existed. Sarenth's leadership was not pre-ordained, nor was their victory.

Noticeably separating herself, King saw and shuffled next to her. "Heck of a grand plan, huh? I grew up a little religious, but I wouldn't say I believe in an invisible string pulling this whole thing together. Do you?"

"Thank goodness there's another brain in the room. No, not one bit. I think the whole idea is dangerous. Where is the recognition of our actions or their effect on the outcome? We should be studying our mistakes and sharpening the skills that led to our progress. I don't like driving blind."

King's brow furrowed. Such a pensive look appeared uncharacteristic, maybe even painful. Red was worried he was suffering a headache.

"Where I come from," he said, "the religious congregation does like to stick its head in the sand. That definitely isn't the best strategy in every situation, but unfamiliar tactics usually develop from unique situations. I don't reckon we can just write it off as patently wrong because we don't understand it. Maybe the positive spirit will give us the wind we need to sail on ahead."

Red rolled her eyes. "I've seen those that carry the flag for the Divine. This," she gestured vaguely toward the soldiers, "whatever this Jangala version of it is, is not it. I'm used to more magical thinking, not saber rattling."

King crossed his arms and smirked. "So, you admit this group of the cloth isn't cut exactly the same way as the ones who let you down before?"

She turned toward him and let out a little sigh. "Okay. You could have a point. I don't know what to expect. I'll just try to be hopeful. Is that what you want to hear?"

He puffed out his chest and cheeks. He made a funny face.

She smiled.

He patted her heartily on the back. "Let's keep our eyes peeled for the rest of them then, huh?"

She nodded without much confidence. Would they be fine without a professional like Inieda? She desperately wanted Sarenth to be right, misplaced faith in the Divine or not.

Sarenth took a datapad out of his pocket and waved Red over. He handed it to her. "I have observed that you are good with information. Here, keep this safe. Dr. Petras encoded it with valuable intelligence she said we should transmit with our message. It speaks of the gates, all our known worlds in peril, the Seekers, and everything we know of the aliens."

She was a little surprised. He did not have the same reservations about her as she did of him. "Of course. Thank you for trusting me." She tucked it into the same pocket as her Journal.

He faced his soldiers. "Listen up! Weapons armed, faces forward. The Earth Princess' field report says we may be greeted by active resistance. Let us go!"

Minnie drew her hands to her flushed face. "You can stop calling me that now…" she said, but barely audible enough for anyone to hear.

They jumped through the portal, snuck past the ever-increasing stacks of Seekers and flying alien ships in the sky, and found the gate that would lead them to Earth. Red stood in front of it, consistently being the last of her peers to enter. Sarenth stood at her side. She stalled.

She had never seen pictures of their home world and it never personally mattered much to her before. But now, with the planet of her ancestors just a step away, excitement bubbled up inside her as well as anxiety over all the knowledge to be gained. Her old-world tongues appeared to be sufficient. Could she possibly find time to converse with the people? Would she learn about their culture or the context regarding the ancient messages her planet had overheard through the gates for hundreds of years?

The Great Answer turned out not to be exactly what she thought it would be, but any information she could bring back might help her people move toward their inevitable post-gate society.

She allowed herself a momentary indulgent thought. The knowledge she brought back may be the most revealing any Rover had ever discovered. The Red Rover would be legendary.

ROVER ENTRY #1083

With an encouraging nod from Sarenth, Red leapt through the gate and into a cavernous, dry, echoing blackness.

Minnie wandered forward. She cast a wide beam of light from a lamp on her suit's chest. They were in a vast, crumbling rotunda with crude paintings and designs decorating what few walls remained. Red looked up. She thought they stood under the open night sky, but there were no stars and she did not hear the wind.

"This is the unexplored zone," Minnie said. She directed her beam toward a rotunda's last intact piece. "Whoa. That ginormous Seeker did a number on this place."

Sarenth's soldiers pointed their weapons up above. The great void absorbed all light.

Minnie kicked rocks out of her way. "It's okay, boys. If the Seeker were still here, I bet we'd know by now."

"Are we underground?" Sarenth asked as he lowered his weapon.

Minnie nodded and sighed deeply. "If it's safe now, please follow me." She ran out of sight.

"Minnie? What is it?" Red shouted after her.

"Wait for us!" Sarenth commanded as everyone gave chase. They followed her out of the rotunda, through a crumbling archway, and onto a dusty street. They found her lifting rocks from a crater in a frantic search.

"Help me, for Divine's sake!"

Red hopped down and grabbed a large boulder. She struggled until Sarenth gave her a hand.

"What are we looking for," she asked.

"He's gone, he's gone, oh my Divine. He's gone." Minnie pulled her hair. "What does that mean?"

"Who?" Sarenth asked.

"Kyle. My best friend was caught under this rubble when I escaped. Could he…did he get out too?"

Sarenth pointed to a soldier to drop his rock. "This is not our mission. We have little time to find the control station." He tugged Minnie's arm. "And because he is not here, down here we should not stay. We may find clues elsewhere during our trek."

She reluctantly followed the group down a narrow street and past primitive buildings.

"Since when have Earth people started living underground?" King asked. "Which one's your house? It's so dark and it doesn't look like you have any electricity at all. Not my taste."

"No," Minnie said. "We found this here. We think it's ancient ruins from humanity's earliest era…or even before."

"Fascinating." Red took out her Journal and sketched the painted art on the walls and the architecture's shape. She did not have any ruins like this at home. She was excited to present these findings at the next Rover conference.

After a long walk, Minnie pointed to a ladder that extended to the stratosphere. "We're gonna make our way to the surface and head across the bridge to Brooklyn. That is where the control station is. Last time I was here, our tunnels were teeming with Seekers. We need to keep our ears open for any weird sounds and our noses active for the scent of smoke."

There were harnesses to clip themselves to the ladder but not enough for everyone.

"I-I shouldn't do this…" Red's teeth chattered.

"You take one of these little doodads," King said, possibly noticing her wringing hands. "I can go without."

"Are you sure? It's awfully h-high." Her stomach was queasy.

"Yeah. I've got two strong hands. If they're not great for gripping metal for dear life, what good are they?"

She secured her clips and began her ascent. As they went higher, she was immensely grateful for the harness. If not for the darkness and nothing below to see, she might have been too afraid to continue. But she ventured upward and, defying her fear, made it to the top.

Minnie offered her hand and pulled Red up. "Oh right," she said approaching a nearby precipice. Small lanterns burned live flames along a cliffside. "The bridge is out."

"Do not worry." Sarenth revealed a telescoping pole from his pocket. He drove the pole into the ground and it popped loudly. Two ropes shot across the divide and clanked as they penetrated rock on the other side. "Place your feet on the bottom rope and use your hands to pull yourself along the top one. At this distance, we can cross two at a time."

Red watched the others traverse across the black void. She could not believe the ladder was looking good in comparison. Trusting a pair of wobbly ropes was terrifying. Dare she say stupid!

When her turn arrived, she creeped back from the edge She said to Sarenth, "I-I don't know if I can do this."

"Come on, Red!" King shouted from the other side. "You've flown to the top of the tallest building and climbed the tallest ladder I reckon anyone's ever seen. What's this rope have on either of those? You can do it!"

"You will be okay," Sarenth said, gently pushing her forward. "The Divine will steady your hands and I will be right behind you."

With the support of her colleagues all around her, she nodded. "O-okay." She grabbed the rope and pulled herself on. "One step at a time," she whispered. She slowly inched her way across. The rope was smooth and cool against her palms. The stillness of the air allowed her to focus. Again, with no bottom to see, she believed this was the only way she could tackle this task.

Adiquis waved from the other side. "Come on! If I can do it, you can too!"

She smiled through clenched teeth and just tried to focus on her footing. She stood about halfway when her stomach plummeted as deep as the chasm. A reverberating roar came from within the darkness. A hurricane of balmy air followed, whipping her hair into her face.

"Give your strength to your grip!" Sarenth barked as the ropes shuddered up and down. He was far behind her.

Red tightened her grasp, but one foot slipped followed by the other. Boots flailing, the rope wobbled in her hands. She refused to shut her eyes afraid that the darkness would snatch her up like a monster if she looked away for a second.

The wind died down. She hung on with vice-like palms.

"Ah! Oh no! Help me!"

"I'm coming!" Minnie climbed back onto the rope and swiftly shimmied her way toward Red.

"We should not have more than two on at a time!" Sarenth shouted. "Support the top line!"

His soldiers grabbed the top rope from the far ledge. The anchored rock cracked and crumbled. The bottom rope popped out and cracked like a whip striking one of the shoulder's shins. It twirled into oblivion.

Minnie pulled herself up and wrapped her legs around the remaining rope. "Can you do this?" she asked as she hung in front of Red.

"I don't think so!"

Minnie swung upside down, dangling by her legs. She grasped Red's wrists. "I'm gonna hold you so you won't fall. Pull your legs up and wrap them around like mine."

Red nodded and swung her legs up. Her left wrist slipped through Minnie's fingers. She screamed and Minnie grabbed her again. After another try, Red managed the deed with all four limbs. She looked back and Sarenth was pulled up as well.

Pain was smeared across his face. "Trust Minnie. She will not fail you," he managed to say. His injured arm shuddered.

They scooted their way to the other side. Sarenth's soldiers helped them down. While enjoying her boots touching dirt again, the last rope snapped and disappeared.

Adiquis jumped. "That was crazy, Minnie! You're like an action hero!"

"Ah," she smiled slightly. "I don't know. I just jumped into it. Maybe that wasn't the smartest impulse."

"You did well," Sarenth said, examining the injured leg of his friend. "Thank you."

"Okay," she beamed. "Come on. Let's get out of here before we discover where that giant Seeker is hiding."

They ran through many corridors. Minnie remarked about the battle that took place at their feet not long ago. They passed a door where she said she almost suffocated inside and another where orphans once lived.

Adiquis had questions about Earth orphans and learned they were treated very differently than on Tenocolis.

They climbed a small staircase and Minnie held her hand up at the top. Everyone stopped.

"Do you expect resistance?" Sarenth asked.

"No, it's not that. It's just that beyond this door is what's left of Earth. I know most of you have never seen it before, no pictures, news, nothing. I just...I hope none of you are disappointed. This isn't how it's supposed to be."

Minnie opened the final door and revealed a sacred ceremony chamber. It was enormous, taller, and longer than any Divine sanctuary Red knew of. Furniture sprawled across the hall in disarray. Red's nose tingled from the stench of sickness and death lingering in the air although the building appeared abandoned. However, the moonlight streaming in through the colorful, partially shattered, elegant windows cast romantic shadows.

"Oh, for Divine's sake," Minnie said, stepping past broken jars and empty tin boxes with red crosses painted across their tops. "Somebody's ransacked the place. They even tore the planks off the windows. Animals."

Red recognized a vague resemblance to the southern settlement's Divine cathedrals. She had visited a few purely out of exotic curiosity, but she had never felt comfortable inside one. Tall, vaulted ceilings descended more dramatically onto carved relief sculptures. The art displayed here was of a grained, dark material instead of the prevalent stone and glass of her home world. Deep rows of long, similarly grained pews stretched to the back of the room. Sandstone benches were instead common back home.

"What are those benches made of?" she asked a soldier near her. "I keep seeing it lately."

"That is wood."

"Fascinating," she replied having no idea what that was. She jotted that down in her Journal. Such an excess of exotic materials on display. This monument screamed of decadence. It made her upset thinking of how many people would shuffle inside week after week and be indoctrinated by a faith built around it. Everything about this place seemed wasteful.

She was anxious to leave, but Adiquis attracted everyone's attention when he sat on a bench and slid across it back and forth. He squealed with delight.

"This looks like the church Father Hannon brought us to on Sundays!"

"This is an epic monument to the Divine," one of Sarenth's soldiers said. "The artistry, the tremendous use of space. It is breathtaking. Please, young child. Treat this shrine with more respect."

Adiquis' smile dissipated. He came to a halt and hopped off.

The soldier knelt on one knee. "Please, join me in prayer, my comrades." Several others joined. Minnie and Sarenth did as well. "If you could, Missionary Sarenth, it would be an honor to hear the words of your conviction."

Sarenth closed his eyes. "Great Divine, knower of all past, present, and future, protect us as we fight for holy victory in your name. Reveal to us the path of conquest and divide our enemies that conspire before us."

"May I?" Minnie whispered. "Oh, Great Divine, lover of their children, please bring us success, peace, and harmony as we attempt this most dangerous task. Your loyal daughter and Princess cries out to you for your merciful eye so it can show her the way forward."

Adiquis ran toward them and tugged at Minnie's arm. "Can I do it too?"

"Of course," she giggled. "What are you going to say?"

"Okay," he whispered to himself. "Just like Father Hannon taught me." He clasped his hands together gleefully. At the top of his lungs, he shouted, "Oh Great Glorious Divine!" Several people were startled, but many others smiled. "Reveal to me the great revelation of my true self! Help me discover my purpose here in this strange place, help my friends discover their purpose, and show us the way, the light, and the truth. For the Divine, I pray!"

"For the Divine, I pray," repeated the others.

Red stood awkwardly at a distance with King at her side. He seemed to watch with relaxed amusement whereas she grew increasingly unsure about the capacity of her teammates.

She leaned close to King. "This again. It seems like a lot for what is supposed to be a smash and grab."

"Yeah, maybe so," he replied. "But even if it's all just a bunch of scrap, it couldn't hurt to shout into the void. Someone or something might actually be listening."

Red shook her head. "Pssh! I wouldn't call this harmless." She pointed discreetly at Minnie. "I thought she was going to be the reliable one. She kept tabs of everybody the other day and fought to get everyone off that rooftop. But now I'm wondering if she's got her head too far in the clouds."

King crossed his arms. "Come on. That's unfair. She just saved your life less than an hour ago. Give her a little credit."

Red swiftly turned on her heels. "I need some air."

She stomped toward a dramatic set of double doors. Before she reached it, she was curious whether anyone was following her. She glanced back toward the crowd. They were watching Minnie step up to an altar.

Minnie placed a hand on its stone surface and said, "I used to pray here with my father. But now…"

A door creaked behind the altar. "Minnie?" an unseen voice called out.

Several soldiers aimed their weapons. Switches flicked, energy charged, and red laser lights crisscrossed the altar. Red did not know whether to run back or take cover.

The soldiers eased themselves when Minnie jumped with glee.

"Kyle?" She threw open her arms and almost squeezed the life out of him. Tears soaked into the ground as she sobbed. Kyle was heavily bandaged and stood with a limp. "Oh, thank the Divine! Are you okay? You look terrible!"

"I'm just glad to be alive! But what about you?" He patted her arms and shoulders, marveling at her attire. "Last I saw you, that Seeker behemoth was bearing down while I slipped out of there. It looks like you found another group and brought the big guns. Are you here to rescue us?"

She stepped back. An elated smile accompanied unsure eyes. "I…"

Sarenth cleared his throat.

She took Kyle's hands. "I don't even know where to start and I don't have the time to try."

Kyle lowered his head with a gentle smile. "It's okay. I know how you are, always running those fetch quests for everyone else. Well, I've been hiding out with the other refugees across town at a new site. I came back every day knowing you'd find your way again. You gotta come with me, even if for a little bit. Your dad, he's going to freak."

"Dad?" She turned and scanned Sarenth's face with wide eyes.

He shook his head, although Red believed he exhibited no pleasure in doing so.

Minnie took Kyle's shirt between her fingers and scrunched it. "Go," she said quietly, "and bring everyone back here. Go deep down and wait by the gate. It's our ticket out and it's safe where we came from. But you can't go through without us. It wouldn't be smart. And be careful down there. I think the giant Seeker is back, but we didn't actually see it. Can you do that? Can you get everyone to wait quietly for us to return?"

He leaned in and took her by the shoulders. "Come with me and tell them yourself!"

"I can't! I have to do something and we're the only ones who can. There's no time and I have to go. Save my dad, everyone. Just promise me, please!"

Kyle scooped up her hands and squeezed. "You can count on me." He hugged her again.

Red watched Kyle rush past her, flash a polite wave, and exit the building. The rest of the team was not far behind.

Minnie placed one hand upon the large, double wooden door. She stared at it. "This drops us in the middle to Eldervalley street. We'll go east for a few blocks and cross the bridge. I think we can creatively fit ourselves inside and on top of my truck."

They all stepped into the cool night air. The remains of a red vehicle awaited them on the road in about as many pieces as one would expect if it fell off a cliffside.

"Dang," Minnie said with an exasperated chuckle. "I guess we're walking."

ROVER ENTRY #1084

Red's boots thumped upon the smooth, unbroken, and weathered walking path. A pleasant breeze lifted her chin and the night sky surprised and captivated her. It did not matter that they were halfway across the galaxy; stars still sparkled the same. But this magical, shimmering sky reignited her Rover passion. The constellations were all unfamiliar. The visible spiral of the galaxy twisted so very differently than how she was used to. She wanted to sketch it all.

"Pretty, huh?" King asked, looking up as well.

She nodded slightly. Her pencil was already on paper.

Grateful for this view, she was surprised they could enjoy it. She expected more light pollution from humanity's civilization center, but she understood why tonight was not representative. Examining the buildings around her next, she recognized the surface of Earth looked more like Adiquis' planet than her own. However, buildings here were constructed of all manner of materials. Stone, metal, this wood she had heard of, and more were all represented. Truly, Earth was a world of plenty and she wondered why her ancestors ever left. She sketched shapes and textures of fauna and architecture that were novel to her.

She walked with the team down the street past residential homes and businesses. Her curiosity tour was derailed by roars of Seekers out of sight. When a nearby explosion overcame her nerves, she let out a yelp. Her Journal fell out of her hands. She scooped it up and scrambled for cover behind a brick garden wall.

Minnie frantically tugged at Sarenth's arm. "Oh no! The gangs are setting fire to the city again! We have to get out of here! We have to run! Or else...they'll…"

She darted toward the bridge alone, barely evading Sarenth's grip. Red could not believe she ran. Something about this city truly was terrorizing her.

"Minnie! It's too dangerous!" Red called after her.

Weapon fire erupted from within a burning building across the street. Dirt and stone sprinkled the sidewalk as deadly projectiles haphazardly sprayed in their direction.

Sarenth waved for everyone to take cover. He pointed to one of his soldiers. "Go after her! Make sure she stays safe and keep her at the bridge until we catch up!"

"Yes, sir!"

As soon as the shooting paused, he said, "We'll stop the shooters and then proceed. The rest of you hold still." He waved toward the short blazing building and led three of his soldiers in a charge. They disappeared out of sight into an alley. Weapons discharged rapidly.

The firing continued as Sarenth's heavy footsteps galloped back alone.

"Run! Get to the bridge!" he howled.

Red jumped to her feet and sprinted after the others.

Adiquis screamed at a soldier, "I changed my mind! I don't want to do this! Get me back to Dr. Petras!" But they shoved him along.

The burning building erupted into a massive fireball behind them. Flames lapped up at the sky casting an almost daylight glow across the street. The ground shook under Red. She had to skip on her toes to avoid being tripped up. Once a good distance away, she turned back to Sarenth who trailed right behind her.

"Where are the others?" she asked.

"They did not survive," he answered through strained breaths. "They gave their lives so we could carry out the Divine's will. We must cross that bridge and find the control station quickly. I believe we are being pursued."

"I thought this armor was strong enough to deflect almost anything!"

"It was not the weapon fire but the burning flames that consumed them."

They neared the bridge, old but massive, and found its center obstructed by large, charred vehicles. A soldier consoled Minnie with some quiet words. "It is okay. You are safe now. Everyone is here."

Minnie looked up and counted the survivors. "No, they're *not*. I've lost more people to the Posse, or the Survivalists, or whoever the heck is terrorizing people now!"

"Please, regain your composure," Sarenth said. "We are here to protect you…"

Minnie threw herself onto a vehicle and climbed up. "Let's just go! No more time for words. I may have forgotten how dangerous it's become here, but I won't let anyone else get caught in its madness!" She scaled the first truck and pulled Red and the others up.

After a hasty climb, Sarenth made it to the other side last. He peered back through a crack in the blockade. Laughter and weapon fire echoed. "We need to move swiftly," he said. "We cannot allow these hooligans to see where we are going."

Several blocks later, Minnie pointed to an imposing square building with a colossal radar dish on its roof. "That's the Galactic Communications Relay. I hope they have an auxiliary power supply. I've only seen the inside on the news, but I know there's a control room which communicates with the orbital signal station."

Sarenth shot the door open. They barricaded themselves inside with small tables and chairs.

The abandoned lobby was small. Floral patterns upon the walls and stacks of magazines with smiling faces on tables made it seem oddly quaint. Rows of chairs hinted at a frequented and popular place for many during happier times. Red questioned a strange, speckled ceiling material segmented with what appeared to be metal rods. Monitors displaying black and white static, while others filled with multicolored vertical bars, broadcasted nothing in particular. There were no functioning light fixtures that Red could see. Or perhaps she did not know how to turn them on and there was no reason to do so at the moment. This building, claimed to be such an important technological wonder for the human species, felt more like a bureaucratic lobby than a monument to progress.

Sarenth surveyed the room. "Identify all windows and avoid them."

Red sat next to Minnie who was slumped in a chair. She needed Minnie to have her head focused even if things were a little screwy in there. "Hey, are you okay?"

Minnie sniffled. "No, I'm not. I keep getting this feeling like everybody close to me gets hurt or worse. It's like I'm some siren of doom."

"That's ridiculous. I mean, you saved my life back there, didn't you?"

Minnie raised her head. She wiped her nose with her sleeve. They both stared realizing the armor exhibited zero absorption capabilities. It was gross. "I guess," she said.

"Thank you for that. You *saved* me." Being *saved* was not a normal word within Red's vocabulary. But in this moment, she felt it was the most appropriate one to help her ally in distress.

"Minnie," Sarenth asked, "can you find the room?"

She dried her nose. "I know what it looks like. Big room, lots of screens, and rows of control consoles. With Divine guidance, give me enough time to poke around and I'm sure I'll stumble upon it."

"Hold up! Don't just go wandering, you rusthead." King jumped behind a desk and searched through several datapads. "Look, a map!" He handed it to Minnie.

Sarenth left two of his soldiers in the lobby while the remaining pair escorted the group through an intricate network of hallways.

Minnie consulted the map as they navigated every twist and turn.

"Why did you take the map?" Red asked. "Don't you have enough faith in the Divine to guide us there?" She did not know why it came out sarcastically. She had just tried to cheer Minnie up. Was she the one conflicted inside?

"I know you don't like the faith."

Red must have looked surprised because Minnie smiled gently.

"It's obvious. We have people like you here on Earth too. I've managed to get along fine with them as long as they let me believe my thing and I don't try to push it on them. I don't think I've done that to you, have I?"

Red fiddled with her pencil in her pocket. "Well, no. And I appreciate that. But we're both involved in a series of pretty important tasks. I find it unsettling that you place your safety, and consequently that of others like me, in your faith which I don't believe amounts to anything." She paused after letting what felt like a fountain of stress flow out. She recognized that Minnie was trying to have an honest conversation with her. "I'm sorry. That came out a little harsh."

Minnie smirked and glanced knowingly at Red. "It's okay. You can't be a daughter of a priest and not get challenged every now and then. I understand your hesitation to roll the dice with me, but I assure you my dice are weighted in our favor. And even if they aren't, I'll continue to lean on you and the others when I'm most unsure. I'm smart enough to not leave everything to chance." She waved the map in her hand.

Minnie was not foolish. While she injected a lot of her faith into her work, she made sound decisions most of the time. And the ones Red did not agree with had mostly nothing to do with her faith. It was her heart that was too big. Red could not hold that against her. Purple was the same way and she was an incredibly competent Rover.

At the rear of the group, Adiquis asked King, "D-do all grownups design buildings to be mazes? First the prison and now this." He twiddled his fingers restlessly.

"No," King replied. "Just the ones who don't want you to find the treasure in the middle."

Minnie pointed to a set of doors ahead. "This should be it."

Weapon fire echoed from somewhere distant. They hurried inside. The room was as Minnie described. An oversized chamber with many computer consoles and a wall-spanning screen. Images of a globe and numerous satellites in orbit indicated at least some systems were intact.

Minnie walked up and down an aisle of small screens. "Now where's the big red button?" She sat at the largest console in the back. Her eager fingers touched sliders and pressed buttons.

"I do not think that is a sound strategy," Sarenth said as he glanced from behind her. "We are liable to do more harm than good if we do not know how to operate this complex device. Are there instructions anywhere in this room?"

"How about this?" Adiquis held up a datapad. "I found it in a desk and there are several schematics of a technical nature on it."

"Give it here." Minnie took it and browsed the screen. "Thank the Divine. There's a troubleshooting tool for total system failure." She typed a command into the console and a loading bar materialized on-screen. "Five minutes? We don't have time to wait!"

A wiry anthropomorphic creature popped on the screen. "I see you're trying to reestablish the connection to the orbital station. Do you need any help?"

"Yes!" She tapped on the creature and a red X appeared over its face.

"I'm sorry. An error has occurred. Please try again."

"Come on!" She slapped its face several times.

"I'm sorry...I'm sorry...I'm sorry..."

"Augh!" Minnie groaned.

"Well then," Sarenth said. "We will just have to defend here until it is done."

Footsteps approached the door. One of Sarenth's soldiers barged inside, nearly knocking Sarenth onto the floor.

"I am sorry, sir! But the building has been breached. We are holding them in the narrow hallways, but they greatly outnumber us and…"

Another voice bellowed from down the hall. "Seekers! They followed the enemies inside and…everyone regroup quickly!"

Sarenth pointed to his remaining people. "You two, follow me." He patted Minnie's back and headed for the door. "We will protect this door and search for an alternative exit. As soon as the objective is complete, call for us and we will return."

Sarenth left and King began pacing.

"Come on, Minnie," he said. "The clock's ticking and we're not even in the final round. You gotta do something and speed this up."

Red did not want to rush her, but King was right. Danger was closing in on them and their escort was dwindling. Had their Divine luck finally run out?

ROVER ENTRY #1085

King paced the room. "What is taking so long? Just dial the satellite and send out the signal."

"Maybe we should go," Adiquis said. "I don't know if we can do this! Dr. Petras could probably, but just us?"

"No, we have to do this." Red faced a worried-eyed Minnie. "King's right. Just hit some more buttons to speed it up. You understand Earth tech, right? Whatever it takes, just do it."

Minnie pounded the console. "It's not so *simple*!" She stared at the loading bar. "This room is normally *filled* with technicians to keep the wheels turning. None of us are computer scientists so we need to let it do its thing. In the meantime, stop hassling me and do something productive! I bet whatever version we're about to unlock is going to be very simplified. Start planning what our short message will be."

Red knelt down next to Adiquis and whispered, "It's going to be okay."

He seemed slightly soothed.

"Well," she continued, "what are we going to say? Has anyone drafted anything?" She looked around, but nobody offered. "What about, 'Help. We're under attack and we need immediate assistance.'"

"But they won't know what the threat is," King said.

"Okay. 'Help. Aliens are attacking. We need reinforcements.'"

"How are they going to find us?" Adiquis asked. "Where are we going to meet?"

"Hmm. We all traveled to Jangala by gate. Should we ask them to do the same?"

Minnie tapped her head. "Perhaps. But there are scientists among the survivors here that think the number of functioning gates remaining in the galaxy may be small. Most of them have probably been buried or destroyed if they're anything like the ones we've seen up close. I mean, King's whole society is built on a series of excavated and scavenged gates buried under mountain ranges. Those things aren't going to work anymore."

"Wait, what?" King scrunched his face and slapped his cheeks. "Whoa! Everything makes so much more sense now!"

"You haven't already figured that out?" Minnie mumbled.

"I think your scientists are right," Red said. "When I was being interrogated by the aliens, I overheard them discussing such a possibility. Wherever the remaining gates are, it's going to be hard for people to find them."

"That's a problem we can't solve right now," Adiquis said spinning in a rolling chair. "Although, I have a few ideas. Let's ask Dr. Petras about that when we get back."

Minnie clapped when the loading bar disappeared. The entire room glistened with flashing lights. The wiry creature returned. "Troubleshooting is complete. Emergency communications will remain open for ninety seconds. You will then be prompted to enter your secure credentials to continue after the system logs out. Please remember to select the correct region and broadcast in the correct language."

"This is it!" King grabbed the microphone and was about to speak before Minnie snatched it back.

"Watch it, quick draw! We only get one chance to get this right and we didn't even account for the language thing. We need to say everything everyone needs to know, across countless human colonies, and we barely know anything ourselves. Who knows the most?"

Adiquis raised a finger. "You could just let the Divine speak through you." He touched the microphone and pushed it toward Minnie's face. "You seem very attuned to scripture. Just start saying everything you know and I'm sure you'll find the right words."

Minnie gently diverted his hand. She looked toward King and they both nodded without a word. They both pointed at Red.

A lump formed in her throat. "M-me? You want me to send a message to the entire galaxy?"

"You've already sort of did it once, right?" King said.

"We're out of time to negotiate." Minnie shoved the microphone into Red's hand and swapped places with her in the command chair. "Forget the succinct, perfect message. Just tell them everything you know and what we need."

The clock upon the large screen was ticking down. Time for arguing was over. Red took out Dr. Petras' special datapad and gave it to Minnie for uploading alongside her message. She pressed a big red button. The satellite on the giant screen emitted curved green lines both toward the planet and into the beyond.

Adiquis consulted the manual and ran his finger across a column of control panel selections. The broadcast amplified. "You are now connected to every human colony capable of receiving."

She drew the microphone to her mouth and slowly parted her lips. They were dry. She was not as nervous as the first time she sent a message to an entire other galaxy, but uncertainty still turned her stomach. She shivered and shook her head. She had to cross this scary boundary. She had to focus!

"Hello. This is Red…wait, never mind that. This is an emergency broadcast from the home world, Earth. The planet has fallen to an alien invasion. Over a week ago, I made first contact with these invaders and learned of a plot to weed us out of the galaxy in pursuit of our natural resources. Colonies everywhere are in danger. A few others from different planets and I have teamed up and we're forming a resistance on the Great Expedition planet of Jangala. We know how to get to the aliens and now we just need your help to fight them! Join us there or search your planet, your solar system, anywhere you can for signs of a wispy, blue glowing gate. Send any help you can and find me…find *us* on the other side!"

"Now, do it in another language!" Minnie said. She continued to upload planetary coordinates and supporting documentation.

Red repeated her message in the five most prevalent languages she knew from a life of pursuing the Great Answer. At the start of her sixth, the blinking lights in the room went dark. She threw down the microphone and followed the others into the hallway.

"Sarenth!" Minnie screamed.

"This way!" he shouted near an exit down a dark hallway. The unremarkable beige walls were now splattered in black sludge and red fluid.

If Red had not known the cause, she might have even called it art.

ROVER ENTRY #1086

Sarenth eyed their retreat as they escaped out the relay building's backdoor. Red stumbled out into a barren yard. The sky was brighter than before. A disturbing crimson glow illuminated the city.

"Head back to the church! Be alert of any pursuers," Sarenth advised. Only two of his soldiers followed her out. Had the others succumbed to the fighting, Red wondered?

Her jaw dropped when she saw what was left of the bridge. The former vehicle blockade was now a pile of flaming, scattered shrapnel. Whatever cleared this out was now behind them. Quickly but carefully she weaved her way through the hazardous gauntlet.

Feet stomped close behind her as she shouted, "Hey! We have a tail!"

Minnie shivered. "No! Don't let them take me too!"

Sarenth grabbed her arm. "We must double our pace. I will not let them touch you." A seeker's roar rattled their bones. "Besides, they have another threat to worry about."

The blazing buildings that Red passed tainted the beautiful environment she previously admired. The glow mimicked a disastrous nightmare in which the twin suns of Abeona-2 swooped down and covered her world in flames.

At the church's steps, a chorus of growls preceded a pack of Seekers emerging from alleyways, over rooftops, and stepping into the street.

Sarenth swung open the heavy doors. "Inside! I will hold the position!"

Seeker feet thumped upon the cold stone street leaving black marks of sizzling sludge. They drew nearer like a pack of wild canidaurochs hungry for their first meal after hibernation. The slicing teeth of one nearing Red gleamed red and white reflecting the flames off its flesh-rendering tools. Or perhaps some of that scarlet tinge was actually the remains of another unfortunate soul before her. Was she to be next within its mouth?

Red fumbled with the pistol at her side but was unable to undo the holster strap quickly enough. Sarenth squeezed his weapon trigger and peppered the encroaching beast with searing light.

"Go!" he demanded.

Red finally rushed up the church stairs. Before she followed the others inside, Sarenth's weapon stopped.

"Shoot!" He waved it through the air. "It is overheating! J-just go! I will…"

"Watch out!" Red screamed as a Seeker charged forward. She successfully drew her pistol and aimed at the beast's side. With her finger on the trigger, she did not feel confident about firing.

"Aim for a weak spot!" Sarenth shouted. "The legs!"

She lowered her sight and fired three quick shots. One cut through the trunk of the hunter. It stumbled and tripped onto its face.

Just as the other monsters snarled and charged forward, Sarenth grabbed Red's arm and dragged her inside. He picked up a plank and threw it against the doors. "Help me!"

She pushed a pew in the way just as the Seekers began clawing at the entrance.

"That is enough. Quickly," he waved. "Below."

They reunited with Minnie and the others down the catacomb's steps and within the dirt tunnel. "Which way?" Sarenth asked her.

A thunderous boom from above plopped dirt on top of Minnie's head. "Follow me!"

The corridors continued to rumble during the entire trek into the enormous cavern, dirt and rocks lodging themselves from the ceiling and walls. Something big and destructive was afoot and Red hoped they were running away from it, not towards.

Staring down into the black sea below, King asked, "How are we gonna get down there?" He steadied himself against the rock wall, not afraid to ensure he was safe. "I don't reckon my knees can take a hop that far."

"This will be the easiest task we do today." Sarenth drove another one of his pocket poles into the ground and shot a rope deep into the darkness. "Grip the rope with your hands and thighs. Release gently to descend. These suits will protect you from the intense friction."

One by one, they slid down the cliff side and sank into the blackness. Their landings were not perfect, but Sarenth caught each of them safely. They followed him back to the infinite ladder's base, through the streets, and climbed into and out of the old crater.

Minnie knew before she saw them. A low hum of humanity whispering and worrying grew louder. She stumbled into the rotunda and shined her light on a sea of people gathered just beyond the gate.

"Bimini!" an old man called out as he shuffled toward her.

"Dad!" She sprinted towards him. A bone-rattling roar shook the rotunda and she stopped. What few walls remained came crumbling down. "Dad, evacuate everyone through the gate!"

Screaming and the cries of children erupted. Sarenth ran to the gate and directed his soldiers through first. "So many people! Regardless, escort the civilians back to Jangala immediately!"

"Sir, but the alien patrol schedules…"

"There is no time to traverse undetected! Defend them from anything on the way at any cost!"

His soldiers dived in and the horde of people followed. Sarenth tapped his suit and a glowing, marigold translucent helmet covered his head. He scanned the ceiling and fired his rifle upward in small bursts.

Red noticed his shots were imprecise. He winced every time his weapon recoiled. She rushed to his side. "Where is it? How can I help?"

"Fire in my direction! This beast is enormous!"

She handled her pistol hesitantly but mustered the courage to point and squeeze the trigger if it meant saving their lives. To her left and right, King, Minnie, and Adiquis took a stand as well.

"You sure you can handle that, kid?" King asked Adiquis with a wink.

"I've seen marbles fire a bigger blast than this pea shooter!"

Red overheard Minnie whispering a strained prayer as they shot into the darkness. She spotted little sparks of impact somewhere far up above. Rocks tumbled past them and an enormous boulder fell and shattered in front of her. It whipped up a vision-obscuring cloud. She stumbled back and coughed. "There's too much dust!"

Minnie coughed too. "That's not just dust! It's smoke! How do we turn on our own little helmet things?"

Sarenth grabbed her shoulder. "Grip and hold until it appears!" A helmet of light encased her head as well.

Red squeezed her shoulder. The glow surrounded her head. Her vision filled with illuminated graphs, charts, and all manners of outlines for what she guessed were structures in the darkness despite being surrounded by impenetrable smoke. She searched the blackness up above and pieced together the green wireframe of a titanic and grotesque monstrosity. The beast alternated between swatting agitatedly at their weapon fire and stretching its limbs to the cavern's ceiling and scraping against it. Boulders continued raining down near the fleeing people below.

"We must draw its ire! Let me try this trick Dr. Petras added to my weapon..." Sarenth flipped a switch on the barrel's side. His instant beams transformed into lobbed balls of light. The rifle kicked back into his shoulder. He grunted in agonizing pain. "You...ah! All of you should go! Ensure all the people make it through the gate and escort the retreat's rear. I will continue to focus this beast's attention."

Each blinding shot elicited an echoing nightmarish howl. Red, King, and Adiquis ran off, but Minnie remained.

"Minnie! Come on!" Red shouted back as King and Adiquis jumped through before her.

Minnie ignored her. "Sarenth, stop being the hero. Your arm's shot so let me cover *you* while you fall back." She barraged the beast with her smaller weapon.

He clutched his aching arm. "No! My duty is to protect you, not the other way around. Almost everyone is gone. Go now!"

"We go together!" She offered her hand.

"I will protect you! I will be last!"

A massive claw swooped down. He shoved her onto the floor. The beast scooped him up and away.

"Sarenth!" she wailed.

King leapt back through the gate. "What are you two still doing here?" He ran past Red and lifted Minnie over his shoulder. The entire rotunda collapsed and giant stones crashed around the gate.

Minnie kicked her feet and pounded upon his back. "No! We have to save him!"

"We're not beating that thing! And that gate is about to be scrap!"

"No!"

The three tumbled through the gate and crumpled on top of each other under the orange sky of Creare. Red untangled herself from King and Minnie's limbs and sat flat upon the cement ground. She wished to hear Sarenth huffing behind her. Instead, the portal filled with debris as its image devolved into a swirly static.

Unfamiliar weapon fire beamed in the distance. Jangalan boots upon the ground thumped much closer. An allied soldier waved Red forward.

"Quickly," he said. "We will cover you and your friend's retreat!" He turned and shot at small gathering dots gathering high atop the wall's steep parapets.

"Get up!" King hopped to his aching knees and yanked the two upright. He pulled them after the Earth people. "Look at that!" he said as they passed more Jangalan soldiers. "The calvary has arrived, right? Olyana is finally buying into the plan!"

Red pulled her goggles over her eyes and zoomed onto the wall's edges. A number of aliens gathered and gawked at them scurrying past. Rather than trying to blast the refugees in this vulnerable state, they pointed and spoke among themselves, seemingly curious. On occasion they ducked from an incredibly inaccurate errant laser.

Last to leap through the gate to Jangala, Red wondered what it would take to fight back through all this and return to search for Sarenth.

Olyana's people, military and civilian alike, ushered clusters of refugees toward the settlement, clothed them in blankets and offered food to the children. From what little Red had gleaned about Jangalan recent history, they were not in a position to be giving resources away. Their show of kindness spoke volumes regarding the colony's virtuous character.

She watched surprise spread across the faces of both the Jangalan and Earth folks. Neither of the two groups had seen a member of the other for almost a thousand years. The Earth folk's skin tone diversity was beautiful compared to the Jangalan's monochrome complexion. Jangalan's were not very inventive with their hairstyles whereas the Earth folk wore their locks long, straight, curly, braided, spiked, and more. Red knew they were worlds apart in many more invisible ways. Was Minnie right to encourage their return here or would this further complicate the only homebase for humanity's resistance?

Wide-eyed Adiquis awaited them near the gate's exit. He ran to Red's side and danced impatiently. "Where's Sarenth? I didn't see him come through yet. Dr. Petras wants to know if her weapon modifications were helpful or not."

"I don't know," she answered, watching the gate and hoping but not expecting to see him at that moment. "But there might be other gates, right? I wager he'll blast his way free and find another one."

"That's…possible," King replied slowly, joining them with Minnie's hand still within his. "I suppose your own planet has a ton of them. But, Red…"

Minnie yanked her fingers through his fist. "Come on, Adiquis. We should speak to Olyana this instant." She ushered Adiquis along toward the ark without another word.

Red and King followed for a time, but King placed a palm on her shoulder and pulled her back. "Hey, hold on for a second."

"What is it? Let's go see Olyana and see what we can do about Sarenth."

"About Minnie. You and I both know Sarenth didn't make it. He was either made into a snack or flattened like a pancake. Why don't we just not talk about him for a while? I don't think she can take it."

Red's face grimaced. "A man probably sacrificed his life for us and you're making a joke out of it?"

He raised his hands in deference. "You're right, I know. I shouldn't have said it like that. I just…I don't want it to get too heavy, you know? If it does, then I have no idea what to say."

Red watched the crowd make their way toward the ark. She sighed. "I don't know. Maybe we should talk about it." She had spent a lot of time as a child wrestling with grief, but she would hardly call herself an expert. She knew talking about it worked for her. It could help Minnie too. "You can't let stuff lie and fester. We have to address it and work through it." She watched Minnie staring at the ground as she entered the ship.

"Yeah." King slowly regained his pace forward. "Everybody needs to heal, her most of all. I'm not saying she doesn't, but neither of us know how to help her. We're liable to do more harm than good. And," he tapped his chin, "is it possible that she had a thing for him? That could make this worse."

Red considered it for a moment. "No, I don't think so. I'm worried because this seems larger than that."

The Gamble

File Under: desperation, anticipation, hope

Location(s): Jangala, Creare

Executive Summary: I did not enter the gate and reemerge with revelations gained through the typical patient and stoic Rover fashion. Danger was omnipresent and it's a wonder I made it back alive. The fact that I was able to transcribe this entry foreshadows my fate. Yet not all parts of me, or the people who helped me, remained unharmed.

ROVER ENTRY #1091

Red trailed the others into the war room. An air of strife engulfed her like a thick haze. She kept her head down as she briskly walked through yelling and finger pointing. An argument was ready to boil over between two women regarding the valuable soldiers lost supporting the unexpected retreat. A man in an apricot coat, swinging a datapad that almost absent-mindedly hit her in the face as she passed, said the aliens' devastating red lasers destroyed irreplaceable equipment. Another agreed and said the entire operation was a poorly calculated mistake.

Red passed Cardinal Murcario commenting to Azul, "Consider this one positive light: I think everyone would be more panicked if not for the aliens' disinterest in chasing us through the gate. As I understand it, they only started firing after one of our skittish recruits shot first."

Azul pondered the notion. "I do not think they much wanted to bother themselves with a nuisance they interpret as pests. That confidence worries me."

Data flashing on a wall of computers reflected off Olyana's focused eyes. She and several advisors discussed charts with heated voices. When she noticed Red and the others approaching, she mustered a smile.

"Ah, the brave galactic warriors return. Sarenth's soldiers report you found the far talk building. However, they suffered great casualties at the hands of Earth's instigators. There is, of course," she sighed, gazing at the ceiling, "the matter of the hundreds of refugees you brought back with you."

"Please," she continued. "Do not worry about the logistics. Volunteers are already integrating your people into the settlement." She took a deep breath and nodded toward Minnie. Could Olyana hear Minnie's heart thumping through her chest? Or perhaps she sensed the guilt overflowing inside Minnie's mind. "Now tell me, Minnie. Were you successful in sending your call?"

"Yes," she said barely above the hum of the room. Her eyes were affixed squarely on the floor. Her thoughts were elsewhere. "Red…she broadcasted to all the modern planets and in several languages. I think anyone who was listening got the gist."

"And did we receive a reply?"

Red raised her hand. "It's okay, Minnie. I can answer that. Well, we only had enough time to communicate outward, so I wasn't able to open a listening channel. However, I can confirm that Dr. Petras' special data successfully accompanied the call."

"Ah. So the plan may still work," Olyana said, patting her chest.

"Yes, but," Red said with a raised timid finger, "that leaves us with a new problem which we haven't figured out." She stepped aside and nodded toward Adiquis.

Adiquis hopped in place. "We're guessing the gates are mostly hidden across the galaxy. We think others may find it hard to find them. I'm hoping to speak to Dr. Petras about a solution based on a few ideas I had this morning."

Olyana nodded. "Very well. Head to her now. She is in the warehouse with Emillee."

Adiquis was gone in seconds.

"Excellent." The room's chattering was dying down. Olyana searched the room. "And where is Missionary Sarenth? His soldiers said he planned on being last during the evacuation. Was he with you?"

Approaching from behind Red, Cardinal Murcario glanced about as well. "My report informs me he held the rear while each of you assisted him in a most glorious defense against a horror of imaginable strength! I must commend the young man."

Minnie struggled to contain short gasps. "He…Sarenth was taken by the Seeker when he pushed me out of harm's way." She tugged at the seams of her suit. Her feet shuffled restlessly. "The size of it. The length of its claws. He…didn't make it through the Earth gate before it lost its connection. I don't know how he could have survived. I tried to…I tried…" She buried her face in her hands. "I'm so sorry!"

Cardinal Murcario immediately clasped his hands together and closed his eyes. He spoke quickly, softly. "Oh, Great Divine. Please lay your holy soldier down to rest and calm his loyal heart. Welcome him into your eternal warrior ranks."

Olyana lowered her head and pounded a fist upon her heart. "Attention, everyone!"

Silence fell upon the room. Everyone turned to her.

"Many soldiers, including a promising Missionary of the Divine, gave their lives today defending our people and those we chose to protect. May they now rest in the place their hearts so believed in."

About half of the room knelt and muttered prayers. Minnie did the same although she barely constructed full sentences through the tears.

When the moment concluded, Olyana said, "Missionary Sarenth was prepared to die. We all are, for war is what we have known for generations."

Minnie staggered to her feet. She was holding back a feeling she desperately wanted to express but seemed too ashamed to share.

Red touched her arm gently. "Are you okay? It's all right to cry."

Minnie snapped out of Red's hand. "I'm not okay! I don't want to cry! I'm a strong daughter of the Divine! But…but, no!" She pointed at Olyana. "Sarenth shouldn't have died! I was right there beside him blasting the same beast. It was time to go. We could've both made it out. Why did he insist on fighting for *me*? Why push *me* out of the way? I was there to help…"

Olyana moved swiftly, pulling Minnie into an embrace. She squeezed.

Azul raised his hand, his lips moving slightly, before simply stepping back.

Minnie's arms squirmed. Her darting legs tried to kick away.

"Life is the price we pay for life," Olyana said loudly. "Sometimes we are the giver of life and other times we are the receiver. Today you are the receiver and I hope you continue to be so for many years to come."

Minnie broke into a wail. She gripped Olyana's shoulders.

Olyana rubbed Minnie's back. "There, there, sweet child. Stand tall and express your heart."

"The Divine was supposed to protect us both. Why only me? Why?"

King glanced toward Red. His eyes darted and sweat gathered at his brow. Red did not know what to say that could possibly help.

After a time, Olyana released Minnie. She slowly walked back to her seat at the great table. Each slow step seemed to echo throughout the chamber that was silent except for Minnie's scattered gasps. It was as if Olyana were trudging through sand, hoping she would never make it and be forced to continue this cruel ordeal.

Once seated, she gestured for everyone to do the same. Her mouth opened but words were delayed. A great sigh, one that slumped her shoulders and drew her head back, preceded. Red thought she witnessed a part of Olyana draining out of her.

"Non-home world travelers, you were able to see the state of that planet," Olyana said. "Is it as desperate as Minnie described?"

"Um…" Red began.

"Yes. It's still burning," Minnie answered with a flat affect.

"What is the possibility that it will be able to lend us any aid, possibly the strongest and most advanced of us all?" Olyana asked.

Red said, "Things do not look great. I wouldn't count on it."

Olyana clasped her hands together. She rested her chin upon her knuckles and glanced at Azul and then Cardinal Murcario.

"Hmm," she said. "Very well. Let us leave Adiquis and the others to continue devising alternatives. We have made much progress in other preparations over the last few days and I must supervise the coordination once again. There is nothing you three need attend. Please rest and be ready for the final confrontation that may be less than a day away."

The room burst into argument. Robes flapped and hands waved all vying for Olyana's attention.

"But Captain, what of our losses?"

"This is ridiculous! How can you possibly justify further action?"

"Enough!" Olyana shouted, slamming her fists upon the table. "Whether because of our invader's technological superiority or their invasive, ghastly pets, they are a threat that beckons a response! I have spent many an hour contemplating our next steps dependent upon the varying outcomes of our traveler's campaign. Thus, it is already decided. *I have already decided.*"

Her brow furrowed, nose crinkled, and what could have been construed as possible tears brewed at the edges of her eyes. Olyana waved to Azul and pointed him toward her chair as she stepped away from it. "Continue bickering over the logistics if you prefer. I must take my leave. There is work left to be done if there will be any chance for our species to retain any of its dignity."

Olyana stepped out into the hallway.

Not keen on sticking around without Olyana controlling the room, Red followed Minnie and King toward the door. She felt the War Council's eyes on her back but not another word was uttered in their presence.

Before the door shut, Cardinal Murcario slipped his hand through and pushed it slightly open. "Wait, please. I want you to know I do not hold Sarenth's fate against any of you. I pray for that promising young man, but Captain Olyana is correct. This is the nature of war."

"Stupid," Minnie uttered.

"Thank you, sir," Red said. "I hope it was worth it."

He nodded. "Know that Dr. Petras has certainly proven to be a mighty asset. I, too, pray your call is worth just as much, if not more. I deeply, painfully pray. Despite Sarenth's fate, his sacrifice may not have been in vain. Thank you." He slipped back inside.

Minnie's feet quickly strode along the metal floor. Red jumped in front of her before she was gone. "Hey! Are you okay?"

"Yeah. I'm fine now." Minnie's eyes were swollen and red. Her fleeting eye contact suggested she was uncomfortable being seen this way. Shallow breaths were more noticeable in the quiet hallway. "Olyana and the Cardinal are right. Sarenth knew what he signed up for…I guess," she ended sarcastically.

"Minnie, I'm worried. It doesn't sound like you believe that. I…I don't really know how to talk about this kind of stuff, but do you want to share what you're thinking with me?"

As if Red had turned a valve, Minnie burst out. "He did everything he should have! He was a devout man who sacrificed repeatedly for others and had faith our plan was protected by Divine favor!" She wet her sleeve drawing it across her cheeks.

With gritted teeth, she continued, "I want to believe he slipped out, but I saw the same thing you did. And because of that, I know I'm supposed to be comforted by the fact that he's probably within the Divine's embrace right now." She let out a shallow laugh. "But he wasn't done here. There was so much more for him to…like all the other young people I've seen…" She choked up. "I can't. I just can't keep myself from crying."

Red nodded, her eyes unsure where else to look but at Minnie's own. Was she doing this consoling business right? "It's…going to be okay. I, uh, think statistically speaking, we have a good chance of pulling this whole thing off. You have a smart plan. We've accounted for many variables thanks to our knowledge of the enemy's technology. Forget about all this faith stuff. I have a lot of confidence in us considering just the facts."

Minnie pushed Red gently out of her way. She flashed a twisted smile. "*Faith* is what holds me together. My *faith* has always given me direction. I don't want anything to take its place."

She slipped past Red and jogged far down the corridor.

Red tried to follow, but King came from behind and grabbed her arm. "Hold on. You're a terrible grief counselor."

She brushed King off. "Let me go. She needs comfort."

"I don't know if she'd want me telling you this, but now that I think about it, you two have this in common. She told me the other day she lost her mom less than a week ago. She was done in by those same gangs that chased us through the city. On top of that, I'm sure she thought her best friend had bit the dust. It's great that he's fine, but there had to have been a period when she started to mourn him. And then the whiplash."

"Oh." Red felt shaken. She had not known Minnie was a girl already grieving and that her recent traumas were further piling onto already deep wounds. "I feel like such a jerk. The way she was acting, I should have known something had happened, but I had no idea it was so terrible. I probably came across callous the last few days. I should tell her I lost my mother too."

"Whoa, Red." King stepped away. "Don't make it about you. I reckon she just needs some time to process alone."

"Maybe. But I was young when I went through the worst of my own mother's death. I had my grandpa by my side. I had a lot of time to come to terms with it, but she hasn't had any downtime to deal with this and she's alone here. She needs our support."

"She's got her prayer. And there's a lot of religious folks around here that, if she wanted to, she could talk to."

"Religion isn't the answer to everything," Red said, rolling her eyes. She watched Minnie round a distant corner. She wished only the best for her.

King chuckled. "You don't need to tell *me* that. Look. I get where you're coming from. You got a thing about the faithful and you reckon if someone just thinks it through enough, that it'll all make sense. But I think this is one of those situations where if she needs us, she'll find us. We don't chase her. We trust her process. Only she knows what she needs."

Red considered this way of dealing with things. Sometimes as a Rover you drove alone for weeks traveling to a distant settlement. If something bothered you enough, you were expected to talk to an Order Arbitrator as soon as you could and clear your mind. However, she knew in practice sometimes you had only your thoughts and your buggy. If she could work through her feelings alone sometimes, then she had to hope Minnie would be fine with time too.

King almost knocked her over with a hearty slap on the back. "Get some rest, you hear? Or maybe you need to update your little book some more. I'm sure things are gonna be different tomorrow. I can feel it." He walked a few paces away. "Well, I'm off to get in a little workout. Gotta be ready to take on Olyana tonight with everything I've learned!"

Red certainly had much to write. The day had been long and the details were fresh. She knew waiting too long could allow facts to start muddling in her mind. Yet, a hint of adrenaline lingered in her body. She wanted to keep feeling that high instead of worrying about all of these very depressing human problems. The incredible stress she had just underwent had not faded and the prospect of watching a man in his prime sweat on a mat may just be what she needed.

"Hey. Is the offer to watch you spar still good?"

King smiled and shook his head. "Yeah, sure. We're meeting up in about an hour. Want me to come by and get you right before? I don't know where your room is but…"

"Room 5660. It's a date!" she giggled.

"Now hold on. Let's not make it out to be something it isn't…"

"Okay!" Red backed into an elevator and waved as the door closed. She pressed a hand to her chest. Her heart raced. She had never said those words before. Green had never given her the chance back home. She was embarking into uncharted territory. Thank goodness she was a Rover and a darn good one. As long as she moved carefully, she could navigate the wilds within the human heart.

ROVER ENTRY #1092

After resting in her quarters for a much-needed quiet moment, Red answered the knock at her door and followed King into the elevator. They rode to another floor and exited onto a sprawling gym. Soldiers worked out in small groups using weights and complex exercise equipment. More people than she anticipated were sparring with each other in this temple dedicated to physical fitness.

"Is that the kind of fighting you do?" Red asked, pointing at the grapplers they walked towards. She had never seen anything like it. She opened her Journal to commit a rough sketch.

"Actually, yeah. It's a helpful style when you're in the face of your opponent. And with my rings, there isn't a projectile that's going to knock me down, so they come to me and I wreck them."

As they approached the practice mat's edge, a woman flipped her partner across the room. "Whoa!" Red yelped as the body soared overhead. "Are they okay?"

"I wouldn't be too worried. These folks are seasoned fighters." He waved at the winner. "Hey! Ready for a real challenge?"

Olyana was the woman left standing. She wore the combat suit of her people unlike the two of them who had returned to the supplied leisurewear. Red admired the suit and the protection it provided the wearer. Thankfully, she had not had to utilize that power herself. Red noted the mat's edge and ensured her feet were clearly off it. She would not survive a minute against Olyana and she wondered if King could either.

Red took a seat on the floor with a splendid view. She opened her Journal and committed an entire page to a detailed portrait of King pacing about. Similar to the canidaurochs, he was like another wild creature to be documented.

"King of Balamanda. I was unsure if you would return after what happened yesterday," Olyana said, wiping her face with a towel.

"Not my official title but I do like the ring of it. And of course I'd be back. I intend to learn as much as I can from you. One little upset isn't going to send me packing. For our final showdown, I have a brand-new strategy that I'm confident you won't see coming. Now about that little throw you did…"

Olyana stepped behind a privacy screen. Her silhouette moved mysteriously. "It is the same that defeated you yesterday. You were wrong when you said the only reason I won was because of my armor."

"Yeah, well it *does* give you a strength advantage over my natural muscles. There's only so much a guy can do."

She emerged from the screen in a different jumpsuit. It fitted loosely and looked exceptionally cozy. "I was under the impression that a professional fighter like yourself would be capable of rising to the challenge. Perhaps the same limits of human physiology compared to technology exist on every planet."

King stepped onto the mat. He rolled his shoulders and stretched his legs. "I don't disagree with that. There's a time for every kind of strength, but at least in a matchup it should be fair." He chuckled and pointed. "So, tell me. Is this new running suit going to inflate and turn you into an assault blimp or something?"

Olyana returned to the mat. She emitted the aura of someone who knew they were about to teach a fool a lesson. An interested crowd gathered. A soldier stepped between them and counted down to zero. He left them alone and the two cast mischievous glances at each other.

"No," Olyana said, "this is not a wonder of any kind. These are simply my favorite workout clothes. They allow for great flexibility and…"

King exploded like a bomb and charged her. At the last possible moment, she took a simple step to the side. As he blew past her, she grabbed his shirt collar and yanked his feet from under him. He fell on his back and she leapt several paces away.

"As I was saying, I am very flexible and quick."

"Okay. So you're strong *and* fast." He jumped up. He stepped cautiously toward her. "I can't say I expected that."

"You certainly have strength. You resist blows like a stone and bounce back like a ball. Yet, you lack any formal style that I can determine. It is as if when you attack, you are flailing. Why is that?"

Olyana instigated first this time. Her fists pumped at King's body like blurs. He dodged a few but resorted to blocking most of her hits with his forearms. True to her assessment, her blows elicited little response from his face and any counter punch he managed to slip in failed to connect with her.

"Go, King!" Red cheered. Her heart thumped. King's physique and his overconfident smile were going to her head.

King rammed his shoulder into Olyana and grabbed her arm. With another hand around her leg, he lifted her over his head. "And with my fans watching from the bleachers, prepare for my signature throw!"

"Too much talk!" Olyana kicked herself free and wrapped her legs around his arm. She swung her body toward the floor like a windmill and sent King tumbling across the mat. She hopped up and pounded her chest as she yelled. "Get up! Your feet are too close together! Your stance lacks steadiness!"

King stood tall, although a bit wobbly, and rubbed his elbow. Swelling on his left cheek was turning purple. "Yeah, okay. I see what you're saying. So, if I just widen my stance a little…"

"Hey!" A child's voice drew the room's attention toward the entrance. The crowd parted and Adiquis ran to the mat. Behind him, a team of soldiers carried King's massive metal suit. "Put it down right here," he instructed.

"Little buddy, what are you doing hauling my gear around?" King said. He stepped next to Adiquis and reached to ruffle his hair but pulled away at the last second. "Right. You don't like that."

Adiquis nodded. "It's done! Dr. Petras, Emillee, and I have, ahem…" He straightened his back, cleared his throat, and used his fingers to make little glasses around his eyes. He spoke with a stuffy voice, "*We have perfected the vibrant steel-to-standard metal adhesion process.*"

"What in the rust does that mean? Is it shiner? It looks shiner."

"Yes! But that's irrelevant." Adiquis pointed sporadically at the suit. "This bad boy is now fully untethered from any power flooring. You can use it, and its strength enhancing capabilities, at full power anywhere!"

The soldiers placed the suit down.

"Mother of metal!" King exclaimed. "This spits in the face of the spirit of the game, but we've got other things to worry about right now."

Red joined them and took a closer look as well. A thin layer of electrically-teeming metal plated the suit's various parts. "Incredible. I've heard of scientists on Abeona-2 experimenting with small fragments of the gate metal. My history texts noted we never could find a way to adhere it to any other material. Also, aggressive metalwork tended to make the steel explosive, absolutely volatile."

"It wasn't easy!" Adiquis said, his face plastered with the proudest grin. "I got to hold all the tools and even simplified the equations twice!"

King hovered his hands near the metal. The rings on his fingers sparked with excitement. "I can't believe it. How did I not think of this? With enough glue, I could've…"

"Now, now," Olyana said, humorously patting King on the back. "If you are anything like me, I bet your engineering skills are worth little to nothing. Your attempt would have looked like a child's craft project."

King laughed. "You're right! It's best I left it to the professionals. What you and I are good at is smashing stuff with tech." He knelt next to Adiquis. "Can I take it for a test run?"

"Dr. Petras said it's ready! Just make sure you only touch the areas marked in red on the outside. The rest of it is…" He shook erratically. "Once you're in, you'll be insulated otherwise."

King unclasped the suit. Before he climbed inside, Red ran to his side and offered her hand. "Here. Grab a hold of me. I'll help you in."

He took her palm graciously. "Thanks, Red! You're always thinking of others like someone else I know. Hey, when this is all over, you got to come back with me even for a little while and meet my girlfriend. She absolutely would love you."

A blossoming excitement shriveled into embarrassment. After he climbed inside, Red released his hand and ran back to the sideline. She had just made herself look like a fool, fawning over such an obviously fine specimen of a man. How did she not realize it would have been statistically absurd for him to be unpaired? How could she let herself fall deeper and farther into his orbit of attraction when it was wholly predictable that there was no existing opportunity? And above all, what disappointed her the most was the slacking of her duty because of this fling clouding her precise Rover brain. She had not written a single page today and the details were fading in her mind fast.

King looked her way, but she averted her gaze.

"Is it something I said?" he asked Olyana, who helped latch his suit shut.

"I doubt either of us smell pleasantly," she replied. "Now then. Are you ready for a real fight? Allow me to return with my warrior suit and you shall have yourself the fair fight you have so desired."

"Fine by me!" His strut looked effortless in the bulky metal. "It feels so light." He gawked at his sparking gauntlets emitting a yellow glow. "It's like I'm getting one-hundred percent of the juice all the time. Hey, Olyana! I bet I could throw you clear out of the ship like this! Blast you off right through the hull!"

Olyana laughed and walked away. She stopped next to Red. "He certainly seems happy to be back in his security suit, yes?"

"Hm. I guess so." Red counted the rivets on the floor.

Olyana knelt and placed a gentle hand on Red's cheek. "What is the matter, Red one? You have lost some of your inquisitive nature."

Red circled her head up in a wide arc to avoid Olyana's stare. She let her eyes wander the ceiling. "It's nothing. I was just being stupid and now I know it."

"That cannot be true. You have not done a single stupid thing since you have arrived here. I have found your judgment to be reasoned and wise. What is it you believe you have done?"

Red twisted herself away. Olyana's piercing emotional intelligence was scary. Or maybe Red was just increasingly transparent.

"Tell me," Olyana tried again. "The heart of a warrior is as important as their limbs."

Red swiveled back with tears brimming on the edge of her lashes. She dared not let a single drop slip out for such a pathetic reason. "I didn't even know he was already a bonded pair! What kind of Rover doesn't do her research like that?"

"Oh." Olyana drew her hand slowly away. "You were developing feelings for the King? But he has not exhibited any flirtatious behavior that I have seen." Olyana looked back at King as he attempted several backflips in a row. "Have you not...are you not versed in the ways of love?"

Red did not speak. She hid her warming face inside her hands.

Olyana placed both her arms around Red and drew her in.

Red allowed a few tears to trickle down her cheeks.

"Oh. Shoo, shoo, shoo, my sweet explorer. Do not cry. Your heart is young and fragile. As my mother once told me, you are no more in control of it than the time the sun rises or the moon retires. Love is a natural force and we are at its mercy. You have done nothing wrong. You are not at fault so do not blame yourself."

Red sobbed into Olyana's soft clothing. It felt rude soiling her garment, but she noticed the fabric quickly dried itself. She felt comforted by Olyana's pats on her head. This motherly embrace mimicked nothing she could recall in recent memory. Only a partially forgotten mental echo prompted her to relax and accept the reassurance.

Feeling her breath return to an orderly flow, Red felt her rational mind returning. With all her trust in the logical and measurable, it was so easy to fall prey to emotions and lose all control. Facts were not the only way to wrestle through a problem. There was a place for feelings, confiding in another, and just stumbling without all the information.

Olyana did not have to say it, but Red heard the words in her mind, *"It's going to be okay"*, and that was enough.

Olyana must have noticed her leveling out. "Do you feel better now?"

Red nodded.

"Good. "Now, if you will excuse me," Olyana rose and headed toward the privacy screen. "I have to remind this man that equipment does not replace technique or discipline."

Red watched the rest of the match with a weight lifted off her mind. She returned to her private quarters promptly after the last blow was delivered. She did not say goodnight and did not turn back to see if anyone was offering her one. Quietly at her desk, she continued to write in her Journal; much needed updating regarding her adventure and the valuable personal lessons she was learning. Exploring the mental facets of human beings was proving perhaps more treacherous but just as exciting as the physical world.

The next morning came early. King knocked on Red's door and she opened it to his giddy face.

"Adiquis figured it out! Wow, are we gonna give it to those alien rustheads!" He took off down the hallway.

She watched him run, feeling only a single grain of emotion from the night before. Her expedition of him had ended.

As he jumped into the elevator, he shouted, "Everyone's gathering at the warehouse! I'll see you there!"

Red dressed herself and managed to find the distant lab again.

Adiquis greeted her at the front. "Red. I'm so glad you're here! You have to see what Dr. Petras, Emillee, and I cooked up! Come on!" His hair stood up in places that were not natural and there were bags under his eyes. They must have worked through the night.

He took her hand. They walked through the workshop and out onto a vacant lot. King, Minnie, Olyana, Azul, and Cardinal Murcario were already there.

Red captured Minnie's gaze for only a moment before Minnie looked away. At least she smiled while speaking cheerfully with Azul. Red decided to continue to give her space. She took her place at the group's opposite end.

Dr. Petras and Emillee emerged from a white spherical craft parked in the center of the yard. Dr. Petras held a sleek, white cannon-like weapon in her hands while Emillee handled a handful of gate shards from the valley.

"Welcome, my esteemed dignitaries!" Dr. Petras said. "Now, normally displays of my promising research are accompanied by booze and money, but I know times are tough so I'll settle for your eternal gratitude and admiration. This doozy of a device is going to go second so please give your undivided attention to my newest fellow genius."

Emillee threw her shards onto the ground and kicked them together into a small mound. "Thanks to our darling Adiquis," she said as he took a small bow, "we learned intense energy impacts upon gate material tend to release a tremendous amount of energy in return. What was first believed to be a temporary explosion has now been observed to present a long-lasting effect."

She donned a pair of goggles and revealed a pistol from her pocket. She signaled for everyone to step behind a metal barrier. Once everybody but herself was safely out of sight, she shot the shards. A thin blue beam projected up towards the sky. "Come on out!"

Red stepped forward and noticed the small pile of gate shards loosely rearranging themselves into a crude circle. In their center, a wimpy portal sputtered in and out of existence. She grasped her chest. "Did you just *make* a gate?"

"Disregard the portal for now," Emillee said. "Instead, please consider the incredible length and intensity of this beam. One might call this a beacon. I know I do!"

Adiquis laughed and reached playfully for the beam. "This is how we get everyone to find their gates!"

Dr. Petras slapped his hand away before he made contact. "Come on! What did I tell you?"

"Whoops!" He giggled. He kicked up dirt and zoomed in circles around the beam instead. "We shoot up the gates on the other side…" He pantomimed shots with double finger guns. "Pew! Pew, pew! They'll radiate out beacons all over the galaxy. Then our friends will see the blue light and find us!"

"Simple, yet effective," Olyana said. "What type of force must we apply to affect the larger metal structures documented in the survey reports?"

Dr. Petras consulted a datapad in her pocket. "I estimate we'll need a blast of about 10.8 gigawatts. So…" She pointed to Emillee.

"…that would be a little less than what our Lightning Tunnels produce per shot. We just need to hit one of the big ones extremely hard. A chain reaction should set them all to beacon mode."

"You can thank Dr. Rashaan for his principle of Electrical Chain Reactions!" Adiquis screamed.

Everyone clapped, including Red until Dr. Petras stepped forward and thrust the cannon device into her hands. She struggled to keep it steady as the doctor paced in front of her.

"Thank you, Red. That was getting rather heavy. Next, I present to you the single most important weapon we'll need when we step through those gates with our game faces on. I think, Captain Olyana, you feel fairly confident our weapons will work against their ground troops. Do you not?"

"Yes. Your recent modifications are remarkable."

"Hah…well, thank you." Dr. Petras did not smile. "But what about our air game? When I strolled through their territory briefly, I saw those big ships in the sky. I'm guessing the minute we try to invade with any force worth our muster, the aliens could declare the area a lost cause and just barrage us with fire from on high. There might not be anything left but scorched soil."

Red shuddered at the thought. That would be an inglorious end to her most incredible journey.

"Your risk calculations are correct," Olyana said. "They are a yet undefendable obstacle."

Dr. Petras nodded. "This is where what I call the Warp Hijacker comes into play. Red, if you could be so kind as to point my device at the weak little portal and pull the trigger?"

Red struggled to aim the hijacker but managed to fire it. A green beam shot out and changed the blue portal to green.

King scoffed. "That's a nice parlor trick, doc. What're green portals gonna do for us? You reckon the aliens are afraid of the color? Have you seen one? They're freaking green themselves!"

Dr. Petras placed her palm on her face and shook her head. "Leave the science to me, young man." She pointed at the warehouse. "Please, Red. Fire at the broad side."

Red did as asked and a green portal appeared on the wall.

Emillee picked up a small rock and tossed it into the portal on the ground. To everyone's surprise, the sound of the rock thumping on the other side of the wall demonstrated guided teleportation.

Emillee walked inside and returned with the rock in hand. "And there you have it," she said. "We can now hijack their portals to transport whatever thing we want anywhere else. Consider firing at their ships and boarding from the ground to commandeer their greatest weapons on the battlefield."

Everyone looked at each other. There were smiles and nods.

"This was one heck of a presentation; don't you all think?" Dr. Petras said. "I do believe our fair lady, Emillee, may be up for a doctor title when this is all over, wouldn't you say, Captain?"

Emillee blushed. "I-I do not know about that. I am just doing my duty."

Olyana smirked. "I alone do not make that decision. It is by committee. But your recommendation is duly noted."

Cardinal Murcario erupted with applause. "Excellent! Truly mind-boggling! I believe we now have just about every piece of the puzzle. With the final flight checks underway, and the pending successful retrieval of our tribe's ship from the fog, we now have two ships of our own."

"There are two of those?" Red scanned the horizon but only identified the one poking above the buildings.

"Indeed, traveler. A joint team of explorers should already be inside the ship. They are preparing to fly it into the portal once the battle starts. We have Dr. Petras to thank once again for developing the portable F.L.A.G. technology that enables such an excursion."

Dr. Petras nodded. "Also, I assure you my mini-atmospheric bubbles will keep your people safe while the main unit is away for at least 24 hours. Beyond that, no refunds."

Red handed the hijacker to Emillee. "Does this mean we're ready?"

Olyana nodded. "Yes. We are as ready as we will ever be. I believe we can take the aliens by surprise. Our small skirmish during the Earth folk's evacuation seemed to draw little concern from them. They do not fear us. However, this time we will strike with more ingenuity than they can possibly anticipate. Our only hope is that with these two new strategies, we will be able to capitalize on the reinforcements you have called for."

"No pressure," King said, "but this sort of all hinges on your plan, Minnie."

"Hey, mine too!" Adiquis said.

Minnie frowned. "All I can do is pray."

After the big reveal, Red caught up to Minnie walking back to the ark by herself. "Hey! Wait up. Can we talk?"

Minnie paused briefly for her. Her eyes were concerned. "What's going on? Is everything all right?"

"Oh! No, nothing's wrong. I just wanted to talk a little about what happened yesterday outside the council room."

"Ah." Minnie continued her brisk pace. She faced straight ahead.

Red had to skip momentarily just to match Minnie's gait. "Well, I just wanted to say I'm sorry about trying to spout my reasoning at you. That's just how I think, but everyone's different. If your confidence comes from your inner faith, then I say lean into that. Let's just both commit to what fuels us."

Minnie's face softened. "Okay…"

"And I also want to apologize for sort of being short with you the last few days. I didn't know how much you've gone through before you joined up with us and…I just want to say I understand the pain."

Minnie raised an inquisitive eyebrow. "Did King tell you?"

"Um…" Red diverted her eyes.

"It's okay. I don't mind."

Red sighed. "Thank goodness. For the record, he said…"

"It doesn't matter. It was just a lot to handle in a short amount of time, but I think I'm going to be okay."

"I'm glad to hear." Red followed silently by her side all the way back to the ship. It was nice to feel comfortable around her.

ROVER ENTRY #1094

Red sat quietly in her quarters updating her Journal. A voice from the intercom in her room said, "All personnel report. The operation commences in three hours."

She slipped into her combat suit for what she hoped was the last time. Olyana's red kerchief brought her comfort but also reminded her of when she was a different person. The Red who only wore one color no longer resided within her. She had changed, evolved since then. She liked to believe it was for the better, but was that objectively true? What would her colleagues back on Abeona-2 think of her newfound thoughts regarding everything from Rover research to the Divine?

She rushed down to the ship's front exterior among the plush grass. Cardinal Murcario stood at the end of a long line which a soldier waved her into. Waiting to receive weapons were Jangalan soldiers, civilians, and Earth refugees. There were many wary eyes. Red picked up that many of these soon-to-be comrades did not fully trust each other. There was a deep history on Jangala which she did not understand.

When she reached the Cardinal, he handed her a rifle she had not used before.

"Sir? I've only used the pistols before."

"Same principle," he said, "but with a bigger, more accurate kick from a distance. Just point and shoot."

Red measured the weight of the weapon in her arms. This beastly tool, of no use against mindless sandstorms, earthquakes, or heat, a thing she was not comfortable handling, did not make her feel safer. It only made her more nervous.

Adjacent to the line, Minnie conversed with Adiquis. A soldier tried to hand him a rifle, but he refused.

"I'm already packing," he said with a unique looking pistol on his hip.

"I saw these whoppers in a museum once," Minnie said, turning her weapon in her arms. "They're ancient energy railguns. I think they're extinct everywhere else because…uh, they were banned. Way too much unstable power, maybe? Maybe sometimes they blow up…?" She examined the weapon with remembered skepticism. "On the other hand, while not ideal when you're holding it next to your chest, we are gonna need to throw everything we got at these punks. Maybe you should reconsider."

"What do you have there?" Red asked, pointing at Adiquis' pistol.

"It's a marble gun!" he replied, proudly turning the grip toward her. Despite his offer for her to inspect it, she politely declined. On the sides, divots hosted marbles imbued directly into the pistol's barrel. "Dr. Petras and Emillee each have one too. Special order!"

"Are you sure that's going to be enough out there?" Minnie said, smiling with her long rifle slung over her back.

Adiquis grinned even wider. "You laugh, but the only thing we need to worry about with these little explosive wonders is anything larger than a building. Maybe it'll take more than one shot, but other than that, we're good."

A passing soldier's mouth swung open. She looked at her rifle and at the pistol.

Adiquis giggled.

Red followed Minnie and Adiquis through the town center and toward the valley. Dr. Petras emerged from a distant building and Adiquis darted off to walk with her.

"Hey. Did you sleep well last night?" Minnie asked.

Red nodded. "I was exhausted. I couldn't have slept poorly if I tried."

"Oh? What had you so worked up?"

Red closed her eyes. She smirked. "Just some silly things. I feel much better now."

"That's good."

The two of them walked beside each other. The streets around them were emptying out in accordance with Olyana's refuge plan. People of the settlement packed their belongings and abandoned their homes and businesses. A man carried his three children on his back and containers of food in both arms. A basket slipped and dozens of tuberous roots tumbled across the ground.

"Here, let me help you sir," Minnie said. She bent down and picked up several roots.

Red did the same.

"Thank you so much!" the man said. "Oh! You two are travelers, are you not?"

"That's right," Minnie said, handing him a root. "How did you know? We haven't met many locals."

"You both just look different," one of the small girls said, perched on top of her father's head.

"That is not nice to say," he scolded.

Minnie smiled. A gentle aura seemed to shine forth. "No, she's right. Everything about us is different."

The man took the remaining roots. "Thank you again. I want you two to know that I am not one of those folks that disapproves of your presence. In fact, I thank the Divine for your arrival. I have hope that you will help us build a better future." He passed the basket back to one of his little boys. "For our children."

"Hope?" Minnie asked. "Ah. I'm not so sure I believe in that the same way anymore. I've seen some good people hope for a lot of things and just not have it pan out for them."

"But not for you," the man said. "And not for all. By the Divine's will, you are still standing. I am still here. My children are still here." He turned toward the valley in the distance. "My wife...she is not. She used all of her strength to get our children ahead of the fog when it fell upon our old settlement."

"I'm so sorry," Minnie said. "That must have been horrible for you."

He nodded. "It was. It still is. And..." He looked into Minnie's eyes. "I see you are haunted by something similar as well."

"I..." Minnie drew back.

"But I am done focusing solely on that. I have decided to do my best to channel my grief into both healing myself and others around me. I may never truly be the same again, but I am alive. Therefore, the Divine has a plan for me." He picked up a child. "I heard you are a Princess. I bet the Divine has a plan for you, too. Even if others had to sacrifice themselves, it was by their own will and intention. Surely they knew what I know. The Divine works in mysterious ways and their plans lead to inscrutable conclusions. It is for us to continue on with our own plan. We honor the Divine by doing so." He headed toward the community rendezvous point. "Hope in ourselves," he called back loudly. "It fuels me. It could fuel you too."

Red and Minnie watched as the man turned a corner. Red waited patiently for Minnie. There was no need to rush her. Minnie's mouth moved slightly as if she mumbled something private. She looked up into the sky.

Minnie took a step forward and said, "It's not that I don't have hope. I never lost it. I just...I just didn't know what to hope *in* anymore. Hope in everyone else seemed to just result in the Divine disappointing me. But hope in myself? I suppose I would only have myself to blame if I messed up. That, I think I can handle. That could be the missing link to discovering my path."

Red smiled, but Minnie did not turn around to see. She did not care about the Divine plan or hope in the spiritual, but she did believe in the power of a person's self-confidence. If Minnie could truly put her belief in herself, then Red would support her one-hundred percent.

ROVER ENTRY #1095

Over two thousand people, humanity's last hope, lined up from the colony ark all the way to the valley's portal in groups of one hundred. Red, Minnie, and King volunteered for the first party led personally by Olyana. Red stood at the portal's edge with her Journal in hand. She found herself reviewing the notes of the plan she had scribbled earlier during a mission briefing. It soothed her to trust in a plan. If they followed it to the letter nothing could go wrong. Or so she desperately needed to believe.

"Send in the colony arks first and draw the fire from our greatest threat: the aliens' aerial fleet," Red muttered to herself, her finger following her scribbles line by line. "We go through and draw the ground troop's attention. The arks will fire upon the gates and ignite the beacons. We push forward in a slow, steady advance attempting to establish as much space as possible between the inevitable Seekers and our incoming science team. Once it's safe, the science team will portal in and begin the hijack operation."

Minnie tapped her shoulder. She managed her first big smile Red had seen in a while. "Do you do this anytime you're about to do something big?"

"No," she grinned back. "It's just that back home everything I did was planned, recorded, predictable for the most part. That type of predictability is comforting to me."

"There hasn't been a lot of that these days, huh?"

Red shook her head. "It's not entirely bad, simply different. I always wanted more than what I was assigned to. I just never knew how dangerous unpredictability could be."

King surprised them both by wrapping them together in his arms and drawing them in tightly. "No risk, no glory! Come on, you two. Big sis Olyana will keep us safe, won't you?"

Olyana took her eyes off her datapad for a moment and cast them a warm glance. Red noticed her smile but was learning to detect the emotions behind people's facades. She deduced the presence of exhaustion.

"It is my duty to keep you safe with all my might," Olyana answered. "Nothing in this galaxy, or the next, will stop us."

"I don't get it," King said, looking back at all the soldiers behind them. "I thought a bunch of galactic folks were supposed to meet us here for the big party. I know the beacon will make it easier, but I expected at least some of them to rush to their nearest gate and help us prevent all-out extinction. Yet, nobody's come through or so much as landed on this planet since the broadcast. What gives?"

"I'm not sure," Red said. "I anticipated reinforcements too. Maybe we weren't convincing enough?"

"No," Minnie said. She pointed at the portal. "They'll come. We'll meet them on the battlefield because we need them to be there. I'm holding on to hope. I believe in my plan."

Olyana placed hands on Red and Minnie's shoulders. "Steel yourselves. It is time."

A tremendous rumble almost shook Red's knees out from under her. From the back of the settlement, the colony ark lifted off for the second time in its career. It hovered low and slow as it approached the portal. Pieces of terra firma littered in its wake crashed through the roofs of houses. King said it looked like a flying tree because of all the dangling roots that hung below and Minnie agreed. But Red did not know much about trees except for the ones she had documented the last few days. These root parts were not captured in any of her sketches of their cylindrical bases and branching tops.

"Oh, wait! Is *that* where wood comes from? Trees? The roots do look like that dark grained material."

"Yep," King said. "Boy, Red. You really are a hoot. Do you not have trees where you come from?" He turned to Olyana. "Hey, if that thing can fly just fine, how come your great, great grandparents didn't just lift off and avoid all this war stuff you've talked about?"

Olyana watched the arks pass overhead. "Both vessels were damaged during their expeditions to different original destinations. By working together among the streaking stars of space travel, both made it here safely and intended to be each other's sibling." She scanned the faces of all those that were following her into battle. She smiled. A well of hope seemed to spring from her feet and bubble up to her face. "It took a millennium for that to finally come to pass. As for the return of their function, it was once again Dr. Petras who gave us a piece of ourselves which we had lost."

Creeping forward, the jungle's fog followed the ark and flooded into the settlement. The abandoned buildings and fields disappeared into the hazy deathtrap. All of Olyana and Minnie's people were huddled together in an intensely illuminated dome that Red could still make out in the distance. She held her breath in solidarity as the fog engulfed them.

"Are you safe?" Olyana asked through a communication device.

"Yes, my Captain!" Azul's voice came through. "The mini-F.L.A.G. is holding steady! All power readings are stable."

With a triumphant cry from the crowd, a second rumbling preceded an additional colony ark. The majestic ship emerged from the foggy valley's opposite side. This ship curiously did not appear to have any effect on the fog as it hovered toward the gate.

Olyana drew the communication device to her lips. An electric hum covered the valley as the arks broadcasted her voice to all. She tugged a small piece of paper from a pocket and unfolded it.

"People of Jangala, Earth, and the Milky Way. This is your Captain speaking. There is no denying the known. We stand at the cliff of extermination, few to our number, and against barely understood odds. The bolstering of our technology has come on suddenly and we are not yet masters of the tools of our destiny."

Red surveyed the crowd. Worried faces were prevalent. What was Olyana doing?

"To my Jangalan family, I have shared this valley with you my entire life, and for a millennium through our ancestors. Our fates have always been intertwined, dependent on the choices of each other."

She took a deep breath. She screamed, "Do not be confused, for today is no different! The person standing next to you holds your life in their hand and so do you of them! They are no longer your enemies across the valley, but your colleague, walking with you hand-in-hand toward your future. Their future. Your descendants' future!"

The crowd hollered. Red noticed the Jangalan people facing each other. There was hope again.

Olyana waited patiently for them to calm before continuing.

"To my hundreds of travelers from across the stars. In more fortunate times, *you* may have been the ones leading the charge during conflict. Yet today I call upon you to aid me in my campaign. I do this for you, for your children, and for your planets." She winked toward Red, Minnie, and King. "Today, do not think of yourselves as separate from the Jangalan family. No. Today, we are all one colony. The human colony!" she cried. "This galaxy is our settlement, and we will claim it and tame it like we have always done! For that is how it has always been!"

The valley erupted with elation. *This* was the leader they needed. Olyana *was* the woman Red thought she was. She did not know how much longer she would live, but she knew if today was her last day, she had experienced one of the greatest expeditions any person had ever experienced across the celestial heavens.

"The operation will now begin!" Olyana declared as she handed her communication device to a colleague.

Red blinked and almost missed the ships being sucked into the portal. She followed her party and jumped through with no hesitation remaining in her heart.

The screams of the children still chilled her bones, but she silently vowed to avenge them. As she had come to understand her Divine cousins, she realized they were trying their best with the limited and unreliable information at their disposal. She, too, had made some questionable calls in her career based on what she was taught, not knowing what she did not know. Now, she recognized that in others. She could no longer hold the Divine wholly to blame for this perpetual museum of shrieks.

The aliens that created the gates had much more to answer for. And she would make them pay with the help of her new colony.

ROVER ENTRY #1096

Red exited from the gate, legs and arms flailing into a steady landing, amid a bombardment of alien weapon fire. Red lasers rained down upon the metal crates near her. Members of her first group were successfully drawing attention down below while the arks positioned themselves to fire on the gates above.

"Get behind the solid crates!" Olyana ordered as enemy lasers melted the concrete at her feet. A beam tore indiscriminately through a pair of Seekers in a barred cage mere meters in front of her. Smoke and oil splattered across the ground. "They are not caring about their tools of terror. Only solid crates!"

Red, King, and Minnie ducked beside a blue container. Several soldiers were blown off their feet from direct hits, but to Red's surprise, they arose and continued onward thanks to their enhanced armor. However, once the alien ships above started firing as well, nothing withstood their massive artillery. Devastating explosions splattered rock, scrap metal, and biomatter across the battlefield.

Red covered her head as a deluge of black goo splashed around them. A Seeker limb twitched in the mess and almost seemed like it would pick itself up and attack her. She was able to tear her eyes away from it when the frightening shots went quiet. She gazed above. The colony arks were deviating from the plan. They repositioned themselves to provide cover from the largest volleys but were now suffering mighty eruptions from their hulls. She wondered how long they could keep that up.

"Do not worry about them, Red!" Olyana boomed, reading the uncertainty on Red's scrunched face. "Our task is to fire from cover and to advance!"

Hundreds of soldiers charged ahead of them amid the enemy attacks.

King jumped back out into the fray and waved for Red and Minnie to follow.

"Get behind me! I can take the shots straight to the face!" Seemingly one to jump first and think second, this time King was right. He clanged his fists together and projected his impenetrable shield of light. Beams converged on him, but none so much as shook his shield. "Get a load of me!"

Red and Minnie dropped behind him and they slowly stepped forward. Red carefully surveyed the top of the great wall that caged them inside. Two large flashes, brighter than the rest, caught her eye.

"Watch out! Something big is incoming!"

Powerful twin blasts propelled King off his feet and pushed the other two onto their backs. King quickly righted himself and recast his shield to protect them from the continuous fire. "Whoa! That was one heck of a mortar!"

Olyana shouted from cover nearby. "Remember your training!"

King nodded. He shifted his legs into a wide stance. He rolled his shoulders back and leaned forward. Two shots flashed again. "Hold on tight!"

The impact was blinding, but King barely budged. They moved steadily forward again. Red fired wearily at the Seekers charging toward them. Their ravenous maws drooled. Their thick bodies carelessly bumped against the container's side that lined their path forward like boulders tumbling down a canyon. She aimed for their legs, like Sarenth once suggested, and they fell and writhed in place. Minnie fired much more freely and peppered the beasts with searing heat.

Behind them, hundreds of groups emerged from the gate and fanned out to create the perimeter they needed. The voice of Chlorian booming from the sky caught Red by surprise.

"Creatures of Galaxy C-94, your attempt at resistance is futile. In fact, you're just making it *easier* for us to achieve our goal. It's rather helpful of you all to come to one place so we don't have to send our organic devourers all over the galaxy looking for you. By chance is there a meal bell you could ring to attract more of your kind?" They chortled. "No matter. At the very least, I hope you're enjoying the chemical adrenaline of your last stand pumping through your primitive bodies."

In the sky, the colony arks completed their maneuvers and fired their Lightning Tunnels at the gates. A massive explosion, fueled by the chain reaction, pushed everyone on the battlefield onto the ground. The entire orange sky turned blue. The beacons shone brightly out of every gate stretching far beyond the horizon.

Olyana ran to Red's side and pulled her up. "Lead your friends forward. Find and secure that little room in the wall that you brought me once. We may be unable to safeguard as much space as I anticipated here. We will need an alternate forward position for the science team to hide inside after they have completed their mission."

Red nodded and waved for King and Minnie to follow. They broke away from their company and weaved between the crates and cages toward the wall's edge. Three small Seekers burst out from a closed crate. King punched each one into an exploding mess.

Once they reached the wall, a beam from above blew the lock off a cage next to Red. A Seeker, five times the size of the rest, stepped out in front of her. Each leg was thicker than a tree trunk. It rolled back its putrid lips and exposed its jagged teeth. She could be swallowed in one snap.

She fired frantically in its direction but failed to deter it.

Minnie shot it in the side. It redirected its rage toward her. "I need help here!"

King leapt between them and drove his fists into the monster's mouth. He gripped the Seeker by the teeth.

"What are you doing?" Minnie screamed. "I didn't mean do something stupid!"

"I know this is crazy, but the teeth are the only part of them that aren't absolutely slimy and a grappler's gotta improvise! Find that secret door and make sure it's safe inside. I got this guy no problem!"

The Seeker flung its head back and lifted him into the air.

"Whoa!"

Red reached the wall first and slapped it. "Up here! Give me a boost!"

Minnie lifted her up. She pounded on the wall until the concrete slid to the side and revealed the room. She climbed and pulled Minnie up after her.

Below, King wrestled his arm out of the Seekers mouth, its fangs failing to fully penetrate his dense armor. He grabbed it by the neck, swung it around a few times, and launched it into the sky far into a tower of crates that went crashing down. He leaped into the room in one single bound.

Red turned on the light. Their hideout remained unoccupied. Protein bar wrappers still littered the floor. She thought she heard an echo of the three of them laughing about a joke she had already forgotten. She would never have thought it possible, but that was a simpler time.

Chlorian's voice over the loudspeaker brought her back to the entrance. "Don't take this as a sign that you're causing me any trouble. It's just that it's getting late and I'd like to avoid overtime if possible. Release all the devourers!"

An unsettling rattle swept over the facility. Cages and crates everywhere unsealed their Seekers. Utter bedlam raged below as the monsters rampaged forward. The desperate screams of humanity echoed across the battlefield.

Red noticed a large group of soldiers breaking off toward her. It appeared they were trying to establish a final safe route for the science team. But could they hold off a wave of insatiable mouths?

"They're gonna get clobbered out there!" Minnie said at her side. "We need to help!"

"That's out of our hands," King said. "Olyana's orders were to secure this site and keep it safe for the science team. We do our job and they'll do theirs. That's teamwork in action."

"No, I…I think Minnie's right." Red said. A feeling swelled inside her chest. It was an exciting buzz. "They need us to act and I believe we can make a difference."

Minnie nodded and leapt out of the room. She ran toward the advancing group.

"Right behind you!" Red jumped down after her.

King rushed to the room's ledge. "Stop, you two! Somebody's gotta watch the room!"

Red trailed Minnie as they passed through the empty cages and crates. They hopped over the smoking bodies of lifeless Seekers. Up in the sky, a colony ark burned and wavered as it took shot after shot from the enemy ships. It slid backward until it touched the edge of a gate. In a flash, it disappeared to who knew where. The remaining ark fired its Lightning Tunnels at the alien vessels, but it did not appear to have much effect.

With half of their sky cover absent, the frequency of orbital barrages increased. Red pointed anxiously above at the twinkling lights of an impending enemy volley. She and Minnie scurried into a crate just before they could have been vaporized.

Teeth-shattering blasts kept them cowering inside. As soon as the attacks subsided, Red tried to push open the door, but it seemed debris had trapped them.

"No!" Minnie shoved Red aside. "We gotta get out of here!" Minnie rammed herself against the door. "We need to keep fighting until backup arrives!"

"Where is everyone? Did anyone even hear our call?" Red said, distressed at the notion.

"No!" Minnie protested. "They're coming! The Divine helps those who help themselves! Good people will answer the call of the home world! I believe!"

She slammed her rifle repeatedly against the door and wailed until she exhausted herself.

She slowly slumped to the ground.

"Don't give up yet. We have options yet to explore." Red shot holes in the damaged, thinning roof. A bit of the sky appeared. She was confused by the scene when what she thought was their colony ark flying overhead did not actually look anything like it. She fired several more shots until she made a sizable hole for her to climb out of.

"Give me a boost."

Minnie lifted herself up and provided her back for Red to climb out. Red pulled her out too.

The pair both stared up in awe.

Thousands of ships were emerging from the sky gates. There were ships of all types and colors. Red had never seen so many spacefaring vessels in her whole life, not even in photos of her school texts. It was overwhelming and amazing at the same time. She barely had the vocabulary to describe the designs, size, and variety of configurations the ships exhibited.

She whipped out her Journal out of elated wonder, forgetting where she was. Before she could get her pencil to paper, the motley fleet opened fire on the alien ships. Scorching neon lasers, frightening fireballs, and the explosions of ships from both sides brought the reality of war violently back to her.

It was not wonderous. It was horrifying.

ROVER ENTRY #1097

Look out!" Minnie cried.

Several vicious claws punctured and carved the top of their crate. A group of Seekers pulled their heads up and peered at their tasty morsels with shifting sets of eyes. Eager jet-black tongues dragged across their teeth.

"We're trapped!" Red exclaimed. She fired at the faces. It only seemed to agitate them. One swiped at her legs. She stumbled back into Minnie and they clasped their hands together.

A narrow, controlled laser beam swept around their perimeter and fried the Seeker pack into boiling puddles. Red searched up above and spotted a ship firing away. She waved with thanks, but it was off to its next task in a flash.

A boisterous clamor grew inside the facility. It was not alien nor beast, but human defiance. Almost too distant to make out, Red noticed a flood of strange people emerging from the gates on the ground. They were dressed in styles of clothing she had never seen before. They charged forth, announcing their ferocity, against a dwindling tide of Seekers.

"Are you two rustheads stuck in here?" King shouted while clearing away debris below.

"We're up top!" Red said.

He jumped onto the roof and laughed. "Well, get a load of this view! What did I tell you? We're gonna weed these aliens out."

"What about the hideout?"

"Don't worry about it. The science crew made it there and boy did they pull up in style. You really missed…"

"Did it work? Did they hijack the gates?"

King pointed toward the sky. "See for yourself."

Several alien ships rotated away from the gates. They bombarded the facility's wall. Colossal chunks exploded and hurtled down to the perimeter's base. Entire towering pillars of crates toppled in a tremendous crash.

It was happening. The tide was turning.

The voice of Chlorian again echoed across the sky. "This is incredibly irritating! You *are* aware this is just a staging facility and you are in no way dealing any significant blow to our grander operations, correct? You're really making me do my job here today and I don't appreciate it! How about we up the ante?"

Clouds of thick, black smoke poured out of sliding gaps high up on the wall like a series of waterfalls. The smoke cascaded over the battlefield.

"Oh dang! We should probably find higher ground," King said.

"It'll be okay. We have our helmets." Red said.

"But *they* don't." Minnie pointed toward the millions of travelers emerging through the gates. "If we have the means to keep fighting, we need to stop the smoke before it takes all their lives."

"I agree. Let's go!" King lifted the two ladies over his shoulders.

"Oh!" Red exclaimed.

"Sorry! We gotta be quick and walking back is pretty dangerous." He leapt from crate to crate. Stampeding Seekers filled the alleyways below making the trip back perilous. Several rammed against the crates. King almost lost his footing.

"Hold on!" He charged the next edge and launched himself into the sky.

"Aaah!" Red and Minnie screamed.

They landed safely inside the storage room. King placed them down.

Adiquis ran to their sides. "Wow! You were like a rocket!"

Dr. Petras and Emillee emerged from inside.

"Nice work out there, young man," Dr. Petras said to King.

"We need to get back!" Minnie said. "Wherever their leadership is, we need to go there and…"

"Give them a big old whack!" King said.

"Oh? Still hankering for adventure?" Dr. Petras smirked. "Well, I can point you in the right direction. I've been studying the extensive reports Red's been submitting to the War Council. I'm ninety-eight percent confident this operation all funnels from the center of the top of the wall."

Emillee showed Red a datapad with a photo of a small building on the top. "We did a little reconnaissance before hiding here. That is where you would want to go. This Chlorian character is likely to be there."

"How did you take this picture? It looks like you were flying."

King waved them toward the room's entrance. "I told you they rolled up in style!"

From the hideout's ledge, Red noticed the white orb parked just below. Seekers were chomping unsuccessfully at its sides.

Dr. Petras stepped next to Red. "Emillee learned to pilot that thing just before we left the planet. That wasn't in the plan, but it was a definite welcomed surprise. Smart cookie, that one."

"Let's clear the way!" Minnie shot down below and Adiquis joined in. The Seekers growled up above and several hustled away.

"It should be clear now. Let's jump in!" King leapt down and hurled lifeless Seeker bodies out of the way. "Hey! How do I open this thing?"

"You do not even know how to drive," Emilee said, dangling her legs off the ledge.

"Well, not this specific thing. But I do have a driver's license!"

"Catch!" Emillee fell into King's arms. Her hand tapped a panel and revealed a ramp.

A large Seeker stumbled forth and tried to surprise them, but Dr. Petras blew it into pieces from above. Her marble pistol smoked. "Get going, everyone! I'll keep communicating with command from here."

Adiquis shuffled to her side. He fiddled with his fingers and gazed up at her until she noticed his staring.

"You too, kid!" she nodded toward him. "I gotta keep blasting portals into those ships, but you're packing the most powerful cannon otherwise! Think you can do it? Consider it training for when we get back to the capital." She winked.

Adiquis grinned from ear to ear.

Red, Minnie, and Adiquis leapt down and piled into the orb with King and Emillee. There was only one pilot's seat.

"A little tight, don't you think?" Minnie said. She stood between Adiquis' and King leaving little room to stretch.

"I believe this recon craft was meant for no more than three, but that is just speculation on my part," Emillee said.

Red took a seat on the floor and tried to steady herself as best she could. "I don't want to fly again! What am I doing?"

"Do not worry. I have become decently skilled with flight," Emillee said. She sat in the chair and ran her hands along an illuminated panel. "Here we go!"

Red did not notice they were already soaring until the wall's summit crested out the front window. The ride was mercifully smooth.

Emillee swiveled the orb around and shot toward the center of the wall in an instant. She slammed on a button and opened the back hatch. "Ready to jump! The top of the wall is just below! I will stay within the area and watch for your retreat for extraction."

"A-already?" Red asked in disbelief. She needed more time to consider her next move now that she hovered hundreds of meters up.

"One punch to the face delivered right to your doorstep!" King cried as he moved around Red and hopped out. The drop was far, but his suit absorbed the landing.

"This is exactly where I'm meant to be!" Minnie leapt out second. King caught her and placed her down.

"King, it's your job to protect me in case things get crazy!" Adiquis jumped out third. King caught him too.

Red inched toward the edge. They were hovering barely adjacent to the wall. The dizzying height just off the ledge almost made her lose her balance. Death from a missed leap at such a height was assured.

"Come on, Red! I'll catch you!" King shouted.

Emillee twisted back in her chair. "Red! If you want, you can stay with me and we will do loops until they are ready. What will it be?" Soaring engines roared past the orb. Alien fighter ships fired lasers near them. "I cannot stay stationary, Red! It is now or never!"

Against her newfound desire for adventure, her reliable, logical brain kicked in. There was no need for her to take this risk. The team had all the strength they needed. She contributed barely any warrior skill. This should be the end of her active exploration. She should hang back, document from afar, and not cross this boundary. After all, was it not her personal mission to learn from her mother's mistakes?

Then why had she not yet sat back down?

The gap between her and the wall was growing while her intrusive thoughts asked if she still adhered to that ethos. Was she still that same girl so resentful of her mother that she allowed her curiosity to be curtailed from across the valley of death? She cannibalized Rover equipment like a rebel. Jumping through the first gate alone was stupidly brazen. Even much of her latest Journal documentation was outside of the Order's scope.

As the wall pulled away and her compatriots respectfully waved her goodbye, she took one step forward. No! Her mother was reckless and unprepared, blinded by the allure of adventure without thinking first, and left her only daughter alone to fulfill all of her responsibilities. But Red was different because…

A laser impacted the orb. The cabin rocked. Red tumbled out of the craft.

Wall.

Ground.

Sky.

Crates.

Cement.

Clouds.

Her vision spun until she righted herself and watched her friends fly past her. Her outstretched hand grabbed for a ledge that was too far away. She tried to scream, but despite being surrounded by open air, there was no more left in her lungs.

"We're coming!"

Minnie, fluttering like a breeze off the ledge dangling by King's outstretched arm, grabbed Red's wrist. Red slammed against the wall. Her goggles upon her forehead shattered. Glass shards, like glittering stars, sprinkled over the facility below.

They hoisted Red up. She sprawled out on solid ground.

"Are you okay?" Adiquis' voice asked, sounding far away.

Red opened her eyes. All three of them stood over her with gazes of great concern. For a fleeting moment while flying through the sky she had cursed herself. She only fell out because she had placed herself in that situation. Just like her mother, she flirted with danger and it only took one surprise to almost take her life.

But she refused to grant that notion a home to fester. With her friends waiting on bated breath for her to speak, the whole galaxy spiraling into chaos with every wasted second, her wellness was seemingly the most important thing in the universe to the people who alone could save it. She recommitted herself to the realization she had before she had prepared to leap out. She had come to trust what Purple said in that cramped tent at the beginning of this journey.

"Your mother was a fearless pioneer…but she did it alone. You are not alone!"

"Yes!" Red grasped Minnie's outstretched hand. She jumped to her feet. "Let's end this together!

ROVER ENTRY #1098

King blew the little building's double-doors off their hinges. At least twenty tall, black armor-clad aliens gawked at them as they stepped inside. Computer-like consoles filled the room and were surrounded by small windows overlooking the facility.

"Th-this is highly unusual!" Chlorian said from far back in the room. "Stop them!"

Brutes aimed their poles and fired syringes at the group. King cast his shield and deflected them until they were spent. They twisted their weapons, igniting electrical charges from the pole's tips, and charged. King bolted toward them and knocked two off their feet. Strikes from the others against his insulated armor had no effect.

"Ha, ha! You think those little tasers are going to do anything?"

Minnie aimed her weapon and fired toward the back. Chlorian covered their head and screamed while dodging her shots.

"Stay still, you home world wrecker!" she shouted.

Two brutes broke past King's blockade and rushed Red. She raised her rifle but closed her eyes as she squeezed the trigger. An explosion jolted her eyes back open. All that remained of the brutes were two unexpected smoldering piles of ash. Her laser marks littered the ground. Red squinted at the spot before her. Her rifle could not have caused this type of destruction.

Adiquis stood by her side, his marble gun smoking from recent kills. "Never take your eye off the sights. Come on. Even I know that and *I'm still just a kid!*" He winked before rushing in and blasting some more.

Chlorian crawled into an adjacent small room and jabbed a button on a console repeatedly. "Full scale retreat! Abandon the facility! All personnel exit through the primary LITS address!" The door to that room slammed shut and it curiously floated up and away.

"They're in an escape ship!" Red cried. "Chlorian's getting away!"

"Right you are, my *dear* Red!" Chlorian said over a speaker. The little room floated over the wall's edge. "Now, if you don't mind, I'd like to get home and start contemplating how to get Galaxy C-94 back on track." Chlorian soared away toward the gates.

"We gotta stop that murderer!" King said, pounding his fist into the last alien brute.

"He's going to escape using a gate." Minnie said. "Wait, let's watch which one he goes through. That'll be the alien's home turf! We can follow and…"

"No way!" Adiquis objected. "We barely avoided getting our butts beat here and this was just, like, an office for their scientists. It'd be stupid to think we can even touch their real army guys."

"Well, then what do you reckon we should do?" King asked. "We can't just let him get away and warn all his cronies about what we did here. We'll be in the same situation when they come back for us!"

Red had several ideas, but one quickly rose above the rest. "He'll never make it back," she said.

She rushed to a control panel. It was strange, had way too many buttons, and had a cryptic language all over it, but she was uniquely up to the challenge. "Adiquis, can you figure out how to use this system, technically speaking?"

"I mean, anything this complex should have a button to turn on and off the entire gate system in case of an emergency, if that's what you're looking for."

"No. I want to turn off one specific gate."

"Just hit them all, then!" King raised his fists to smash, but Red threw up her hand.

"Stop! I need to turn off one specific gate at just the right time. There are tons of our people coming through all the others. I don't want to cut us off by the knees down there."

"If you say so," Adiquis opened every drawer he could find.

King rummaged through the pockets of the aliens beaten unconscious on the floor.

Minnie stood next to Red and watched Chlorian's ship approach an enormous floating gate. "What are you thinking?"

"I know what I'm doing. I am using every scrap of knowledge I have, every piece of evidence, and placing it all on the hope that it'll all work out just as I've observed. This is alien technology that I don't understand, but there's a chance I could be right."

"Putting it all on hope. I believe in you, Red."

"I got something!" Adiquis hopped toward Red with what appeared to be a datapad. He pressed a button and its screen glowed to life. "I have no idea how to read it, but…"

"You've done enough. Thank you!" Red scrolled through the menus and clicked on everything she could. The text was not that far off from Orderlish but it was still unique. She scanned the text looking for any patterns. The mechanisms of her mind unscrambled the glyphs. Her years of study, combined with this excellent specimen of an alien lexicon, made her realize that no matter the species, language developed more or less in the same way. The varied dialects of humanity were an exceptional example of what once seemed infinitely complex being, in truth, interconnected and simple when analyzed from a distance.

"This…and this!" Red toggled a switch on the console. She flipped seven levers and turned a giant dial. "And…" She typed a string of digits into a keypad. She lowered her goggles to enhance her vision but was reminded they were shattered.

"Is Chlorian there yet?" she asked, gazing across the facility.

"Almost!" King answered. "Almost…and…now! He's right in front of it! He's going in! Now, now, now!"

With the crushing power of her fist, the same fingers that breached the first gate, the same hand that reached out to her comrades and brought them together, she slammed a big red button.

"Wait! It didn't work." King turned a confused face toward Red. "He went right through."

"No. It did." Even from this distance, she could tell the wispy portal had changed to static. It looked once again just like she had always known it to be. "I disconnected the gate from its other end. He'll be stuck hurtling forward, in inexplicable pain, to a destination with no end. Possibly forever."

Several of the remaining alien ships fled into that same gate. Realizing what had happened, further ships avoided it and instead blinked into space. The alien troops upon the wall stopped firing and retreated elsewhere. What few Seekers remained across the battlefield were being hunted down. With another check of the datapad, Red shut down the waterfall of smoke.

"Oh Divine! We did it!" Minnie jumped at King. She pulled Red into the embrace as well.

King chuckled. "Cool your jets, young lady…"

Adiquis wrapped himself around Red's leg. "You did it! You're a smarty pants just like Dr. Petras."

Tears streamed down their faces.

Their journey was over.

Humanity was safe.

For now.

Informal Appendix

ROVER ENTRY #1209-01.A

Since my presentation of the attached report at the 701st Annual Rover Conference, I completed this summary entry regarding the proceeding events after the Great Answer Crisis. Often requested by my colleagues, the following complete, informal and personal account of my thoughts is now included to serve as a thorough and accurate record of the results that will continue to affect our new era.

A few days after we uprooted the aliens out of Creare, I found myself writing quietly in my resting quarters aboard the Ark of the Endeavor. There were many celebrations occurring across the Jangalan settlement, but I chose not to attend. While inscribing within my Journal, I reflected upon having lived through the First Intergalactic War. I aptly named the conflict as such because I absolutely anticipate a second. Although Chlorian was dispatched to the same eternal doomscape as the children of my colony, not all alien ships stumbled into the same fate. Sightings of their strange vessels have been reported across the galaxy and all are heading toward the perimeter. I would be surprised if they were not flying home the old-fashioned way. I don't know how long the aliens live or how fast their crafts can travel. But if they manage to make it back home, our ancestors can expect a rude reunion with their interstellar neighbors.

Still on the Jangalan settlement, while the colleagues I had grown to care for and trust were raising cups to success, I continued writing. I was determined to ensure fair representation of the many worlds I had traversed.

The Rover Order claimed it was the duty, no, the life's purpose of a Rover to meticulously record gate knowledge for the benefit of the settlements. But I had come to believe the knowledge of everything, not solely of just the gates, was of a greater purpose. A cornucopia of new knowledge would grace our settlements soon and I was eager to help make sense of it all.

For starters, the gates on that alien world were now the property of humanity. Jangalan and Earth scientists were able to determine that Creare was near the center of our own galaxy. All the portals still shimmered, although not all led to a functioning gate on the other side. Indeed, many connections must have deteriorated or were unwittingly dismantled by humanity during what King taught me was a historical period called the Metal Rush.

While humanity had a lot to unravel concerning alien technology abandoned at the facility, galactic travel was going to be a lot easier and I was going to make it my personal mission to ensure the lives of Abeona-2's people would improve as a result.

Regarding technology left behind, there were a lot of weapons. There was a frighteningly tense day after the war when Olyana's soldiers had to point their arms against fellow humans. Scavengers were making off with dangerous devices and it almost seemed like chaos had taken a hold of the facility. Olyana's young Jangala Leadership Council, evolved from her War Council, took decisive action and secured the artifacts until a later time when researchers could scour the area and safely catalogue the technological advances.

My surprise friend, Minnie, wasted no time after the battle and promptly returned to Earth with her refugees. Although her original gate was destroyed, there were several others for her to choose from. With a heavy heart, none of them contained our friend and hero Sarenth on the other side. With renewed faith in the Divine, Minnie was eager to begin the cleansing and restoration of the home world. There were more than enough alien weapons left behind for her to secure a cache through the Leadership Council. An Earth battalion felt confident about their chances to restore order to a temporarily lawless world.

Minnie and I no doubt had our differences, but we both agreed years of difficult struggles lay ahead for her collective people. While I worried about the pragmatism of a young woman leading an entire planet through restoration alone, Minnie said there were many examples of young leaders in the Divine scripture. I have to admit, I had no idea. No matter how it happened, Earth would need to stand again if humanity was to unite permanently as one across the stars. Minnie was confident the Divine would shine luck down upon them. I was comfortable telling her she was probably right. Whatever the guiding light she chose to follow, Minnie was an amazing person and I did not need any further evidence to prove that.

During our last conversation when I transcribed her story, I told her how much I'd grown to admire her ability to give her whole self to others, a trait I'd never learned to value. Minnie said she felt compelled to be that way, but she did not recommend it if things were working just fine for me. She also told me to keep in touch. I don't have a communicator that can reach across the galactic divide yet, but I'll be visiting Earth with the inaugural Rover Galactic Expedition Team once they graduate in the near future. I'll have to touch base with her and see what method she had in mind for continued connection and collaboration. Her friendship is one I do not want to neglect.

Adiquis and Dr. Petras planned on staying on Jangala for a little while. They were recruiting soldiers to return to Tenocolis with them and join the fight against the Autocracy. There were also scores of dangerous steelys to reclaim from their enemy. Their recruitment efforts were having some real success among the career soldiers. From what I had heard, many predicted an uncertain future for themselves with peace in the valley. In addition, tales of the Autocracy and their method of rule across their empire did not align well with the new Leadership Council's edicts regarding human rights. Many of the Jangalan people were looking for a cause and an opportunity.

To my great dismay, the Leadership Council decided certain actions of war could no longer be overlooked. This same council Olyana helped establish considered the action she took to end the Perennial War a horrendous act committed against the deceased Jangalan people forever entombed within the fog. There were those in her inner circle that argued the situation at the time and her decisions were far more complex than the council could possibly understand. But the reality of the politics trying to govern and provide solace for a quarter of their population being formerly Divine made anything short of a condemnation seem tone-deaf. In response, Olyana released a statement in which she believed it best to keep herself from becoming a distraction in the new Jangalan era.

I was stunned when I heard she had volunteered to step down as Captain of the colony and exile herself. I sought her out and found her alone in her private quarters packing a bag. I asked how she could walk away from her home like that, one she carried upon her back like a woman worthy of her own legend. She said charting her own original course was more her style and she was hopeful for what was ahead for both her and the people she would leave behind. Her advisor, Azul, would become the first Captain in recorded history to not be the child of the former. She believed this would not be a catastrophe like some thought. It was another step in a new and exciting direction. She and Emillee planned to depart with Dr. Petras and Adiquis when they were ready to return to Tenocolis. They were the first two to join the next fight. I asked her if she was tired of conflict and war. I could see its effects etched permanently by way of lines upon her face.

She said to me with a brave, bright smile, "War is all I have ever known. The day I tire of it will be my last."

King introduced me to his bonded pairing, Tillie Sue. In retrospect, it is now obvious he had someone waiting for him back home. He never stared back at me the same way I, on occasion, ogled him. As to how I was able to meet her, apparently during the great battle she and a whole army of muscled brawlers, like King, burst through their home's gate. Tillie Sue was a security official on her planet and was familiar with firing a weapon. She led the recruitment effort and charge after hearing my broadcast on her planet's media and recognizing King's unforgettable voice in the background. Unlike the ruthless warriors she came through the gate with, Tillie Sue told me she shot three aliens during the battle and cried about it the entire following evening. I told her I had not stopped crying about what I had seen on the battlefield and it was okay to let your emotions out. We consulted together with a crises arbiter on the ship to help us come to terms with our shared trauma. I think we might be friends now.

King shared a secret with me. He said he was going to propose to Tillie Sue after they returned home. I do not know what he ultimately proposed, but I hope it was a well-deserved vacation. Maybe somewhere humid and warm like Creare, but with significantly fewer aliens. Those two appeared happy sharing in a celebration with the other brawlers as they returned from battle. I guess their people spend most of their time fighting one another where they come from. I hope by now they have found a way to put their differences aside and have become allies.

As for me, as soon as I returned to my quarters, I opened the drawer and slipped my mother's glove back on. I once told Minnie it held no unique significance like the Divine artifacts of her religion. However, I realized this was exactly what the glove meant to me. I wondered about my mother and how her insatiable curiosity got the better of her. I questioned if, when she was young, she had any experiences like mine that stoked the flame of exploration in her heart so hot she knew it would never subside.

I could not see myself ever judging her again and probably would now actively seek the unknown to see it for myself. Where I once feared being compared to my mother, someone who pushed the boundaries so far it snatched her away from her beloved family, I questioned if I would mind the comparison anymore. I know my mother had made grave mistakes.

Now I had made some as well, but the difference was I felt experienced and supported enough to avoid some of the same consequences. I may be able to now accept all the good things about her and make peace with the parts that are best left forgiven or undisturbed.

On my last Jangalan day, I connected with King, Adiquis, and Olyana one last time and reviewed the stories they dictated for me. I was so completely absorbed with recording every minute detail of their adventures before we met that Azul had to tell me the news twice before I stopped peppering Olyana with questions. He brought word that Abeona-2's gate had been identified.

This miracle occurred because two brave, wide-eyed teenagers came through to Creare carrying bags upon bags of survival gear. They were dressed like they were walking into a sandstorm and Azul said he instantly knew they were from my planet. He assured them I was safe and directed them back home to await my arrival. They were not cooperative and they hassled him greatly for information, true to Rover form. I never knew Green and Purple had it in them to try something as risky as me. That was their first daring act that indicated their conviction for things far greater than ourselves. They have repeatedly shown me great courage and have proven to be my best allies when championing reforms here at home.

Green and I have started collaborating more frequently. Now that I am working out of Alpha settlement alongside Rover leadership with greater frequency, we are situated closer than we were before. If we plan well enough, we can carve out a little time in the evenings to conduct lengthy independent field research just outside the city. There are so many non-arch discoveries waiting to be made from creatures, fauna, to geological and it does not take much to spot them once you start looking beyond the Great Answer. Yes, a Rover tent filled with equipment does not make for comfortable overnight quarters, but we…make do. And to think that I was looking for something on the other side of the galaxy that I already had back at home. Well, I sought at least a connection that was interested in exploring the same future as me and that expedition is now concluded.

I had hoped I would witness my grandpa's pride when I returned with the tales of the Red Rover and the lessons she learned of resilience, hope, and courage. Yet, I was saddened to learn his last grain of sand had dispersed while I was away. I was told by the medical attendant who was present when it happened that witnessing me forge boldly, selflessly into the gate was the greatest moment of his life and of our people's history. My last memory of him was of his belief that I would find my mother on the other side. In a way, I did. Now only time will tell if the Red I became the day I returned was the new me that I will forever be. Or if, as I have come to suspect, I will continue to forever explore new parts of myself like a good Rover should. How to understand people, as it turns out, is the still greatest unknown answer.

Thank you for reading!

Please visit my website and help me continue to write.

- Leave a review!
- Join the mailing list!
- Go on another literary adventure!

www.choustore.com

Other books by Daniel G. Chou:

Candii's Quest, a musical fantasy novella

The Martian Connection, a sci-fi romance novella